# *Sinners of Magic*

*Lynette E Creswell*

Published in 2012 by FeedARead.com Publishing – Arts Council funded



First Edition



A CIP catalogue record for this title is available from the British Library.

***This book is dedicated to my mum, Shirley,***
***who loved my story with a passion,***
***but never lived long enough to see it in print.***

## *Acknowledgements*

Many people have given me valuable encouragement, support and constructive criticism during the writing of this book which will eventually be a trilogy. Thank you to:

Andy, my long suffering husband for believing in me and being so supportive; Jamie, my son for helping me sculpt the first few chapters; Kristian, Arron and Alex for listening to a new chapter over and over again; Hannah Clark, my daughter in law to be, for her friendship, enthusiasm and ability to reread; Cheryl my daughter in law, for her funny suggestions and bags of wit.

Also a warm thank you to my new friend Sheila Cutting, who not only reread my story at the most crucial point of my books existence, but also helped in ways too numerous to mention. And last but by no means least, Phil Moss who painted the most amazing cover.

# *Prologue*

The forest seemed calm and settled for the night, until a storm broke high above the whispering trees, causing dark shadows to sweep across a narrow mud track. A solitary figure hurried along the darkened trail. Hunched over to protect himself from the biting wind, he dragged the hood of his cloak down over his brow. A lock of hair managed to escape his grasp and it danced to and fro across his forehead until he grabbed hold and pushed it behind a pointed ear. An unexpected flash of lightning filled the night sky, revealing his two crimson eyes and he pulled his hood closer to block out the sudden blinding light. A second spear brought forth a curse as he tried to regain some of his night sight, struggling to penetrate the darkness yet again.

It had been a long journey, plagued with worry and mindless stress over what was yet to come and although he was a shape-changer of considerable talent, he was forbidden to use any of his powers out of his own realm; it was the law. He had travelled therefore in his human form, avoiding unwanted attention from his own kind and maintaining a low profile.

The rain changed to hail, stinging his eyes and freezing his toughened skin. He was cold and tired, but aware he was almost at his journey's end, which gave him the strength to carry on. A memory flashed; it was brief but sharp and he strained his eyes into the darkest part of the wood. The cold began to blur his vision making everything around him look hazy, but his memory showed him the path he should take.

As he followed his instincts, he was able to make out the dark silhouette of a small rounded door, hidden in a mesh of brambles and thick foliage. It was old and neglected, just as he remembered, and its ivy-covered hinges were crudely carved within the trunk of the huge oak tree.

His small, slight frame moved off the track, heading for the cover of thick vegetation. His cloth-wrapped boots stepped without a sound over debris and hidden roots and he listened to the whispering sounds of the forest, afraid to hear any intruders or spies who were close on his trail.

A hard thudding was beating inside his chest and he put his hand to his heart as though to quieten it. In retaliation, the hairs on the back of his neck stood rigid and sharp when a twig snapped beneath his feet. He took in yet another deep breath, calling upon a calm state of mind, preparing himself to convene with a powerful force known to be much stronger than his own.

With the cold, driving rain chasing at his heels, the king's advocate braced himself and grabbed hold of the slippery latch. With only the briefest hesitation, he pushed his way inside the witch's domain and prayed he would live to see the sun rise.

'Who's there?' snapped the witch on hearing the door creak open. ''Ave you no manners? Ain't anyone ever taught you to knock before entering?'

At her fury, the elf made a small bow before mumbling some kind of apology.

'Oh, it's you, Tremlon,' she muttered, sounding somewhat disappointed. 'Close that damn door before I catch me death.' Tremlon closed it immediately, before untying his rain-soaked cloak and allowing it to fall onto the small stool by his feet.

'You're late,' the witch snapped, pointing a bony finger at him. 'Where've you been till now?'
Tremlon's brow furrowed.

'Lilura, you know I've travelled far,' he said, sounding terse. 'Is this any way to greet a guest?'
The witch watched him with a crooked smile playing across her thin, stretched lips.

'There's a lot of things I'd call you, and a guest ain't one of them!' she spat. Tremlon frowned. It was obvious she had no intention of making this visit anything less than uncomfortable for him. He felt his eyes roll over his host's attire.

Lilura was dressed in long, dark robes, which rested on the straw covered floor. The hem of her clothing was tatty with age, a string of dried dirt clinging to the bottom of her garment. She was old enough to be his great-grandmother, and her skin was dry and paper thin, wrinkled in some places and stretched to the point of splitting in others. Her face was haggard beyond any recognition, but her eyes were sharp and alive. He felt himself redden when she caught him watching her.

'I'm soaked to the skin,' he ventured, when she didn't offer for him to sit by the fire. 'Will you not allow me to be warm and dry this night?'

'If you feel you must,' she said, pointing to a spot where he would not be in her way. 'Just don't go making yourself too comfortable!'

A fire blazed in the farthest corner of the room, and he watched in wonder when a prism of bright shimmers bounced softly against the unusual angular walls. Her lair was as he remembered. Each dark corner was filled with eerie objects and deadly beasties. The strong aroma which filled his nostrils was not of death as one would expect, but from the flowers which she used either for their healing properties or her deathly poisons. Inflorescent clusters dangled along the roofline, like an upside-down, dehydrated meadow. He noted the wattle and daub surfaces were still smooth and clean, absent of the sooty texture normally left by a fire. It struck him as odd that although there was no chimney of sorts, the air seemed clear, as though the smoke had found some natural way to escape.

As he approached the flames, the witch nodded towards a large twisted root which she used as a table.

'Sit over there,' she commanded, turning to view her visitor with shrewd eyes. 'I've been paid to feed you b'fore we leave.'

Tremlon felt a slither of apprehension creep down his spine at the thought of her offering him food. He knew it would not be wise to decline her offer and sensed the danger she put him in, forcing the chill in his bone to deepen.

'You'll not be poisoned this night,' she said with a cackle. 'I've been paid well by your king for this conspiracy, enough it seems to spare your wretched life this night.'

Tremlon dropped his gaze, trying to keep his turbulent emotions well hidden from her. Secretly, he chided himself for his carelessness; she had been able to read his thoughts too easily. There was a moment's silence as he closed his mind to her.

'I told you to sit,' she snapped, turning hostile, when she realised he'd severed the connection.

Reluctantly, he did as he was told, afraid of the glare still burning in her eyes, aware of her unpredictability.

'The child's not here then?' he said, trying to sound nonchalant. The old crone let out a hiss between her rotting teeth.

'No, she isn't 'ere yet,' she answered, moving slowly towards a brewing pot. 'Time enough for trouble,' she added, twisting her body to shoot him a menacing grin. She flicked her tongue along her lips, tasting the fear that emanated from his life force, giving her cause for a moment of satisfaction. She picked up a ladle and filled a coarse, wooden bowl with a thin broth she had made earlier in anticipation of his arrival.

'Be at ease, elf,' she said, adding one more spoonful. 'The wind will bring the babe soon enough.'

She turned, placing the bowl before him, together with a crudely carved wooden spoon.

'It'll give you the strength of mind you seek, along with the gift of courage you so lack,' she hissed, her eyes still golden with wickedness.

Tremlon felt himself bristle and a tremble of anger rippled down his spine. His lips pursed at the slight, but he remained silent. He disliked the old woman intensely, but was no fool to her powers. Instead, he picked up the spoon and placed the first mouthful of the watery broth to his lips. She turned away from him and stared into the flames.

Slowly, the elf started to chew, grimacing with embarrassment when his stomach growled from hunger.

'Damn cold night for a babe to be travelling,' he remarked, mustering some courage to break the eerie silence and hide the rumble from his stomach. Lilura moved towards the warmth of the fire, watching with interest the long, dark shadows created by the flames.

'And to be a long one for us,' she said, her eyes turning cold.

'My humble thanks for the food,' he replied, ignoring her menacing stare.

'It's what's expected of me,' Lilura answered, with a shrug of a bony shoulder. 'But be warned, my kind deeds have run dry.' Before he could answer, the door burst open, causing huge droplets of icy rain to blow in the witch's face.

'Be off with you, stranger!' Lilura screeched, when the dark silhouette of a man blocked her small doorway. 'You have no right to be here.'

'It's Bridgemear!' shouted Tremlon, feeling relieved to see the magician. 'It's good to see you safe and well.'

The newcomer was a larger man than the elf, tall and solidly built. His clothes were filthy from the track, but the dirt did nothing to hide the ice-blue eyes. He stepped forward with wide strides, a confidence born only of the powerful. A nod of his head was his only acknowledgement that he had heard the elf as he stepped inside.

Bridgemear was well over six feet tall, born within an elite realm of sorcerers, and the room was made even smaller by his presence. He wore a long draping coat, and pulling back the hood, he revealed plaited blonde hair falling either side of a strikingly handsome face, with lines of worry creasing what would otherwise be a smooth complexion. His menacing stare rested on the shape-changer.

'Tremlon,' he said, his eyes becoming hard like pieces of flint, 'I have the child, as arranged.' Closing the door with the heel of his boot, he took a step towards them. The roof was low, almost touching his head; he flicked his gaze across the room. A spare chair moved to his side, he sat without invitation.

Disturbed by the sudden mayhem, a mangy cat slipped between the unwanted intruders, unnoticed it crept towards the magician. In a flash, its claws were outstretched seeking his flesh, and with one vicious swipe, it latched itself onto his calf.

'Get away!' cried Bridgemear, kicking the startled feline aside. 'I have no time to mess with familiars.' The witch moved surprisingly quick for an old crone, grabbing Bridgemear's arm in retaliation. She instantly regretted her impulsive action when hot pain seared through her fingertips and up her arm. She bit her lip to stifle a cry, releasing her grip and leaping back in shock. Bridgemear chuckled, but his eyes flashed like cold steel.

'Foolish one,' he chided, beginning to unfasten his tunic. 'You of all people should know your darkness cannot touch the light.' She stole to the rear of the room, still rubbing her arm.

'I ain't even been told what all this is about yet,' she lied, when the pain in her fingers began to subside and her anger had no choice but to cool.

Bridgemear's lips tightened. 'You know too much of my business already,' he spat, causing his eyes to narrow. 'You know only too well, what you have to do.' Peeling back his cloak, he revealed the half-naked body of a sleeping child. 'You must ensure the babe is switched with one that has died in the ordinary world.'

'Is this your daughter from the princess?' she asked, while her mouth tightened with spite.

Bridgemear's face flushed. 'Enough questions!' he hissed, his face contorting with inner pain.

'So she is then,' said the witch, flashing a crafty grin. She looked upon the babe's sweet face and was surprised to see how peacefully she slept.

'The child is to be named Crystal,' Bridgemear said, allowing a deep sigh to escape. 'It was her mother's choice, not mine.' He made to scoff at his own remark, but a weak rasp escaped from his throat instead.

'Give the child to me,' said Tremlon, his arms eagerly outstretched. 'She'll be fine in my care. I promise I'll look after her and ensure no harm befalls her.' His eyes locked upon the magician's, willing him to give up the child.

It felt like an eternity, a whole lifetime, before Bridgemear began to untie the child from his breast. His strong fingers tore at the fabric, releasing his hold, allowing his daughter into Tremlon's care. Smears of blood stained her body from the birth and a sense of sadness appeared to engulf them both.

'There's something else,' Bridgemear added, pulling at a leather pouch secured to his belt. He lifted his hand and displayed a beautiful chain of bright golden orbs, placing it with care upon the table.

'What have you there?' asked Tremlon, sounding rather confused. 'It looks like the amulet which belongs to the inner circle of my people.'

'It did belong to your people, or rather a certain person,' said Bridgemear, his voice thick with genuine sorrow, 'but it's Crystal's now.'

The necklace had a plain metal clasp with silver entwined, and in the centre lay an exquisitely cut jewel that shone fire-red. Tremlon reached out a trembling hand and retrieved it. He interlaced his fingers between the orbs that made up the thickest part of the chain, becoming absorbed by its natural beauty. He brushed his fingertips over the stone, watching in awe when tiny sparks of light ricocheted from inside it. Mesmerised, he saw the colour swirl from red to a deep purple, showing him his feelings of utter despair.

'Without the amulet, Princess Amella will be unable to return to her people,' Tremlon stated, his own words making him realise he would never see her again. 'She can't do this,' he insisted. He glared dangerously at the magician, his eyes turning to slits. 'I won't allow this to happen; she's our only princess.'

'Calm yourself and be reasonable,' roared Bridgemear, becoming infuriated. 'Don't you think she knows the consequences of what she's giving up? I tried to make her keep the amulet, but it's her wish that the child should have what would have been passed down to her, if she had been born legitimately.'

'Why would she destroy her own life for this child?' Tremlon gasped, releasing the necklace and watching it fall helplessly onto the table. Guilt washed over him as he looked down at the sleeping babe who Bridgemear had so trustingly nestled into the crook of his arm.

'We broke the law!' Bridgemear cried, jumping to his feet and banging his head on the ceiling. 'Amella felt she could no longer honour her father and people after what we did and has taken a life of exile.' Tremlon averted his eyes, while the sorcerer cursed and his gut tightened at the thought of his inadvertent betrayal of his princess. It had just been a little love rivalry; he had never meant to be the one who told the king of her secret love affair with Bridgemear.

'It's no use fighting between ourselves,' said Lilura, edging her way to the door. 'What's done is done. My lord it's time you left.' Bridgemear's eyes filled with regret.

'I only did what the Elders forced me to do,' he said, sounding pitiful.

'Then take peace in the knowledge that you did only what the law-makers asked of you,' she replied testily, 'you could do no more.' With hard eyes, she lifted the latch and exposed the dreadful night.

'Forget her,' she advised. 'Your terrible secret's safe forever. You must understand that we cannot have her here, as in time her powers could be far greater than all the elite magicians put together. She could so easily destroy us all.'

'I think you're over-exaggerating,' said Bridgemear, refastening his tunic and looking beyond her into the night.

'My lord,' the witch said, bowing her head, 'I exaggerate nothing.'

Slamming the door behind him once he'd left, Lilura cackled almost to the point of hysteria.

'Stop your noise,' Tremlon snapped, when he could stand her hysteric's no longer. 'You don't know what he's going through.'

'Oh, and you do,' the witch snapped back with a hiss. 'Why is that, I wonder?'

Tremlon glared at her, a look of repulsion spreading over his face, but her own facial features merely mirrored his own and he read his secret in her eyes. *She knows what I've done,* he thought aghast. Blanching, he dropped his head in shame.

'It's time we finished his dirty work,' she told him, before picking up his cloak, and with a swift movement for one so old, she threw the garment towards him.

Catching it with one hand, Tremlon spun the cloak in the air until it fell neatly upon his shoulders. 'So be it,' he said with a bitter twist of his mouth. 'The dirt must fall at someone's feet; it may as well be mine.'

*

The moon cast an ominous glow through the large open window. Death's dark shadow crept across the bedroom wall of the sleeping household until he willingly slipped back into the darkness from whence he came. Tremlon stepped out from his hiding place and knelt, head bowed towards the lifeless babe lying in its crib. The room felt icy, and Tremlon could not decide whether he shook from the cold or from despair. The misery surrounding these terrible circumstances clung to his heart with invisible fingers, causing him to feel the pain of loss once again that night. After a moment, when his composure had slipped back into place, he lifted the tiny, lifeless body from its resting place and laid it with care on the floor.

'Hurry,' he urged, searching the darkness for the witch's shadow. She heard the desperation in his voice and stepped forward, placing Bridgemear's daughter into the crib, a baby who appeared almost identical to that which Tremlon had just removed.

'It's done,' she said, bowing her head. Respectfully, she picked up the dead child and wrapped it in a fine woven cloth that she took from inside her robes. She placed the bundle gently back upon the floor.

'Away, child,' she said, her voice soft. 'Go now, for it's time to rest amongst your own.' She closed her eyes, her lips moving as she reached down and touched the cloth. Slowly, the small bundle flattened until all that was left was empty material. An unexpected sigh escaped from her lips. Tremlon stood up and moved towards her. She drew back, her hand still clutching the silky material. The cloth began to unravel carelessly in her grasp and for a moment he felt afraid, until he saw the material no longer held the tiny body.

Turning to Tremlon, Lilura said, 'We've got to be on our way.'

'I must wait awhile,' he argued, 'to be sure the mother does not suspect.'

'I have laid an enchantment,' said the witch. 'The plain folk will not sense a thing. Why stay?'

'I have my orders.'

'I should have known your king wouldn't trust me,' she said flashing a scowl. 'Shall I wait with you?'

'If you wish,' he answered, shrugging his shoulders, 'but I have no need of you now.'

As dawn finally broke, the witch and the elf moved closer to the shadows, and slowly their shapes began to melt away. Arms and legs dissolved, creating a different shadow to grace the walls where, only moments before, two human outlines had been displayed. Within the blink of an eye, their clothes faded to nothing, replaced in a breath by velvety feathers. The witch took the shape of a large black crow while the elf had chosen his natural change, to a dove.

Moments later, his beady eyes watched with anticipation for the mother's arrival. They both sat on the windowsill, waiting in silence for the king's wicked plan to take effect. His eyes locked upon her when she finally entered, and his head bobbed up and down as he strained his neck to get a better look. He observed the young woman who bent over the crib and lifted the mage's baby into her arms. He held his breath in expectancy, releasing it only when she began to kiss the baby's forehead and stroke her cheek with a delicate finger.

The black crow crowed by his side, her dark feathers blowing gently in the cool morning breeze.

'We must leave before they suspect,' she urged.

Outstretching his wings, Tremlon flapped them simultaneously. The beautiful white feathers caught the sun's warm rays and they bowed together before the tips of their wings touched; then Tremlon vanished. The crow followed a moment later, but not before she watched the new mother place the baby safely back inside her cot. She noticed her hesitate, before rummaging her fingers between the sheets. A moment later, the glow from the amulet lit her surprised face. She had found the string of orbs that had been placed between the sheet and soft blankets, a gift left by another mother.

'Live long, princess,' the witch cawed; 'live long and pray your life in this world will be easier than if you were in your own.' Startled, the woman's eyes shot to the window pane.

'Shoo,' she shouted, waving her arms in the air like a lunatic. She rushed over and pushed the window wide, intent on making the bird fly away. 'Get away, you horrible bird!' she yelled, still flapping her arms. 'Go and find yourself an abandoned churchyard to haunt.' For a moment, their eyes locked; jet-black held silver grey. A cold shiver forced its way down the woman's slender spine, and in that instant she felt the crow to be a bad omen.

'Beatrice!' a voice called out. 'Close that damn window before you catch a chill.' The crow took flight and the woman watched it move towards the horizon.

'Meg, something's wrong,' Beatrice told her friend when she came into the room and placed a caring hand on her shoulder. 'Look what I've found, some kind of necklace.'

'Well aren't you the lucky one; bet it's only a bit of costume jewellery though. What with your crib coming from the charity shop, I bet it was under the mattress or something; these things do happen from time to time.' Beatrice agreed that her theory had a ring of truth, but deep down she knew the necklace hadn't been there when she put the baby to bed.

'Come on, let's get you back into bed,' said Meg, shaking her head. 'You know you shouldn't be up so soon after the birth.'

'Something's not right,' Beatrice persisted, heading back to her child. 'I've only just lost my husband; I can't lose my baby too.' Hot tears hung on her dark lashes, threatening to spill down her flushed cheeks.

'Look, everything's fine,' Meg insisted, sweeping her eyes over the sleeping infant.
'It's only natural that you should be feeling fretful after what you've been through. Now, let's get you back to bed where you belong.'

With some resistance, Meg was able to guide her charge to her own room, directly opposite the nursery.

'Your baby's going to be fine,' she soothed, turning on the bedside light, 'you just need plenty of rest.' Beatrice sat on the bed, her face turning pale and drawn.

'But you don't understand,' she bleated, her eyes still shining like glass with her unshed tears. 'That crow's a sign of bad luck.'

'Nonsense, dear,' Meg insisted, pulling at Beatrice's slippers. 'It's just a silly little bird that's all. You know there's dozens of them around here. Why, you should see my place; there are hundreds of the damn things living on my roof!'

Meg covered her body with a soft bedspread and Beatrice breathed in the scent of soft, fresh linen. When she laid her head on the pillow, a whispering voice called out to her somewhere in the back of her mind. She focused her senses, unsure where the voice was coming from, until a whispering murmur brought with it a name that seemed to be balancing on the tip of her tongue.

'Crystal,' she said, aloud.

'What's that, dear?' Meg asked, glancing over her shoulder. 'Have you come up with a name for your baby?'

'Yes,' Beatrice answered, trying to stifle a yawn. 'Yes, I have. My baby, she's to be called Crystal.'

'That's an unusual name,' said Meg, pulling a face, 'and it's certainly different.'

Beatrice looked up into her friend's kind face and saw only her smile, yet her instincts were telling her there was something wrong, but she found she couldn't quite put her finger on it. Her eyelids were beginning to feel heavy with sleep and she felt herself drifting off. The last images held in the swirl of her subconscious came swimming to the surface as soon as the darkness penetrated her thoughts. She began dreaming and saw her dead husband William, standing in a place she could not recall. So vivid was the dream that she tried to call out to him and touch the man she loved, but no matter how hard she tried, her fingers could never quite reach him. He floated closer, his handsome face much clearer and her already outstretched arms pleaded for him to allow her a moment's embrace. But then horror exploded in her mind and a sharp pain erupted in her heart when she focused on something small and lifeless lying in his arms. A silent scream left her numb and trembling lips when she realised he was clutching the limp body of a dead baby to his blood-soaked chest.

The horror of what she saw sent her mind into utter turmoil; was this more than just a nightmare she was suffering? Fighting the agony of watching those she loved slip away, she sobbed inwardly when William's tear stained face turned from hers and began to shimmer like an illusion on a hot summer's day. Slowly, the two figures disintegrated into minute particles of sparkling dust before her very eyes, and in her sleep she wept an ocean of tears.

# *Chapter 1*

'Books back in two weeks,' cried the librarian, crushing the date stamp on the blank page of the lender's book. She snapped the last cover closed, pushing it across the highly polished desk and the visitor grabbed hold, shoving them all into an old school satchel, before turning on her heels and heading for the nearest exit.

Crystal watched the old lady's hasty retreat and smiled to herself. She loved it here, in the town's local library where her mother had dropped her off for the rest of the afternoon. She was often found to have her nose buried in a novel of some kind, and here inside this old library, she felt safe within the confines of the solid brick walls. Her love of books and thirst for knowledge had given her the courage she needed to overcome the ghost stories she had heard concerning the library as a small child.

She focused her concentration back on her favourite novel, Emily Brontë's *Wuthering Heights*. The story had woven its magic within her soul many times in her short life, with the pages portraying a lonely and bitter life entwined with love and ultimate tragedy. Her gaze fell back to the printed page and she became lost once more on the cold and lonely moors with Cathy and her volatile lover, Heathcliff.

While her mind conjured up colourful images of times gone by, an unexpected burst of giggling drifted down the long, cool corridors and was caught by her sensitive ear. With her concentration broken, Crystal closed her book and placed it back on the shelf, momentarily forgotten. Her inquisitive nature pushed her eagerly towards the source of the disturbance, her mind still filled with ghosts of long ago.

Almost on tiptoe, she hurried between the oak-panelled bookcases, careful not to make a sound. She passed row upon row of ancient literature, each book begging for a reader to reach out and pluck it from obscurity. The columns loomed high, each one branded with a large fancy gold letter of the alphabet placed there to help the untrained eye differentiate between the novels by the author's name.

The giggling was beginning to grow louder and more boisterous, making it extremely easy for her to detect where the noisy culprits were hiding. Cautiously, she moved even closer. Someone let out a yelp.

'What the hell!' said a startled voice, when a dark silhouette appeared against the pale, even walls. It only took a moment for Crystal to realise she had been detected, and without delay she revealed herself to the two surprised visitors.

'Hi there,' she said, jumping out of the shadows. 'I'm sorry if I scared you, but I heard you laughing and just wondered who was down here.' She looked with interest at the two teenage boys, who were sitting wide-eyed in her direction.

'Hi, my name's Alfie,' said the smaller of the two lads.

'That's Matt over there,' he added pointing a stubby finger towards his friend. 'He's my best mate.'

She nodded a greeting.

'My name's Crystal,' she explained, giving them a nervous smile. 'I come here a lot, but I don't think I've ever seen you two in here before.'

A short silence engulfed them when no one spoke, until her eyes lit up with silvery sparks when she hit on an idea. 'Perhaps you need help finding something?' she probed, letting a slight smile hover around the corners of her mouth. 'If you do, I can help, because I pretty much know this library inside out.'

'Well,' said Alfie, clearly toying with the idea for less than a second, 'I think we're alright, actually.'

'Oh,' said Crystal, feeling a stab of disappointment. 'Are you sure?'

Alfie nodded his head and shot her a look which told her he didn't want any help from some know-it-all. Crystal let out a sigh and stared at him with a sudden critical eye. She thought by the way he was dressed that he looked younger than her, although Matt looked around the same age, sixteen. Alfie was wearing blue jeans and a personalised football shirt. She decided his blonde hair was in desperate need of a good haircut and sensed his behaviour was bordering on childishness.

'Hey, speak for yourself,' Matt suddenly shot back, grinning at her.

'Really?' said Crystal, flashing a smile and feeling intrigued. 'Tell me, what is it you need?' She watched him stand up and walk towards her. She hadn't realised he was so tall, with thick, dark hair and unusual green eyes. His limbs were long and athletic, and he wore a faded denim shirt with cut-off sleeves, accentuating his lean physique. He was what she would have described a teen heartthrob and she lowered her gaze, slightly embarrassed for labelling him in such a way.

'You've caught us arguing over our homework on the British involvement with the African slave trade,' he explained, oblivious to her burning cheeks. He offered her the book he was reading.

'We're trying to find out why they actually got involved in the first place,' he continued, 'but none of the books we've found so far have given us any real information. Everything seems to give a brief outline and it's just not enough material to get us at least a B grade in English.'

He gave her a pleading look, raising his left eyebrow in good humour.

'Any ideas, gorgeous?'

Crystal laughed then.

'I really don't know why you're looking in this old thing,' she said, flicking through the dated text. 'But if you really do need such detailed research, why don't you follow me and I'll show you exactly where to look.'

'By all means, lead the way,' said Matt, grabbing his jacket from the back of his chair. He nudged Alfie's arm, gesturing that he should follow.

'Come on then,' she urged, her eyes shining with enthusiasm. 'No time like the present.'

Crystal slipped through the uneven rows of books followed closely by Matt and Alfie. Alfie just couldn't resist goofing around and he flicked Matt's ear, making him squeal in pain.

'Ouch, that hurt,' gasped Matt, rubbing his reddening ear with his thumb and finger and trying to alleviate the pain. He threw an angry glare in Alfie's direction and shook his fist close to his nose, giving him a clear warning.

'Are you okay?' asked Crystal, turning to peer into his face.

'I'm fine, just fine,' he said, still rubbing his skin. 'But someone else may not be so lucky if they continue to act like a complete moron.'

Alfie focused straight ahead, struggling to control a snigger that tickled the back of his throat; he never could take

Matt too seriously and besides this place took the word 'boredom' to a whole new level.

'Believe it or not, but there is an actual section in here dedicated to slavery,' Crystal said, pointing to the specialised selection, before herding them like sheep towards the shelves. 'Here we are, I think this is just what you need,' she said, pulling out a hardback book and placing it on a table.

'Bloody hell, that looks old,' said Alfie, pointing to the dusty cover and noting its protective wrapping was torn.

'Yes, it is,' she agreed, 'so you'd better be very careful with it.'

Crystal used her delicate fingers to turn the musty pages, showing them the beautiful illustrations contained inside. She gave her full attention to the book, becoming more enchanted with each turn of the page. Unable to find what she was looking for, she cast her gaze over the table of contents.

'Ha-ha, this should be just what you need,' she said with a smirk. 'Within the pages of this book you will get a complete overview of the whole history of the British involvement with the slave trade. This book is amazing. It will tell you about the world famous anti-slave campaigner, William Wilberforce who worked tirelessly for most of his life after taking on the cause in 1787. It will explain why the British actually got involved and why they chose African slaves. You'll probably get an A-star.'

The two boys gave her a look of pure delight, before pulling up a chair. Matt's eyebrows shot up to his hairline.

'This is just fantastic!' he said, giving her a heart-warming smile. 'It's really good of you to take the time to show us this section,' he added. 'Thanks a lot.'

Crystal felt a warm glow reach her cheeks for the second time that day.

'I'll leave you to it, then,' she answered, feeling suddenly redundant.

'It was really nice meeting you,' Matt nodded, his eyes absorbing the invaluable text. 'Thanks again.'

As she turned to leave, a wave of nausea burst into the pit of her stomach, followed by a crushing pain in her skull. She grabbed hold of a vacant chair to steady herself. If she waited, surely the moment would pass.

'Are you alright?' asked Matt, realising she had become unwell.

She opened her mouth to answer, but felt only spears of hot pain shoot through her brain causing her to gasp. Her limbs grew heavy with an intense pressure as though huge boulders had been placed upon her shoulders and she felt herself edging towards the floor. Then the coloured images within the library started to spin away in a spiral of dense fog and unknown voices invaded her mind while she fought to stay conscious.

Alfie felt his stomach lurch.

'What's happening?' he cried, feeling a stab of unease. 'You're not going to throw up or anything like that, are you?'

'Death will take the innocent!' she shouted, forcing the two boys to stare at one another in astonishment. Alfie's face turned blank, and Matt's head snapped back as he took a reality check.

Her body language was strangely stiff, but her eyes were huge and lucid, moving rapidly from side to side.

'Beware of the water, for he hides there!' she cried out. Small beads of perspiration were forming on her forehead, sparkling like diamonds in the bright sunlight. Confused, Alfie moved his chair closer to Matt's.

'There's no water here,' Matt soothed, trying his best to reassure her. His eyes switched to the library, looking for signs of an imminent tidal wave.

Crystal's facial muscles tightened as her mind was taken over.

'Don't get in it!' she pleaded, her arms reaching out, but her fingers touched nothing but emptiness. 'I beg of you, listen to me.'

The vivid images they couldn't see were so extraordinarily real to her and her alone, and she was coherent enough to realise she was experiencing some kind of extrasensory vision. Her distress was mounting and she held the chair tighter, her knuckles turning white. Without making a sound, Matt pushed his chair away from the table.

'Stop right there!' Crystal shrieked. Huge sobs broke from her body and Matt tensed.

'The darkness has won,' Crystal wailed, her eyes pouring with tears. Her hands suddenly flew to her throat and a choking scream echoed from her lips, as though she was suffering some kind of a constriction around her windpipe. Her eyes flickered for several seconds and then she fell unconscious to the floor, her arms lying limp by her side, her breathing a faint whisper.

Matt was petrified. Dropping by her side, he shook her fiercely, calling her name and trying to wake her. At first, there was no reaction and niggles of acute apprehension pricked sharply at his brain until he admitted to himself that he didn't know what to do to help her. Finally, he received encouragement when a moan touched her lips. So soft was the sound that escaped that he thought for a moment he had merely imagined it. She groaned again, louder this time, and relief enabled his blood to flow freely once more.

'Go and get help!' he shouted to Alfie, rubbing her frozen hands with his. 'Go and get someone quick.'

A woman's voice broke his train of thought.

'What's going on here?' she demanded and before he could answer, the stranger was by his side and a firm hand gripped his arm, trying to pull him out of the way.

'Is she hurt?' the woman asked, sounding genuinely concerned. 'Come on, please move out of the way and let me get a better look.'

'Who are you?' asked Matt, feeling somehow responsible for Crystal's welfare.

The stranger eyed him critically.

'I'm her mother,' she said, tight lipped. 'Now, let me get a closer look.'

Dropping to her knees, Beatrice stooped over Crystal's shivering body. Concern was knitted deep upon her brow.

'Who has done this to her?' she gasped, throwing Matt an accusing stare. 'Are you the cause of this?' she demanded, her eyes flashing angrily.

'We didn't do anything,' Matt said in his defence. 'She just started saying loads of strange stuff and acting really weird.'

Beatrice turned her attention back to her daughter, brushing her hand over Crystal's cool skin.

'You need to understand that my daughter is very special. By that remark, I don't mean she has any physical or mental disabilities. What I mean is she is different, she can sense things.'

She turned her attention towards Matt.

'Tell me, what did she actually say to you?' Matt shrugged his shoulders.

'I'm not sure to be honest, none of it made any sense.'

'What about you?' she asked Alfie, raising a quizzical eyebrow, her expression already doubtful. 'Can you shed any light as to what has happened to my daughter?' Alfie shook his head and then knelt at Crystal's side. His hands were shaking and he twisted a bit of his shirt between his fingers in an attempt to give himself courage.

'She was mumbling something about the darkness winning,' he told her, stroking Crystal's clothes as if she was a puppy. He fixed his gaze upon Beatrice, his huge eyes pleading for a look of reassurance.

Crystal murmured something unintelligible and then began to stir causing Beatrice to shift her daughter's head onto her knees so that she could use her lap as a pillow.

'She's waking up,' she said, her eyes sparkling with relief. 'You can go now if you wish.'

'Are you sure?' asked Matt, looking reluctant.

'Yes, of course,' Beatrice insisted. 'There's nothing more you can do for her.' She caught the pained look in his eyes, realising he only meant to be helpful.

'She's going to feel pretty embarrassed once she comes round,' she explained, heaving a sigh. 'Please, don't make it any harder for her than it already is.'

Matt nodded. 'Okay,' he said, hesitating, 'if that's what you think is best.'

Beatrice nodded. 'It is, my dear,' she replied, allowing her lips to turn into a tight smile. 'Everything's going to be just fine.' The boys said their goodbyes, but both were unwilling to leave. Dragging their heels, they made their way out of the building and onto the main street.

'What on earth was all that about?' mumbled Alfie, once he felt they were well out of earshot, his eyes still fearful. Matt didn't answer; he had noticed his hands were shaking and he shoved them into his pockets in an attempt to make them stop.

'Beats me,' he said, turning to view the library in a new light, 'but I was really scared for her back there.'

'What do you think she was trying to tell us?' asked Alfie, concentrating on picking his nose and wiping it on the front of his shirt.

Matt pulled a face. 'Do you have to be so disgusting?' he hissed, shoving his hands deeper into his pockets. A nervous twitch formed above his right eye when a droning noise filled his ear. He tilted his head and watched a honeybee buzz close to his ear; it was big, black and golden. He moved out of its way, allowing it to pass, watching the small, plump insect race along with the wind, busy, alone, yet with such purpose to its life. His thoughts returned to Crystal, wondering what he had just witnessed.

'I just think Crystal's lost her marbles,' Alfie said, frowning; 'what other explanation could there be?'

Matt shook his head in dismay.

'I don't know what to make of it, but one thing's definite; I ain't ever going back inside that library again.' He made his way across the road and headed for a side street, his face tightening when he mounted the pavement. 'In future, I think we'll just stick with the Internet.'

Alfie laughed, slapping Matt playfully on his shoulder, the incident already becoming a distant memory.

'Come on, mate, cheer up. I've just remembered the footy's on tonight and we're having fish and chips for tea. I'm sure there'll be enough left over to put a smile on your face; what do you say?'

'Now that's food for thought,' said Matt, suddenly producing one of his famous grins. 'Hah,' Alfie chuckled. 'First one home gets to eat the scraps!'

'You're so gross,' shouted Matt breaking into a run. His strong legs took huge, wide strides, allowing him to take the lead almost immediately.

'Get back here!' Alfie shouted, stumbling. 'It's not fair, you have an advantage with those beanpoles for legs.' He stopped for a moment to catch his breath.

'Come on, loser,' cajoled Matt, slowing down when he realised his friend was miles behind.

*Conceited swine*, thought Alfie, who was anything but amused. *Why did Matt always have to make everything so bloody competitive*? He started to run again, his determination getting the better of him. *One day,* he thought to himself, *I will show Matt what I'm really capable of.*

*

Crystal opened her eyes and winced. Her head hurt beyond belief and she raised her hand to feel the back of her swollen skull. Her fingers probed for the source of the pain; a large egg-shaped bump was making its way to the surface. Although coherent, her head throbbed from the impact of hitting the hard stone floor, making her feel rather woozy. As her eyes came back into focus, she realised her mother was bent over her, holding her in a protective embrace. She groaned, turning her head away in embarrassment.

'Come on, love,' her mum urged, 'let's get you onto this chair; it's a bit more comfortable than the floor.'

Gritting her teeth, Crystal used all her strength and tried to stand, grasping her mother's arm for support. With some reluctance, she allowed Beatrice to help her get into a sitting position, before managing to pull herself up off her knees and onto the chair.

'What happened to you?' Beatrice asked, with a flash of anxiety reaching her eyes. Crystal lowered her lashes as though to hide from her and turned her face away.

'Don't you want to talk about it?' her mother pressed.

Crystal lifted her head and met her mother's gaze. She noticed the worry lines etched deeply in her skin and felt a twinge of guilt. Her mother didn't deserve to have this weight of trouble put upon her, yet Crystal had no one else to turn to. She took a deep steadying breath.

'I saw one of those boys die,' she said, fighting a sickening knot that invaded her gut. She brought her fingers to her mouth and started chewing her nails. It was clear her nerves were bordering on collapse.

'I tried to tell them what I'd seen,' she blurted, looking deep into her mother's troubled eyes. 'I tried to warn them, but the dark side jumbled up the scenes in my head, trying to stop me from telling.' Tears of frustration filled her blue eyes as she begged for her mother to understand.

'I scared them away,' she said, sounding miserable, 'and all I have to go on are their first names.' Her words faltered and the tears that had been brimming so close to the surface now ran unchecked down her face.

'I don't know what to say,' said Beatrice in bewilderment. 'You're getting yourself all worked up over something you can't control,' she added, busying herself with her daughter's crumpled clothes and ruffled hair.

Crystal shook her head in dismay. It was obvious her mother just wasn't grasping the seriousness of the situation. Her soft, calming tone was soothing to her daughter, yet her lack of understanding irritated her immensely. Crystal rose to her feet, setting her hands on her hips in a gesture of defiance. Her cheeks were streaked with tears and her eyes shone with those yet to be shed.

'You know I have a special gift,' she snapped, searching her mother's face for some sign of comprehension. She reached out and squeezed her mother's shoulder.

'Tell me you know I'm different.'

It was Beatrice's chance to turn away, but Crystal's grasp was far too strong and their eyes held one another.

'I do understand only too well my darling, probably more than you realise, but this is not the time or place to discuss it. Let's just get you out of here and back home where you belong.'

Crystal let her go.

'You know I have to try and help them,' she said, while the evening sun crept through the windows, casting a wonderful golden light above her head and causing her to look like a fiery angel.

Her mother gave her head a solemn shake. 'Look, just be very careful what you do,' she warned, holding onto her hand. 'This is all new ground for you and you don't know the penalty for dabbling in these dark arts.'

'You know I'm not dabbling, and they aren't dark arts,' Crystal snapped with rising frustration. 'I can't just sit back and do nothing when I know someone is in danger. I feel a real sense of power deep inside me, one which I don't quite know how to use yet, but in time, I'm sure I will. All I do know is that one of those boys is in serious peril and I'm going to do my very best to save him.'

'Sometimes I think you have come from another place,' Beatrice said, feeling a stab of cold apprehension.

'I think that's exactly it,' said Crystal, making light of what her mother said. 'I think I came from somewhere like the planet Krypton.' Beatrice managed a weak smile.

'I'm serious,' she chided. 'You know when you were born, I used to have the oddest of dreams, nightmares really, and I would wake up believing someone wanted to take you away from me, that you weren't actually *my* daughter.'

A soft smile lingered on Crystal's mouth. She had heard this story many times in the past and had never taken it seriously.

'You should be so lucky,' she chuckled. 'No one's going to take me away Mum, not ever; that's all they were, just horrible dreams.' Her expression softened and the atmosphere around them turned lighter. 'I'm all the family you need,' Crystal added, flashing her brilliant blue eyes and enabling her mouth to lift at the corners, just a little. She took a step forward and slipped her arm around her mum's full waist, giving it a tight squeeze.

'Nobody will ever change who we are,' Crystal whispered, when her mother returned her warm embrace. 'It's just you and me, like it's always been and that's how it's going to stay for the foreseeable future.'

# *Chapter 2*

Only a single day had passed since the drama in the library, but to Crystal it felt like a lifetime. She sat huddled over the breakfast bar in her warm kitchen and scanned the local newspaper for any clues or stories that could inadvertently help her save a life. She probed each column of print, in search of crucial information involving water, but everywhere she looked, she found nothing that could help.

Beatrice entered the kitchen from a side entrance, leading from the dining room, and headed for the sink. Placing a used cup and saucer in the washing-up bowl, she eyed her daughter; aware of how much she had matured over the last couple of months. She stared at her delicate features and thought, not for the first time, how she didn't resemble anyone in her immediate family.

She had been such a good baby. Once settled into a routine, she had rarely cried and grew into a gentle and caring child. Her placid nature and quick wit showed at an early age, but she had to admit that the nagging doubt of her being some kind of an impostor was still there, eating away at her, bit by bit, day by day.

She remembered how she'd slept fitfully that first night of Crystal's birth, worrying the child was not truly hers after the harrowing dream she'd suffered as soon as she'd drifted off to sleep. Since that night, part of her always believed that the real mother would one day make her way to her tiny cottage and steal her beautiful baby back. Logic told her she was being completely ludicrous; what substantial evidence had she ever found to support the wild accusation that roamed uncontrollably in her head? Yet she knew, deep down in her soul, that the child she held dear was not her own. The dreams had been too real and too regular, and the reality of day had been unable to chase away the dark shadows that had so readily grasped hold of her subconscious mind; it was like an itch that could not be scratched. But she loved Crystal with all her heart and no one would ever take this child from her without a fight.

She studied Crystal once again, watching as her hair fell over her face while she devoured the contents of the weekly tabloid. Her long auburn hair had been allowed to grow out of its girlish bob and it fell down her back like a moving cascade of hot lava. It was so rich in colour and thickness that it was outrageously sinful, the deep russet tones accentuating her eyes, which were a dazzling shade of sapphire blue, protected by a row of long, silky lashes. She was a willowy creature with slender limbs and artistic tendencies. There was not a shadow of a doubt; Crystal would mature into a strikingly, beautiful woman.

Beatrice looked down at her own hands and saw only the wrinkled lines of age and felt a pang of despair. She was growing old there was no denying it, her youth already a distant memory. Her own hair was peppered with grey, yet she made no effort to hide it, her only priority was Crystal. Raising a child on her own on a widow's army pension was no easy feat and money was always tight, but they somehow managed and Crystal was her one beacon of hope for the future.

While Beatrice continued to think about the years ahead, a more recent incident scrambled to the surface of her thoughts, yet another reminder that life was not quite so 'normal' with Crystal around. Only a few days ago, there had been a minor incident when Crystal cut her finger while assisting in the kitchen. She was preparing fresh vegetables for dinner when the knife she was using slipped, slicing open the tip of her finger. Blood oozed onto the stainless-steel draining board, creating a dark-red watery pool. Crystal grabbed the nearest thing she could see, a clean tea towel, and wrapped it around the wound to try and stem the flow. While the blood soaked into the cloth, she ran to her mother for help. There'd been a flurry of panic as they raced to the medical cabinet looking for a clean bandage and some tape. Beatrice removed the cloth to find there was no cut to attend to; the wound had miraculously healed itself. They both stared in disbelief, the blood-soaked towel lying abandoned on the bathroom floor, a startling reminder of what just occurred.

Back in the kitchen, the radio was playing softly in the background. The music was mellow and easy listening and in-between the songs the presenter talked about his impending retirement. Suddenly conscious of watchful eyes upon her, Crystal threw her stare directly at her mother.

'Penny for them,' she said, searching her mother's doleful expression.

'Not worth halfpence,' retorted Beatrice, trying to force a smile. A profound sigh escaped Crystal's lips while she crumpled the newspaper into a tight ball.

'There's nothing written in here that's going to help me,' she said, throwing it into the bin in disgust. 'But there has to be something somewhere which will give me some kind of clue,' she said scowling, 'but I just can't find it.'

'Come on, love, stop tearing yourself apart,' her mother soothed. 'You tried to help those boys as best you could, but I don't think there's anything else you can do.'

Unconvinced, Crystal resorted to tapping her fingers lightly on the table, humming to a tune she recognised on the radio and then she started mumbling the lyrics to herself.

*'Mmm, I swear I left her by the river, mmm, I left her safe and sound.'*

With a cry of inspiration, Crystal leapt out of her seat, startling her mother who took a step back in fright.

'Of course, the fishing lake, that must be the place!' Crystal shouted, her eyes shining with enthusiasm. 'It's the only deep water I know of; it would make perfect sense.'

'You're not going!' cried Beatrice, becoming fretful. 'I mean it, absolutely not!'

Crystal flushed. 'Mum, you know I have to do this.'

Grabbing her coat from the back of the chair, she kissed her mother hard on the cheek as she flew past.

'Look, you mustn't worry, I'll be alright.'

'No, child, you mustn't go,' Beatrice cried, sounding flustered. 'You don't know for sure if you will be able to stop anything happening, you might even make matters worse, and you're just a young girl who has no experience of life or the paranormal.'

Crystal chose to ignore her mother's harsh words, concentrating only on what she must do. She moved to the other side of the kitchen and opened a stiff, wooden drawer. She pushed aside the few knick-knacks that had been stored there to reveal the amulet. With nimble fingers, she placed the necklace around her throat before glancing in the small opaque mirror to admire it.

'There! Now I'm safe from harm,' she said, pawing at the necklace. Her slim fingers brushed the red stone and the jewel rippled at her touch, producing a rich, golden glow.

Beatrice raised an eyebrow when she saw the amulet change colour.

'You know we don't know for sure what kind of charm that is,' she said, shaking her head with worry. 'You've always been able to sense things, but it's not necessarily because of the necklace.' Crystal turned away from the mirror and pushed her arms through the sleeves of her jacket, the tight band on the wrists proving troublesome. Then, she made her way to the back door and opened it. Cold air wafted in and Crystal turned towards her mother, her face softening upon seeing her look of anguish.

'Look, mum,' she said, trying to defend her own reasoning. 'What you say may well be true, but I always feel safer when I'm wearing this necklace. The truth is, I do feel different when I wear it, I feel a bit like ... Wonder Woman,' she said, trying to force a grin.

'Please don't go,' begged Beatrice, still unconvinced. 'I think it could be really dangerous, especially with it involving the lake. I couldn't bear it if I lost you too.'

Crystal felt her heart miss a beat at the mere thought of her dead father.

'Don't try to make me feel guilty by using dad,' she said, her eyes burning with a sudden fury. She felt a wisp of sadness cling to her at the memory of the man who had died before she was born.

She took a step outside, breaking the last invisible bonds of her childhood and she unconsciously stroked the orbs, feeling a wave of calm rush through her body at its touch. For years she had accepted she was different, she had just never been sure in what way. After the episode yesterday in the library she knew she had a special gift, something unique. Now her strength was growing and with it a sense of bravery which she hadn't experienced before.

Her mother called out to her, one last time.

'There will be no turning back,' she said, reaching for her daughter and grabbing nothing but fresh air. 'Your fate lies in your own hands and I have to admit, that frightens me.'

'You know deep down, I have no choice but to do this,' Crystal shot back, her eyes still showing signs of hostility. 'My gut instinct tells me I have to unravel the crazy puzzle which I have seen inside my head. I may not be sure how to use my gift yet, but I'm positive I will know soon enough.'

'This is sheer idiocy,' Beatrice declared, her eyes narrowing. 'You're just a girl!'

'Mum, please stop being difficult. Why can't you see that I feel like a volcano ready to erupt. This strange burning sensation which ignites while I sleep grows stronger with each passing day. You know I'm not normal, so why try and play these silly games with me?'

Her mother looked beaten and her lips stayed in a tight line, still unable to comprehend her daughter's sudden wilful streak.

'Look, I'll be back as soon as I can,' Crystal promised, when she saw her mother's stunned expression. 'Just don't go worrying yourself stupid.'

*What the hell just happened?* Beatrice thought when Crystal left. She massaged her forehead when a banging sensation hit against her temples. She had almost felt intimidated by her daughter's maturity as she stood her ground. Something had changed, shifted between them. She moved to the stove and grabbed the kettle. Taking it over to the sink, she turned on the tap and watched it fill with water. The loud gushing noise grated on her nerves, making her turn off the gas and place the not-quite-full kettle on the draining board. She turned and looked out of the kitchen window, her eyes drinking in the endless green of the rolling hills lying in the distance. Her mind was in turmoil. What on earth was happening to them? Her eyes filled with tears when she wished for the support of a loving husband, something she had wished for many times in the past, but no one else had entered her life in that way. Her vision became bleary from unshed tears wavering on the very tip of her lids, testing her ability to keep it together. Her throat ached with hurt and fear, and she reached out and filled a glass with water.

'Come back to me Crystal,' she heard herself plea. 'Don't leave me like your father did.' Her body straightened as though a whip had hit her spine. She felt her hands reach up and cover her face and her resolve broke and a flood of tears poured down her face. She was no longer in charge of her daughter's life; somehow the tide had turned. Her future rested in her own hands and the child who was her only piece of priceless treasure, was becoming harder to keep safe from the rest of the world. Then, while she wiped away the endless stream of tears with the back of her hand, the feeling of having lost her precious daughter suddenly deepened.

*

It took Crystal some time before she reached a safe place where she could climb onto the grassy bank that surrounded the lake. She stumbled upon a dry stone wall which had crumbled away enough for her to gain easy access. Glancing around, she checked that no one was watching her, not wishing to draw attention to herself – a girl alone. Satisfied she was unobserved; she made her way through the gap and onto the stony path. It seemed such a lonely place and she trembled with apprehension. She zipped up her jacket to protect herself when a blustery wind appeared from nowhere and made her shudder, making her stuff her hands into her pockets for added warmth.

A small brook twinkled prettily down a slight embankment to her left and she watched the water trickle over the muddy earth, seeping over mossy stones and slippery rocks in search of its final resting place, making the path wet and dark. She continued on her way and within minutes, passed a solitary man fishing. His stature was well built and he stood close to the water's edge on strong, sturdy legs. His fishing tackle was strewn over the pathway, making it difficult for her to pass but she manoeuvred around him, annoyed at his lack of consideration for others. She stole a glance his way, noticing his eyes were closed and that his mouth was covered with something that resembled blood...

*'What the?'* She gasped, sensing danger. She forced herself to think, realising she had to get away from him - fast. She averted her eyes and then broke into a run. She prayed he wouldn't drop his fishing rod and give pursuit, convinced this was his immediate intention.

On hearing her running footsteps, the man turned and opened his eyes. Deep within him, something evil began to stir. The festering ooze of a supernatural being, malevolent in character, was hiding itself inside the mortal body of the man, and the force of his greed dripped from his twisted mouth. On earth, people called this presence: *The Shadow of Death*; in the extraordinary world he was named *Abaddon – the Destroyer*.

He continued watching her while she fled from his sight, becoming ravenous for her unusual kinetic energy which surrounded her and he sensed she was powerful. He had felt her supremacy when she had closed in on him, and he wanted it all for himself. He was known to be a force external to nature, controlling forty legions of souls, and each soul was sent to him to suffer an immortal life of purgatory and he fed on their fear and loathing.

Now he wanted Crystal.

As she ran, Crystal forced the growing niggles of danger aside, pushing herself on and evaluating what was important. In the strong sunlight she was beginning to look tired and drawn.

*Stay focused,* she told herself, when her mind reverted back to the stranger and she suffered a shiver of fear. Scanning the lake, her eye caught sight of something oddly familiar. Her gut threw her an almighty punch when she realised what she had spotted in the distance. Against the haze of the sun she made out the shape of a rowing boat, she'd seen in her premonition. Bobbing against the tide it drifted on the surface of the water, creating a scene of serenity before her troubled eyes. Then she saw two small, dark shapes messing inside and knew instinctively who was on-board. The overwhelming feeling of panic forced her to break into a sprint. The boat seemed so far away, and she needed to get there – fast. Adrenalin pumped through her veins and strong muscles, giving her the burst of energy she so desperately needed. With a will of their own, her legs ran faster, her determination and strong spirit urging her on.

'Get out of the boat, get back to the bank!' she screamed until almost hoarse. However, her cries were swallowed by the sheer vastness of the space between them. It felt like she was never going to reach them, and she realised time was already against her.

*

It had been without hesitation that Alfie and Matt had rolled up their trouser legs, shoes forgotten on the bank, and waded into the water to rescue the abandoned rowing boat.

'This is just the coolest thing,' laughed Alfie, grabbing the oars and checking they weren't broken. 'Let's row to the middle,' he said, passing a paddle over to Matt, 'it'll give us something to do.' Matt clipped the oar into the holder, creating a splash when it hit the surface of the water.

'Hey, watch it!' laughed Alfie good-naturedly. 'I don't want a bath just yet.' Matt chuckled to himself while they both larked about, happy to be outside on such a pleasant day. The wind had died away and the sun was shining down on their naked heads, the water refusing to entertain a ripple, just what you would want to create a perfect afternoon. They made their way to the centre of the lake and noticed they were alone.

'I'm surprised it's so dead out here on such a lovely day,' said Alfie scanning the horizon for bodies.

'Yeah I know what you mean, it's usually busy down here this time of year and we could have made the most of it if we'd thought to bring our fishing tackle,' said Matt staring down at a passing trout.

'You're right, it would have been great fun to do a spot of fishing, especially with us finding this boat,' answered Alfie with a cheeky grin. 'I wonder what kind of fish are down there? Bet there's salmon, and I heard my dad say there's carp here too.' He stopped and thought seriously for a moment. 'I wonder if there are any piranhas?'

Matt let out a genuine yelp of laughter. 'You're such an idiot at times,' he said, shaking his head in disbelief. 'You know, you don't half come out with some right tripe at times,' he added, placing the oar back in the boat and settling himself down.

'No I don't!' retorted Alfie, feeling a stab of resentment. 'Don't say things like that to me, you're supposed to be my mate.'

'I can't help it,' Matt teased. 'You should hear yourself.' He searched for an example. 'Like the time you believed you get newborn babies from Tesco's!' He let out another peel of laughter. 'That was so funny.'

'That's not fair,' said Alfie thinking of a way to defend himself. 'That was my older brother's fault, that's what he told me, and I was only five at the time.'

Matt was starting to enjoy himself. 'Okay then, what about that time you went to the toilet, and an hour later your mum videoed you fast asleep on the loo, with your trousers round your ankles and showed it to half the street.'

Alfie's head jerked back at the reminder, humiliation burning his plump cheeks. He could feel the heat from his face creep all the way down to the pit of his belly. He opened his mouth in protest.

'Oh yeah, I forgot you're so bloody perfect,' he hissed with such venom that Matt was quite startled. 'Who's the one in double figures that can't even swim then, smart arse?' A wicked glint appeared in Alfie's right eye; something dark surfaced from inside him and he decided it was time Matt drank from the cup of humiliation for a change.

*

Crystal managed to cover some considerable distance in a relatively short time, but her body screamed out from the physical exertion. Her legs hurt, her chest was tight and her long hair clung in a damp cluster across her face. Beads of sweat were visible on her pale skin, but she wiped them away with the back of her hand as though they were nothing more than a group of annoying gnats. She was determined to make it to the boat, but she still had a fair distance to cover before she would be close enough to enable the boys to hear her calling them back to safety.

It took her by surprise when she found herself falling, and trying to save herself she thrust her hands out to break her fall. Crashing hard upon the stones and baked soil, she realised she had been taken down by an obstinate root and had landed badly. Wincing in pain, she thought perhaps she had sprained her ankle. She bit her lip, forcing herself back onto her feet. She felt hot pain shoot up her leg and immediately sat back down. Grappling the soil, she forced herself up with the help of a thick branch she spotted close by. The pressure of her foot touching the ground caused her to wince in pain again, but with each passing moment the throbbing appeared to ease. She wasn't far from them now; she knew she couldn't give up. Struggling to calm her beating heart and fill her lungs with much needed oxygen, the terrible scene she had seen only the day before in her mind began to unfold before her very eyes.

Back on the boat, Alfie had started to rock it from side to side and it was clear anxiety was mounting by the look on Matt's face, but this only fuelled Alfie's desire to scare him all the more. Matt shifted his gaze and peered below the surface of the lake. He thought the water had an eeriness about it, as though strange shapes were moving through its dark tangles of weeds and he gave an involuntary shudder when he realised he couldn't see the bottom.

'Don't even think about it!' shouted Matt, attempting to read Alfie's mind and when Alfie turned to look at him, he realised Matt was genuinely frightened.

'I mean it, pack it in!' Matt cried, when he was almost jolted out of his seat. 'You know damn well, I can't swim.'

'You're not so tough now,' Alfie sneered in delight. 'You don't like it when someone else is in control for a change, do you?'

Matt's green eyes rounded in shock and Alfie's smile turned into a ghastly grin. He gave the boat yet another sharp tug and this time, it almost capsized. Matt clung to the sides, yelling obscenities in fear. He found he couldn't move a muscle and his knuckles had turned white as he used all of his strength to ensure he didn't fall into the lake.

'I'm going to wring your bloody neck when we get back on dry land,' Matt screeched while his face turned red with fury.

'You're in no position to threaten me,' laughed Alfie, clearly enjoying himself. 'I'm in control for once and we'll go back when I'm good and ready!'

'Please, enough's, enough,' Matt pleaded, noticing the look of madness in Alfie's wild eyes. 'Come on, let's get back to shore and forget all about this.'

'Not on your life,' Alfie spat, lifting his chin in defiance. 'Because today's the day, I teach you a very valuable lesson.'

Abbadon looked on from the safety of the shore and relished the thought of what he was about to do. He calmly made the fisherman put down his rod. His eyes were burning red as scorching coal embers inside the man's head and the torturous pain the demon was inflicting, tasted savoury and sweet. Releasing himself, the demon began to shake free from his human cover.

The possessed man shook and squealed from the internal pain like a slaughterhouse pig, but the demon only chuckled with infinite pleasure. Invisible claws ripped at the man's flesh and tore through his entire body, bringing death to him in an instant. The demon, intent on escaping the confines of his mortal shell, poured from his hiding place like the plague, vaporising into a black mist which choked the air like coal dust. The empty carcass fell to the floor; the lifeless body discarded, his soul already devoured.

Abbadon licked his evil lips wanting to taste fresh, young souls and applauded himself when he spotted the two boys messing about on the lake, victims rich with life.

He quickly made his way over the water, floating through the air only inches from the surface. Dark clouds filled the once blue sky, swirling and thick, and sat in abundance above the lake amidst the rumbles of thunder.

Crystal felt the malevolent presence before she saw it, and with all of her might she screamed her warning one last time. On hearing her cry, Abbadon formed a ghostly body. Then he extended his arm and opened his long, bony fingers, seizing her words in the palm of his skeletal hand. A dark sound escaped his blackened lips as he crumbled her words to dust, before allowing the ash to fall into the water like scattered cinders. Crystal could only watch in horror when Abbadon flew with purpose, towards Matt and Alfie. He hovered over them like some prancing Halloween effigy and both boys flinched when he shot to Matt's side. Then with one quick flourish of his hand, he knocked Matt straight into the water.

Matt was under the surface before he knew what hit him. Shock clasped Alfie like strong hands around his throat. He hadn't actually intended for his friend to fall in and had never expected any intervention by some black, deadly ghost. He sat frozen to the spot, unable to move as though rigor mortis had somehow invaded his trembling body, his senses told him his best friend was fighting for his life, but he was unable to move.

Matt surfaced only once and while he struggled for breath, the water covered his head once more and he disappeared under its cold surface. He fought to make it back. Thrashing his arms and legs, he tried to reach the boat, confused as to why Alfie wasn't trying to save him. His sodden clothes dragged him under the murky water and he was unable to re-emerge. His lungs screamed out for oxygen as he tried to breathe underwater, his nose and mouth could no longer suck in air and his lungs contracted in pain. His eyes grew wide with terror, watching his world slip away and he floated down to where a watery grave lay waiting.

With evil intent, Abbadon dived into the freezing water, feeling nothing but excitement under its cold surface. The girl temporarily forgotten, he swam in circles around Matt's body, faster and faster he spun, disorientating him in seconds. Matt was unable to cope, his brain couldn't decipher the sluggish messages it was receiving and his mind fled to the safety of unconsciousness, allowing his legs to finally still. The sweeping grasses hidden below reached out for his feet and slipped their slimy leaves around his ankles, tightening their hold, obeying the Destroyer.

'Your time on earth is almost over,' they whispered sadly.

Abbadon was thrilled. He could almost taste the boy's life force as the weeds dragged him further towards the darkness.

Back on the surface, Crystal's heart was thumping so hard in her chest that she thought she was about to have a heart attack. She knew if she didn't use the light, the burning power she held inside herself, Matt was as good as dead. Determination and fear were growing deep within her causing a strange tingling sensation to wash over her entire body.

Closing her eyes, she focused her mind on Matt. Then, she touched the stone in the centre of the amulet and a golden aura formed around her body. She glanced down at her hands feeling the glow penetrate her skin and caught sight of a bright light in-between her fingers.

Clasping the amulet in both hands Crystal once again closed her eyes. Her lips parted and words that she had never heard before slipped easily from her mouth. The language she spoke was not one she recognised, but it flowed from her tongue like a dam bursting its banks.

Her mind saw only a ball of light; the bright golden rays sent tendrils of energy through her body. Her nerve endings became filled with heat, her veins full of fire. Her mind pulled at the fiery strands as though they were cotton threads dangling tantalisingly towards her, touching her, teasing her, enabling her to pull more and more energy from them. Her rich voice was rising, becoming more forceful and she outstretched her arms towards the lake as though she was summoning something to come to her.

The stillness of the water broke before her closed eyelids and waves started swelling against the water's edge. Then something rippled and uncoiled a few metres away from the boat. It was at least twenty foot long and silver-grey in colour. It dived under the water, swirling its slippery body with ease and made its way to the motionless body tied down by a multitude of weeds. It watched Abbadon take hold of his victim, ready to suck out the last breath that kept the boy in the world of mortals.

Without warning, the creature attacked Abbadon and taken by surprise, the demon let go of its prize. The creature swam with purpose, wrapping its enormous thick trunk around Matt, much like a python, obscuring the victim from view. Abbadon was furious, believing the creature wanted his trophy for itself. Attacking the serpent, Death howled like a banshee, clawing at the creature, fighting for his rightful possession. The creature screamed when vicious talons ripped at its bare flesh. Recovering from the shock, the serpent made its way to the shore, and forcing itself towards the alien world of mortals, it sprang from the water. Using all of its strength, the magnificent creature unravelled its colossal body from the lifeless boy it was trying so desperately to protect.

With a flick of its long finned tail, the serpent catapulted Abbadon's victim through the air and towards the shore. Matt landed with a loud thump, only inches away from Crystal's feet. He lay there on the ground, like a dead fish that had been plucked from the water by an unsuspecting fisherman.

Crystal opened her eyes at the sound of the thud and immediately ran to Matt's side, dropping to her knees she felt for a pulse. Fear numbed her brain when she realised there wasn't one to find.

'No!' she shrieked, pushing him over onto his back. His arms dropped like heavy weights by his side and she didn't know what to do; his face was so white, his body so still. She was filled with terror. Her head lashed back as she tried to remember how to give the kiss of life. Bending his head and neck back to open his airway, she tried to breathe life into his dead body. Particles of her breath still carried the magic from the chant within it, and the ghostly molecules drifted into his lifeless shell.

Crystal faltered when she watched his skin turn grey, not knowing if it was all too little, too late. She pumped his stomach and then pressed against his ribcage, clamping her strong hands around his chest, beside herself with worry. Aware of losing him, she kept her rhythm going, before pouring air into his lungs again and again.

'Please wake up,' she begged, checking again for a pulse. 'Damn you Matt, I won't let you die,' she hissed.

His eyelids fluttered, before he opened them and took a sudden gasp of air. He shuddered and water spewed from his mouth and she turned him over onto his side so that he didn't choke. Sheer relief filled her body as she coaxed him to get as much water out as possible and he coughed and spluttered beside her for several minutes.

Once his breathing was more regular, she pulled off his wet t shirt and shirt and replaced it with her jacket. Pulling it around him, she hugged him tight.

'I saw what happened out there,' she said, watching the colour return to his cheeks, but Matt's face was blank of expression.

'Really?' He said, shrugging his shoulders in bewilderment. 'Well, I can't remember much after getting into that boat, except when I close my eyes, I can see some kind of black phantom, trying to suck my face off,' he said, shivering. 'Anyway, enough of me, where's Alfie?'

'Alfie?' she repeated, glancing at the boat and seeing him curled up safely inside. 'Yeah he's doing just fine.'

Matt pulled the jacket closer and Crystal thought he still looked dazed.

'Don't worry, you're going to be okay,' she said, trying to reassure him, pulling the zipper up to his chin.

Glancing back at the lake, she saw Abbadon and the serpent both emerging from under the water. They were still fighting and the shrill noise they made each time they made contact made her recoil. The serpent took hold of Abbadon, trying to shake him senseless, but Abbadon didn't know when to call it a day, he was furious at losing the boy and soon had the serpent in his grasp. He became aware he was being watched and looked across at Crystal before throwing the serpent down into the water as though it was nothing more than paper. He knew he had been cleverly outwitted. Although aware he had lost the battle, he took comfort in knowing he would always win the war.

He soared high into the sky, levitating high above Crystal and Matt. His dark shadow flowed like torn ribbons against the blackened sky, blocking out any light which dared to peep through the thick cloud. He took one final look at Matt, who returned his gaze without a glimpse of fear showing in his eyes. He had stared Death in the face and lived.

A howl escaped the lips of the demon before he exploded into a thousand bellowing crows and the cawing of the birds while they flew away blew a spear of dread along the wind. Silence followed, before calm swept over the lake; smooth, like icing smeared on a wedding cake.

'I can't believe you managed to save me from that thing...' Matt said, unable to express his gratitude.

Crystal looked gravely at her new friend.

'I'm just thankful you're alive,' she replied, glancing over her shoulder. 'You gave me one hell of a fright out there.' Matt nodded, still clearly unsure as to what had actually happened.

The water lapped against the sides of the grassy bank once more and the newly exposed sun shone down on their frozen backs.

'Look, Alfie's drifting closer to shore, I'd better go and get him while I have the chance,' Crystal said. 'Will you be alright for a minute?'

'Yeah, sure,' said Matt, shifting uncomfortably on the grassy bank. 'I'd rather you tried to get him to be honest, I'm not sure I can face going back into the water just yet.' He tried to force a smile.

'Alright then,' she said, poking him in the chest. 'But don't you dare move from this spot until I get back or I'll crucify you.' He laughed then and she got up, noticing her limp had completely vanished. She checked her ankle for swelling unable to believe her eyes, but there was nothing there, so she rolled up her trouser legs and waded into the lake.

Just as the water reached her knees and the chill seeped way into her bones, something stirred around her feet and for a second, she thought perhaps the serpent had returned and her eyes locked onto the rippling water to see if she could catch the flicker of a silvery tail.

Crystal took a step forward, only to retract her steps when she felt a dragging sensation pull around her toes. Alarmed, she decided to head back to the safety of the shore; Alfie would just have to get himself back on dry land. She went to turn, but the strong current wouldn't allow her to move as though invisible weights clung onto her legs. She was starting to feel afraid, unsure what was happening when a few metres away, the water became a bracelet of silvery foam, creating a large swirling whirlpool.

Hysteria floated inside Crystal's head and she cast her eyes back to the bank where she had left Matt only moments ago. Her eyes widened when she realised he hadn't done as he'd promised and had wandered off. Panic rose in her throat. She waved her arms to try to alert his attention and she shouted both Alfie's and Matt's names over and over again but to no avail. She got no response from Alfie who lay in the hull as though he was comatose and Matt unaware of her dilemma, simply waved back while he searched for his socks and shoes a few hundred metres away. Crystal lowered her arms in defeat. Her gaze drawn to the centre of the whirlpool, mesmerised as it swirled and bubbled wildly.

She felt herself turn cold and her heart skipped a beat when a human hand broke through the swirling vortex.

The hand, slim with long, beautiful fingers, was followed by an equally impressive arm. Crystal caught her breath. She turned towards Matt once again; surely he could see this too? Although she had begun to question her sanity, she watched the image of a woman rise before her. The figure ascended majestically from the shadowy depths, her long robes clinging provocatively around her curves and the shimmering gown she wore was the colour of aquamarine. Long, golden hair waved in a thick layer down her back, entwined with two herringbone combs to hold her thick tresses in place. She stared at Crystal, her body hovering over the water. It was then that Crystal noticed the long slithery tail and she drew back, forcing her hand to her mouth while she tried to stifle a scream.

'Do not fear me,' the creature soothed, 'I'm not here to harm you.'

When she spoke, her voice seemed light and sweet, floating towards Crystal like a butterfly that drifts from flower to flower. The panic died in her throat when she realised the creature felt no animosity towards her, but the fear refused to leave her.

'Have we met in a past life?' asked the beautiful apparition, edging closer.

Crystal found her mouth was so dry she thought she might choke and merely shook her head in answer. The creature smiled, sensing her fear and with agile grace, pulled one of the herringbone combs from her hair and swept it through her golden tresses. Shimmering strands fell from the teeth and dropped into the water and calm swept over the lake and through Crystal.

Crystal watched her replace the comb.

'Now then child, wasn't it you who called me to save the mortal?' the creature asked, flicking her tail unexpectedly. Crystal dropped her gaze.

'I don't know if it was me who called you. I mean, I did need help, and I believe I was chanting some kind of incantation, but I didn't quite know what I was doing, so I'm not sure if it was actually me who brought you here.'

The beautiful creature giggled like a secretive child and a spark of curiosity lit inside her sea-green eyes.

'My name is Gzhel,' she said, curtsying daintily. 'I am a wandering water spirit, a drifting soul of a time gone by. You called me with the spell of Egoth, a spell known only to the elfin bards who were destroyed many centuries ago.'

Crystal was dumbstruck. She stared into Gzhel's eyes and realised she somehow spoke the truth, but she didn't know what to say.

'You conjured a very powerful spell,' Gzhel continued, 'and I am not absolutely certain how a young inexperienced witch like yourself managed to awaken me from my unfathomable slumber.'

'I'm not a witch,' Crystal cried in surprise. She heard her voice rise with disdain. 'I desperately needed help, that was all,' she added. 'I just closed my eyes and used my mind, praying someone would come and save my friend from that terrible ... *creature*.'

'You did more than that,' said Gzhel, ignoring her outburst. Her beautiful face looked sad. 'Because of the powerful magic you used, I was brought here. Now my mystical strength is very weak. Deep inside my body, I have internal wounds that will take many suns and moons to heal. These wounds were caused by my fight with the Destroyer. However, even with the strongest will, I could never physically beat him. He is filled with such evil and you know him in this life as the Shadow of Death; and as you are well aware, no one will ever beat Death. My courage came from a thousand dreams of hope, a bravery forged by a desperation to be forgiven. My strength is from centuries of hardship and despair, something you may also taste in your many lives upon this lonely earth. The Elders, an elite council of mages, banished me from my own world for things that cannot be undone. I will be punished for a thousand years or more; pray the same will never happen to you, sweet child.'

A cold wind blew across the water, causing Crystal to shiver.

'What did you do that was so terrible?' asked Crystal, feeling a stab of intrigue. The words fell easily from her lips. She hadn't meant to pry, but she couldn't help being inquisitive. What possible sins could this fascinatingly beautiful creature be guilty of?

'It is not for me to tell,' said Gzhel with a heavy sigh. Huge tears ran down her soft cheeks, shining like diamonds against her peachy skin. 'I am merely here at your request and nothing more.'

Crystal was struck with guilt. Her eyebrows arched as she contemplated what she'd actually done by awakening this supernatural being.

She opened her mouth to apologise, but before she could speak, Gzhel was pointing a slender finger towards the necklace, a fleeting smile crossed her lips and her bright eyes danced with mischief.

'Aah, I see how you roused me from my slumber,' she said, her gaze fixed upon the stone. 'The amulet you wear has a name, it's called the 'Spirit of Eternity' and it's *this* amulet that helped stir me from my deathly sleep. Tell me, from where did you get it?'

'My mother found it in my crib when I was a child,' Crystal said, placing her hand protectively over the orbs. 'It isn't worth anything to anyone but me.'

'I find that hard to believe,' said Gzhel, giving her an odd look. 'It's plain to me that you are a child of the extraordinary world. These two worlds are often linked together for one reason or another, but I'm curious as to why you're here in the world of mortals? Still, that is none of my business and as for the amulet I feel it could very easily be your birthright to have it.'

Crystal shuddered again; confusion splintered her mind into thousands of unanswered questions, her hunger for knowledge, dripping like oil onto a burning flame, fanning a need so intense she felt her head was about to explode.

'That's just impossible,' she heard herself saying, 'really it is.'

Gzhel pondered for a time. 'Do not fret over your origin,' she said at last. 'I have a strong suspicion you will know the truth soon enough, but believe me when I say you are *not* from this world but from another. You need to put your unanswered questions to the council of Elders. My foresight tells me they will have the answers you seek.'

'But how can I get to these people?' asked Crystal, becoming caught up with the excitement of what the spirit told her. 'I don't know how to find them.'

'Your question is simple to answer; you hold the key to all knowledge in your hands.'

Crystal felt frustrated and her mind raced ahead, searching for clues. She didn't have any key, only a weird necklace.

'I have said enough,' said Gzhel, her eyes focused beyond, as though sensing something that made her feel ill at ease. 'I cannot help you any more, my task here is done, I must leave you now.'

'Thank you for saving my friend,' Crystal blurted when she realised the creature was preparing to plunge back into the icy water. 'Please believe me, I never meant to hurt you.'

Gzhel watched Crystal closely, before giving her an important piece of advice.

'Beware, daughter of magic. Death has been cheated here today and he won't look kindly on that. Mark my words he will be back, if not for your friend then for you. You have certain bearings of the supernatural, which a mere mortal can never obtain. Hear my warning: you have not seen the last of him, for he will not forget today, and *will* seek you out in the future.'

Before Crystal could protest, Gzhel whipped her silver-grey tail, around her body. In a flash, the lake withdrew the water, revealing the moist sand beneath. Frightened fish jumped in the air, quivering, their own silvery tails flashing in the sunlight while they used them as an emergency rudder, wishing only to penetrate the surface and return to the safety of their silent world. The dark water surged forward, erupting into an enormous fountain. The torrent towered high above the spirit's head for what seemed like an eternity until she turned and dived inside. The cascading flow ultimately subsided and then eased into a fine mist of delicate silver droplets, each melting away until any trace of her was gone. The lake, always respectful, settled back into a picturesque setting.

Crystal raised her hands heavenward.

'I saw her with my own eyes, I actually spoke to a mystical being,' she whispered, pinching her arm to check she had not been hallucinating.

Her chest muscles relaxed enough for her to breathe freely again. Crystal lowered her hands and glanced over to the boat. To her surprise, she saw it was making its way towards her, pushed by an invisible hand. It glided on the calming water, stopping only when her fingers reached out and touched the bow. She peered inside to see Alfie rolled up in a tight ball, his eyes screwed shut with his hands over his ears. Without saying a word, Crystal turned back towards the bank and guided the wooden boat safely to the sandy shore.

# *Chapter 3*

'I still can't get my head around what happened yesterday,' said Matt, grasping the handle and opening the great double doors of the library. His eyes, however, were extremely vigilant when he stepped inside. Crystal shrugged her shoulders.

'I don't presume to have all the answers,' she said, throwing herself into the first vacant chair they came across, 'but at least you're alive and kicking.' Alfie cleared his throat.

'You know, I really am sorry about what happened. I honestly don't know what came over me.'

'Oh, it wasn't your fault,' Crystal said, stretching the tension from her shoulders. 'You were a pawn in a terrible game out there yesterday, but thankfully, in the end we were not the losers.' She breathed in the heady smell of beeswax mixed with the natural aroma of furniture polish. It smelt so good and the tension in her shoulders slowly ebbed away.

'Let's just forget about it,' she said, giving him a warm smile to show she felt no animosity towards him.

'I agree,' said Matt, slapping his mate on the back for good measure, 'and to think we're back in this place,' he added, screwing up his nose and taking the seat next to Crystal. 'You know, I wasn't going to step foot in here again after meeting you.'

. *An unfortunate beginning to an unusual friendship,* she thought secretly to herself.

'Yes, I have been known to appear a bit strange,' she said instead, shifting in her chair and frowning. 'You see, I'm not entirely sure of the powers I possess,' she explained reaching for a magazine, 'but as long as it all works out in the end, what does it matter?'

Alfie moved towards a set of three oak bookcases situated close behind them, showing a tantalising display of hardback books. He thumbed along a few of the spines, but it was obvious nothing held his interest. Instead, he dropped like a sack of potatoes into a leather armchair and watched Crystal leaf through the pages of the magazine. Crystal caught his stare, and he forced a tight smile unable to hide his bout of boredom. Somewhere in the building, a clock chimed the hour.

'Can you hear that?' Alfie suddenly asked the others. Cocking his head to one side, he strained to hear a distinct sound. Crystal was amused to see his eyes appear to dart in several directions at once and Matt made the gesture of putting his hand to his ear, to help him focus on the noise.

'Probably bats,' Matt said, losing interest, however Crystal wasn't totally convinced.

'That's strange,' she said, sounding wistful, 'I'm here most of the time, and I've never heard constant tapping like that before.'

After a minute or so her face tightened, the noise was clearly irritating her.

Tap, tap, tap, the noise continued. Crystal felt the earlier tension in her shoulders returning.

'Do you want me to go and investigate?' asked Alfie, his voice sounding weak. He didn't really want to, but didn't want to appear spineless after yesterday's performance.

'It's probably just a broken branch or an overgrown twig banging against the window,' said Matt, thinking of a rational explanation. 'It's hardly anything to worry about.'

It was a slow, regulated beat, precise in its elemental rhythm: TAP, TAP, TAP.

'What the hell is that?' Crystal snapped, throwing her magazine down in frustration. She folded her arms and narrowed her glare to rest upon Matt, making it obvious she wanted *him* to investigate. He accepted the challenge and jumped to his feet and she watched him with keen interest, noticing how his eyebrows arched in concentration.

'Look, it's coming from that window,' Matt said, pointing to a small circular hole above them.
Alfie started shaking in his boots.

'What do you think it is?' he whimpered, with a crackle in his voice exposing his anxiety. Matt's face softened. 'Oh, it's nothing more than a little bird,' he said, pointing to something white. 'Look, it's pecking like mad to come in.' Alfie followed his gaze, suddenly smiling broadly.

'Phew,' he said, shivering with relief, 'it's not something nasty then.'

Climbing on a bench, Matt reached up and fiddled with the latch. He could see storm clouds forming, blowing high in the sky and scudding in front of the sun. He switched his attention back to the handle. It was stiff with age and he was struggling to open it. There was a clap of thunder before the drizzle fell and he gave a small cry when the latch gave way, allowing fine rain to splash onto his face. He pushed the window wide; laughing with pleasure, his hands wet and slippery, when the bird dived past him.

'Well, there's the culprit,' Matt stated, jumping down off the bench. 'It's a white dove and it was adamant it was going to get in through that window.' Crystal walked over to the bird which was resting onto the back of a chair. Something had caught her eye.

'Why, it's got a strange marking on its left wing,' she pointed out, moving closer and craning her neck to get a better look. The bird flapped its wings clearly startled, before folding them back and settling with a 'coo.'

'It looks like a fingerprint,' Crystal stated in surprise. 'No, actually it's thicker, more like a thumbprint; how unusual.' The bird cooed at her once again, bobbing its neck as though in greeting.

'I wonder if it's tame,' Alfie pondered aloud. 'Looks like it to me.'

'Mmm, you could be right, but look, it has the weirdest coloured eyes I've ever seen,' Matt said.

'It's plain freaky!' said Crystal, clearly ruffled by the bird's presence, 'I think we should get out of here and go and grab a coke.'

'But it's pouring down,' said Alfie, whining. 'I don't want to go out in the rain.'

'It's okay we can stay if you want to,' Crystal said, shifting her shoulders uncomfortably, 'it was just a suggestion.' A peculiar wave of internal intrusion washed over her then, like something was trying to tap into her psyche, and she grabbed her stomach, feeling slightly sick. The dove spread its wings and took flight, landing on the bench, its eyelids closing sleepily. She frowned turning to look at the bird.

'I'm sorry,' she said, sounding confused, 'but I suddenly don't feel well.' Crystal looked at both Matt and Alfie as she spoke, her blue eyes turning troubled. 'I know this sounds silly, but I feel like something is trying to take me over.' She became agitated, chewing her bottom lip in distress. 'It's like someone else is here with us and they're trying to get inside my head, I can feel it.'

Alfie gulped. *Please, God, not another vision*, he thought to himself. After the day he'd had yesterday, he couldn't face another drama.

'I'm getting some sort of mental vibe,' Crystal said, trying to explain herself better. 'I just need time to clear the fuzz inside my head,' she rasped, realising she sounded completely batty. Matt glanced around the library, his shoulders were tense but he was relieved to see there was nothing sinister lurking in the shadows.

'Do you want to be alone, is that it?' he asked, raising a dark eyebrow. 'Just say the word and we're out of here, if that's what you want.'

Crystal knew he was being perfectly reasonable, but it annoyed the hell out of her all the same.

'No, of course not, silly, leaving me isn't the answer. It's hard to explain, truly; just give me a minute to pull myself together.' After a moment Crystal looked as though the pieces of the puzzle were finally falling into place.

'It's all getting clearer,' she said, putting her fingertips to her temple, 'I can see a picture in my mind... I can just make out the faint outline of a male figure. He's small, with blood red eyes, and he's extremely anxious. His natural movement is strange, quite jerky and I believe he's neither human nor animal, I just can't quite see his face...'

She closed her eyes and then blinked them open, turning her attention back towards the dove. Unexpectedly, she dived onto the bench. For a moment, she thought her legs would turn to water and flow away like a broken raft when a strange feeling zapped her energy. With sweating palms, she grabbed hold of the bird; it was clear it had been taken by surprise and when she tightened her grip, it tried in desperation to get away from her grasp. The terrified bird pecked fiercely at her fingers, but Crystal refused to let go.

'What are you doing!' Matt gasped, unable to keep the shock from his voice.

Crystal glanced over at him, but her attention was snatched by the strange black mark on the dove's wing. She drew a shuddering breath before letting go of the bird with one of her hands and she placed her own thumb over the black mark and pressed down, hard. There came a guttural cry. A blaze of green and red light erupted like a flame from a faulty firework, followed by a rich stimulating aroma, which no one could later identify. A breathless enchantment darted through the smoky atmosphere, causing a shiver of uncertainty to descend between everyone in the room.

Crystal felt herself dragged to the ground by a sudden heavy weight and lost her balance. Her eyes were blinded by the intense blur of colour, but her fear of the unknown only tightened her grip. The hazy glow faded away and in its place sat a figure with Crystal's hands clasped around a bare throat. They both lay there, stunned, for what seemed like eternity until a voice rasped in Crystal's ear.

'Would you mind letting me go?'

Crystal was scared, unsure of what she'd done and refused, until she felt the intruder surge to his feet, forcing her to follow, both of them white faced. She stared at the strange looking man for several seconds without releasing her hold and she saw that fright competed with fury in his eyes. She absorbed the dark hair, his unremarkable face and his rather pointy ears. Her eyes ran over his sallow complexion and stopped at his eyes, for they were red as blood. He looked almost human, but it was clear he was not, even though he was dressed in simple clothes, a plain linen shirt and dark woven trousers. From his belt hung a small silver dagger intricately carved with a complicated design. The hilt flashed when he moved his hip, a warning of its potential to kill.

'Who are you?' Crystal mouthed, unable to stop trembling.

'Isn't it obvious?' the creature replied, pulling a grim expression.

'Well, no, it isn't actually, but the main question is, are you going to hurt us?' she asked, suddenly tightening her grip.

'Hardly, and anyway, aren't you the one with your hand around *my* neck?' the creature hissed, flashing his hard eyes at her. He flicked his gaze to Matt and Alfie and saw only their cold stare in return.

'Why is someone like you here in our world?' Crystal asked, her lips drawn tight. 'What do you want with us?'

'Well, if you let me go I will try and explain,' the half human shot back. 'Of course, we could always stay like this,' he added, placing his cold hand over hers. 'It's your choice.'

She felt his cool fingers touch her skin, but she was too afraid to let go. Matt walked over and pulled gently at her arm.

'Let him go,' he urged softly, but his eyes were filled with concern. 'I think you're hurting him.'

'Well, Hall-elu-jah,' the creature said, when she relaxed her fingers from around his throat, feeling his neck and making sure his windpipe was still intact. 'You have quite a grip there, young lady.'

'What do you want?' Matt interrupted, pulling Crystal to a safe distance.

The stranger took an unexpected step forward.

'In answer to your question, my name is Tremlon and I am a messenger sent here by the Elf King Gamada, who rules the Kingdom of Nine WInters.'

Alfie screwed his hands up into fists and raised them to his chest.

'Do you have a message for us or something then?' he demanded, flexing his jaw. Crystal stepped back and clutched one of his hands. She raised her eyebrows, shaking her head at his unreasonable behaviour.

*She's got a nerve,* thought Alfie with a huff, *especially after the performance she's just given.*

'Well no, not exactly,' Tremlon replied, looking sly.

Crystal cast her gaze back towards the elf, and he nodded to a chair for it was clear he needed to sit down when his legs buckled underneath him. Tremlon's movements were surprisingly swift, but he sat heavily on the cushioned seat, his sharp eyes searching for the nearest exit.

He heard Crystal speak and a question he had not been expecting reached him as quick as rainfall on a cloudy day.

'Are you here to tell me I am like you?' she asked, looking slightly foolish.

He sounded wistful when he replied.

'So, you fancy being an elf do you?' he asked, with a hint of amusement trailing through his voice. He rubbed his neck when he spoke; where angry, red welts were forming, a reminder of what she was actually capable of.

'Oh, an elf! Is that what you are,' Crystal declared, her eyes widening. 'I have spoken to Gzhel, a wandering water spirit and she told me I could be from another place.'

A tense silence fell between them.

'Yes, alright, it's true, you belong to the extraordinary world,' Tremlon admitted throwing her a wary look, 'but your origin is not so well defined as mine.'

Crystal shifted from one foot to the other.

'You're not making any sense,' she said, clearly unsettled. Frozen by the chill in her eyes, Tremlon knew he could only bend the truth a little.

'We have been watching you for some time,' he told her, sitting back in his chair. 'We already know you called Gzhel, the spirit of the lake, which is how we were alerted to where you were and the fact that you were using old and forbidden magic. You see we were never sure what powers you would possess, nor indeed if you would ever inherit any natural Elvin tendencies with having Oakwood blood flowing through your veins.'

Crystal held up her hand, signalling for him to stop.

'What, you knew of my existence already?' she blurted, feeling her breath leave her body. He heard coldness seeping into her voice and he appeared to struggle with his conscience before being able to carry on.

'I think you had better sit down,' he said, patting the seat next to him.

Crystal hesitated. Her mind was racing ahead and thoughts of who she might be leapt around her brain like an opened sack of jumping beans. She dragged her gaze towards him and eventually obeyed. Clearing her dry throat she said, 'I think you had better tell me what's going on.'

'I can tell you only what I know,' Tremlon answered, clasping his small hands together and trying hard not to stare. His face turned serious and sadness shot from behind his eyes.

'Your beginning was a terrible time for all of us,' he said finally, unable to turn his face away.

Nobody heard the delicate footsteps that echoed down the empty corridor. No one heard them edge their way closer. Matt and Alfie had pulled up a chair, forming a small semicircle, with Tremlon placed at the centre. One by one they each became engrossed in what Tremlon was saying.

'Hello guys!' came a cheery voice, startling them all. 'What are you doing hiding down here?'

Taken by surprise, Crystal spun round in her chair. Tremlon's eyes grew wide at the intrusion, instantly transmuting back into a dove. He flapped his wings, taking flight before Crystal had chance to pin him down again and he flew to the safety of the rafters, hiding along the wooden beams.

Crystal gasped, screwing her eyes up to try to catch a glimpse of him, but he was nowhere to be seen. Fury filled her heart and consumed with anger, Crystal turned on the intruder. Her rage fell on her victim like boiling water poured over an unsuspecting ant.

'You stupid, stupid idiot!' she cried. 'Have you any idea what you've just done!'

'Err, I'm really sorry,' said a trembling voice. 'I didn't realise I was interrupting anything important.'

Matt jumped out of his seat and viewed the young girl standing before him with angry eyes.

'She's my sister!' he revealed, showing obvious contempt. 'Camilla, what the hell are you doing here?'

'Why? What's the big deal,' his sister replied, suddenly pouting like a spoilt child. Her large, brown eyes locked onto his when she added, 'I didn't realise it was against the law to come and find my brother.'

'But you never come here,' Matt insisted, grinding his teeth. 'Why choose today of all days to change a habit of a lifetime?'

Camilla bit her lip and looked sulkily at the floor. Exasperated, Crystal bolted forward, pushing the girl aside and it was Alfie who reached out and grabbed her. Her face was shiny with tears and she paused, mid-step at his touch.

'Oh, what does it all matter?' she muttered, trying to make light of the heart break she was feeling inside. 'Tremlon's probably gone for good and so I'll never know the truth now.' Alfie stared at her with his sad, puppy dog eyes but Crystal's head was so scrambled with damning revelations that she didn't see the pity welling inside them.

Her exposure was no real surprise to her; in fact it was nothing more than unexpected confirmation of what she had always known. A secret she had held at arm's length, the whisper she had kept silent for so long. The skin around her beautiful blue eyes tightened just a little while she accepted who she might be. In reality though, who was she? Was she different because of her father? The father she had never met, the man who had died before she was born? Was he the one from this other world, an elven creature like Tremlon? She had been so close to a major discovery about herself, but now any chance of finding her real identity was shattered. She brushed Alfie's hand away and without looking back, walked from the library and into the arms of a torrential downpour.

Matt watched her leave. He wanted to rush after her and tell her it would all work out, but he didn't know that for sure and he realised she probably needed time alone.

'I really feel for her,' he said, raking his fingers through his dark hair, 'she's in a place we don't even know exists.' He turned towards his fourteen year old sister. 'I could quite easily murder you right now,' he said, allowing his anger and frustration to escape.

'What did I do?' Camilla wailed, clearly unaware of the dilemma she'd caused.

'You followed me here!' Matt snapped, pointing an accusing finger. 'And to think, you've never read a book in your life!'

'Dad told me where you'd gone actually,' she blurted, sounding hurt. 'All I wanted was someone to hang out with.'

Matt bit his lip when he caught her wretched expression.

'It's time we left,' he said, slipping his gaze over her for the final time. 'You've done more than enough damage for one day,' he added, marching off down the corridor, with Alfie close at his heels.

'Wait for me!' she suddenly begged, rushing after him. 'Don't go leaving me in this horrible place all on my own.'

High above the rafters, hidden from view, Tremlon watched them leave with a quiet mind and a calmer spirit. The king had given him so many responsibilities and there were too many plans to keep secret. He would return to the king and inform him of his first meeting with the princess. She had been so very clever, this young, intelligent, almost magisterial creature, using a natural source of sorcery known only to the antiquated bards who had not existed for thousands of years. He spread his wings, content to be returning to his own kind in one piece and as he vanished, he wondered, not for the first time, if King Gamada actually realised he was playing with fire.

# *Chapter 4*

It was nearly a week before Matt managed to see Crystal again. He'd visited the library every day since the episode with Tremlon and his sister, but each time he was disappointed to find there was no sign of her anywhere. Alfie tagged along a couple of times, but finding it boring, eventually produced a feeble excuse so as not to have to go back again.

Matt stood alone outside the solid structure of the central library. His eyes swept over the large square stones holding this remarkable building together and he was impressed by what he saw. Above the door sat a sombre plaque, both weatherworn and showing signs of age, explaining it had been built in 1801. The huge clock dominating the centre of the building, chimed a deep, bellowing welcome.

While he was studying the impressive architecture, the sky was suddenly hijacked by a flock of pigeons and small, brown birds. Dropping from high above, they swooped to earth, landing on the verges and soft green lawns of the grounds, close to where Matt stood. Their small beady eyes fell on the rich, dark soil in search of small insects and anything remotely edible. Hungrily, they pecked at leftover crumbs and stale crusts dropped by fleeting visitors over the lunchtime period that were in a rush to fill their empty bellies.

Matt kept a watchful eye, searching for a glimpse of the white dove with the black mark on its wing, but once the ground was clear of every crumb, the birds moved on, and so did he. With purpose, he climbed the grey stone steps that led him to the mouth of the library. Swinging the gigantic double door that led into the main hall, he felt its sheer immensity fill him with an overwhelming feeling of insignificance. It had taken him more than a little time to appreciate just how awesome this place really was, but he had gotten there. The perfectly smooth walls were solid, with strong oak beams placed high in the painted ceilings, creaking and groaning a long tune of eeriness whenever anyone dared to enter.

Matt approached the heart of the library and his pace slowed when he reached the section of books clearly marked 'W'. He glanced at the famous names written in black and gold, embossed with a firm indent on the spine of each book. Williams, Wodehouse and Wordsworth. None of the authors' names meant anything to him, yet he knew they should and a stab of ignorance twisted in his gut.

He reached out and grabbed a book, trying to show a spark of interest. He flicked through the musty pages, unable to focus on the words with his mind being someplace else. Regretting his lack of concentration, he replaced the volume back onto the shelf. He tried again, the tip of his finger moving towards a light, silver binding and he pulled at the spine, but then a sudden movement behind him made him let go. He spun on his heels, his nerves taut with expectancy, but he soon felt foolish when he realised there was nothing behind him except innocent, fleeting shadows. His breathing was heavy and the small hairs on the back of his neck stood up like soldiers waiting to be inspected. He realised his imagination was running wild and he took a deep breath to calm himself.

'Who's there?' he called out, suddenly convinced he wasn't alone. His eyes moved in search of what made him uneasy, but nothing but silence answered his call. The acute sense of isolation surrounded him making him aware of his own vulnerability and he called out once again, his voice sounding on edge.

'Be quiet boy!' a shrill voice commanded. 'This is a library, not a playing field.'

He recognised the voice to belong to the librarian and he let out a sigh of relief. He peered out into the gloom, but it was clear the librarian was well out of sight.

'I'm outta here,' he mumbled under his breath, still feeling foolish. 'There's nothing here for me but trouble.' He pursed his lips and started to whistle to give himself courage but then an elderly man with his ageing wife came into view and Matt let the tune die in his throat. He headed for the bright green signboard that pointed to the exit and stuffing his hands into the sanctuary of his pockets, he thought about where he could go to kill the rest of the day.

'Were you trying to grab my attention?' asked a familiar voice. He recognised it immediately and his mouth broke into a broad grin when he saw Crystal appear from behind one of the huge, white pillars.

'Hey, fancy finding you here,' he said, genuinely pleased to see her. He accepted the welcome of her smile, but he thought she looked tired and a little drawn around the eyes.

He watched her move to a small writing desk, hidden between two marble columns. A table light throbbed above her head, making her hair glow like fire. Matt stared at her for a moment too long before he spoke, afraid if he said the wrong thing she would disappear again. She was hurting he could sense it and he didn't want to upset her by opening his stupid mouth and saying the wrong thing.

'I'm sorry about what happened the other day,' he said, trying to strike up a conversation. 'I know how important it was for you to speak to that bird-thing.'

Crystal was reading a book and ignoring him.

'So, what have you been doing with yourself?' he persisted, changing tactics, 'have you been up to much?' Her eyes glanced up from the page but she appeared to look straight through him.

'Come on, you must have been doing something?' Matt gasped, when she still didn't answer him and she pushed a wisp of her long, thick hair which had fallen across her cheek away from her face instead.

'I've just been doing some research,' she told him when the curl slipped back over her eyes. He felt a shiver run down his spine.

*God, she's so beautiful,* he thought to himself.

'What are you reading?' he enquired, swallowing hard. Her reaction was guarded and her face was set, resolute, and he instantly regretted asking the question when she snapped shut the cover of a large book and he let out a sigh of frustration.

'What's so top secret that you can't tell me?' he snapped, offended by her actions. Crystal blushed when his eyes flashed with anger.

'I'm sorry,' she said, lowering her dark lashes. 'I know I can trust you of all people.'

Matt heaved a sigh.

'So, are you going to share what you've learned with me then?' he asked moving to her side. He thought back to that unforgettable day at the lake knowing he had a lot to thank her for. She had saved him and, in return, he would try and do the same for her – one day.

Crystal's eyes clouded.

'I've found this old book on mythology,' she explained, shrugging her shoulders. 'I thought it might help me understand a little more about sorcery or that bird-man, who, if my memory serves me correctly, is called Tremlon.'

He nodded, remembering the moment when the bird had transmuted before his very eyes.

'None of us will be the same again after seeing him,' he said, threading his fingers through his hair and pushing it away from his face. Crystal broke into a bitter laugh.

'You're so right there,' she said, pushing the thick, leather-bound book towards him. 'None of us will ever be the same again, especially me.'

He reached out and felt the cool binding touch his fingertips. His eyes inspected the dark cover. The book smelt of damp and old age, and a bronze clasp in the shape of what looked like a Celtic symbol grasped the numerous pages firmly together. He had never seen a book of this calibre before, and it needled him.

'Where'd you find it?'

'In the fantasy section, though I swear I've never seen it there before.'

'It's not like you to miss a book of this size,' he said with a smirk that reached his eyes. 'I thought you said this place was your second home.'

Crystal pulled a face.

'A mere oversight,' she said, rising from the chair and motioning for him to sit. 'Come here and I'll show you what I've found so far.'

His keenness showed as he obeyed her. The warmth of her body trapped within the wood of the chair, made his body tingle.

'You've got a warm bum,' he teased turning shy. They both giggled; two teenagers learning how to become close friends. A slight draught brushed against his left cheek and he bristled, his eyes alert.

'Did you feel that?' he asked, spinning in his chair.

'Feel what?' Crystal replied, her attention returning to the book. She leant over his shoulder and started to thumb through the pages but Matt suddenly felt very ill at ease. He didn't know if it was because she was so close, or if it was because something else was closer still?

'Matt, you okay?'

'No,' he said, his eyes hooded. 'I guess it's just my vivid imagination on overdrive again.'

Crystal mumbled something about being silly and tried to nudge him out of the way.

'So what's so good about this particular book?' he asked, shuffling his chair to make room for hers.

'Well, for a start the cover is not actually leather, but made of human skin,' she told him, brushing her fingertips over the odd ripples that covered the surface. 'If you look closely, you can see all the lines that make up the membrane.' She had shocked him and Matt recoiled, pulling his own fingers away from the cover, momentarily repulsed.

'That's disgusting,' he told her flatly.

'You don't believe everything you hear, do you?' she replied, her eyes filling with amusement.

Matt bit the inside of his lip. 'It looks real enough to me,' he said feeling his jaw tighten. 'In fact, it's bloody gross.'

'It's just a legend,' Crystal said, ignoring his outburst. 'The story goes that the skin represents an influential magician who believed he could one day be brought back from the plateau of the afterlife. His bones were buried in a secret location and he ordered his skin to be peeled and soaked in the amniotic fluid of his first-born son, the water that had protected the foetus in the womb. Once this was done, the skin was turned into parchment, before being made into this unique book.' He shut his eyes and allowed the vision to form behind his lids.

'Nope,' he said, his eyes still closed, 'that just doesn't cut it for me.'

'You have to be more open minded,' she told him, not the slightest bit amused. 'After all, if you're hanging around with me you're going to have to lose some of your scepticism,' she added. His face relaxed and he opened his eyes to see hers, bright and wary, fixed on his. He noticed her arms were folded under her small breasts and he blushed before having the decency to look away.

'Anyway, I've managed to find out what Tremlon meant when he said I had Oakwood blood,' she told him, unaware of Matt's bright red cheeks.

'Oh yeah, what's that?' he asked, thankful for the diversion.

Crystal laughed.

'Apparently, the bloodline can only be found from the realm of Oakwood Wizards.'

'Wow, that sounds very mythical, doesn't it?' he said, grinning. 'So tell me, what evidence have you found telling you all this?'

Crystal shifted uncomfortably before reaching out and turning the thick vellum to a page she had bookmarked earlier. He felt a slight tremor move through his body at her even closer proximity.

'See here,' she said, pushing the book right under his nose and pointing to a specific paragraph. He followed her gaze and slid his eyes over the beautiful handwriting, written over a thousand years ago. The pages were large and thick, and the lettering was amazingly clear considering its age, with sweeping illustrations inscribed with meticulous detail. Matt pulled his chair closer, drinking in the startling information, he felt the enchantment woven within the pages begin to magnetise him, coaxing him to concentrate. He felt a thrill of excitement when he traced his fingers over the thick, gold letter imprinted at the start of each new page. The words were written by a fluent hand, filling him with wonder.

'This is just awesome,' he murmured, with eyes wide with delight. He brought a finger to his temple in concentration. Silence welled and his mind opened to the spells and charms, lying like a mountain of goodies for him to digest. The faint light of the library unfolded down on him and he was unaware of the dimming surroundings. He turned over the next page, transfixed. Drawings of colourful wizards jumped out of the page at him, and the words of sorcery, waved like a magic wand before his eyes, creating wonder in his mind. He eventually went back to the paragraph Crystal had earmarked and, glancing up, he pulled the table light closer so he could see the writing more clearly.

*...But there were others, others who were special far beyond what we would call a normal wizard or sorcerer. These wizards were born with incredible powers, which were released with age and maturity. They were given these gifts to protect the ordinary and the extraordinary worlds. We have little knowledge of this band of mages. The evidence we do have, tells us they came from the realm of Ravens Rainbow. These wizards were strong, their sorcery not from the darkness but from the white spear of light. If they disgraced their own kind, the penalty was heavy, possibly even eternal purgatory. However, there has been known to be a slither of leniency, which was not always acceptable to the one who was judged. If the magician was found to be guilty of a crime committed against the realm he could, if granted by the Elders, be pardoned. Banishment was only a minor luxury, but if they so chose, the guilty party would have to give a living part of themselves to the ordinary world. Whatever part they gave had to be done so freely, only then releasing them from their sentence...*

'This is pretty heavy stuff,' sighed Matt, mentally exhausted. 'No wonder you're so troubled. Can you imagine having to give away your arm or leg?'

'Well, I'm not completely sure that's what it means,' Crystal said, pulling the book away from him and taking her turn to gaze at the paragraph once again. Matt sensed her turmoil.

'We aren't knowledgeable enough to understand all this,' he said, trying to ease her confusion, but then he saw a shadow cross over her face.

'Come on, out with it,' he demanded, his eyes turning to slits. 'I can see you're not telling me everything.'

Caught at a vulnerable moment, Crystal decided to come clean and tell him all about what happened at the lake and the full version of events, followed by her life and her fears of who she might be. She spilled the beans to her newfound friend, having a burning need to release the torment that was eating her up inside.

Matt listened spellbound for the next few minutes while she poured out to him the constant dreams and visions she had suffered since early childhood. She shared with him her innermost secrets of how she had saved him and what she had awakened deep below the surface of the waves. She stopped only to draw breath, exhausted by the rush of words that spilled like wine from her lips. Only a moment's silence engulfed them before it was shattered by an intruder's voice.

Simultaneously, Matt and Crystal's eyes darted into every dark corner and deep recess having recognised the voice. Uncertainty wafted between them and Crystal worried as to how much the bird-man had overheard.

'And so we are to meet again,' Tremlon trilled, manifesting before them like a ghost and Matt sprang out of his seat in surprise.

'Bloody hell!' he said, pointing his finger accusingly. 'It's the bird-geezer again. I knew he was here, I felt him creeping about earlier but thought it was just my stupid imagination.'

Crystal shrank back into the shadows, taking the book with her.

'Don't worry about that old thing,' Tremlon said, releasing a sly smirk and pointing to the book. 'I'm only too pleased you were able to enjoy what's written inside; I thought it might help you understand our kind more.'

'Why, you scheming son of a bitch!' she yelled, clutching the book to her chest. 'I knew it wasn't there before.'

Tremlon gave a hearty chuckle and the book was torn from her fingers by an invisible force, landing with a loud thud on the cold stone floor only inches from his feet. Crystal rushed forward in panic, uncertain what he would do next. She desperately wanted to keep the book, but she was too scared to try to retrieve it and so instead it sat like a vast rock between them.

Tremlon clicked his fingers and the book vanished into thin air. Crystal gasped.

'I've merely archived it,' he said, in a peevish tone, unaware of her look of dismay. He clasped his hands together and brought them up to his mouth as though in prayer.

'Crystal, I have a proposition for you?' he said, cocking his head to one side, unconsciously imitating a bird. He watched for her reaction with curious eyes. 'Tell me; are you interested in broadening your horizons?'

She looked bewildered, aware only of her ribs moving up and down as she breathed.

'What are you talking about?' she asked, jutting out her chin in disdain. She feared him, loathed him even, but deep down she knew he was the key that could unlock the dark secrets that would tell her who she really was.

Tremlon looked into her beautiful blue eyes and saw raw hunger.

'I believe it is your wish to visit my world, is it not?' he probed, watching a pulse twitch at the side of her temple. 'After all, didn't Gzhel advise you to seek out the Elders?'

She hesitated, unsure of herself and that moment of delay sealed her fate.

'I have come today at the request of the elf king Gamada,' Tremlon explained, exchanging glances. 'You've heard me speak of him before,' he reminded her with a toss of his black head.

She nodded; feeling her own curiosity ignite and she peered over at Matt and noticed he was looking rather fractious.

Tremlon followed her gaze and frowned. He sensed Matt's devotion to the princess for it was clear he adored her and this made the shape-changer all the more cautious.

'It would appear the king needs your help and he thought he could perhaps strike an unlikely bargain with you. You help the king, and in return he will take you to speak with the Order of the Elders so you can learn whatever your heart desires regarding your actual birth right,' he said, leaning his shoulder against a marble column. Crystal looked at him in surprise.

'How could I possibly help an elf king?' she asked, forcing her eyes to connect with his.

'Well, I'm not sure, I'm just the messenger,' Tremlon stated, shrugging his shoulders. 'However, the king must believe you can do something to help him otherwise he wouldn't have wasted my valuable time sending me here to find you.'

'You're messing with her head,' Matt snapped, rushing towards him, his fists raised in readiness to punch him. His eyes glared dangerously at the shape-changer, his body taut with expectation.

'Hey, calm down,' said Tremlon, backing away and showing the palms of his hands in surrender. 'I'm not here to cause any trouble.'

'Don't leave!' Crystal begged, fearful Tremlon was about to vanish and Matt turned to see the look of panic in her wild, blue eyes and immediately lowered his fists and rushed to her side.

'I'm sorry if you think I've just made matters worse,' he said, putting his arm around her shoulders and pulling her close. 'I was only trying to protect you.'

He felt the electricity from her skin rush through his body, sending a strange sensation to register in the pit of his stomach.

'Calm yourselves,' said Tremlon, when the atmosphere crackled with uncertainty. 'There's no harm done, I never meant to intimidate either of you.' Matt saw Crystal attempt a weak smile and he in return, smiled back.

'Look here,' said Tremlon, trying to lighten the mood, 'let's start over.'

He held his breath, allowing a gentle current to fill the atmosphere and he transmuted his body into another shape. He changed so quickly, that Crystal's heart, like her eyes, filled with alarm. Her legs buckled and Matt grabbed her, her fingers digging into his flesh when she clung to him for support.

The elf changed into the figure of a woman; not just any woman, but that of Beatrice, her mother. Crystal noted she was dressed in the wrong era of clothes, making her look strange and out of place, but there was no mistaking the remarkable resemblance to her mother: the greying hair, the plump yet firm body. It was all much too real.

'No way!' Crystal gasped, taking a step back. 'You're not my mum, you freak!' Her mind swam with suffocating confusion. Did this mean that the shape-changer had been part of some terrible conspiracy against her all these years? Had Beatrice only been make-believe, a person created through Tremlon's ability to change into a human being?

'It's just an illusion!' Matt yelled, trying to reassure her. 'It isn't real, it's just a trick of the mind,' he insisted, covering her hands with his own and trying to make her see sense.

'It looks real enough to me,' she cried, pushing him away. 'Tell me is this some kind of sick joke?'

There was a mumble in the air, a whisper of words and Crystal saw Tremlon change back into his human form. He tweaked at his clothes as though preening his feathers, unaware of the distress he had just caused her.

'That wasn't bloody funny!' she roared, and her eyes filled with tears. She started to cry and Tremlon lowered his gaze and bowed to her in apology.

'Forgive me Crystal,' he said in earnest; 'please, dry your eyes, for it was not my intention to upset you.' He reached inside his trouser pocket and walked over to a spare table. Crystal could see his fingers were curled securely into a fist. It was obvious he was holding something tight in the palm of his hand and she strained her neck to get a better look. She watched him open his fingers and release golden particles, no thicker than a grain of sand onto the surface of the table. The sand moved when he swept his hand away, moulding themselves together into a type of soft pyramid. A blue flame ignited on its very peak and lazy wisps of smoke trailed into the atmosphere. Tremlon bent his head and pursed his lips, blowing out the flame and the sand scattered like rain to reveal to them an incredible miniature, winged dragon.

Crystal's tears vanished.

Tremlon looked up and was pleased to see her face was filled with wonder and he let out a sigh of relief. Crystal took a hesitant step towards the dragon, her confusion and fear of Tremlon momentarily forgotten while she peered in fascination at the tiny creature. Its beautiful dark wings were stretched with a bat-like skin and its body was dark green with scales of silver-grey woven into a hard membrane running down its back. On its head sat five horned peaks of flesh. Its eyes were the colour of amber, giving an effect of hot, bubbling lava floating around the cornea.

'Is this dragon for real?' Crystal gasped, her troubled eyes lighting up with newfound curiosity.

Matt appeared at her side, peering with disbelief at the remarkable creature. The dragon was so tiny yet perfect in every way; a real piece of magic.

'Yes,' said Tremlon with a smirk. 'It's as real as you and me.'

'It's truly amazing,' Matt said, almost lost for words. 'Why, it's beautiful.'

Tremlon opened his mouth to speak, but a short snort came from the dragon's mouth and an energetic flame of fire left its nostrils, taking them all by surprise. The flame only narrowly missed their clothing, and landed on a pile of abandoned books left by a previous reader on the opposite table. The books exploded into flames and smoke bellowed towards the ceiling and Tremlon was startled when the fire alarm went off.

'Oh no, we need to turn it off,' Crystal cried, grabbing a magazine and wafting the air above her head. 'You'll have the fire brigade here in minutes if we don't get these flames out.'

Tremlon reacted by pressing his thumb gently against the dragon's back. The creature let out a wail of protest and was forced to transmute. Tremlon stood back; the dragon was gone but in its place stood a perfectly formed white stallion. The miniature horse snorted and whinnied in panic, kicking out its legs and its front hoof caught Matt's hip.

'Ouch!' Matt said with a jerk. 'Tremlon, will you stop messing about! Just forget the party tricks and concentrate on getting rid of this smoke before we end up in trouble!' Tremlon nodded and then took a long, deep breath; before blowing cold air into the direction of the burning books. Ice and snow flew from his mouth, and like a fire extinguisher, the white mixture concealed the flames, putting out the fire. His lips had turned blue and he wore a white, icy moustache just above his top lip which in Crystal's opinion made him look like Jack Frost.

'Will that do?' he said, wiping the ice from his lips with the back of his hand. Crystal and Matt smiled with relief when the alarm suddenly fell silent, their fear of him for the moment relinquished.

'I am willing to take you to my world if you're ready?' he said, assessing the situation. Time was moving swiftly, and if he failed to bring the princess back the consequences were something he wasn't ready to think about.

He moved towards her, trying to coax her to come with him.

'I promise you, no harm will come to you while you are a guest in my kingdom,' he said, extending his hand. 'If you agree to come with me, then we must hurry and make our way to the Kingdom of Nine Winters,' he cajoled.

'Why does the king want me of all people?' asked Crystal, hearing the urgency he was trying to hide in his voice.

'All I know is that the king fears an uprising from another realm,' Tremlon explained, looking slightly shifty and she noted he was unable to look her in the eye.

'But that still doesn't explain what that has got to do with me,' she argued, realising she still held the rolled up magazine she had used to waft away the smoke.

'I don't know,' Tremlon admitted, lowering his gaze and looking at his feet, 'but the king has made it clear to me that he needs you, and I'm sure you would benefit from a visit to our land, of that I am certain.' Crystal looked torn and threw the magazine onto the floor.

'It's the chance of a lifetime!' Tremlon pressed, pulling his lips into a tight smile, 'and you won't get another chance like this again.'

'But how will I get there?' she asked, glancing at Matt and shrugging her shoulders. 'It's not like I can just vanish into thin air!' A sudden bustle of noise brought them back to reality.

'Where's the fire!' shouted the librarian from somewhere down the hall. 'Can anyone see any flames? We'll have to evacuate, I can smell smoke.'

'Quick! We haven't much time,' Tremlon hissed, realising his mistake with the dragon. 'Crystal, are you ready to come with me?' He grabbed the white stallion and slapped it between his hands causing sand to spray out of his fingers and all over the floor.

'We must leave now before I am seen,' Tremlon said, backing away towards a dark corner, unable to hide the fear in his eyes. Matt looked down at the table and noticed a pile of manure left by the horse and he screwed up his nose when he saw it steaming.

'That's disgusting!' he said, appalled. 'Why don't you clear that up as well before you leave?'

'Are you coming with me?' Tremlon asked Crystal, ignoring Matt's outburst. 'It's now or never.'

A prickling at the edge of her senses warned Crystal too late.

'Yes, we'll come,' she said, looking at Matt for a sign of encouragement.

'We!' said Tremlon taken by surprise. 'There is no we.'

'I'm not going anywhere without Matt,' she stomped, turning stubborn.

'Hey, do I have a say in this?' Matt interrupted with a grin spreading over his face, clearly pleased that she wanted him by her side.

'No, you don't,' she said, giving his hand a quick squeeze. 'We're in this together.'

'So be it,' said Tremlon, closing his eyes in concentration. He whispered words in the old language, creating a spell. Crystal shuddered and something shifted inside her; excitement, expectation. She felt a rush, and then at her feet dropped two thick animal skins, landing with a thump on the floor. Taken by surprise, Matt picked up the one closest to him and stroked the thick pelt; it felt soft against his skin.

'Why the hell do we need fur coats?' he asked, sounding confused. He bent down and retrieved the second coat before offering it to Crystal.

Tremlon winked and gave them a huge grin. 'Why on earth do you think it's called the Kingdom of Nine Winters!' he said bursting out laughing. 'Come on now, isn't it obvious?'

# *Chapter 5*

The wagon was rickety and the horses in need of rest and a decent meal. Crystal and Matt sat huddled together inside the wagon for a slither of warmth and a slice of humble security. The wooden wheels, worn from many years of use, wobbled dangerously upon the road, and each bulky stone they went over, rattled their bones.

Tremlon had somehow catapulted them all into the extraordinary world, and when they arrived the group had been greeted by five elf warriors who wore black livery and dismal expressions.

'Nice welcoming party,' said Matt, eyeing a threatening warrior with a sideward glance. He turned his head and caught the attention of a black, beady eye and gave a shudder.

'Remind me to never bump into one of those guys on a dark night,' he mumbled aloud, 'why I've seen friendlier faces on death row.'

'These are good elves,' Tremlon interrupted, annoyed at hearing Matt's unfounded comments. 'And they have been sent by the king to protect you.'

'Why should we need protecting?' Matt asked, throwing a suspicious glare towards the distant hills in search of sinister shadows. 'I thought you said we would be safe? You never mentioned anything about being in any danger and, how come we have to travel so far to meet the king? I'd assumed your spell would take us straight to him.'

Tremlon's hand gripped the leather reins.

'We have a long ride ahead of us, and we don't know who or what we may encounter on the road. These are dark and troubled times and we must stay extremely vigilant. The soldiers are here to help defend us, should we meet anything untoward. You may think our magic can shield you from harm, but it doesn't work that way here. You see you have to understand, strong magic is forbidden outside of our kingdom, but not everyone abides by the rules.'

'Where is here?' Crystal interrupted. She was beginning to take more notice of the lush green countryside and wide-open spaces that surrounded them, suddenly aware of how vulnerable they could be to an attack.

'This is the passageway known as Cleric's Ridge,' Tremlon explained, flicking his head towards the horizon. 'Once we arrive through the gates of our kingdom our magic is no longer bound and we will be safe.'

'So why aren't you allowed to use strong magic outside of your kingdom?' Crystal asked, wishing to understand the strange restriction a little better.

'Our laws tell us we should only use magic in our own kingdoms so as not to dominate the weaker realms,' Tremlon explained with a sigh.

'Well, what about our world does the same rules apply there,' Matt asked, setting his face in a hard scowl, 'I mean, let's face it, you were about as subtle as a brick back there!'

Tremlon's eyes narrowed and he flicked the reins hard, causing the horses to almost jolt him out of his seat and when Crystal turned to look at him, she thought Matt looked quite angry.

'I'm sure we're going to be alright,' she soothed, holding his hand and trying her best to ease the glare in his eyes.

'What were we thinking coming here?' Matt gasped, his anger still simmering. 'We're virtually prisoners, and it's all our own doing.'

Crystal let her hand fall, the truth hitting her like a slap in the face. Matt was right, they were at the mercy of these mystical beings; how could she have been so stupid to come here so willingly? It was too late to turn back now; she knew Tremlon would never let her go. She had inadvertently put them both in great danger and a hard lump filled her throat.

'I'm so sorry,' she whispered, causing Matt's glare to soften. 'I should never have asked you to come here with me.'

The sun was already showing signs of setting when one of the guards made his way to the side of the wagon and suggested they stop for the night.

'There's a tavern just north of here,' he told them, pointing ahead. 'We can stop there and carry on again in the morning.' Crystal grabbed hold of Tremlon's arm, forcing him to look at her.

'How long are you expecting us to stay?' she asked, looking at his face for a sign of a clue.

'Don't worry about that,' he said, shrugging her hand away. 'Time has stood still in the earth world; so when you return, it will be as though you have never left.'

'Are you sure?' she pressed, her voice wavering with un-spilled emotion. 'Because I don't want my mum frantic with worry, thinking I've been kidnapped or worse...'

'You're going to have to learn to trust me and listen to what I say,' said the shape-changer, drawing his lips into a tight line. He pulled at the reins and slowed the horses.

'You've got a lot to learn little one, and it will take much time for you to understand our ways. Do not fear your destiny, for it is your fate that you should come here.'

'Don't say stuff like that,' Crystal snapped. 'Why, here I am, in the middle of God knows where, with God knows who, with creatures out there that would willingly hurt me, and you're telling me it's my destiny!'

'Listen to me!' Tremlon suddenly hissed. 'You are unique, the only one of your kind; without you, we could all be lost.'

'So it's true, you do know more than you're telling me,' she retorted, her eyes flashing with hostility. 'I damn well knew it!' Tremlon glanced away.

'Perhaps we can talk later,' he said, staring ahead. 'Look, we are approaching the tavern.'

As the sun finally set, Tremlon stood at the side of the wagon, his hand resting on his leather hilt.

'Men, inside!' he shouted, directing the elves towards the main door of the tavern. He turned to take Crystal's hand to help her from the wagon. She took it and slid down by his side. She felt uncomfortable being so close to him, sensing his fearful mood.

They entered the tavern as weary travellers, and Matt was relieved to find it was warm and cosy inside. Crystal felt the heat enfold her body and she let herself relax, a little.

A huge log fire burned in a large, open grate, filling most of the back wall. The heat soared from the orange and red flames that licked at the wood with a devilish madness and Crystal hoped they would be seated close by. A young girl soon approached them. She was dressed in simple clothes but there was an air of sophistication about her that caused Crystal to wish she was dressed a little smarter.

'Good evening, my lady,' the girl said, before welcoming the others each in turn. 'I believe you are in need of a room and a hearty meal this night?' Crystal nodded and then followed her to an unoccupied table. Tremlon pulled out a chair and gestured for Crystal to sit down and Matt slipped into the seat next to her, forcing Tremlon to sit on the opposite side of the table. An angry glare left Tremlon's hooded eyes but his sign of hostility was wasted on Matt who simply pretended not to see his furious stare.

'Your food will be with you shortly,' said the girl, departing with an unexpected curtsey. Her feet appeared to glide along the floor and both Crystal and Matt thought it looked rather freaky.

The foot soldiers, who had also taken residence, sat on carved, wooden benches, with their swords still strapped to their sides. They were chatting amongst themselves about their journey, pleased it was almost at an end and their laughter filled the air. Two helpers came from behind a dark, heavy curtain. Their hands were filled with frothy tankards and loud cheers and wolf whistles soon reached everyone's ears. Once the tankards were in the soldiers' grasp, they wasted no time guzzling the amber nectar and it wasn't long before cries for more burst from their eager mouths, their mood happy and jovial. Crystal turned to see Tremlon passing her a tankard of her own.

'Here, take this,' he said thrusting it into her hand.

'What is it?' she asked, feeling rather overwhelmed. He smiled unexpectedly, showing a row of small, white teeth.

'It's a type of woodland wine,' he explained with a grin. 'It's grown from the local vines and I think you'll find it quite to your liking.'

Matt cupped his drink to his lips and emptied the vessel of its contents in five large, greedy gulps.

'Ease up, boy,' said Tremlon, with a smirk twitching the corners of his mouth. 'I can't have you falling over drunk, now can I?' Matt grunted and wiped his mouth with the back of his hand. He set the empty tankard back on the table and looked around the room, hoping for more.

'He's right,' said Crystal, looking at him with concern. 'Don't drink too much of that stuff, after all you don't actually know what's in it.' Matt tried to protest, but then three serving girls came into the room and his voice died in his throat. Their arms were laden with large, oval platters, decorated with an attempting array of specially selected meats and freshly cooked treats. One girl came over and placed a large dish in front of Crystal; giving her a warm smile.

'Welcome,' she said. 'My name is Nienna, and I will be here to serve you for the rest of the evening. If there's anything you need, please don't hesitate to ask.'

Crystal smiled her thanks and Matt nodded his appreciation, but shouted out that he needed more wine, whilst pointing to his empty cup.

'I will fetch it as soon as I can,' said Nienna, furrowing her brows at his tone, a shout from one of the soldiers distracted her and she glanced across the room, noticing they were becoming rowdy.

'I will just help to feed your men and then I will be back,' she mouthed back at him, but it was clear her mind was already elsewhere.

'I can wait,' said Matt, feeling a stab of disappointment, 'but my throat is very dry,' he added, rubbing his Adam's apple for effect.

Tremlon turned in his seat and watched the soldiers becoming boisterous, clearly eager to have their empty bellies filled, and let out a hearty laugh.

'They won't be quiet until their stomachs are full and they've drunk the owner dry,' he mused. 'Sooner they're fed the better for everyone.'

Crystal ignored the soldiers and watched Nienna instead. She decided the girl was actually quite stunning, in an elfish kind of way. She noticed her well-defined features, like her eyes, which were protected by long, thick lashes and her smooth, flawless skin looked like porcelain. Her dark hair was pulled back, showing off her pointed ears and Crystal couldn't help but stare at them. Nienna caught her looking at her and Crystal swept her gaze towards her food, embarrassed at being seen and her cheeks flushed pink.

'Look at all this odd grub,' said Matt, catching her attention.

'Will you try it first?' Crystal asked, feeling a bit of a coward. 'But don't go eating like a savage like him,' she added, flicking her gaze towards Tremlon who was munching through his meal as though he hadn't eaten for weeks. Matt picked up a fork and gingerly prodded the dark, brown substance on his plate and Tremlon noticed him hesitate.

'Don't worry, it won't fight back,' he scoffed, pointing to his own plate with his greasy fingers. 'It's mainly Feefalas; a kind of wild bird that's plentiful in these parts.'

Matt forced a weak smile that looked unconvincing, but his belly rumbled with hunger, telling them he was starved. Regardless of the species, he knew he had no choice but to eat what had been placed before him.

'Umm, it actually tastes quite good,' he said, taking a bite and trying to entice Crystal. 'It reminds me of roast duck.'

Half-heartedly, Crystal made a conscious effort to slice into a piece of meat. She brought it to her uncooperative lips and took a nibble. She chewed at the soft flesh, while her taste buds investigated what she had put in her mouth and after reaching for her wine she admitted that it hadn't tasted quite so bad after all, and Matt was right, it did have a distinct flavour of duck. While she ate, she switched her attention to some of the other guests.

In a corner stood some other soldiers dressed in dark clothing. These men had a golden crest on their chests and fury in their voices. Her own party of guards appeared unperturbed when these voices rose, enjoying instead the free flowing wine and a night of good company and so her gaze flickered towards a wizened old dwarf, sitting alone by the fire. He was small in stature and reminded her of a character from one of the fairy stories she had read as a child. He sat acknowledging no one, uninterested in making casual conversation or making friends. With his head bent low, he stared into his drink, perhaps she thought, to look for the answer to the problem that appeared to trouble him so, but she soon lost interest and scouted the rest of the room for someone more appealing.

To her right, tucked almost out of sight, lay a small, cosy snug and two young elves were playing some kind of game. She couldn't make out what they were playing, but small tablets that looked to be made of stone were floating in the air and bright, shiny coins lay haphazardly on the table, glistening yellow-gold, caught by the flickering firelight. Muffled curses rang out at random, followed by merry belts of laughter while each elf tried to outfox the other.

Eventually she grew weary of trying to work out what they were playing and switched her attention to the elf warriors instead. By now the soldiers had finished their supper and were moving from the dining room into the main hall. A few belches were heard followed by heavy laughter; it would appear to those who were interested that the soldiers would be content for the rest of the evening.

Crystal and Matt eventually started some idle chit chat and Tremlon, still very much the outsider, listened to every word his human visitors had to say with eager ears, making it difficult for them to discuss anything in private and their conversation eventually became stunted. Just when the silence was starting to become unbearable, the solider that'd approached the wagon earlier made his way over to their table and nodded in greeting before turning his attention to Tremlon.

'Yes, Arhdel, what is it?' Tremlon asked, shooting him a look of impatience.

Arhdel cleared his throat. He had a presence that automatically commanded respect, and although not a tall man, he had a broad physique and arms that were powerful and strong. A wispy beard, coarse and wiry with flecks of grey fell from his chin in spiky tufts. His leathery face told the tale of many a bloody battle, and a thick scar, red and inflamed ran from his left ear to underneath his chin; he had the kind of face you could never forget.

'The rooms are ready, sire,' he said in a low rumble, 'and I have taken the liberty of having your bag taken straight to your room.' Tremlon nodded his appreciation, but Arhdel hadn't finished.

'Unfortunately sire, the tavern is quite full tonight and only two rooms were available. Naturally, I have given the young lady a room of her own, however, due to unforeseen circumstance; it appears you will have to share with the mortal this night.'

He glanced at Matt and then averted his eyes. 'I'm sorry, but it's the best they could do at such short notice.' Tremlon gulped down the last of his wine before slamming his tankard down hard on the table.

'Well, I don't suppose I have a choice,' he growled.

'No, sire, I'm afraid you don't,' Arhdel agreed, 'but at least you're not with the horses unlike the rest of us.' Tremlon turned then to the soldier.

'I see your point,' he said, heaving himself out of his chair, 'and on that note I think it's time we called it a night.'

Arhdel bowed again before clicking his fingers and Nienna approached from the main hall and watched them with expectant eyes.

'Your guests would like to retire,' Arhdel instructed, gesturing for her to take charge.

'Of course,' Nienna replied, throwing out her hands and leading the way, 'why, please follow me and I will show you to your rooms.'

Tremlon turned his attention to Crystal. 'You should try and get some rest tonight, you look tired and we have an early start tomorrow.' Crystal simply nodded and Arhdel interrupted her thoughts by bidding her goodnight, and once he left, the three guests followed Nienna through a well-lit passageway.

From the outside the tavern had looked quite small, but once inside the building took on a whole new spectrum. The ceilings were high, with strong, wooden beams jutting out from the roof with lots of windows cut into the stone walls, making the whole place seem light and airy. They had left the rosy cheeked landlord serving a couple of the guards and they could hear him laughing at the soldiers' somewhat pathetic jokes.

They reached a wooden staircase stretching upwards and curving to the right. This set of stairs led to a long corridor of bedrooms and their shoes made a 'thudding' noise as they ascended. Small oil paintings and prints dominated the white walls and Crystal noticed there were no portraits or pictures of people amongst them, and horses, pigs and dogs appeared to be more to the collector's taste. They continued to climb three flights of stairs before Nienna stopped and pulled out a large key from her pocket. She unlocked a door and then pushed it ajar.

She gestured to Matt and Tremlon.

'This will be your room,' she said, stepping back so they could enter. 'I hope you find it to your liking.' Tremlon appeared to hesitate, turning towards Crystal once again.

'I will wake you for breakfast,' he said, grasping the door handle, 'please don't leave your room without letting me know where you're going.'

'Is there a problem if I do?' she asked, feeling her eyebrows knit together with concern.

'Er no, not exactly, but you are not from this world and I don't want you getting yourself...' Tremlon paused, searching for the appropriate words, 'into a situation you can't get yourself out of.' Tension filled the air and it was Nienna who intervened.

'Should you need anything in the night milady,' she interrupted taking a step towards her, 'you'll find a lever by your bed; just pull it and I will come and assist you.' Crystal nodded her thanks.

'I will,' she promised, producing a weak smile, 'but I'm sure I'll be fine.'

Only slightly pacified, Tremlon entered his room whilst grabbing Matt by the scruff of the neck, shoving him inside and slamming the door behind him with the heel of his boot. Nienna reached out and put a gentle hand on Crystal's shoulder.

'He's always been a bit tense, so don't take it personally,' she said, opening an adjacent door and gesturing for her to enter.

'Thanks,' said Crystal with a grin. 'I'm guessing you've met him before by that comment.'

'Oh, yes,' Nienna said, with a nod of her head. 'He's stayed here many times over the past few months.'

Any thoughts of Tremlon were swiftly wiped away when she took a step inside her room.

'Wow! This can't be real!'

'Is something wrong?' Nienna asked with genuine concern. 'Is there a problem, don't you like it?'

'But it's just like my bedroom at home!' Crystal gasped in astonishment. Running to her bed she grabbed the cuddly toy sitting on her pillow.

'Hercules!' she cried with joy. 'What are you doing here?' She was so pleased to see her favourite stuffed toy and she hugged him fiercely, feeling the first pang of homesickness wash over her. She looked over and spotted the heavy framed picture of herself and Beatrice sitting on the bedside table. Still holding the bundle of fluff, she rushed over and picked up the colour photo, gazing at it with love glowing in her eyes. What the hell was she doing here in this strange world anyway? Would all this secrecy and knowledge really be worth it in the end? She placed the photograph back on the table.

'How did you get this room to look like mine?' she asked Nienna, fascinated with the concept of all she saw.

'Why, it's a standard feature in most of the taverns,' said Nienna laughing with surprise, 'didn't you know?' Moving a thick curtain aside, Nienna exposed a metal grid attached to the wall. It looked to Crystal like some kind of combination.

'This,' Nienna pointed, 'is what we call a room dial. It isn't actually a dial, as you have to push the buttons,' she shrugged her shoulders. 'I don't know where the name came from but anyway, you punch in a number and the room will change to any theme you wish, as long as you have the right combination, of course.'

Punching in a code as she spoke, Crystal watched the room change before her very eyes into a ship's cabin. The room swayed with the roll of the sea, causing her to feel slightly nauseous. The hammocks tied to the ceiling swayed to and fro and the water jug placed at the centre of the table slid from side to side to match the movement of the rolling waves. A single round porthole gave her a view of the deep blue ocean. It was real, as real as anything she had ever seen and the sea sprayed against the window causing her to giggle with sheer delight. She could make out colourless shapes under the water, shapes that were swimming closer to her and she shrieked with excitement when beautiful mermaids jumped from the icy waters in a huge synchronised display. Their large tails flapped playfully in the foamy bluish water and their long golden tresses were wrapped around their bodies to cover their modesty.

'I can't believe what I'm seeing,' Crystal exclaimed, unable to accept what her eyes were telling her to be true. 'This really is another world; you do have magic here.'

'It's not magic,' said Nienna, shaking her head thoughtfully. 'What may appear to be magical in your ordinary world is not necessarily so in ours.' She punched a number back into the dial to recreate Crystal's bedroom once again. The room blurred for a moment making Crystal feel slightly dizzy before it settled back, but Crystal was too impressed to let that bother her.

'Tremlon's right though,' she said, turning to face Nienna, 'I do have a lot to learn and even more to understand about this world.' Nienna smiled, the corners of her mouth softening, just a little.

'Sleep well, milady,' she said, after turning the bed down for the night. 'Remember, if you need anything at all, just pull this lever by your bed and I will come straight away.' Nienna showed Crystal how it worked before replacing it to its correct position.

'Please don't fuss, I'll be fine,' Crystal insisted, jumping on the bed and hugging Hercules for the thirtieth time.

'Very well, then I will bid you goodnight,' said Nienna leaving her side and heading for the door and once she had closed it, Crystal went back to hugging her dog, oblivious to what was about to happen to her in the next twenty-four hours.

# *Chapter 6*

Amadeus sat on the ridge waiting for a sign that the wagon was approaching. He had waited all night, sitting under the stars with only the moon and the baying of wolves for company. The elf king had ordered him to watch and wait for the daughter of the Oakwood Wizard Bridgemear to arrive, trusting no one else with such an important task.

Amadeus was seen to be a solid man, heavy boned with unsmiling eyes and hair that was thin and wispy. He had been born the son of a smithy, but had taken the oath of the king after his seventeen birth moon. His gift as an elf had been his strength and none could beat him with either fist or sword. Now, In his later years, although more weighty than when he was a boy he still had what it took to be the best warrior the king ever had. He sniffed the air, causing his nostrils to flare; the wind blew to the east and with it the scent of someone approaching. Alerted to the intruder, Amadeus held his sword tight, ready to strike, thus enabling him to have the element of surprise.

'Amadeus!' a voice he recognised called out and he relaxed the grip on his sword.

'Hello Phaphos,' Amadeus said, lowering his guard, but feeling suspicious. 'Tell me, what brings you all the way out here?'

'I've a message from the king,' said the warrior, clutching his strong hand in his. 'He instructs you to proceed without delay to Raven's Rainbow with all possible speed. The king has given you his finest beast to help you on your journey.'

'But why the sudden change of plan?'

Amadeus noticed Phaphos's lips tighten. 'The king wishes you to go and seek out Bridgemear, the Oakwood Wizard and not wait for the wagon as first planned.'

'But why has the king chosen me to go? I am no match for Bridgemear's magic especially if he should greet me with animosity.'

'You are to go as the king's envoy,' Phaphos explained. 'You must track Bridgemear down and although that may not be easy, the king believes that you are the only one who will find the mage.'

Amadeus studied Phaphos further with his startling hawk eyes and felt a cold touch worm down his spine.

'What am I to say to him?'

Phaphos stiffened. 'Only a handful of the king's advisors and I will know about this. You must tell Bridgemear news which will change our history forever.'

'What news?' Amadeus asked, already feeling a knot in his stomach. 'What does the king wish me to tell the mage?' Phaphos waivered and Amadeus's foreboding deepened.

'You must tell the magician that the penalty he once paid for his debt against the realm has been quashed. Tell him his daughter, Crystal, the child born of Amella our princess, will arrive shortly in the Kingdom of Nine Winters.'

'But Bridgemear is no prince, and could never lie with Amella,' gasped Amadeus, astounded by such a revelation. 'Why, what you say is simply preposterous!'

Phaphos shook his head and sighed. 'It is not for us to lay the law, but only to abide by it. What I tell you is the truth; how this happened, I know nothing of it.'

'This cannot be true,' Amadeus insisted clutching at his sword as if it gave him inner strength. 'No one from the realms has ever done such a terrible thing and lived to tell the tale. Yes, I was told Bridgemear had a daughter, the very child I was waiting to meet and escort to our kingdom, but not that her mother is Amella, why, I simply cannot believe it.'

'Calm yourself,' said Phaphos in a firm tone. 'As you are aware, the girl is already in our lands, and you must go and tell Bridgemear that his once banished daughter has re-entered our world with permission from the Great Order of the Elders.'

Too confused to speak, Amadeus merely stared at him in shock and only shifted his gaze when Phaphos left his side, then he turned on his heels and made his way towards the edge of the ridge. Facing the cool, orange sun he felt its weak rays try to penetrate his weather-beaten face.

'So be it,' he said, his face grey and ashen. 'My allegiance has always been with the king therefore my duty I am sworn to do.' He spoke these words aloud against the breeze, unable to quell the red-hot fire that burned in his gut. With a heavy sigh, he turned and ran towards the king's horse. Mounting, he cried out his command for the beast to run like the wind and thus began his immediate ride to Raven's Rainbow.

*

Tremlon tapped on Crystal's bedroom door and waited for a reply. Inside, Crystal was hidden under the covers with Hercules, tucked safely under her chin, not wishing to be disturbed from her fitful sleep. One of her slim legs poked out of the bottom of the bed while the other was covered, snuggled into the warmth of the sheet. She ignored his knock at first, dreaming of life at home and being pampered by her mother. The dream was comforting; her mind convinced she was home, safe and sound.

Tremlon knocked a little harder, becoming impatient, wanting to have his breakfast and leave. The smell of freshly baked bread filled his nostrils and the noise of others already filling their bellies made him less tolerant than he might usually have been. Startled, Crystal sat up and rubbed her eyes. Her body was still heavy with sleep and it took her a moment to get her bearings.

'Are you alright in there?' Tremlon called out, suddenly afraid she was gone.

Crystal pulled back the covers and promptly charged towards the door. She pulled it open with such force that Tremlon drew back in surprise.

'What is it?' she snapped, standing there with her hair all awry and messy.

'We're leaving in twenty minutes,' Tremlon told her, regaining some of his composure. 'I just wanted you to know that your breakfast has been ready for some time.'

'Fine, I'll be down in a minute!" she yelled, slamming the door in his face. Bemused, Tremlon made his way along the passageway and down the stairs to where Matt sat waiting.

'She's certainly not a morning person,' Tremlon told him a moment later, when he joined him for breakfast. Matt shrugged his shoulders and gulped some ale.

'That's women for you,' he said, reaching for the bread which had just been placed under his nose. 'If she's anything like my sister, I would stay well clear; they're all hormonal and as snappy as a croc first thing.' With a grin, Tremlon grabbed a slice of bread and took a thoughtful bite.

He didn't quite understand what Matt meant, but he believed he got the gist. The fairer sex had always been a mystery to him; time and age had never altered that.

'I don't think she'll be long,' Tremlon said, taking another bite of his bread. 'So let's just enjoy the peace while we can and be thankful for small mercies.'

Back in her room, Crystal put on the same clothes she had worn the day before. She sniffed at her clothes finding them suddenly offensive. She sat on her bed, her legs dangling over the edge and simply marvelled at it all.

Then she had a brainwave.

She dived across the floor and reached out to open one of the wooden drawers in the dressing table. She clapped her hands with delight when she looked down to find some of her clothes from home were in there. She pulled out an unworn jumper, a cream hand-knitted Arran brought back from the Highlands of Scotland last year. Crystal smiled; she had screwed her nose up at this gift, but now, here in this Godforsaken place, it was the answer to her prayers. Closing the drawer, she opened another to reveal clean underwear and socks. She felt slightly miffed that her underwear was in there, neatly folded, but grateful nonetheless. She grabbed her clean clothes and headed for the wash basin and then dressed. Once she was happy with her appearance, she pulled open her wardrobe and sifted through the mountain of junk lying at the bottom. She found what she was looking for, her bright pink rucksack and filled it with clothes, a hairbrush and a few odds and ends.

Once she was satisfied she had everything she needed, she flung the bag over her shoulder and closed the wardrobe door. Picking up Hercules from the floor, she gave him one last kiss and a pat on the head before placing him on the bed.

'See you later,' she said, with sadness slipping into her voice. 'I'll be home as soon as I can.'

She descended the stairs, two at a time, before meeting a wave of activity. She noticed Nienna busily scurrying from one table to the next with plates piled high with food. The smell of something that resembled bacon drifted under Crystal's nose, causing her to seek out the others. She joined them with a friendly greeting. Matt was only half way through his breakfast, eagerly tucking in when Crystal pointed to her face to alert him to the fact that egg was dribbling down his chin.

'Did you sleep well?' Matt asked, pulling a piece of cloth from under his plate and wiping around his mouth and upper jaw.

'Like a log,' she mouthed, turning her attention to the shape-changer. 'Good morning, Tremlon, I hope you slept well?'

He cast a wary look and grunted something that sounded like 'yes' before returning to his breakfast.

'What's up with that miserable devil?' she whispered in Matt's ear. 'Looks like he got out on the wrong side of bed to me,' she added with a smirk.

Matt sniggered and reached for the salt.

'Never mind about him. Tell me, what did you think to your room? Wasn't it the coolest thing ever? Ours was actually split down the middle and my half was just like my old room back home, but Tremlon's changed into a billet, like what soldiers have and it was very sparse and I was so glad to have my own soft bed to sleep in.'

Crystal giggled.

'Yes, isn't this place fantastic,' she agreed, pulling the rucksack up from underneath the table. 'It was so nice to have my own things around me; I even managed to pack some of my stuff.'

Matt looked at her with a very blank expression.

'Oh, I never thought to do that,' he said, suddenly looking down at the clothes he was wearing from the previous day. 'Perhaps I could pop back after breakfast and collect a few things,' he added, brightening up.

'You'll not have time now,' Tremlon interrupted, wiping his mouth on the cuff of his sleeve. 'We leave in five minutes.'

Nienna walked over with Crystal's breakfast.

'Good morning, milady,' she said, placing the food on the table. 'I hope you slept well?'

'Yes, I did, thanks,' Crystal replied with shining eyes. She looked at the goats' milk and sugar paste that were already in bowls on the table along with square, glass jars filled with jam and honey and gave Nienna a warm smile.

'Get tucked in,' Matt urged, stuffing more food in his mouth, 'these mushrooms are sooo juicy.'

Crystal had to admit the food did look inviting. Eggs, sizzling meats and large flat mushrooms looked up from the huge platter, begging to be eaten and she finally couldn't resist tucking in and enjoying the mouth-watering flavours that flooded her taste buds.

'Come on,' said Tremlon, finishing the last of his meal, 'it's time we were on our way,' and without waiting for them to finish, he rose from the table.

Crystal let out a squeal.

'We can't leave now?' she declared, her eyes rounding. 'I've only just started eating!'

'The king awaits our return,' said Tremlon giving her an impatient grunt. 'We simply don't have all day to wait for you.'

Crystal turned stubborn.

'I'm sorry Tremlon, but I'm not leaving until I've finished my breakfast,' she snapped, breaking off a piece of crusty bread and mopping up her yolk. 'I'm sure your king won't mind if we leave a few minutes later than planned,' she added, stuffing the last of a juicy, black mushroom into her mouth. 'Why, this food is simply delicious.'

Tremlon stared at her long and hard. Then he said, 'No, I told you, it's time to leave. You may have Oakwood blood running through your veins, but we must leave while there is much light.'

'What's the rush?' asked Matt, sensing his urgency. 'Are we in any danger?'

'Perhaps, I cannot say for sure, but the sooner we reach elf territory the better. Crystal, the men are waiting.'

Dragging her heels, Crystal reluctantly ventured outside. Both the men and the horses were ready and Matt helped Crystal into the wagon while the familiar look of worry filled her eyes.

'We'll be alright, just as soon as we reach this Kingdom of Nine Winters,' he muttered almost to himself.

'How can you be sure?' she asked, settling down on the hard seat and leaning the rucksack on her leg. 'There are no guarantees for our safety even if we manage to make it there alive.'

'Then we will just have to trust what Tremlon told us,' Matt said, moving her along so he could sit next to her. 'It's obvious to me that these warriors would have killed us already if that was their intention.'

Arhdel approached the wagon and he fell silent. The warrior called to them as he walked by.

'All the horses are well rested and eager to leave,' he said, moving towards the beasts and checking their mouths. 'Hope you enjoy the scenery,' he added, when he caught Crystal's stare, 'I'm sure you will find it all rather pleasing to the eye, once we reach the outskirts of Nine Winters.'

Tremlon called out to the soldier, who responded by leaving the horses and moving to his side.

'My eternal gratitude to you and your men,' Tremlon said with unexpected sensitivity, 'you have all done well to keep us safe from harm.' Arhdel rubbed at his scar; the angry red mark appeared to glow upon his face.

'We have many more miles to cover yet, sire, let's not be too hasty.'

'Yes indeed, you're right,' said Tremlon, pulling his dagger close, 'I'm speaking prematurely and we should not let our guard down too soon.' He jumped onto the wagon with one swift leap.

'Better get your furs on,' he shouted to his travelling companions, pulling his own pelt closer. 'It's going to get a lot colder from here onwards.' He dropped his goatskin bag on the floor before settling himself and picking up the reins.

'Once we get over that group of hills,' he said, pointing to the north, 'the change in the weather will be dramatic.' Tremlon clicked his tongue against his teeth and the horses jolted into life. The soldiers walked two in front and two behind, and only Arhdel walked by the side of the wagon. The sun, a pale ball of orange, was just peering over the horizon ready to claim the day, its rays unable to penetrate the chill in the morning air. The wagon lolled from side to side, and the small group were soon deep in their own thoughts.

It was early afternoon when the weather turned cold and the cloud thickened to form a grey blanket over the sky and the horses snorted in disapproval.

'How much further?' asked Matt, when the chilly effects of the weather made his hands ache with cold. The bitterness was starting to penetrate through to his bones, even with his fur pulled tight.

'A few more hours, if we're lucky,' answered Tremlon, clicking his tongue at the horses. 'We've just crossed into dwarf territory, so we haven't got much further to travel.' The horses stepped up their pace with a crack of the whip but within minute's snow began to fall, making visibility extremely difficult. The white snowflakes fell thick and heavy on the ground, the wheels of the wagon falling silent.

As they rode deeper into the chill, the two soldiers walking in front could barely be seen and Arhdel called out for them to wait when they started to blend into the foreground, camouflaged by the thickening snow. However, after only a short while, Arhdel's concern grew when they disappeared from view altogether. Hitting the side of the wagon with his fist, Arhdel signalled for Tremlon to stop and the shape-changer pulled hard on the reins and halted the horses with a snort of warm air.

'What's wrong?' Tremlon shouted, realising the soldiers were no longer visible. The wind was whipping around his ears creating a frenzy of noise, making it almost impossible to hear what Arhdel was saying.

'I'm not sure,' Arhdel shouted against the wind, 'but I need to go and take a look.' He signalled to the two soldiers at the rear of the wagon.

'You, stay here,' he said to the elder of the two, 'and you, come with me,' he said to the other. Without looking back, Arhdel marched off with the young warrior close at his heels. They carried on for only a few yards before Arhdel dropped to the ground. He pulled off his thick leather gloves and stroked the surface of the snow with his fingertips, searching for the soldiers' footprints and a wave of unease swept over him when he realised they had ended abruptly. The heavy snowflakes fell onto their tread, covering the tracks in a matter of seconds; Arhdel sensed more than bad weather lay ahead.

A delicate crackle, almost inaudible to the human ear, caught Arhdel's immediate attention. He turned his face, straining to locate the sound, before a blow to the head sent him to the ground. A second later, the soldier lay unconscious by his side; with a slow trickle of blood oozing from his head, staining the crisp, white snow.

Back on the wagon, Tremlon waited for Arhdel's return. Apprehension was niggling at his senses and anxiety was making his shoulders stiff with tension. He twisted his neck from side to side in a gesture to relax his tightening muscles but they refused to ease and he glanced over to Matt and Crystal who were huddled together for warmth like two new born lambs. A sudden shrill cry split the solitude and echoed through the air, taking Tremlon by surprise and before he knew what was happening, a pair of large, brawny hands was upon him and something fierce and dressed in dark clothing was clinging to his throat, threatening to throttle him where he sat, momentarily stunned, he was unable to transmute. Instinctively, Tremlon grabbed the strong hands and tried to prise the huge fingers apart. He pushed the attacker with all his might and forced him to stagger backwards. Tremlon reached down for his blade. It flashed when he drew it from its hilt, but his attacker had already recovered and was upon him yet again. A fierce fight broke out and his dagger was no match for the attacker's skill at arms, and within seconds the knife left his hand and lay buried in the snow.

Tremlon punched his attacker full in the face and then tried to reach the goatskin bag. The horses whinnied their confusion and pulled at their slackened reins, frightened by all the commotion. They gave a sharp tug as their nerves jangled, causing Tremlon to lose his balance. In an instant, he fell from the wagon and landed with a dulled thud on the ground, the snow breaking his fall, but his attacker was still attached. Crystal screamed, terrified. She clung to the side of the wagon, cowering away from the fight, unable to digest what was happening until she came to her senses and screamed for Matt to do something to help the shape-changer.

Although frightened, Matt found his nerve, and jumped from his seat, landing on the back of Tremlon's attacker. He flung his arms round their neck, pulling tight against their throat, trying to force the intruder to let go. The intruder retaliated by elbowing Matt in the gut, and he fell to his knees in agony, before crouching into a ball in the snow, unable to breathe. The attacker's full attention therefore turned towards the shape-changer. A second assailant who had been hiding downwind hit the back of the wagon and overpowered the solitary guard. There was a kafuffle, the soldier clearly no match for the huge powerful frame which attacked him and a sword pierced the soldier's heart, killing him with one, single thrust. He fell like a stone and hit the ground with a soft thud.

For the first time in her life Crystal didn't know what to do, everything was happening so fast. In a panic she threw herself onto the bare wooden floor of the wagon, searching for some kind of weapon. She grappled with the few bits of clothing and dirty rags that lay strewn about, but her eyes filled with terror when she could find nothing to hand. She pushed her rucksack out of the way, already aware there was nothing inside that could help her, but caught sight of the goatskin bag and a glimmer of hope ignited in her eyes. She reached out and grabbed it, but before she had time to open the silver clasp, a dark-skinned hand, smelling of horses and dried dirt, came out of nowhere and assaulted her. She squealed when dirty fingers covered her nose and mouth and she reached up, clawing at the hand which threatened to suffocate her, her fingernails digging into the cold flesh.

Her attacker appeared undaunted by her struggle, simply gripping her tighter and forcing his free arm around her waist. His solid frame, which she felt against her back, was strong and unyielding. Fear filled her eyes when she was dragged from the wagon, and she felt bile rise in her throat when she caught sight of Matt lying face down in the snow. A rough voice barked an order and the ambushers' ran, taking her with them. It was clear she was being kidnapped and once her kidnappers' had reached their horses, a large canvas sack was pulled from a saddle bag and shoved over her head.

They secured their captive well, using strong rope which was bound around her waist and Crystal cried out, begging them to let her go, but her pleas simply fell on deaf ears. Her arms were pinned to her side making it impossible for her to move, the rope was pulled so tight it cut her flesh. Then she experienced a feeling of weightlessness and was forced off her feet, she cried out again, her legs kicking wildly as she tried to find solid ground. Stolen laughter was all she could hear. She felt a rush of air before she connected with a hard thump to her belly and was placed onto the back of an awaiting mare. Although disorientated, she heard men's voices low and menacing seeping through the sack and although she only caught wisps of conversation, it was enough to turn her blind panic into fear.

'We must ride straight to Forusian's castle without delay,' said a triumphant voice. 'The girl must be in his possession before King Gamada gets a whiff of what has occurred here.'

Snorts of agreement filled the air, and Crystal could hear them ridiculing the elf king while they hitched up their horses ready to ride. From their muffled conversation, Crystal guessed they were no more than three kidnappers. Her mind swirled with confusion. What did they want with her? What had happened to Matt and Tremlon? Were they seriously hurt? She blanched when she thought back to the scene at the wagon and shivered. They'd been unable to fight off these intruders and she gave a silent prayer in the hope that they were both still alive. A cry broke out, and the horses set off at a fierce gallop. Their hooves pounded the snow, the hard ground underneath their feet was solid like stone and unyielding and her mind raced ahead, confused and frightened.

They had been riding for many hours when there was a commotion, and some kind of vocal command rang out between the riders. Crystal's stomach ached from the bumpy ride and the queasy feeling she felt in her stomach would not leave her bruised gut. As the horses slowed, she feared what was going to happen to her once she reached her final destination.

'Where is she?' demanded a voice she didn't recognise. She took a breath when strong arms dragged her from the horse and she fell to the floor, the impact almost winding her. Rough hands picked her up and she struggled until she was thrown over someone's shoulder, her legs kicking out in fury.

'Careful, you idiots,' the voice scolded, 'I told you she is not to be harmed and take off that stupid rag thing that's covering her face. I want to see my prized possession in one piece and not as damaged goods.'

Crystal was thrown onto her feet and from somewhere behind her a guard stepped forward and cut the rope that bound her wrist with one swift slice of a dagger. The sack was then whipped off her head and as soon as it was lifted, daylight blinded her and she raised her hand to protect her eyes. Her damp hair was clinging to her face and her clothes were torn and dishevelled but she saw none of this and once her eyes grew accustomed to the glare of daylight she concentrated on rubbing her aching wrists which were bloody and sore. Soon horror filled her eyes when she turned and stared at the guard, for he had removed his hooded clothing to reveal he wasn't anything remotely human and a blood curdling scream left her stricken lips.

'Oh, my god!' she shrieked, trying to control the instinct to run. 'What the hell are you?' She stepped away, unable to look at the hideous creature for a moment longer and turned to face the person who owned the voice of command.

'Oh my, we have a feisty one here,' said her captor, shading his eyes to get a better look. 'Now, let's stay calm, no one's going to hurt you.'

'What?

'Mmm, I see,' he continued, scrutinising Crystal from head to toe, 'you're not what I expected at all.' The male standing in front of her shifted from one foot to the other, unable to take his sharp, green eyes off her.

'Now before we go any further, let me introduce you to my loyal subjects,' he said, pointing towards the guard. 'These creatures are the Nonhawk, a powerful combination of pure muscle, self-pity and greed, yes they are a little strange looking, but their loyalty to me as king is beyond all doubt.'

Crystal looked back at the guard, he was the closest thing to an alien she'd ever seen. Its green skin was thick and cratered and its eyes were nothing more than two black holes in its huge, ugly face, staring back at her, dull and lifeless. She turned back to glare at her captor.

'Who are you?' she demanded, feeling the welts on her wrist disappear. 'And why is it you're so different to them?'

'Well, well, my manners are known to be appalling,' he said, giving a little snort. 'Let me introduce myself. I am King Forusian, ruler of the Nonhawk and I see it hasn't escaped your attention that I am not of their blood, but I am their king, anyway enough about me. Are you alright? I'm sorry about your little "detour" but I'm afraid my needs are foremost.'

The person standing in front of her was indeed no Nonhawk warrior, and she couldn't help noticing how young and handsome he appeared to be. His thick raven-black hair was smooth and sleek, falling against his forehead and softening his face. His eyes were the greenest she had ever seen, like the ocean in the middle of summer and his smile, totally dazzling. He was not a tall man, indeed his height could be seen as a disadvantage. His legs were thin and bony, almost wasted, and it appeared only the top half of his body could ever be appealing.

Crystal bit her lip; she sensed an underlying danger behind those soft green eyes.

'Come, come, don't be shy,' Forusian said, waving his hand for her to follow him. 'I wouldn't want my new guest to think me unwelcoming.' The guard pushed the butt of his sword into the crook of her back. She flinched, turned and glared at him, but he ignored her penetrating stare.

'Keep up, keep up, there's a good girl,' ordered Forusian walking away. 'That's it, just follow me, I'm sure you would love a tour of the castle, everyone does, you know.'

It appeared the castle was perched on a high cliff face at the very edge of the sea. A solitary seagull sent a hysterical cry above her head, and the shrill of its wail pierced the grey sky and Crystal shivered.

'Where am I?' she asked, noticing that not a single flake of snow had fallen here.

'Why you're in my kingdom,' Forusian answered with a pearly, white smile, 'and you're my most welcomed guest.'

The guard grunted for her to move on and Crystal took a step forward, reluctant to obey. Gravel crunched under her feet when she made her way to the main entrance, following Forusian who took her into a great hall.

'Well, what do you think, do you like it?' He asked, waving his hands in the air when they entered. Crystal fell silent and Forusian appeared not to notice.

'I was given this castle as a *present* from a scheming goblin owing me a considerable amount of money due to bad investments. I gave him an offer he couldn't refuse: either surrender his abode to me or die,' he let out a sudden chuckle. 'So, here we are.'

Crystal pulled her lips tight; realising he liked the sound of his own voice to echo from the four walls. She needed to know why she was here before she could work out a plan of escape, so she decided to bide her time and try to stay out of trouble. She didn't know if Forusian was dangerous, but her intuition told her to be wary, very wary.

'Here we are at the King's Hall,' he said, laughing as though he had said something amusing. He turned to her, his face bright and cheerful. 'Well, it is a hall and I am the king, so I guess that's as good a name as any don't you think?'

The two Nonhawk warriors guarding the doors to the King's Hall pushed them aside to allow the king and his entourage to enter. The room was spectacular, with fine, tall lancet windows and a hammer-beam roof. The dining table placed on a raised platform in the centre of the room was made from the highest quality walnut and looked to be able to sit at least sixty people with ease. Crystal noticed the table was already set with silver cutlery and the finest cut-glass crystal. Nine candelabras stood in a row, creating a wonderful display of grandeur. The ornate mantelpiece framed the fireplace, which crackled with life. Hanging high above the mantle sat a larger-than-life sized portrait of King Forusian.

'Isn't it a wonderful painting,' he gushed, when he caught her stare. 'I just love looking at it, it's so me!' he giggled, putting his hand to his chest in an act of self-modesty. 'I really am a lucky fellow to be blessed with such devilish good looks and to have all the power which I possess. I guess you could say I got the cake and ate the hand that baked it too.'

Forusian moved towards Crystal with a light step.

'You're quite a delightful dish to feast my eyes upon, and I just love your deliciously long hair. What colour is that? It's in fact quite dazzling.' Crystal stared at him in disbelief; was this guy for real?

'Cat got your tongue, eh? Well, I guess it's not every day you get to be in a castle with a real king, you must be quite in awe of it all, sweet girl. Still plenty more to show you, so let's not sit and chat here or we'll never get finished.'

Forusian took Crystal on a tour of the castle, which lasted for over an hour, and all the time she was followed by two Nonhawk soldiers. Afterwards, he led her back to the King's Hall, which also gave access to his private chambers.

'I have decided to put you in the red room,' he told her. 'I thought it would be appropriate with the colour of your hair. Dinner's at eight and I don't expect you to be late. I thought we could eat in the drawing room, it's much less informal in there.'

Forusian nodded to the guard to take Crystal away. He gave her a sharp nudge and once they reached her room, he pushed her inside and locked the door behind her. His footsteps melted away and she gazed around the bedroom taking in her surroundings. She could see why it was called the red room, the main feature being a solid oak four-poster bed; delicate carvings of beautiful young maidens were portrayed in great detail on the wooden bedstead, each bolster wrapped in a rich-red velvet curtain, finished off with twisted gold braid trimmings. The chairs were covered in a rich scarlet fabric and a bright-red chaise longue dominated her view of the window, which was barred.

A tall, thin cabinet stood against the far wall covered in gold and on the top sat a realistic figurine of a fawn which reminded her very much of Mr Tumnus, with his cloven hooves and human face and when she reached out and touched his horns with her fingertips, much to her amazement he started playing a haunting melody on his pipes. It took a while, but once she grew tired of him she noticed there was a small door which opened to the bathroom, and she pushed the door ajar and took a peek inside.

The room was surprisingly sparse, but a silver swan was perched on the far wall, with its wings cradled to catch the water that flowed from its smooth, elongated beak. Fresh towels sat on a set of carved wooden drawers each embroidered with a regal 'F' and she thought the shape of the toilet looked decidedly unusual. She noted that clean clothes were draped over a chair and looking down, realised her own were filthy and torn.

She washed and changed and after what seemed like hours later, the sound of her door being unlocked brought her attention back to Forusian. The guard was waiting for her when she found the courage to open it and he told her briskly that King Forusian requested her attendance at dinner.

She stood in the doorway wearing a pale blue dress, shaped like a sari but with a fuller skirt. Her necklace shone deep purple around her tender throat, showing her despair.

'This way,' the Nonhawk soldier barked, pointing his sword down the corridor.

Crystal felt her spine stiffen.

'Whatever you say,' she barked back. 'It's not like I have a choice is it!'

When she entered the dining room, Forusian was sitting at the head of the table.

'So glad you could make it,' he said in amusement. 'Please, come, take a seat.'

The guard pulled out a chair and Crystal sat down. A troll came to her side and poured sparkling wine into her goblet; once filled, he bowed before the king and left. King Forusian rang a small, silver bell and two more trolls appeared, this time with large, silver platters perched high above their heads. They placed them on the table and a wonderful aroma filled the air.

'Tuck in,' said the king, waving his hand in the air. 'I'm sure you must be hungry and I can't have you wasting away.'

Forusian reached out and grabbed a large drumstick; he took a bite, pulling the white flesh from the bone with his strong, perfect teeth.

'I do hope you're not one of those fussy vegetarians,' he said with his mouth full, 'but if you are, I can always get you something else to try.'

Crystal pushed her plate away.

'I'm not hungry,' she said lowering her lashes. 'I just want to go home.'

'You can't go home,' Forusian spat, his eyes turning cold and he threw the drumstick onto his plate, having suddenly lost his appetite.

'But I don't understand why I'm here; what *do* you want with me?' Crystal argued. Forusian reached for the silky material which served as a napkin. He wiped his mouth several times before he spoke.

'So, you wish for me to cut to the chase and tell you why you're here?'

'Well, I didn't think it was just to show me your damn castle,' she snapped, feeling her anger rising.

'True,' he said, turning serious. 'However, it is really important to me to make sure we have a good relationship during your stay.'

'What do you mean?' she asked in dismay, 'how could we possibly be friends after you kidnapped me?' Forusian wiped his fingers one by one and then threw away the silken cloth.

'Well, let's just say having you here with me will help me in more ways than one, and I would like us to be friends.'

'You're talking in riddles,' she replied, frustration filling her voice.

'I'm sure it will all become apparent to you in time,' he said, wagging a firm finger, 'something I feel you will have plenty of while being my guest.'

'I am not your guest,' she boomed at him; 'I am your prisoner.' Forusian shifted uncomfortably in his seat; it was clear he wasn't used to being spoken to in this manner. Once again, he gestured to her to eat, preferring to ignore her sudden outburst.

'Don't worry,' he told her, picking up his goblet and taking a large gulp of wine. 'You'll be pleased to know that if I have my way, we will become closer than you ever thought possible.'

Crystal looked exasperated and a deep chill seeped into her bones. How could he even think they could be friends, but more importantly why would he ever want them to be?

# *Chapter 7*

Matt and Tremlon entered the elf kingdom in disgrace. When the wagon did not appear at the gates at dusk, Phaphos had been ordered by the king to send out a small search party. The snow lay thick upon the ground, but the blizzard had long since passed. It took much time to cross the frozen lands, and the bitter wind and freezing conditions hindered their task, but eventually, the remains of the wagon stood on the horizon, the frozen carcasses of the horses lying like ice statues where they fell.

'Build a fire!' shouted Phaphos, urging his men to do the task quickly. 'Then bring any bodies you can find towards the flames.' They found three bodies close by; the first was beyond anyone's help. The dead warrior's blood had run like an icy river, changing the pure white snow to a deep, dark crimson. He lay face down, his throat cut from ear to ear and what blood was left inside his body was frozen in his veins for all eternity.

The search party stared in disbelief. The scene before them was nothing more than savagery. Dragging the second body to the fireside, Phaphos helped strip the soft pelt from Tremlon's stiffened body and began to pinch the unconscious elf's ears and nose before slapping his face. The fire soon took hold, and huge crackles rippled through the darkness as the flames licked towards the stars. The golden glow flickered while the wind blew forcing dark shapes to dance upon his pale skin. Tremlon's eyelids fluttered, then a moment passed and his body suppressed a groan and he opened his eyes. He stared at Phaphos without really seeing him at all, disorientated, he blinked at an alarming rate before bolting upright in panic, unable to grasp his bearings.

'Be calm, you're safe,' exclaimed Phaphos, grabbing his hands in restraint. 'It is I, Phaphos; don't be afraid and tell me, who did this?' With trembling limbs Tremlon fought to get to his feet, pushing Phaphos aside. Worry clouded his judgement when cold comprehension shot to the surface of his mind. He stumbled, losing his footing and he grappled in the snow, desperate to reach the place where Matt was laying, cold and still. He crawled on his hands and knees, his breathing laboured for he was weak from the attack and his incompetence at protecting the boy rang loud and clear inside his brain. He reached out and brushed the snow off Matt's back and then turned him over. The boy's limbs fell with a sickening 'thud' onto the bed of soft snow and Tremlon blanched when he realised they were probably too late to save him.

'Phaphos, over here!' he yelled, pulling at the boy's ears and nose with no effect.

'Is he mortal?' asked Phaphos, dropping to his knees and examining the boy's body, 'because pinching his ears won't do any good if he's not one of us; you need to warm him and give his lungs air.'

A soldier threw more wood on the fire and it roared into life. Tremlon covered Matt with thick blankets brought by the soldiers and he checked his vital signs to find they weren't good. His pulse was weak and his pupils dilated, but he was alive.

He dragged Matt's body closer to the fire, placing him as close to the flames as possible. The bonfire crackled and hissed, spitting heat towards his frozen body and eventually, Matt's cheeks turned pink and his skin was warm to the touch and he opened his eyes. Tremlon although not a sentimental elf, cupped his hand around Matt's head and pulled him close; he would always be eternally thankful the boy had not died whilst in his care. Once satisfied Matt was out of danger, Tremlon called to one of the elves, asking for something hot for Matt to drink, which Matt readily accepted and whilst the warmth seeped down to his belly Matt's thoughts drifted back to his last memory before his brain had shut down, like someone flicking a switch off inside his head.

It had been so difficult to know what to do when Crystal was taken. The kidnappers had knocked Tremlon out with one too many blows to the head and killed the warrior without mercy. Matt had known fear before, but in a different world and in a different place. Here, he was out of his depth and he could never win against those who were deemed to be mystical beings. His eyes misted over and he shivered involuntarily. He realised what a fool he'd been to accompany Crystal to this place. He had not fled on a horse, which perhaps a wiser man would have done. Instead, he'd fought with the bitter wind to cover Tremlon's motionless body with the dead warrior's coat, searching for anything that might prove useful in saving the shape-changers life. He'd no idea how far he was from the Kingdom of Nine Winter's, so he'd sat and waited to be rescued, alone and vulnerable, until his blood turned to ice.

A shout rang out and two of the search party were seen dragging Arhdel's body towards the fire. They had found him lying only a few yards away with the young warrior by his side. The deep snow which acted like a blanket had saved both their lives. The soldier revived Arhdel from his icy slumber and warm rugs were flung around his shoulders and a mug of something hot and sweet, shoved into his trembling hands. The warrior's attention was fixed on the flames which danced and licked the air until Tremlon moved to his side.

'Who did this to us?' Tremlon asked, sitting beside him and warming his numb fingers.

'Nonhawk, it was Nonhawk.'

'Do you have proof?'

'I don't need any, I know how they work.'

'Arhdel, they've taken the girl.'

'Then they have probably taken her to their king.'

'Why, what would he want with her?'

Arhdel shrugged his shoulders, making it clear he didn't know.

'Getting her back is not going to be easy,' he said instead. 'King Forusian is a very powerful king; he has a considerable sized army and his magical powers are supreme within the Nonhawk.'

'What do you know of the Nonhawk?' asked Tremlon, trying to keep calm. Arhdel chose his words carefully before continuing.

'As you may be aware they are a mixed breed; they are impure, once created between goblin and elf. However, their leader King Forusian is not of their blood. He was once an Oakwood wizard banished for his crimes against his realm and sent to a life of exile. It was written many centuries ago by the wise men of our time that no future races should ever be mixed again because of what it produced. The Nonhawk became an evil breed; goblins came from the dark side of magic and the elves from the light. Mixed together like fire and oil they made a deadly concoction.

Legend has it that when our world was created, having been split from the ordinary world, the Nonhawk decided they would take over the ordinary world and rule it and when the two worlds separated, the Nonhawk jumped from our world to the next. Thankfully, they jumped a fraction of a second too late and the divide had already taken place. They fell in between the two worlds and saw only darkness, where they lived for many centuries. The ordinary world would not forgive them for their betrayal and decreed a law banishing them from ever entering their world again. The extraordinary world, for some reason perhaps known only to a few, took pity on the Nonhawk and allowed them access back into our world on two conditions: that they use magic only in their own territory and never try to rule another realm again. They were given a kingdom of their own, but in actual fact they were cast out.'

Arhdel placed his empty mug in-between his feet and pulled the rug tighter around his shoulders to keep out the chill which threatened to return.

'I am starting to have terrible feelings about all this,' he continued, his voice flat. 'I just know in my bones this is all Forusian's doing. He is ruthless and has never tried to hide his perverse desire to take over the extraordinary world and become the ruler of all. Now Crystal has somehow become ensnared while he conspires against us, I'm afraid she may somehow hold the key to Forusian's future plans.'

'How will we get to her?' asked Tremlon, his voice betraying his jangled senses. 'What do you know of his castle?'

'Unfortunately, a great deal,' Arhdel answered. 'I know you can only access the castle by crossing two bridges over the outer moat and entering through the main gatehouse on the eastern side.'

'Can't we attack from the sea?'

'No, that would be futile. We would have to approach by land, however the castle has a twin-towered gateway barring unwanted access and it's the only way in.'

'Okay, so say we somehow manage to get inside, what do you know of the layout?'

'Well, I know the castle has two imposing turrets which houses the prisoners and the soldiers. One of the turrets leads to the cliff face and the other is where the portcullis mechanism is kept and where Forusian tortures his victims and gains access to the murder holes.'

Tremlon heard himself gulp.

'So what will he do with Crystal?'

'I have no idea; however I feel he will want to keep her safe if she is valuable to him.'

'Do you know where his private chambers are?'

'No, but that wouldn't be difficult to find out.'

'How come you know so much about him?' asked Tremlon, eyeing the soldier warily.

'Let's just say I had the misfortune of staying as his unwanted guest for quite some time,' the warrior replied, touching his scar with his frozen fingertips.

Tremlon's face fell.

'We must find Crystal and bring her back immediately,' he said, realising Arhdel's words confirmed his worst fears. 'If what you say is true and we don't succeed, then we will lose our realm to the Nonhawk and live as slaves for generations to come.'

'We must first speak with King Gamada,' said Arhdel, rallying with infuriating swiftness. 'He will know what we must do.'

'Then to the palace we go,' said Tremlon, already throwing his drink into the fire. 'Phaphos!' he shouted, his courage igniting. 'We must leave immediately.'

*

They rode like the wind, the horses sensing their rider's urgency and galloping with haste. Matt sat on the back of Tremlon's horse, his arms wrapped around the elf's waist and his fingers locked together in a tight grip. When at last they arrived at the gates of Nine Winters, there was no warm welcome. Instead, many warriors dressed in black and holding long pointed spears stood in line waiting to escort them to the king. When the group of horses rode between them in a swirl of sleet and snow, the soldiers rounded upon themselves, shoulder to shoulder, to stop them from turning and making their escape. Tremlon blanched, realising they were under arrest and he tightened his grip on the reins.

Matt was oblivious to their dilemma and was busy enjoying the scenery, finding the mountains spectacular and he called out to Tremlon to tell him his home reminded him of Liechtenstein in Bavaria and that he almost expected someone to pop out from the top of a mountain and start to yodel.

Tremlon shook his head at the boy's ignorance and sighed.

'Where's the castle?' Matt asked him, searching the horizon for a sign of a battlement.

'There isn't one,' Tremlon answered, sounding tiresome. 'The king lives in a palace, inside the mountain.'

They rode the rest of the way in silence until they were urged by the guards to dismount. Muttering and complaining Tremlon, Arhdel and Matt jumped down onto firmer ground. The guards appeared cautious when they forced their prisoners towards a wall of rock and once they could go no further, it was Phaphos who outstretched his hand and touched the stone. Matt was surprised to hear a low rumble from within the mountain and while he watched in awe, a deep crack appeared within the surface of the stone and then the rock crumbled away and a passageway became exposed.

'Off you go,' insisted one of the guards, pushing the tip of his spear in the small of Tremlon's back. 'The king awaits your return.'

Tremlon almost snarled but took a step inside instead and both Matt and Arhdel followed with Phaphos somewhere behind them. Inside the rock was a labyrinth of long, dark corridors and echoing passageways. Watery pools filled with silvery liquid had produced a city of stalactites along the roofline and the temperature was ice-cold. The small group travelled deeper inside the mountain and large naked flames licked at the rocks when the soldiers lit several sconces.

Eventually they approached what looked like a large floating ball of purple mist which hovered over a stone archway, blocking their path. Matt wanted to touch it, to feel its soft consistency, but he knew better than to let his curiosity get the better of him and it was Phaphos who once again took charge. He outstretched his palm, allowing his fingers to mingle inside the mist and he stepped forward, pushing his hand deeper inside, searching its core. The mist started to disintegrate until it floated away in wisps of trailing vapours.

'What would have happened if a mortal had touched it?' Matt whispered in Arhdel's ear. The warrior couldn't help chuckle.

'You would have been vaporised and become part of the mist,' he said, allowing a tight smile to hover around the corners of his mouth.

'Go on ahead,' interrupted one of the guards, pointing to the entranceway with his spear, 'we can go no further, but you must enter at once.'

Tremlon became agitated.

'I am sure we can find our way,' he snapped, taking a step inside and nodded for Matt to follow. 'It isn't like I haven't been here before!'

The transformation once they passed through the doorway was truly exceptional. The stone corridors changed to columns of polished marble and the design was smooth and incomparable. To their left, an arrangement of unique gemstones lay on slabs of solid gold. The gems shone like polished stars and the vibrant colours of fire opals and dragon's breath, teased their sparkling eyes. Petrified raindrops dangled like chandeliers from the ceilings and prisms of light dazzled them with the colours of the rainbow.

'Wow!' said Matt, utterly mesmerised. He had never seen so many jewels before, and black and white diamonds the size of plums were sat in bowls of white crystal. His fingers reached out and brushed against a bunch of red rubies, the gemstones sat like fat berries waiting to be plucked and he cradled them in his hands, not wishing to put them back.

'Put them down!' ordered a stuffy man who suddenly appeared from nowhere. He wore a tall, silver and black pointed hat and a heavy robe stretched with difficulty around his plump waist.

'Didn't you hear me!' the voice boomed, when Matt turned deaf. 'Why, I'll have you skinned alive boy if you don't do as I say immediately!'

Matt bristled and reluctantly let the rubies fall from his grasp. The Lord Chamberlain raised a quizzical eyebrow at Tremlon and Arhdel, before waving a theatrical hand and motioning for two large doors to open.

'The king is awaiting your arrival in the throne room,' he said, shooing them along like lost sheep. 'And it would be wise not to keep him waiting.'

When Matt entered court, he immediately spotted a few hostile stares from the elder courtier's who made him feel rather uncomfortable and he moved closer to Tremlon's side. He noted their clothes were very different from his own. The young women wore long, ceremonial dresses which clung provocatively to their well-shaped bodies and Matt felt himself gulp when he was unable to avert his eyes. The men wore clothes that were just as regal and their eye sought his when he passed them by, their eagerness to see a real, live mortal written all over their faces.

The usher made his way to Matt's side; he was a short, dumpy man with dark hair and equally dark, liquid eyes. He gripped Matt's arm with vice-like fingers and pulled him out of sight along with Phaphos. Matt tried to protest, but Tremlon shot him a look that made the words die in his throat and so he watched Arhdel and Tremlon make their way to the king's throne instead.

'Well, well, well, my most faithful servants have returned,' said the king when they approached.

'Your majesty,' Arhdel began.

'Silence, you imbecile!' roared Gamada, clearly infuriated. 'Don't you think I already know how you have failed me?' He stared in disgust at Tremlon and Arhdel who had fallen to their knees, there heads bent low in shame. Yet wasn't it he who was truly at fault? Wasn't it because he had been so naive to believe Forucian would not have known when Crystal entered their world?

He cursed himself for his own stupidity, taking his vengeance out on his two most loyal subjects. He had to think of a plan to get his granddaughter back or the whole kingdom and his future as king could be in serious peril. He took a moment to compose himself while both elves squirmed beneath his feet. He placed his cold stare on the back of their necks and toyed with an idea that was starting to form behind his hooded eyes, and he became more pensive.

'Get to your feet,' he ordered, gesturing for the Lord Chamberlain to hurry to his side, 'for I have decided, there is much for you to do.'

# *Chapter 8*

Amadeus sat on the king's horse looking down at the lush valley below. It had taken him three days to reach the valley of Raven's Rainbow and now he had finally arrived he was filled with an unexpected sense of foreboding.

Since an ancient law was broken here many years ago, elves were no longer welcome and he felt his shoulders knot with tension. His horse made its way down the steep ravine and Amadeus held the reins tightly when the mud slipped from the sides of the slope, causing his horse to stumble over loose rocks and large sods of earth. He headed towards the river and the horse broke its surface with an unexpected splash and she whinnied in dire protest when the icy water rose up to her belly.

Kicking his horse on, he urged her through the freezing current until they reached the other side of the bank and then he pushed on towards the cover of trees. He needed to make it to the traveller's rest before nightfall. He was weary and wanted to be fresh when he finally came face-to-face with the wizard, Bridgemear.

Unfamiliar noises filled the bristling trees while Amadeus rode through the dense forest. Tension tightened the muscles on his shoulders as taut as piano strings and his eyes darted from side to side in his attempt to be vigilant. A sudden movement caught his eye and he reached for his sword, manipulating his horse to turn so that he could ensure no one was planning to attack him from behind. He wished he hadn't come, wished the king had chosen someone else. He pushed his horse on while the wind died and a gentle stillness settled around him. The trees spoke to each other in secret whispers and calm settled over the forest.

It was a few lonely hours later when he broke through a set of trees and found himself in a less dense area. He followed a track going east to Fortune's End, where he planned to rest for the night. It had grown dark, but he managed to make out the minute hut which sat alone in a small clearing. He got off his horse and immediately felt the presence of another but he was not afraid; this was neutral territory, even for elves. He unfastened his saddle and the horse gave a snort of appreciation.

Out of the shadows, a small gnarled figure came to greet him, with a dented lantern held securely in his hand. He had short legs and fat arms, his face was drawn with many lines across it and his age had been forgotten long ago. He wore only a shirt and a pair of trousers, but the evening was strangely warm so there was no need for anything more.

'Welcome, weary traveller, come in and rest the night,' said the keeper, gesturing for him to approach. Amadeus relaxed his shoulders and pulled the bed roll off his mount. He was relieved to see that the man he had sensed was not a wizard.

'That would be very much appreciated,' said Amadeus walking towards him with a smile.

'Come in, come in,' said the keeper, stepping aside to allow Amadeus to enter. 'There is no need of a fire tonight, but I have hot food. Please, come and place your bed down while I pour you a drink to wash the dust from your throat.'

The keeper placed the lantern on a small pine table, the light sending gigantic shadows across the walls. The room was sparse but clean, and the keeper reached for a goblet from a shelf, pouring a sparkling liquid into it from an old, battered carafe.

'You speak the words I have longed to hear,' grinned Amadeus, when the keeper offered him the goblet.

'I can tell by your clothes you have travelled far. I will see to you first, and then I will see to your horse.'

'You are very kind,' said Amadeus, taking a gulp of his wine and finding it refreshing.

'My name is Nekton,' said the dwarf closing the door, 'and as you may have guessed, I am the keeper here.' They shook hands, and Amadeus noticed the dwarf had a strong grip, a sign of sincerity.

'The washbasin is in the back,' Nekton explained, releasing his grip. 'You'll find what you need to clean yourself there.'

Amadeus was soon washed and changed, and he sat expectantly at the table. Nekton was as good as his word and presented him with a hearty meal.

'Oh, I love Feefalas cooked this way,' said Amadeus, when he saw what he'd prepared. The meat had been cooked in rich, dark gravy seasoned with black pepper and garlic, and was accompanied with fresh vegetables and a mountain of potatoes.

'This reminds me,' Amadeus continued when his mouth stopped watering, 'of when I was a boy and my mother used to cook for me and my brothers.' The memory of his childhood flashed before his eyes; they had been good times.

'Dig in my friend, while I attend to your horse. I am sure she is just as hungry, but definitely not as thirsty as you,'

Nekton chuckled, while he watched Amadeus fill his goblet for the third time.

It was black as pitch when Nekton ventured outside to see to the horse. There were no stable as such and the only shelter for the horse was at the side of the hut. The horse was tethered to a ring nailed to the outer wall, and she snorted her appreciation when she saw the dwarf approaching with a bundle of hay and a bucket of oats.

'Easy, girl, I guess you want your supper too?' he said, placing the food in front of her. He patted her gently on her rump while she ate. She whinnied unexpectedly, scraping her hoof in the dirt and Nekton gave a puzzled expression.

'What's troubling you?' He asked baffled. 'Why, you're not one of those fussy eaters are you?' The horse became restless and Nekton started to feel uneasy. The horse was sensing something, but what? He shook his head, for he knew there was nothing to fear here. He stroked her strong neck to calm her; she was of good stock and a purebred, which could make them temperamental at times. Eventually, she nudged him with her warm nose and Nekton forgave her irrational behaviour and headed back inside the hut.

A while later, Amadeus lay on a lumpy mattress rolled up in a horsehair blanket. He was unable to sleep, yet the night was turning cool and windless. He lifted his head when he thought he had heard something and listened – nothing. Then he heard it again. He rose from his bed already fully dressed, just his boots lying abandoned on the floor. He grabbed them and shoved his feet inside. He made not a sound when he crossed the wooden floorboards. Nekton lay asleep in a makeshift bed situated on the other side of the room, and for privacy he used an old torn and threadbare sheet for a curtain, which he draped over a piece of taut string.

Amadeus went to the window and looked outside. The night air was becoming sharp like glass and the stars were sparkling in the sky, clear of any clouds which might dare to drift across them and dim their brilliant light. The trees surrounding the hut stood like stone statues in the background, not even the leaves trilled, and then Amadeus saw the eyes. He took an involuntary step back, for the eyes had no face or body. He knocked over a chair and sent it crashing to the floor, causing Nekton to jump from his bed, startled by the sudden noise.

'What was that?' he called out, pulling back the curtain and rushing to light the lantern before going to Amadeus's side. Even before he spoke, Amadeus knew he would sound crazy, but he knew what he had just seen. 'There are spies out there watching me,' he bellowed. 'I've just seen them.'

'Seen who?' asked Nekton, confused. He was the keeper and would know if someone approached the hut. 'There is no one here but us,' he said, trying to calm him. 'Perhaps you have had a bad dream?'

'No,' said Amadeus turning angry. 'I was not asleep. I saw with my own eyes three sets of yellow pupils staring through the window.'

Nekton was in despair. Amadeus had obviously had too much wine.

'You must be mistaken,' he said, taking a tone of voice which he thought may pacify his guest, 'but if it makes you feel better let's take a look outside and see if your eyes are still watchful.' Amadeus walked over to his bed and took his sword from underneath it.

'You cannot use that here,' warned Nekton, pointing to the blade. 'Are you not aware it is neutral soil here and no one must be harmed?' Amadeus tensed; he knew what he had seen, but he also understood the law of the magicians. If he was to break such a law, he would be punished, perhaps even put to death.

'Very well,' he said, sounding resentful. 'I'll leave my sword behind and we'll take a look together.' Nekton looked relieved.

'Come on then,' he urged opening the door, 'you go first.' Amadeus shot Nekton an expression of distrust, which spread like butter over his face.

'If there's nothing out there, then why don't you go first?' he asked, a hard look reaching his eyes.

'Fine, I will,' Nekton snapped. 'I just thought because you are a warrior and I'm a dwarf you would wish to defend me. I haven't a problem with who goes first, as I don't believe anyone is actually out there.' Amadeus gave a broad grin. Nekton was right; how could he even think of sending out the dwarf? What on earth was he thinking?

'You're absolutely right, my dear fellow,' he said, genuinely ashamed of his outburst. He targeted Nekton with a hefty slap on his back, almost sending him reeling out of the door.

'Hey, stop that,' said Nekton, looking un-amused. 'I'm only little.'

The two of them walked outside keeping a few metres apart, with only the lantern and the stars to help illuminate their way. The warrior and the dwarf checked the area for anything suspicious. At last, Amadeus was satisfied they were alone and called to Nekton to call it a night.

'Well, I won't say I told you so,' said the dwarf, grinning with satisfaction. 'And, now that we've cleared that up, I'll just check your horse one more time, before I go back to bed.' Amadeus nodded, appreciating his consideration and made his way back to the cabin.

He entered the doorway and felt fatigue fill his bones. He sat on a chair to take a moment's rest and a cold warning rippled down his back. They were both ill prepared for the attack. Flashing their silver swords, strange shadows came out of the trees and headed straight for the hut. They were practically invisible to the naked eye, using forbidden magic on the orders of their king. They had been waiting to attack the soldier Amadeus who was known to be a mighty warrior and who would not be taken without a fight.

They had not planned to take the dwarf but now realised they had no choice. It would be easy to capture him, although this would cause a great calamity if the wizard of Raven's Rainbow was to find out who had taken him. Without a sound, they edged themselves closer to the keeper and three of them surrounded him without him being aware. Another four waited for the signal that Nekton was captured before attacking Amadeus.

They pounced on Nekton causing him to fall against the horse. She whinnied a warning for the second time that night, but it came far too late. Invisible hands grabbed him from behind and another covered his mouth so he could not alert the warrior. They gagged him with thick material, his teeth biting down on the cloth, forcing his lips apart and causing his mouth to turn dry. They tied his hands together with rope, tugging sharply to make sure he could not make his escape. Fear showed in Nekton's beady eyes. This was Fortune's End, the one place in the extraordinary world where no one could be harmed, and yet here he was being exactly that.

Moments later, Nekton heard a cry, followed by heavy scuffling. The sharp noise of glass crashing to the floor made him flinch; they had attacked the warrior also. It took the assailants only a few minutes to defeat Amadeus. He could not see them, and although he put up a brave fight he was no match for their illegal magic. He was pulled out of the hut in the same way as Nekton, bound and gagged. Fury burned in his eyes and hatred showed in his twisted features when the same invisible hands pushed them to the cover of trees.

Their captors had them walk only a few metres before coming across a group of horses. Nine stallions stood fastened to a rope that had been tethered to the branches, and then Amadeus and Nekton were forced to mount and then their hands were bound to their saddles. More rope was used to tie two horses together while a leash was stretched from the leader's horse to their own. A cry echoed through the forest and then they were gone.

The party travelled for miles and were following the main route out of Raven's Rainbow when the enemy removed the spell that had given them anonymity. Amadeus was confused when he clapped eyes on them, instantly recognising the crest of the Nonhawk embossed on their armour. He was no fool and soon calculated the reasons behind his capture. These were Forusian's men; they had captured him before he reached the wizard Bridgemear.

He rode along the bumpy road with his mind racing ahead. There was something going on here more than first met the eye. For the Nonhawk to break the sacred laws of the land and risk the wrath of the wizard Bridgemear, it had to be something extremely serious. It was clear to him that Forusian did not want Bridgemear to know his daughter had arrived in the extraordinary world, but why? This was the burning question to which he had to find the answer. He knew he must stay alive at all costs, for he realised that king Gamada had never needed him as much as he needed him now.

# *Chapter 9*

Tremlon awoke in his chamber to find the sun was rising and Arhdel to be sitting beside him.

'You have a terrible fever,' Arhdel told him, turning to pick up an empty cup and fill it from the pitcher that lay next to him. He placed the cup to Tremlon's dry lips and he drank thirstily.

Tremlon's head was throbbing with a terrible ache and the pressure behind his eyes gave him cause to believe a hundred elves were slamming pickaxes on the top of his skull. He was also suffering from the symptoms of hyperthermia, and even with his bed full of blankets and the warmth of the sun flooding through the window he shivered with cold. Arhdel gave a solemn rasp.

'It's just as I thought,' he said, pulling a blanket under Tremlon's chin. 'You are seriously ill and we must get the healer to you as soon as possible.'

He glanced over at Matt, who stood waiting for him at the bedroom doorway.

'It's the effect of being in the snow for so long,' Arhdel explained. 'Warriors are very versatile to the bitter weather –

we adapt according to our climate with ease, but Tremlon is no warrior, his inner strength is not the same as the soldiers and he was unconscious in sub-zero temperatures for far too long. To be honest, it was a miracle either of you survived.'

Matt looked gravely at the shape-changer lying in his bed, sick and helpless. He had started to like the temperamental shape-changer who clearly suffered with a bad case of attitude, but he had concluded that he was just a strange bird-man burdened with a heavy conscience.

Arhdel called out to a passing servant and whispered urgent instructions. She hurried away, making her way down the polished marble steps and through the long corridors to seek out the king's healer, Sawbones.

It wasn't long before the healer arrived laden with a long, willowy stick and a brown leather pouch and he proceeded to the bedside table before opening the drawstring bag and delving inside. Pulling the bed covers away from Tremlon and placing them down to his waist, he listened to his patients wheezing chest with mounting concern. Tremlon's breathing was becoming irregular and his skin was grey and clammy. Sawbones held a small red bottle in his hand and he dislodged the cork with his teeth. He continued by pouring a thick, brown liquid onto his fingers before smearing it over Tremlon's chest.

'It will help his breathing and make him sleep,' he explained to Arhdel when he caught him staring. 'This elf is in a critical condition and we have no time to lose; we must take him to the Altar of Vitality and ask the guardian of the catacombs for her help if he is to have any chance of survival,' he said, replacing the cork. He didn't wait for Arhdel to speak before collecting his belongings and replacing the covers over the shivering body. Matt was numb. He had never seen anyone look so poorly, even when his granny suffered a stroke. She had died at the age of seventy-two in her sleep, but even in death she hadn't appeared as grey or as lifeless as Tremlon did now.

'The king must be notified at once,' Sawbones added, moving towards the door.

'Yes, of course,' Arhdel agreed. 'I will go immediately and tell him myself.' He turned to Matt. 'Can I trust you to escort Tremlon to the Altar of Vitality while I report to the king of Tremlon's sudden deterioration?' Matt nodded, with keenness glowing in his eyes.

'Good, it is settled then; I will meet you there.'

'Is he going to die?' Matt blurted, swallowing hard. Sawbones took a deep breath and puffed out his chest to show his authority.

'I'm afraid it isn't looking good; unless we can convince the guardian to use her powers to restore his health, he won't stand much chance of recovery. However, I must warn you that these types of elves – shape changers, are not good at fighting infection, and her powers will only bring him back from the shadowy place where his soul is lurking if it is not his time to leave us. If she agrees to help us and manages to bring him back, he will still be weak and in need of much care.'

Two guards with strong arms and rippling muscles entered the chamber. They had been assigned by Arhdel to transport Tremlon to the altar. The altar was set only a stone's throw away from the palace in a small catacomb carved deep into the rock close to the mountain and the guards laid Tremlon down on a stretcher, ensuring he was secure before making any attempt to move him. Matt picked up the blankets that had fallen to the floor and fussed over him like a mother hen making sure he was kept warm, but Tremlon's symptoms were changing and he was becoming hot. Instinctively, he kicked at the blankets to cool himself and beads of sweat wound their way down his forehead to soak his pillow.

Matt watched Tremlon finally fall asleep and in a sombre procession they made their way to the catacomb. When they entered, the cool air was a welcome kiss on Tremlon's clammy skin and for the first time the shape-changer looked at peace in his induced sleep.

Once inside the catacomb, the air became damp and the earth underfoot changed to an orangey red. Matt noticed the healer was already waiting for them by a table made of rock; he had changed his clothes and resembled a Benedictine monk with his long, brown robe, short only of the halo of shaved hair. The catacomb was eerie and smelt of decomposing matter and Matt saw that long hollows had been dug out of the rock and what looked like mummified bodies were wrapped in decaying cloth, protruding like trophies of death.

'Bring him to me,' said Sawbones with a new urgency to his voice. 'We have little time to spare.' The two stretcher-bearers gave a deep bow before proceeding to the table. With gentle hands for such strong elves, they placed the shape-changer onto the cold slab. Matt was surprised to see the shape-changer didn't awaken when his body touched the cold limestone or cry out with shock; instead he lay perfectly still. Sawbones began the ritual by placing Tremlon's hands palms down upon his chest and then sprinkled a handful of what looked to Matt like some sort of blue powder over his abdomen. A deep groan slipped from Sawbones' lips and he waved a shaking hand over the whole of Tremlon's body.

Candles in many different shapes and sizes adorned the cracks and crevices of the catacomb, creating an aura of artificial brightness all around them but a sudden gust of wind blew down from the abyss above, causing the candles to flicker and all but a few were extinguished. The healer clearly unfazed by the strong, blast of air and consuming darkness, continued to chant. Then the strange powder changed colour, glowing silver like the moon and a ghostly apparition materialised before their eyes. The figure shimmered, illuminated by the bright glow until the light faded away to reveal an old crone. Matt thought her appearance was completely unnerving. She was nothing less than grotesque, and her wizened and gnarled body shot painful messages of unbearable ugliness to anyone who had the misfortune to place their gaze upon her. Her face, pockmarked and red-veined, showed years of neglect. Bony hands tapered to scrawny fingers, with long, blackened fingernails displaying razor-sharp points, which could evidently be used as instruments of destruction if she so desired.

The guardian stood by Tremlon's feet while she waited for the healer to acknowledge her and once he had done so, she took a step forward to take a better look at the sick elf.

'Who is this creature?' she hissed, her voice hoarse with age.

The healer cleared his throat; he had great respect for the guardian, but feared her sometimes volatile behaviour.

'His name is Tremlon; he is a shape-changer and he is extremely ill.'

'And what do you expect from me?' she asked, while a cunning smile played along her purple lips.

'We ask for you to use your magnificent powers to heal him,' he responded with a bow.

'And what will I get for me efforts?' she asked, with a shrewd glint in her eye. Sawbones smiled already one step ahead of her.

'I have brought you a gift in return for the favour we ask of you.' The old crone shot him a look of interest. 'Show me your gift!' Vanishing behind the altar, he reappeared with a crisp white cloth held in the palm of his hand. He peeled away the corners to reveal a small, perfectly formed butterfly. The colours and size Matt could not see from where he stood, but the hag sucked in a gasp of sheer delight. She was known to desire living creatures, fascinated with their beauty, craving vibrant colours from outside her world which consisted only of misery and semi-darkness.

'What do you say, guardian? Is it worth the trade?'

'Oh yes, yes, definitely yes,' she said with obvious glee. 'I have always wanted one of those; why, just look at the fine, elegant structure of the wings.' Her eyes became hard. 'Can I have it now?'

'No!' said Sawbones, withdrawing his hand. 'Do we have a deal or not?'

'Very well,' she sniffed. 'I will see what I can do.' She turned her attention to the motionless body lying before her.

'He's close to death,' she told the healer, her voice flat. She watched his face tighten like a clenched fist. 'I will not make any guarantees to save this elf. The decision will rest upon the effect of the poison when it reaches his heart.' Matt, who had been silent up to that moment, took a step forward and challenged the guardian.

'You cannot use poison on him, or you'll kill him!' he roared in panic.

The crone spun round on her heels with startling speed and faced him, her mouth twisted in a bitter grimace.

'And what do you know of my ways?' she spat, causing droplets of saliva to be sprayed from her mouth into the atmosphere. Matt was repulsed, but stood his ground. He had to try and protect Tremlon from this evil witch.

'Do not meddle in matters that are way beyond your understanding,' snapped Sawbones, furious with the mortal for interfering. 'The poison will either kill him or cure him, it is not for you to decide,' he fumed and while he apologised to the guardian for the mortal's behaviour, Matt moved back into the shadows.

'Then I shall continue,' said the witch, giving Matt a smug grin and a hush fell over the catacomb. The guardian placed her fingertips over Tremlon's forehead and glided her hand over his skin, stopping only when she reached his abdomen. She noticed his breathing was shallow and his chest could barely be seen to rise. A cry left her lips and she stabbed the elf in the stomach with one of her long, lethal nails. She ripped at his flesh, causing blood to ooze from his gut and run along the alter. Tremlon's eyes flew open and he shot up into the sitting position. Red eyes met black.

'Sleep,' the old crone commanded.

He fell back, his arms flailing by his side, once again unconscious. Matt felt bile rise in his throat and he blinked back hot tears which stung his eyes; she had made him literally sick to the stomach. While crimson blood still flowed down Tremlon's side, the guardian made an awful noise in the back of her throat before she spat into the wound. Matt felt sick fill his throat and an uncontrollable river of vomit flowed from his mouth.

'You're weak,' said the hag, with fury burning in her eyes. 'You're not of our world and you should not be here.' Matt wiped his mouth with the back of his hand and tried to compose himself. He looked up to see she was rubbing Tremlon's wound with a surprising tenderness, and a bright light moved underneath the wound, before spreading into each of his veins. Tremlon's body was unable to stop the poison which was carried in the guardian's saliva, and so it travelled unleashed to every part of his body. The light burned inside him like a fierce fire, rushing along his veins in search of his heart. The moment the poison touched the barely pumping muscle of life, all of the other channels of light disappeared, creating one single aura around the centre of Tremlon's chest. It was so bright it was blinding and then it died away.

'It's done,' said the hag with a wave of her hand. 'Now leave me.'

The healer signalled for the stretcher-bearers to come forward.

'How is he?' asked a voice in Matt's ear. Arhdel had returned.

'I don't know,' Matt answered, turning to face the warrior, his face grim. Arhdel shook his head in sympathy. 'I hope he makes it,' he said in a sad voice.

'Well, we're not just going to sit here and do nothing, are we?' Matt flared, showing his frustration.

'No, indeed we're not. I have just spoken to the king and he has decided to involve you in a very important task.'

'What kind of task?' asked Matt, surprised the king even knew of his existence.

'The king has no choice but to send us to try and bring Crystal back from the Nonhawk.'

'Nonhawk, who are they?'

'They are an evil breed. I told the king I believe King Forusian, the ruler of the Nonhawk, was responsible for the kidnapping of your friend. The king appeared to agree with this theory. Unfortunately, we cannot take Tremlon with us. There's no doubt he would have been very useful on this journey, but we must go it alone. However, on no account must you tell another living soul what we plan to do. This is to be our little secret, for only the three of us will know. I have already disgraced myself because Crystal was captured while in my care, I cannot fail again.' Excitement ignited in Matt's green eyes.

'I don't care what it takes; I just want to help get her back.'

'It's going to be dangerous, my young friend, and we must prepare ourselves, not just against the threats we can anticipate, but –' Arhdel broke off, pressing a firm hand onto Matt's shoulder in a gesture of their alliance. 'I've suffered in ways your imagination could never comprehend at the hand of Forusian; I've endured pain beyond your wildest nightmares and I do not look forward to going back and taking you with me.' Matt felt the palms of his hands begin to sweat.

'Did he torture you?'

Arhdel stiffened. 'Yes he did.' He broke Matt's stare and cast his gaze to rest on the pale and bleeding body of the shape-changer who was being taken back to his chamber.

'We must get ready for our journey,' he continued, his voice gruff with raw emotion.

'I am ready,' said Matt, feeling a glimmer of exhilaration. 'Just tell me when.'

'Then we go now; the horses are saddled and it is better to leave before nightfall.'

Matt agreed and so they left the catacomb, becoming part of Tremlon's entourage. Tremlon awoke from his slumber, his vision blurred with the effects of the poison. The pain in his chest was excruciating and he was having difficulty in breathing. He gasped in distress and both Arhdel and Matt ran to his side, pressing a caring hand on both of his shoulders.

'It's okay, just lie down and calm yourself; you're in good hands,' Matt comforted, trying to get him to lie still.

'Crystal,' he rasped, 'where's Crystal? I must tell her the truth about her mother.' Arhdel became agitated by his words and called to the healer to sedate him.

'He is delirious and doesn't know what he's saying; calm him,' he advised with an anxious glare.

'Why's he saying that?' asked Matt, unaware of Arhdel's twitch of nervousness. 'What does he mean,' he added, sounding confused, 'you know, about Crystal needing to know the truth? Does he know her parentage or something?'

'I don't know,' Arhdel said, looking slightly shifty. 'He is very ill and his mind is playing tricks on him. Best to let him rest; once the fever has broken, I'm sure he'll be back to his old self.'

Although not completely satisfied with Arhdel's explanation, Matt allowed him to lead him out of the catacomb and towards the stable block where two horses were waiting.

'We must stay focused if we have any chance of getting Crystal back,' said Arhdel, giving Matt an encouraging pat on the back. 'We will ride to the castle of King Forusian, and as we travel I will explain Gamada's plan to free Crystal from her captor.' Matt saddled up, the reins feeling as alien to him as his surroundings.

Arhdel kicked his horse into life and the dust rose.

'Arrgh,' Matt boomed in the horse's ears. 'You heard him, let's go.' The horse, unwilling to be left behind, finally broke into a desperate canter. They rode to the south, the wind howling its presence in the thick mountain air. The deep rumble of the horses' hooves drummed a constant beat while they rode along the frozen plain and their thoughts become tangled with determination and hidden doubt.

In the evening around the campfire Matt dozed while Arhdel guarded him with his sword. In the wavering firelight Arhdel pondered over the revelations the king had thrust upon him that very afternoon. He felt a barrier rise between him and the boy and he couldn't help feel saddened. He liked Matt, but his loyalty was to the king. Neither Matt nor Crystal knew the truth to who her natural parents could be and the king wanted it to stay that way, (for the time being).

Arhdel had been shocked, although he had managed to hide his despair from the king's piercing glare. Amella, his princess, had disappeared many years earlier and only now did he know the reason why. The shame she had suffered for loving a wizard would have been hard enough for anyone to bear, but to then have her baby taken to save Bridgemear's life would have undoubtedly destroyed her. The ancient laws had been written so many centuries earlier that no mixed breeds were allowed because of what the Nonhawk had tried to do in the world of mortals, their love had been doomed from their very first kiss.

He shook his head in dismay and with a stern expression, threw a piece of dry wood onto the fire; it crackled and hissed before igniting. The flames settled, and Arhdel nudged Matt for him to take his turn on lookout. Although tired, Matt rose from his bedroll and allowed Arhdel to take his turn to catch a well-deserved couple of hours' sleep. Tomorrow they would carry on until they reached Nonhawk territory and from then on there would be no sleep for either of them until they returned victorious with Crystal by their side.

Matt soon became lost in his own thoughts while he sat gazing into the golden flames. He knew Arhdel had changed, that something had shifted between them. Their relationship seemed a little strained, and he guessed it was because of his visit that afternoon to the king. All he wanted to do was get Crystal back, safe and sound. He let out a miserable sigh. Lies and deceit, that was all anyone held dear in this place. He felt depressed; he missed Crystal and just wanted to get her home.

A cool breeze started to blow, the evening temperature dropping to its chilliest. Matt pulled his jacket closer and watched Arhdel pull his blanket tight around his body. Turning his face away from the flames, he shut his eyes and allowed the darkened images inside his mind to dance behind his lids.

'Are you okay?'

Matt jumped, startled.

'I didn't mean to...' Arhdel came and sat beside him, resting his hands on his knees. His gaze was upon the fire. 'It's going to get much worse,' he said into the flames. 'It's a terrible risk we take, not even knowing if we are going to succeed.' He turned his head and saw bewilderment illuminating Matt's face. 'It's an experience you never wanted,

I know, and you find yourself in the midst of a battle which you should never have been part of.'

'You're right, I shouldn't be here,' Matt snapped, a little too harshly. 'This was never my fight from the very start.'

'Evidently, but you're here to fight for Crystal, are you not?'

Matt winced.

'Yes,' he said, still feeling grouchy, 'and I won't leave here without her.'

'Then your fate is sealed,' said Arhdel, looking troubled. 'My only hope is that you live to tell the tale and get her home safely.'

# *Chapter 10*

Crystal had been a prisoner in Forusian's castle for five days. For most of that time she'd been locked away in her room, allowed out only for meals and the occasional walk in the grounds, followed at all times by a Nonhawk soldier. Since her arrival Forusian had acted the part of the perfect host, but he'd upset her by taking her amulet claiming he was keeping it simply for safekeeping. He still hadn't explained why he'd kidnapped her or of what value she appeared to be to him and when she tried to broach the subject at dinner, he simply changed the topic with a flurry of his hand.

The sun was setting when the guard knocked on her bedroom door and proclaimed it was time for supper. When she arrived in the drawing room, Forusian was sat at the head of the table just like he did every night. Candles were lit and the fire tended but Crystal sensed something was different. She looked down at the table. The food was just as lavish, the wine plentiful, but the atmosphere was - charged.

Forusian waved for her to sit down and once she was seated they ate in silence, which was rather unusual. The fire crackled, breaking the eerie silence that was growing between them and Crystal shifted uncomfortably in her chair. She saw the king was dressed in a new suit, and his crisp white shirt stood out against his clean, tanned skin. She thought he looked extremely smart dressed in that particular shade of blue and felt her eyes draw towards his handsome face. She dragged her eyes away and sliced through the ham which had been placed on her plate, trying to concentrate on chewing her food instead. Forusian suddenly cleared his throat and she looked up expectantly and she watched him wipe his mouth, before taking a gulp of wine.

'I hope you are not missing your home too much,' he said, placing the goblet on the table.

'Why do you care?' she asked, her long lashes hiding a sudden awareness in her eyes. A shadow appeared to pass over his face and she sensed he had something important on his mind.

'Do you like my castle?' he asked, flinging out his hand and pointing to the four walls.

'Well, what I've seen of it, yes,' Crystal replied, replacing her knife and fork back onto the table. 'However, I wish you wouldn't have me shut away in my room like some common criminal,' she added, pushing her plate aside, her food barely touched. She looked at him thoughtfully for a moment and then she said, 'tell me Forusian, what's wrong with you tonight?'

'Oh, why nothing my dear, I would just like to see you more settled that's all.'

'You would? Why is that, have you suddenly found you own a conscience?' Forusian almost chocked on a piece of meat and his fingers reached for his goblet and after taking a huge gulp of wine he said, 'tell me Crystal, could you actually learn to like me?'

Crystal looked shocked by his question, and the glow from the fire did nothing to hide the redness held in her cheeks.

'That's a very strange question to ask someone who you are holding against their will,' she answered in a huff.

Forusian sighed deeply and was just about to say something when there came an unexpected knock on the door; or was it expected, Crystal wondered, when he shot her a devious glance and she watched his demeanour change before her eyes.

A soldier entered the room, his clothes were dusty from the road and he looked uncomfortable when he saw the princess sitting at the table.

'Forgive me, sire,' he began, 'but I bring important news from Raven's Rainbow.' Forusian jumped to his feet and flashed a look of excitement towards the messenger. He pushed his chair away from the table with an eager hand and then proceeded to lead the soldier to the library. He turned suddenly, remembering he was about to leave Crystal all on her own.

'Excuse me for a moment my dear, while I talk to my messenger. Please make yourself comfortable, for I won't be too long.'

Crystal watched him leave through a small side door and after waiting only a few seconds she quickly followed him. In his excitement, Forusian had forgotten there were no guards to stop her from doing so and she saw him enter the library, before tiptoeing slowly towards it.

She pushed her red hair behind her ear and then pressed it against the wooden door. She could hear them talking but their voices were muffled and she strained to hear what was being said and so she pressed her ear a little harder against the panel.

'That is excellent news,' Forusian was heard saying to his messenger.

'So my mole really did know the soldier was going to alert Bridgemear.'

'Yes, indeed sire,' a voice replied.

'You were not seen?'

'No, my lord. We used the spell you gave us to make us invisible; the wizard will never suspect it was you who set up the ambush.'

'Marvellous, this really is good news for I mustn't have Bridgemear dropping by and spoiling all my plans. No, you and your men have done well,' Forusian said, and Crystal heard someone gulp down a drink.

'Also, I need to add that we must ensure that no one from the elf kingdom knows we have captured one of their warriors, otherwise I will have them knocking at my door and this could lead them straight to my hidden jewel.'

Crystal digested every word, conscious she was probably the jewel he was speaking of. Hope filled her heart though when she learned someone from the elf realm had been captured, believing it to be Arhdel or Tremlon; if it was true and one of them was really here in the castle then perhaps she could free them and in return they could help her escape. But as she listened a little longer, she was distraught to find out it was no one she knew at all.

Their voices changed to laughter and Crystal realised their conversation was concluding so she rushed back to the drawing room, a cloud of disappointment following close on her heels. Her thoughts were filled with worry. Where were Matt and Tremlon? Was it possible they had not figured out she had been captured by this mad king? Perhaps Forusian had been clever enough to cover his tracks?

She slid back into her chair; her heart thumping against her ribs and her breath was turning short. She inhaled, trying to calm herself so he would not suspect she had been eavesdropping on him and flustered, she grabbed at the goblet of wine, accidently knocking it over and spilling the contents all over the beautiful cloth. She struggled to soak up the wine with her napkin, but there was far too much to make a difference and all she managed to do was spread the stain a little further. Forusian re-entered the drawing room and watched her trying to mop up the liquid as best she could.

'Come, come,' he said, sounding relaxed, 'don't worry about that, it's only a little wine and I have many more of those frilly things to cover my table.' He walked over to her and touched her hand with his.

'Leave it,' he commanded. 'The servants will clear it away.'

'I'm so sorry,' she said, pulling her hand away. 'I'm not usually so clumsy.'

'Forget it at once and come and sit by the fire, the nights are chilly and I wish to speak with you about something which concerns you.'

'Oh, what is it?' she gasped in surprise. 'Is it something serious?'

'Well, it's just that I have something important to ask you,' he said, seemingly struggling to find the right words. 'More of a proposition really.'
He gestured for her to sit by the fire.

He pointed to a particular chair situated close to the flames and Crystal found herself drawn towards it. She sat down and started fidgeting; causing the light from the flickering flames to dance upon her skin and Forusian caught his breath at her beauty. He had to admit she was like a newly formed rosebud, ready to be plucked from the stem of life and her frightened eyes made him pull his own chair closer. No sooner had he made himself comfortable, he was jumping from his chair as though he'd been electrocuted, throwing himself at the mercy of her feet.

Startled, Crystal pushed back her chair and tried to stand, but he held her feet fast and her hands flew to her mouth, unable to hold back a choking sob.

'Do not be afraid of me,' he pleaded seeing the terror in her eyes, 'for I wish you no harm.'

He sighed, shaking his head.

'I shall just come out with it,' he declared, sitting up and bending on one knee, his face lifted with expectancy when he tried to grab her hand in his.

'I know this may seem a little unexpected, but Crystal, child of the elf realm, will you do me the greatest honour and become my wife?'

# *Chapter 11*

Deep in the belly of Forusian's castle ran a maze of dark and dangerous dungeons. Nekton and Amadeus had been thrown into prison by their captor and they sat huddled together in the dirty stench of a fleapit. When they arrived at the castle, fighting and clawing at the guards, they had expected to be tortured by the Nonhawk but instead they were taken down to the murder holes and kept there like caged animals, fed only pitiful scraps of rotting food to help keep them alive.

'We've got to get out of here,' said Amadeus, when the guard threw yet another lump of foul-smelling mess onto his plate.

'And how do you propose we do that?' asked Nekton, when his own food plopped in front of him.

'I'm not too sure,' said Amadeus, flashing him a look, 'but I can't stay in this hellhole for very much longer.'

Nekton reached out for the plate and began to eat; he went to take a second mouthful but stopped midway, his face turning green. He dropped the plate to the floor, turned and heaved the contents of his stomach into the farthest corner.

Maggots spewed from his mouth and Amadeus's lips hardened in disgust.

'You're right,' Nekton choked, wiping his mouth with the back of his hand. 'We must get out of here soon. If I stay in this stinking place much longer I will die from starvation, for I refuse to eat maggots, whether they be full of protein or not.'

'Then we must come up with a plan,' said Amadeus, nodding in agreement. 'I think I could have one almost hatched inside here,' he said, tapping the side of his head. 'It's time we put my half-cooked idea into action; after all, we have nothing to lose but our lives.'

Amadeus bent down and drew a sketchy plan in the dirt with his fingertips. Nekton grew excited with each detail Amadeus added to the earth.

'It might just work,' said the dwarf with an encouraging smile, his stubby fingers traced the outline of sand. 'Anything is worth a try.'

'Let's do it tonight,' said Amadeus, his eyes glistening with excitement. 'I've noticed we're watched by only one guard once they have finished dishing out that slop they call food.'

Their bid to freedom came just a few hours later when the guards changed shift for the night.

'Help!' shouted Amadeus sounding desperate. 'I think my companion's dead.'

A solitary guard looked through the spy hole in the centre of the door and watched Amadeus lean over the dwarf. The solider noted Amadeus's distress and sliding back the bolt, opened the door with extreme caution.

'Get him out of here,' Amadeus begged, jumping away from Nekton's still body. 'He's probably riddled with disease.'

'You,' said the guard, pointing his sword and twitching it to the left, 'move away from the door.'

Amadeus did as he was told, dropping his gaze in an attempt to portray submission. The guard was holding his sword in one hand and a slop bucket in the other. He placed the bucket on the ground while he locked the door behind him and cautiously made his way towards Nekton. He bent over the body to get a better look, nudging the dwarf with the tip of his sword.

In a flash, Nekton rolled over and grabbed his leg, taking the guard completely by surprise. Before he could yell for help, Amadeus was upon him from behind, gagging him with his huge hands and pulling him to the floor. Nekton grabbed the sword from the soldier's grasp and twisted it with a flick of his wrist; a flash of metal held his stare, before he stabbed the Nonhawk clean through his heart. His cry was stifled by Amadeus's suffocating hand, the blood from his wound pumping freely like water from a well.

With not a moment to lose Amadeus grabbed the dead soldier's belt and searched through the mountain of keys dangling from it, desperate to find the right key before another sentry came looking for his comrade. His palms were sweaty and his fingers slipped while he tried each key in the rusty, old lock.

'Hurry,' urged Nekton, becoming anxious when the seconds ticked by, 'or we'll never make it out.'

'I'm doing my best!' Amadeus snapped, his jaw tightening. 'Pressurising me at a time like this is not exactly helping!'

At last they heard a 'click' and both gave a huge sigh of relief, but they couldn't rest on their laurels for they were not free men yet. They fled from the dungeon, unsure of the castles layout and their sense of direction was dulled due to the lack of food and sleep.

'Do you know where you're going?' Nekton hissed; his frustration mounting. 'Only I heard that somewhere inside this castle there's a narrow corridor leading from the dungeon to the cliff top; it's where Forusian has his prisoners thrown to their death.'

'Yes, I've heard this story too,' said the warrior, checking behind to see if they were being followed. 'But more importantly I have heard there is a path which leads from the cliff to the shore.'

Nekton shuddered.

'Then we must find the corridor that leads to the cliff face.'

Amadeus stopped dead mid step, raising his hand for Nekton to fall silent. Straight ahead, a group of guards were sat by a glowing fire, laughing and joking, oblivious to the two prisoners who had almost walked in on them. They doubled back and at a fierce pace raced away, feeling bursts of anxiety and claustrophobia engulf them, caused by the close confines of the stonewalls. They swerved to the right when a V-shaped tunnel split into two but panic rose in their bellies when time and time again they found nothing but dead ends. Each time they were forced to turn back, retracing their steps until once again yet another blank wall greeted them.

'We're going in circles,' Nekton gasped when his breathing became more laboured. 'I really thought for a while that we had a chance.'

'We're not beaten yet, old man,' Amadeus hissed, feeling a thread of fresh air blow on his face. 'Nekton, we're so damn close, I can almost taste the sea.'

They bore left, running with a sudden spurt of energy and their hands gripped the damp walls of the narrow passageway to steady themselves and when they came to the end of the outlet they could see the waves crashing against the shore and the blue of the sky, but their access was barred by a metal gate filled with rusty ironwork.

'What do we do now?' whined Nekton in despair. 'We're well and truly trapped; there's no way we could break through these.'

Amadeus stared at the bars, weighing them up before grabbing hold of the two in the centre with his bare hands.

Nekton looked at him in astonishment.

'You don't honestly believe you can bend them, do you? Why, that's just pure crazy.'

Amadeus ignored him. He closed his eyes in concentration, working his mind on channelling all of his strength down through his arms and into his hands. He had been born with great strength and he was going to use it to get them out. With a determination that would have impressed even the king, Amadeus pulled with all his might and his body shook with his efforts, but the bars didn't budge and he gritted his teeth, unwilling to be beaten.

'It's no good,' said Nekton in dismay, 'you're strength alone is not enough.'

A low growl escaped from deep within the warrior's throat and he gripped the bars once more. Power pulsated from inside his body and sweat ran down his cheeks as he continued to channel his energy to where it was needed most. A faint creaking seeped from the rusty bars followed by an eerie squealing sound. Amadeus heaved a sigh, before standing aside to expose a gap large enough for both of them to pass through. Weakened by the amount of energy he had just used, he leant on the wall for support. Nekton stood by his side.

'Come on,' he yelped in delight, 'you've done it; you've managed to set us free.' He tugged at Amadeus's arm, but the warrior didn't move.

'I need a moment's rest,' he gasped, his arms hanging limp at his side. 'I must get my strength back.'

'We have to keep moving, you know as well as I do it won't be much longer before they realise we have escaped.'

'Just another minute,' Amadeus insisted, still weak, 'that's all I ask.' Nekton could see Amadeus was totally exhausted, but time was of the essence and he could rest later. With a firm grip, he took hold of Amadeus's arms; the warrior was a big man, but it was Nekton's turn to use his own strength.

'We cannot stay here,' Nekton insisted, gasping for breath when he realised just how heavy his comrade really was. 'I'm much too old to be experiencing such an adventure,' he added, when a spark of vitality twinkled in his watery, blue eyes.

He dragged Amadeus through the opening and then dropped him like a stone on the velvety, soft grass. Amadeus gave a feeble smile.

'I'll never live it down if word gets out that I was saved by a dwarf,' he scoffed, with a grin.

Nekton hauled him to his feet and they trudged the rough and winding pathway until they found the steps cut in the cliff that led to the shore. The steps were slippery from the sea spray, making them treacherous underfoot and they made their way with much caution, forever glancing over their shoulders in fear of being caught.

Once they hit the shore they hugged the shoreline until they made it to a road and then headed straight for the seclusion of trees. The night was drawing in and neither elf nor dwarf knew the woodland through which they roamed. Amadeus took the lead and Nekton followed close behind. They walked for many miles, wanting to stop and rest but fearful of the consequences, knowing they had to get out of Forusian's territory if they were to have any chance of survival.

Eventually, Nekton could go no further and he called to Amadeus to rest; although Amadeus was reluctant to do so, he realised he had no choice, for Nekton had done well to keep up for one so old. Amadeus finally succumbed to his companion's needs and decided they should take this time to find something to eat. The woods were alive with animal activity: owls hooted alerts on their leafy branches and bats flew low in search of their own tasty morsels of food. Amadeus was swift when he needed to be, and when he spotted a plump rabbit several feet away, his elf feet moved like lightening.

Nekton sat against a tree, resting his weary bones on the mossy bark. He lifted his head when he heard his friend return, grateful to him for allowing him to take a much-needed rest.

'I have dinner,' said Amadeus, holding up the dead rabbit. 'We cannot stay here for the rest of the night and we shouldn't really light a fire, but we are ravenous so we will eat a little, rest a little and move on.'

'You speak wisely,' Nekton agreed, 'but I am old and cannot keep up with you; my legs have given up on me, I cannot move another step.'

'Nonsense,' scoffed Amadeus, while he searched the ground for something he could use to skin the rabbit. He picked up a few flat stones, throwing them down again before finding one which he felt was sharp enough to do the job.

'You don't give yourself enough credit; you have kept by my side and have not faltered once. We haven't much further to travel before we enter the realm of the dwarfs. There we can get horses and stock up with fresh supplies.'

Nekton rose stiffly from his comfy spot and set out to find tinder and twigs to make a fire, contradicting what he'd just said about his feet.

'What did you mean when you said 'we' can get horses and fresh supplies?' the dwarf asked, lighting the fire with the ease of one who had done it many times before. 'You wouldn't need much in way of supplies once you reach my realm, why, you're only a day's ride away from your home.'

'I'm not going home; no, I'm going with you to Raven's Rainbow to find the wizard, Bridgemear.'

'Is that the reason why you came to Raven's Rainbow in the first place?' asked Nekton, blowing gently onto the fire and watching it crackle into life.

'Yes, I have orders from the king to tell him his daughter from the elf world has returned to the Kingdom of Nine Winters, but I was obviously intercepted by Forusian's men to stop me from doing so.'

The dwarf looked surprised – a wizard has a daughter by an elf? Could this be true?

'How did Forusian know you were going to seek Bridgemear?' he asked instead.

'That's a good question. There were only two other people who knew I had been asked to go on this quest; one of them was the king and I don't believe for one minute it was him. No, there has been treachery here by another, and I know exactly who he is and I will seek him out and ensure he pays for his betrayal.'

Amadeus finished skinning the rabbit before making a spit from an available branch. They ate by the light of the silvery moon, talking in whispers until it was time to put out the fire. They travelled throughout the night and by dawn somehow made it into dwarf territory.

The sun was rising into a ball of orange when Amadeus turned to Nekton and swore an oath that he would make sure Bridgemear knew of his daughter's return, even if it was the last thing he ever did and Nekton knew he meant every word.

# Chapter 12

The damning news of the dwarf's abduction finally reached the ears of the wizard Bridgemear. Suspicion was raised when a weary, weather-beaten traveller in great need of shelter and a bed for the night found the hut at Fortune End to be deserted.

His disappointment soon changed to concern when he saw a horse tethered to the side of the hut and once inside, found startling signs of a struggle with shards of broken glass covering the floor.

Bridgemear was filled with outrage, for who would dare to violate the laws of the land laid down by his ancient forefathers? The primordial magicians' had ruled this land with strong hearts and justifiable morel standings and their voices filled his mind, like a phoenix rising from the ashes.

*...And the land shall have safekeeping, owned by none, ruled by neither, a place where the lonely traveller can rest without fear of interrogation or reprisal for his sins. No man, wizard, elf or dwarf will ever have the right to harm a hair or claim a soul from another. If the wish for peace is ever*

*broken then the one who kisses the lips of death will willingly stumble upon his own demise and know his soul to be lost forever…*

His eyes flashed icy to match his mood, but they were as clear as running water. He looked down at the magician's staff held in his clenched hand. It was a magnificent piece of magic, a stave passed down from generation to generation and embodied with mystical enchantments. The tip held a small, golden globe, inside something mysterious and cloudy swirled about, a sign of the unique power created by those who were now a part of Bridgemear's ancestral descent.

The wizard's mind ran wild.

*Heavy will be their loss*, he thought when a bitter smile touched his lips, *but first I must find out who has taken the keeper.*

Pointing his stave at a sixty-degree angle, his voice sounded strong and determined when he spoke an incantation. The golden sphere started to revolve, producing a dazzling bolt of light. The beam condensed into a long, thin tunnel of white, creating a projection of luminosity within the atmosphere.

'Awaken, Adlanniel!'

A face of immense beauty materialised from the prism of light, but her greatest asset was her voice; soft, husky, like music.

'What do you wish of me, master?'

'Show me Fortune's End.'

'I will take you to wherever you heart desires,' she said, her voice smooth as silk. She melted away into the vapour which formed around her. To her magician, the spirit revealed the lush, green woodland that was known to be Nekton's home.

Everything looked peaceful and serene and Bridgemear was disappointed to find there were no telltale signs of foul play. Frustration played upon his mind; for he needed to know who had taken the keeper.

*It was someone clever who took him,* he thought, *someone who knew the consequences of their actions and are not playing games.*

He made an instant decision: he must call together the other wizards of Oakwood and begin a quest to find and punish those responsible. He thought about his blood brothers, Elveria, Mordorma, Amafar and Voleton and how they would be eager to ride by his side, but where would they start? It would be tricky; but there were already rumours of an elf warrior who had been seen making his way through the woods the very night the keeper vanished.

Bridgemear knew he was no longer welcome in the realm of Nine Winters, not since his affair with princess Amella and agonising memories of her rushed inside his head and he winced in physical pain. He shook his head in a bid to shake her image from his mind but it was no use; she would always haunt him. He had lost his heart to her many years before, his beautiful Amella; yet he had been the one to betray their love and the cold touch of truth made him shiver.

When the Order of the Elders found out what they had done they had turned cruel, using the ancient scriptures and written laws of their time to punish them both for their crimes. Amella had suffered the most. They had taken everything from her including her child, all in the name of justice and for what gain? Bridgemear winced, if only she hadn't given the child the amulet, the key to her realm, she could have returned to her people, but Amella had wanted to give the child something other than the gift of life.

The Elders explained the consequences to which they would accept the child as an offering to the realm. At the great table of wisdom, it was decreed what fate had in store for their daughter. It was proclaimed the child would be sent to the ordinary world to live with the plain folk, banished for her father's sins and given to a mere mortal. A woman who's new born child would die from cot death and therefore be replaced with the mage's own flesh and blood.

Amella loved Bridgemear so much she'd agreed to their terrible terms, fearing for her lover's life. Bridgemear was overwhelmed with only one emotion – relief and Amella's continual stream of tears for her unborn child did nothing to soften his heart. He saw the babe only as a crucifix, a burden to be carried until such time they would be free of it. He believed the child had changed everything, ruining any chance of a life together, and so he wanted no part of it. Shortly before Crystal was born the love they shared grew strained. Resentment burned between them like a raging fire, until the anger and misery they suffered finally erupted, tearing them apart. The final nail thrust deep into his heart was when he was told he was forbidden to ever set eyes on Amella again. This was a condition set to punish him by the Elders for all eternity and he felt the pain of her loss every day.

A cry of rage escaped from his tormented body and ricocheted from every corner of the room faster than a bullet from a desperate soldier's gun. He knew he must keep focused on the problem at hand and not stray onto the path that led to the past. He must forget Amella as best he could and find instead the one responsible for taking the keeper but sometimes her memory would not lie low.

The wizard made his way through his many chambers to the outside world, which brought him to the waterfall of Valandil. He wasted no time in stripping off his clothing and plunging naked into the icy waters, the shock of the freezing water cleansing his mind of all his agonising thoughts. Once revitalised, he swam with confidence, diving under the water and breaking through its surface until he was gasping for air. The waterfall fell about him in a rapturous cascade, the noise of the falls almost unbearable to his ears, but he loved the noise, for it allowed him not to think.

He eventually pulled himself from the sanctuary of the water and his naked body glistened in the bright sunlight. He felt none of the inhibition of a mere mortal. Nature had found peace within itself here, captivated by the consuming beauty of its surroundings, embarrassment did not exist.

His jaw flexed when a breeze whipped the air and he shook his body, eager to be dry. The cool wind wrapped itself around him, forming a cocoon of air and once dry he returned to his den. He decided tomorrow would be soon enough to start his journey, today he would simply rest and prepare himself for what was yet to come.

The following morning, a warm sun protruded the white, fluffy clouds and Bridgemear came out of his den with a calmer spirit. He would leave his stave behind due to the laws of the realms but his sword would never leave his side. He flung a thick, black cloak about his shoulders and fastened it with a dazzling jewelled brooch. He stroked the brooch absentmindedly – it had been a gift from Amella.

He saddled his horse and then visited each kingdom within the realm of Raven's Rainbow and gathered the four Oakwood mages' by nightfall. They stayed in Elveria's den, a place carved inside the hill of Quintel. Bridgemear stood by the silvery windows of Elveria's moon room, a place he used for his guests and the wizard felt pleased to be surrounded by his brothers.

Elveria was the elder mage. His lined face was devoid of humour and his eyes were sunk deep into their sockets. His beard was long and white, reaching almost to his waist and he tucked it into his belt to help keep it from rolling up to his chin The wandering spirits which roamed the mountain had already whispered to him of the disappearance of Nekton and because he was the most feared, they told no one else of their findings.

'I'm sure we will find out what has happened at Fortune's End,' Elveria said, turning to Bridgemear and showing his eyes were filled with concern. 'However, I feel there are a few things we need to clarify before we go any further. Would you mind if I start by asking you a few questions?'

'No, not at all,' replied Bridgemear, moving closer. 'Why, ask away, for I will tell you anything I can.' Elveria nodded looking pleased.

'You know we have had our differences over the years, especially with what occurred with you and Princess Amelia, but with this disgraceful situation upon us, I wish to set those disagreements aside.'

'Bridgemear appeared to squirm under his watchful eye.

'So, start by telling us what you know to be fact,' said Elveria, observing the red glow of humiliation burning on Bridgemear's cheeks. Bridgemear cleared his throat but could not look the elder mage in the eye.

'It is as I said earlier; the traveller went to the resting place at Fortune's End and saw it was deserted. Upon closer inspection the keeper was nowhere to be seen and the place was found to be completely ransacked. However, one thing is strange.'

'Go on,' urged Elveria, with a wave of his hand.

'Well, it would appear the intruder who was seen riding in my woods left his horse tethered to the side of the hut. Now who would do this for it would mean they would have to leave Fortune's End on foot?'

'I smell serious trouble,' interrupted Mordorma. He was Bridgemear's closest brother.

'Mmm, I don't like the sound of this either,' said Voleton, who was one of the younger mages. 'For I believe this attack was planned.'

'I think you're right,' agreed the youngest wizard, Amafar. 'Nekton wouldn't just vanish into thin air without a trace.'

'Indeed,' said Mordorma, nodding his head in agreement. 'Whoever took the keeper made sure they didn't leave any clues.'

'So, tell us,' said Elveria, turning his attention back to Bridgemear. 'Couldn't your stave identify the culprit when they approached the keeper's rest?'

'No, surprisingly not,' said Bridgemear dropping his head in frustration. 'But I have heard there was an elf warrior seen riding through my woods and who stayed at Fortune's End that very night.'

'Then we shall ride to the elf kingdom and see what King Gamada has to say for himself,' said Elveria, his eyes narrowing with suspicion.

'But I am forbidden to enter the elf realm,' gasped Bridgemear, astonished at the mere suggestion of entering Amella's realm.

'Yes, you are,' agreed Elveria, 'but this is different; their people are just as welcome in our realm as you are in theirs. I think it only fair that you come with us to the Kingdom of Nine Winters, after all what's good for the goose...'

Bridgemear blanched.

'I'm not sure if I can...'

It was Mordorma who came to his rescue.

'You will not be alone,' he said in a soothing tone. 'I know it won't be easy for you to return, but we must unite as one if we are to gain the answers we seek.'

Bridgemear held his gaze.

'I know you're right brother,' he said turning pale, 'but what if I see - her.'

'That will never happen while there are stars in the sky. Amella is long gone, no one has clapped eyes on her for many years and you should not worry yourself which such thoughts. Be strong and look towards the future for the past holds nothing but pain for you.'

The next morning, the four wizards rode at Bridgemear's side, their frustration worn like a warrior's mask on their taunt faces. They would deal with whoever had defied their laws with a penalty worth a wizard's wrath and so they rode to find answers and to defend their forefathers' wishes.

After crossing much land they began to tire and Bridgemear slowed his pace.

'Do you really think it was the elf that took the keeper?' asked Voleton, pulling hard on the reins to manoeuvre his horse to walk beside Bridgemear's.

'It's possible,' he conceded. 'No one can be absolutely sure either way, but he is the only lead we have. The one thing that puzzles me is that for some reason my magic could not help me trace him, which I find hard to comprehend.'

'Do you think they used forbidden magic to disguise the attack?' asked Mordorma. Who also moved closer on hearing snippets of conversation from behind Voleton.

'Again, It's possible,' Bridgemear answered, kicking his horse with his stirrups, to force her on.

'Who would want to do this?' murmured Voleton when Bridgemear was well out of earshot.

'Someone who feels they have a lot to gain,' said Mordorma, aware of a sudden chill in the air.

'It has to be someone willing to take a huge risk,' Voleton remarked.

Mordorma turned in the saddle and looked him straight in the eye.

'Then we had better make haste and find the culprit before they have chance to cause more chaos.' Voleton was about to agree when something caught his eye and he called out a warning.

'Look, two riders are approaching,' he said, pointing over to the west. 'Can you see, over there, on the horizon.'

Each mage stopped and turned their horse, straining their eyes to look to where Voleton still pointed. Sure enough, two small, black specks were making their way closer, the haze from the sun causing their outlines to shimmer like an illusion.

'One of the rider's is an elf warrior,' said Elveria, closing his eyes to slits, 'and the one who rides with him,' he added, raising his thick eyebrows in disbelief, 'is the one we seek, for it is the keeper of Fortune's End.'

Stunned by Elveria's announcement, no one attempted to meet the two riders; instead, they sat in silence, deep in their own thoughts, and waited for them to draw near.

The thud of the horses' hooves vibrated through the hardened soil, a beat which was in rhythm with the pulse in Bridgemear's temple. The two riders approached and with watchful eyes rode towards the band of mages. Bridgemear pushed his horse forward.

'Welcome back, keeper of Fortune's End, you look like you have come from afar. Please tell us what has happened to you.'

Nekton merely grunted; he didn't look well at all and beads of sweat were trickling down his face.

'Sire,' Amadeus interrupted. 'My name is Amadeus and I am a messenger sent by King Gamada.'

'I know who you are,' said Elveria, his voice thick with contempt, 'what we want to know is what you are doing with our keeper.'

'My lord, I was captured while staying at Fortune's End; my attackers lay in wait for me hidden in the woods. To overpower me they used a magic spell which made them invisible except for their eyes, for their pupils shone yellow against the night sky.'

'Who was it that attacked you?' demanded Bridgemear, furious at the thought of someone using forbidden magic.

'It was King Forusian, ruler of the Nonhawk; it was his men that came that night and took us captive.'

'Why was it so important to him to capture you and take the keeper?' asked Voleton trying to contain his surprise.

'I believe it was because I have a message from King Gamada for the wizard Bridgemear, and I have since come to realise King Forusian did not want the message I hold to reach his ears, as for the keeper, he was simply a witness to the crime.'

'What message could be so important it would warrant a move against us and with it the possibility of war?' asked Mordorma, his horse becoming restless and snorting in protest.

Amadeus opened his mouth to speak, but Nekton was no longer able to hold onto his horse and fell to the ground in a heap.

Amadeus jumped from his mount and bent down on his knees scooping the ailing dwarf in his strong arms. Bridgemear dismounted and placed his cool hand on Nekton's damp forehead. He felt his fever burn his fingertips and he closed his eyes. A blue light glowed above his hand and travelled down his fingers. Muttering undecipherable words, Bridgemear whispered a spell, letting the light melt against the dwarf's skin. Nekton's eyes fluttered and he suddenly sprang to his feet and then looked down at Amadeus in surprise.

'What are you doing down there?' he asked, clearly puzzled at the warrior being on his knees.

Amadeus rose to his feet and smiled, grateful Nekton was looking much better.

'Thank you,' Amadeus said to the wizard in gratitude, 'he has become a good friend.'

'There is no need to thank me,' said Bridgemear moving his hand onto his hips, 'he is my keeper and therefore my responsibility; I will always watch over him.'

Amadeus took the slight rebuff on the chin and then concentrated on guiding Nekton back to his horse before remounting.

'So,' said Amafar, who had been silent up to now. 'What is this message from King Gamada? It must be something pretty important to risk the wrath of an Oakwood wizard.'

Amadeus turned towards Bridgemear and watched the wizard climb back on his horse. Taking a deep breath, he faced the wizard's look of scorn.

'Bridgemear, wizard of Oakwood,' he cried, feeling all eyes boring down on him, 'I must inform you of the return to the extraordinary world of your daughter, Crystal, born of Princess Amella.'

Bridgemear almost fell off his horse and the beast whinnied in protest when he grabbed the reins too tight, forcing the mouthpiece to cut into her flesh. It was clear to those who looked on that he was astonished by the unexpected revelation, his face a picture of confusion.

Elveria frowned, his mouth pulled in a disapproving line.

'I always knew your past would come back to bite you on the arse,' he hissed like a venomous viper.

Bridgemear ignored him. His mind was too busy whirling over the fact that his daughter was back in his world, and he felt despair; the Elders would be furious when they found out. His brain worked overtime - why was she back? Had she come to seek him out?

'Where is she?' Bridgemear cried, trying his best to ignore the roar of raised voices and words of despondency.

Amadeus shrugged his shoulders.

'I assume she will have reached Nine Winters by now,' he said, grabbing his horse's reins. 'I have not been to my kingdom since I was captured by Forusian's men and only visited the realm of the dwarfs to gather horses and food for this journey.'

'Then we carry on to the Kingdom of Nine Winters,' Elveria cried out. 'We must find out what she is doing here and more importantly why the Nonhawk king tried to stop us from finding out.'

# *Chapter 13*

Matt and Arhdel sat on their horses and looked at the dark silhouette of Forusian's castle. They could only legitimately enter the castle by crossing two bridges over the outer moat and entering through the main gatehouse. They already knew that was not possible and instead planned to use the limited information given to them by king Gamada.

They turned their horses and made their way down towards the sea. Their plan would start with gaining entrance to the castle via the underground system. This was not a pleasant way to gain access, but the only way they could get in without being detected.

Arhdel was the first to jump off his horse and onto the shingle. The crunch of it under his feet sounded loud in his ears but the noise of the waves crashing against the rocks disguised his steps and the taste of salt soon entered his mouth. Matt was less enthusiastic to leave his horse and Arhdel waved to him and urged him to follow.

*The boy must learn to grasp the importance of courage,* thought Arhdel, scanning the shoreline and checking they hadn't been seen. He would try to teach him as best he could and believed Matt would not be slow to learn.

From his belt the warrior pulled out a small dagger with a jewelled hilt and once Matt was by his side he presented it to him. It was pleasing to the eye and Matt was stunned to be offered such a gift.

'I don't understand,' Matt stammered, refusing the dagger and pushing it away with his fingertips.

Arhdel closed his eyes, trying not to lose his patience.

'Take it, it's yours,' he insisted. 'You will need a weapon worthy of a warrior while you fight by my side.'

Matt paled.

'I'm really grateful to you,' he said, touched by his generosity, 'and deeply honoured, but I cannot accept such a gift.'

Arhdel looked puzzled.

'Nonsense lad, I'm giving you the dagger because you will most likely have to kill to stay alive.' Without ceremony, he thrust the blade into Matt's hand.

Matt gulped; in his naivety he hadn't really thought about anything as drastic as killing someone.

Murky clouds began to roll in from the sea and obscure the light from the stars and then huge drops of rain splashed down from the heavens, landing with a plop onto Arhdel's armour.

'Damn it!' Arhdel cursed, 'that's all we need.'

Grabbing hold of both sets of reins he pulled the horses onto a grassy bank set well back from the sea.

'They'll be alright here,' he advised, when the rain turned heavy. 'The sea doesn't come this far and the rain will not last forever.'

The rain was bitter cold and Matt felt sorry for the poor beasts.

'We must hurry and find the entrance,' stated Arhdel, pulling him away, 'or I'll turn into a rusty tin can before your very eyes.'

As nimble as a squirrel, Arhdel began to climb the steep incline. Matt tried to keep up but the short stumps of grass dotted here and there were slippery underfoot and he kept stumbling.

'Come on, in here!' called Arhdel from some way up. 'I've found the entrance we were looking for.'

'Are you sure?' Matt tried to shout against the wind, but his words were lost to the sea and so he carried on in silence.

Arhdel checked to see if they were being followed before entering a small cave. The ceiling was exceptionally low, forcing him to crouch on his hands and knees as he made his way through. He could see a hole about a foot square, a squeeze for anyone bigger than a small child to get through let alone a chunky warrior wearing plated armour.

Matt tracked him down and appeared at the rear. He stared briefly at the small hole that Arhdel told him they must use and unconvinced his eyes searched for an alternative route.

'You can't be serious,' he gasped, when he realised there was nowhere else they could go.

'It's the only way in,' said Arhdel, brushing a calloused hand over the stone.

'See this wall? It's already crumbling, and if we concentrate on this area here,' he said, pointing to where the stone was disintegrating, 'we should be able to make a hole big enough to enable us to get through.'

His eyes darted around the cave, surveying its structure.

'Let's just hope it doesn't collapse on top of us,' he muttered under his breath when he caught Matt's look of scepticism.

'How are we going to do this? We don't have a shovel or any tools with us,' Matt complained, reaching the warrior's side.

'We use our hands and feet,' boomed Arhdel in his ear. 'Come, lad, are you a man or a tiny, furry mouse?'

Matt shook his head in despair but joined the two large hands which were already tearing at the mud and stones. It was a very slow process; his nails were soon cut to the quick and the silt ingrained itself into his smooth skin. Dirty water was oozing through the hole and in no time at all it seeped through most of his clothing; soaking his skin.

It seemed to take hours, but after much hard work, the opening was just large enough for them to crawl through. Arhdel went first, pushing his bulky frame through the jagged hole; causing shards of decaying stone to break off and fall into the water.

'I'm almost there,' called Arhdel, still pushing his way through. 'But it's my damn armour,' he roared, 'it's stuck on a chunk of granite.'

'I'll push from this side,' Matt yelled, grabbing the soldier's shoulders and giving them a shove. 'You just need a little more power behind you that's all.'

Arhdel wriggled and squirmed while Matt pushed from behind, the granite unyielding until a final push made it give way and Arhdel fell straight into the stinking water below. The water wasn't very deep, less than waist high, but he was soon gasping for air and cursing.

'Are you okay?' Matt shouted, scrambling to his feet and peering down at him.

'Get in here!' ordered Arhdel, having finally lost his patience. 'I haven't all day to wait for the likes of you.'

Matt grinned. It was the first time he'd seen the warrior lose his cool. Without a second thought he jumped into Arhdel's awaiting arms and was grateful when he caught him with a splash.

The tunnel was much wider than Matt had expected and the water colder too. It was dark inside the tunnel, but Arhdel had come prepared. From inside his vest he pulled out a wand the colour of milky tea. He scraped it against the wall like you would a match and a bright glow illuminated their path.

'What's that you've got there?' Matt asked.

'It's a candle that never dies,' Arhdel replied, checking about for Nonhawk soldiers. 'They're quite rare nowadays and were given to soldiers many centuries ago to aid them in the darkness. It's called a 'wickercal.'

'Wicked,' said Matt, with a broad smile.

'No, it isn't bad magic,' said Arhdel, misinterpreting Matt's meaning. 'It's a tool created only for good.'

'That's not what I meant,' said Matt, realising his mistake. 'In my world the word 'wicked' means fantastic.'

Arhdel shook his head in dismay. 'No wonder your kind's all messed up,' he said, rolling his eyes in consternation.

They carried on through the brown, rippling water, stopping only when the tunnel turned into a crossroads.

'What do we do now?' Matt asked, shivering with cold and aware his lips were turning blue.

'I'm not sure; the king only knew about the way in and nothing else. I guess we will have to use our instincts and hope we don't get lost.' Arhdel moved the wickercal to view each tunnel in turn.

'Let's go this way,' he said, pointing his hand in the direction he thought looked the safest.

'How do you know if it's the right way?' Matt asked.

'I don't,' Arhdel replied, shrugging his shoulders, 'but we'll soon find out if I'm wrong.'

He turned left, wading further into the darkness and Matt felt his tremble deepen, anxious in case he should be accidentally separated from his mentor.

'What are we actually looking for?' Matt asked when he caught up with the warrior.

'We're looking for an open grate or door which will lead us to the kitchens.'

Matt nodded and so they wandered purposely looking for some kind of an opening which would lead them inside the castle, but found nothing.

'We're going around in circles,' Matt complained when he recognised a worn stone ledge they'd passed several times before.

'Yes, I can see that,' Arhdel snapped, when he saw it too. 'It's not as if I'm blind.' The warrior decided to take a moments rest, and moved to lean against the ledge.

'We'll have to go back to the crossroads,' said Matt, stating the obvious.

'Oh, so you're the expert now,' said Arhdel, wiping a crust of dried dirt from his face.

'Well no, of course not, I'm just saying it's the only thing we can do,' said Matt, feeling Arhdel was being rather unreasonable.

Arhdel glanced away and a small hole chiselled neatly in the stone caught his eye and wondering what its purpose was he pointed the wand closer. Shadows danced against the stone making the opening look even more intriguing and Arhdel reached out and put his hand inside. He grappled around and felt something soft and furry touch his fingers and he gasped, quickly pulling his hand away.

'What's wrong with you?' asked Matt, when he heard the warrior suck in his breath and then he saw a huge, black hairy spider with sixteen red eyes charge out of the hole, waving its front legs in the air in a menacing dance towards him. Matt jumped back repulsed by such a creature but Arhdel simply chuckled, looking slightly foolish. The spider eventually lowered its venomous quills and headed back to its nest, but those numerous eyes never left Arhdel's sheepish stare.

Once the spider was gone, Arhdel placed his hand back inside the crevice, but this time he gripped hold of something solid and pulled. A creak echoed eerily down the tunnel and a secret doorway slid open, showing them an entrance into the castle.

'Well, what do you think about that?' grinned Arhdel, turning smug. Delight danced in his eyes and Matt saw a glimpse of the boy he had once been.

'About time,' Matt teased. 'Finally we can get out of this stinking hole.'

Arhdel's tone changed abruptly.

'Now we must be on our guard. I don't know where we are in the castle and this makes everything far more dangerous for us. We must tread carefully, and always, always, do as I say.'

Matt nodded, moving quickly to Arhdel's side. He respected the warrior and would never disobey him on purpose.

Matt touched his dagger.

'I will do whatever you ask of me,' he said to prove his allegiance.

Arhdel patted his shoulder.

'I know I can count on you.'

They went through the door and into an abandoned passageway. The corridor was dry, but the air was thick and musty. Cobwebs hung over their heads as though fisherman had cast their nets, and repeatedly dropped in their faces.

'This stuff is disgusting,' Matt muttered, wiping yet another shroud of web from his face.

'It's not for long,' Arhdel told him, throwing his hands in the air and dragged away more spidery webs with an exaggerated swoop. 'We'll soon be out of here.'

Sure enough, the corridor ended with a door blocking their path and Arhdel pondered what to do next.

Arhdel pressed his ear to the door and listened. He could hear loud banging on the other side making it difficult for him to detect if anyone was about. He paused for a moment and then put his finger to his lips and Matt nodded to show he understood. Pulling his sword from its sheath, Arhdel drew the blade in readiness. There was only one way to open the door, so he signalled to Matt to press his body into the wall while he activated the door's release mechanism.

The tension between them was electric. Arhdel held his sword tight, his knuckles almost white and with his other hand he waved it across a glass panel and the door swished open.

Arhdel pounced on an unsuspecting guard who was standing on duty. Stabbing him repeatedly in his back and neck, he attacked the soldier until he fell to his knees, dead. Without hesitation, the warrior pushed his arms under the soldier's armpits and dragged the body into the passageway and out of sight.

'Let's go,' Arhdel said, once he checked it was all clear, 'and whatever you do, stay close.'

They found themselves stepping onto a metal overhang, perched some twenty feet in the air. Arhdel peered over the rail and saw there was no one about; so he moved quickly to get out of sight with Matt following close at his heels. Although afraid of heights, Matt stomached a sly glance down. He saw that directly underneath him sat a huge vat of bubbling fluid. Bubbles burst, and plopped like volcanic lava, pushing enormous clouds of steam towards him; the temperature was excruciatingly hot and the dry air burnt his throat.

Arhdel tapped him on the shoulder and they ran along to the end of the bridge, until they came to a staircase which led away from the scorching heat. Arhdel took three steps at a time, but Matt's legs weren't so strong and he struggled to keep up. Beads of perspiration were forming on Matt's forehead and he grew thirsty.

Once at the top of the stairs Arhdel scanned the area for a way out. Matt spotted a small alcove, which hid a door, and Arhdel signalled for them to make a run for it. The noise and heat stopped the moment they closed the door behind them and they clasped each other's hands in a sign of victory.

They found themselves in a large, expansive room, which was being used as some kind of a laboratory and was filled with row upon row of long oblong caskets made from some type of toughened glass. Matt thought about Snow White and the glass coffin until he saw they were each connected to a set of strange looking cables and he could see magic flowing through them, a colour that was as blue as the morning sky.

'I've never seen anything like it,' Matt hissed, looking from one tub to the next. 'What the hell are these things?'

Arhdel shook his head and they both moved closer.

Matt noticed the tubs were filled with a gooey liquid. It looked thick and sticky, and the colour had a similar tint to what he had seen in the vat. Matt felt a stir of curiosity and tipped the box with the palm of his hand. The fluid inside rushed from one end of the casket to the other, but apart from that nothing interesting happened. Matt's fascination grew and he chose to ignore Arhdel's plea for them to leave. Instead, he messed about with a dial that was set at the side of each casket, spinning it like a safe combination.

'Stop touching,' scolded Arhdel, still searching for a way out.

'It's not like it's doing anything,' said Matt, shrugging his shoulders and letting out a sigh.

'And what will you do, if it does?' Arhdel retorted, pulling at a door which he found to be locked.

Matt spun the dial as far as it would go and his fingertips were still on the control when something shot out of the gloop and grabbed his arm. Matt screamed in terror – unable to digest what was happening because he was being held by a large, blue hand covered in thick slime. The limb was unbelievably strong and it held him tight, squeezing his upper muscle until he thought it was about to explode.

In a flash, Arhdel was by his side pulling at the hand with all his might but the bony fingers only dug deeper into Matt's flesh making him squeal in pain.

'Get it off me!' he yelled, causing panic to make his voice sound high-pitched.

'I'm trying!' Arhdel yelled back, clutching the fingers and trying to force them free, 'but they won't let go.'

Matt reached out his trembling fingers towards the dial and turned it to zero, immediately the hand drooped back into the liquid.

'What was that- disgusting thing?' Matt demanded. His breathing was rapid and he wiped the slime off his arm and onto the floor in disgust.

'That was a hand of a goblin,' said Arhdel, still alarmed. 'What bothers me more is that if there is a hand in this casket then what the hell is in the others?'

'Do you think there are goblins in every one of them?' Matt gasped, wiping the last of the slime away.

'Yes, I do,' Arhdel said, with dread filling his voice, 'and if I'm right, we're in serious trouble.'

He walked over to another casket, and after checking the dial was on zero, he plunged his hand inside and pulled out the limb of a leg. The leg was one of an adult goblin; the foot displayed only four toes.

'But there's hundreds of caskets in here,' Matt wailed, watching his companion drop the limb back in the goo and then wipe his hand on the side of the glass.

'Could be even more than that,' said Arhdel, with worry lines creasing his forehead. 'It looks to me like Forusian has his own factory of body parts in here. There are enough goblins in these glass coffins to create a small army. I'm afraid we may have stumbled on something which could get us killed quicker than I first thought.'

'But how is he getting the parts to stick together?' asked Matt trying to think logically. 'He can't just sew them together, can he?'

'I don't know, but magic cannot bring back the dead so he obviously has a plan or he wouldn't be doing this,' said Arhdel, still looking worried.

'We must destroy them, right now,' said Matt. 'We can't leave here knowing he's got parts of an army in here.'

'You're right,' said Arhdel, rushing to the cables, 'we've got to try and stop him.'

Stretching his arms out to the main supply, he pulled at the connectors, desperate to detach them from the wall.

'Stop!' yelled Matt, panicking. 'You need to find the main source of power.'

'That's easier said than done,' shouted Arhdel, still tugging at the leads. 'There must be some kind of generator somewhere, as it couldn't possibly be run by magic alone.'

'How do you know?' asked Matt, scanning the area for some kind of switch.

'Because,' Arhdel gasped, 'no single sorcerer would ever hold such an amount of power.'

While he was talking, one of the cables came loose. The bolt of electricity was so powerful that it shot straight through his body, throwing him several feet. He lay winded, his beard and eyebrows singed, and a strong smell of burning flesh filled the air. A loud blast from a siren bellowed overhead.

'Now you've done it!' Matt shouted, helping Arhdel to his feet. 'You've set off some kind of alarm.'

Before he could reply, an interconnecting door was flung open and a mob of angry guards fell through, each flailing a sword with murderous intentions.

Arhdel caught Matt's eye.

'You're right,' he said, laying his sword down on the ground and raising his hands in surrender. 'I think I've just blown it.'

# *Chapter 14*

The velvety night sky was home to a darkened moon and the stars, covered with a thick layer of cloud, gave no light to the shadows that were scurrying like rats beneath them.

In Forusian's castle, the Nonhawk guards were a force to be reckoned with. Fierce and cruel, they had delighted in capturing the two unexpected intruders and on closer inspection one of the Nonhawk soldiers had recognised Arhdel from his previous capture. The soldiers were unsure of Matt, having never seen a mortal before and they handled him with mild caution until they realised he could do them no harm. Then the two captives were forced down into the dungeons where they were beaten and then moved to one of Forusian's murder holes to await his decision on whether they should live or die. The guards taunted their captives for several hours and their eagerness to execute the pair became increasingly obvious as time ticked by. They craved revenge for Amadeus and Nekton's escape and wanted these two prisoners to pay the ultimate price.

King Forusian however, sat in his chamber, filled with rage. Only a short time ago his captain of the guard had knelt before him, relinquishing the news of the two captives having been found trying to destroy his life's work. He slammed his fists hard onto the table, the force allowing his nails to dig into his flesh and draw blood. His mind was in turmoil; things weren't going quite as planned and he was enraged.

His mind raced along with the tide that was not far from his window. He had already taken the decision to move Crystal into hiding, realising that if the warrior Amadeus managed to get back to the elf kingdom he would undoubtedly return to leading Gamada straight to her. But now there was Arhdel to contend with. He was not quite ready to go to war with the elves but events were moving much faster than he had anticipated, his hand was being pushed a little further than he wished, but he was still confident that he had the upper hand.

He slipped from his chamber, making his way without the protection of an armed guard to one of his murder holes. Many of the thick, stone steps were worn away from years of use and sconces were already lit with bright light to guide him on his way.

His murder holes were set away from his dungeons. Indeed, the dungeons were for his everyday captives, thieves and vagabonds; his murder holes were for his special prisoners, prisoners he wished to torture and maim without the help of his guards.

Reaching a solid doorway, Forusian pulled back the heavy bolt barring his access. The door groaned when he pulled it towards him, revealing his two hidden treasures. He entered, feeling like a child who had stumbled upon his Christmas presents early.

Forusian cast his evil gaze upon his prisoners. Matt was chained to the upper ceiling in a wrought-iron cage and he saw blood congealing on his mouth and nose from his earlier beating. He was suspended in the air by a row of thick iron links and the cage rocked with each movement he made, causing it to swing like the pendulum of a clock. Arhdel was placed directly beneath the boy. His face, swollen and bloodied, stared vacantly ahead. He stood half naked, stripped to the waist, and each of his hands had been placed in shackles that were connected to a length of wood which ran horizontal to the walls. Forusian sniggered. He would definitely be enjoying some fun with these two tonight.

The cell was damp and icy cold. Stagnant water slid down the dark, grey walls where terrifying weapons covered in dried blood hung like trophies along the parapet. Forusian glanced over at the sickening array and his gaze stopped at the spider, a weapon designed specifically to mutilate women. The long ripping claws, which Forusian liked to heat before using, hung like vicious talons against the wall. A slither of disappointment slid down his back; he felt it unfortunate that they could not be used on Arhdel.

He observed the ocular speculum, a contraption used on the eyes. Its disturbing effect was to separate the eyelids from the eyes by engagement of the ocular side of the eyelids, and a spring lever attached to the side of the gadget forced the conjunctival fornix to split. His lips curled into a malicious grin; here was a weapon that might just come in useful.

Forusian placed his hands behind his back and inspected his prisoner. With a meticulous step, he circled the elf, like a snake circling its prey.

Arhdel paled, but his eyes did not betray the dread that was rising in his gut.

'So we meet again,' said Forusian, under hooded eyes. A smirk slid across his tight lips. 'I didn't expect you back so soon. Tell me, did you enjoy my hospitality so much that you just couldn't wait to come back and taste more?'

Arhdel pulled at his shackles, and he winced when pain pierced his cut wrists.

'Oh behave and stop that,' said Forusian, sounding irritated by his prisoner's attempts to break free. 'I hear you have been snooping around my castle uninvited; not something one does really, is it? A little birdie's told me how you've stumbled upon my little secret. That's a shame you know, because now I won't be able to let you go.'

'You had no intentions of letting us go!' Arhdel roared, still pulling at his chains. 'That's why we're down here!'

'Ooh my, we are a little touchy today, aren't we?' Forusian teased, enjoying Arhdel's outburst. 'A right little tiger you're turning out to be. Still, not to worry, if you cooperate with me then I promise I won't give you too much of a painful, slow death; however, if you do decide to be tiresome and difficult, then I will pay back the favour by torturing you for at least a week, so, tell me, what will it be?'

'Go to hell!' Arhdel shouted, his fury rising. 'I will tell you nothing you piece of scum.'

Forusian's smile dropped.

'Mmm, that's not really a good start, is it? Perhaps I should concentrate on the boy, maybe try and loosen his tongue?' he said, turning his eyes to rest on the tongue slicer. 'It's your choice Arhdel, how shall we play this?'

'Leave the boy alone,' Arhdel hissed, gritting his teeth, 'your fights with me.'

'Now, that's not quite true, is it? You're in this together, partners so to speak. So, tell me why are you both here? Did you accidentally stumble over my secret or were you sent as a spy?'

Arhdel turned his head and stared at the wall, knowing his silence would seal his fate. Forusian's face changed to a fireball of anger. He moved towards the warrior with fury burning in his eyes and he came so close to his face that their noses were almost touching and Arhdel noted he had minty breath and he couldn't help but give a chuckle.

'I asked you a question and I expect an answer.' Forusian shouted and his hand flew under his tunic and a second later he held a knife to Arhdel's throat.

'Cat got your tongue eh?' he asked, with a devious smile. 'You're not so cocky now I hold a blade to your gullet.'

'Tell him what he wants to know!' Matt shouted, unable to keep quiet when he saw the flash of steel. 'It doesn't matter if he knows why we're here.'

'Wise boy,' said Forusian, flicking his gaze to the cage. 'He's a bit brighter than you, isn't he Arhdel?' he scoffed, sliding the blade out of sight.

Arhdel clenched his fists. Hatred for the evil king seeped once again through his throbbing veins, his blood curdling at the thought of what atrocities Forusian was planning to do to them.

'Alright, this is your last chance,' Forusian warned, finally losing his patience. 'If you don't cooperate with me this instant then I'm going to persuade you the hard way.'

A dark shadow crossed his face, changing his handsome features to a vision of pure ugliness.

'I'm up for it, are you?' he growled, loosening his tight-fitting tunic and freeing himself from the bounds of the bright, crested fabric.

Matt stared down from his cage and watched in horror as Forusian took a coiled whip down from the stone wall. The whip was curled in a spiral of leather and Forusian unravelled it before he gave it a flick with a twist of his wrist, making it crack when it hit the floor. The 'thwack' of the whip when it connected with the ground made Matt almost quake in his boots.

'I'll ask you one last time,' Forusian roared, circling the whip around his head like a lasso. 'Tell me, what you are doing here!'

His arm pulled back ready to strike and Arhdel's skin glistened with uncontrollable sweat. The soldier closed his eyes, ready for the first lash to strip his back of its flesh but Matt was shouting for Forusian to stop and Arhdel shook his head in despair.

'Please, don't hurt him!' Matt begged when the whip gathered speed. 'I beg you, if you stop what you are doing, I will tell you anything you want to know.'

A whoosh filled the air when Forusian ignored his words.

'I swear I will tell you everything,' cried Matt, his voice rising in desperation, 'even about Crystal!'

Forusian's arm froze in mid-air. The boy had said *her* name, and his brain slammed on the brakes, just in time.

'Who are you, boy?' Forusian demanded, lowering the whip. 'Tell me now, before I strip the skin off your friends back!'

'Matt, my name's Matt.'

Recognition crept over Forusian's face.

'Surely you're not the same Matt who is the mortal friend of Crystal?' He gasped aloud, dropping the whip to the floor.

Matt nodded, looking forlorn.

'So, YOU are the friend she speaks so highly of?' he asked, when his curiosity ignited. 'This is all extremely interesting and I have to say changes all my plans. Pity, I was so looking forward to seeing Arhdel scream a time or two this night,' he added with an exaggerated sigh.

'Well, well, well, this really has dropped a spanner in the works,' he said, refastening his tunic and heading for the door.

'You're not leaving us down here to rot, are you?' Matt shouted, shaking the bars of his cage. 'Hey, come back here and another thing, where's Crystal? We know you have her hidden someplace.'

'Don't you fret, she's just dandy,' Forusian replied sounding smug. 'I'm afraid however that you're going to have to be my guests for a little while longer,' he said, securing bolt.

'You can't keep us down here forever!' Matt shouted, kicking at the bars in frustration.

'Pull yourself together, lad,' said Arhdel, when he saw how angry Matt was becoming. 'It's no use getting upset; we'll be here until he decides what to do with us.'

Matt accidently bit the inside of his mouth.

'But what if he doesn't come back? Isn't there some chance we could escape?'

Arhdel sighed deeply.

'No, lad, not this time. Look at me, my wrists are shackled and you're twelve foot in the air. There's no escape, we just have to hope that the end is quick, I'm just sorry I got you into this mess.'

'It's hardly your fault,' said Matt, shaking his head in despair. 'I wanted to help get Crystal back; I knew the risks when we set out for this place and I only have myself to blame.'

'You're too kind, boy,' said Arhdel, with sincere regret. 'You knew nothing of Forusian and what he's capable of. I should have known better than to take you along, but now it's too late and again, I apologise for everything you may have to endure by his hand because of me.'

Matt dropped his head onto his chest when Arhdel's words began to sink in.

'We'll get through this,' he said with conviction. 'Somehow I just know we'll get away from here.'

'Well, don't hold your breath,' said Arhdel, shaking his head, 'because inevitably you may not live to see it.'

*

Forusian raced up the steps two at a time, his thin wispy legs struggling when he reached the very last stair. He extended his fingers and clasped hold of a chair sitting close to the entrance. He couldn't decide whether his breathing was tight due to the exertion he had just displayed or the immediate flurry of excitement he felt deep inside. He just couldn't wait to tell Crystal the good news.

He flinched when he thought back to the night she had refused his marriage proposal and his eyes turned to slits. Thanks to the arrival of the boy, that was all about to change. He chuckled softly while he made his way back to his chamber. If she tried to turn him down again he would warn her of his intention to kill the boy.

A Nonhawk soldier stood on duty and when the king approached he pulled back the outer door to allow him access to the main corridor. Forusian felt a shiver of contentment. Before the moon was full he would have Crystal as his wife, of that he was sure. He wanted her by his side and he was damn well going to have her too. He stepped inside his chamber and quickly changed his clothes. He would go and see her, tell her his good news, strike while the iron was hot.

His nerves were taut with anticipation when he called for the guard to saddle his horse. He moved to the window; the wind was blowing, the night heavy, but he was thankful to see there was no rain. The moon was hiding between an array of thickening cloud but in a matter of days it would be full for all to see.

Forusian smiled and the evil in his heart deepened. It was only a matter of time before he became the most powerful magician in this world and once the marriage to Crystal was consummated, she would have to bend to his will and then there would be no holding him back...

Within minutes his horse was saddled and two of his most trusted bodyguards were ready to ride. By his side he carried the Sword of Truth, a blade he had stolen from the body of a dead goblin murdered by his own hand many years ago. The sword was enchanted and it would protect the bearer against any other sword or dagger. Forusian very rarely went anywhere without it.

The night was eerie and the riders rode like the wind, covered with black masks and long, dark cloaks to help them blend into the darkness.

Forusian's mood was euphoric when he finally arrived at Crystal's hiding place. He scanned the surrounding woodland for spies and when he thought it safe; he climbed inside the trunk of a large burnt tree, his bodyguards close behind him. Once inside, he took a flickering sconce off the wall and used it to guide his feet along a narrow path. Tree roots sprouted unevenly under the soiled floor making it hazardous underfoot and he cursed aloud when several times he almost tripped.

At the end of the tunnel was a door. He had used magic to keep it closed from unwanted visitors and it creaked loudly when it opened. He found Crystal sitting at a small table. She looked up, startled by his sudden appearance; she had not expected to see him tonight.

'My dear, there you are,' he said, as though he had merely stumbled upon her.

'Good evening, King Forusian,' she replied looking wary. 'What have I done to deserve this honour at this time of night?'

Forusian gushed, not hearing the sarcasm in her voice.

'Oh, my dear, I have had the most wonderful day, I really have.'
He came to sit by her side, the guards positioned outside the door.

The room was small, but adequate for one. It looked very much like a tree house, but was underground. There were two rooms at Crystal's disposal. The first, her living quarters, were sparse but habitable. There was no fire to keep her warm, but a small stove lay hidden in the corner.

The only other door in the room led to her bedroom. This room was smaller than the first, having just enough space for her bed and a water closest. It was extremely basic, with one woven rug on the floor.

'I hope you don't mind being down here too much,' he said, feeling a twinge of claustrophobia. 'I know it's a little *cramped.*'

Crystal squirmed in her chair.

'What's wrong?' she asked, sensing that something was playing on his mind. 'Has something happened?'

'I have heard people from the ordinary world like a brew called tea,' he said, playing for time. He jumped up and walked over to a hand-carved dresser which held a few pieces of crockery.

'Shall I make us some?'

He looked to see if she was interested in his proposal and his smile dropped when he realised she wasn't the least bit keen. He reached for the tea set anyway, which was painted in a deep-blue design, and placed two cups with saucers down on the hard wooden dresser. His actions were clumsy; he clearly had no idea what he was doing.

While he busied himself, his mind whizzed with his ideas. He so desperately wanted to tell her about the boy he had dangling from his ceiling, but now he was here he didn't want to upset her. He wanted to use him as a weapon to get her to marry him, but looking into those beautiful sapphire blue eyes made him feel weak. He felt a disconcerting emotion when he realised he wanted her to marry him of her own freewill, almost causing the cup to fall when he lost concentration.

'Shall I help you?' she asked, getting up and moving to his side. She reached out her hand and took the teapot from the shelf, accidentally brushing her hand against his. The shock of her touch forced him to pull his hand towards his chest, the power from her skin so immense that he thought she had physically burnt him.

'Are you alright?' she asked, unsure of what just happened. 'Have you hurt yourself?'

Forusian's mind flashed with the memory of her touch, and he blushed before recovering his composure.

'No, I'm fine,' he gasped. 'I think I just got an electric shock from you.'

'Oh, I'm sorry, I didn't feel anything.'

'Not to worry, I'm fine now.'

Crystal moved to the stove and put the small pot she used to heat water on to boil.

'Would you like milk and sugar?' she asked, pointing to the teacup.

He frowned.

'I don't really know,' he said, pulling a face, 'but I think I'll just go with the milk for now.'

The pot was soon ready and Crystal gave it a stir. With nimble fingers she poured the dark liquid into each cup, before adding a little milk to them both. She offered him the drink and he bowed his head in gratitude. Crystal noticed how he didn't hold the cup with the handle, which would have been expected with someone of his breeding. Instead, he held the rim with his thumb and forefinger, drinking his tea at this strange angle.

'So tell me, Crystal, have you given anymore thought to my proposal of marriage?' he asked, searching her eyes.

She felt her mouth go dry and averting her gaze, she picked up her own cup and gulped the hot liquid, causing her to burn her tongue. The pain moved to her belly, but it was a painful distraction, one which she readily accepted. Her mind whirled with a rush of excuses; like, why couldn't he just leave her alone?

The burning sensation in her throat died away, but the fire it created would not leave her. She felt a hot surge reach her lower lip when her mind went into blind panic. An awareness of an extrasensory perception smothered her, and then the room fell away.

She saw Matt in a cage. Although her mind was cloudy, she understood more of her vision this time. She knew not to call to him, already surmising that he couldn't hear her. She saw a flash of colour, a crest of a shield and instantly recognised where he was being held.

Forusian stood up and pushed his chair aside.

'What's wrong with your eyes?' he demanded, his jaw clenched. He knew she was the daughter of a powerful mage, but she was young and inexperienced, therefore naturally deemed powerless without the amulet. He unconsciously bit his lip, aware this should not be happening?

'Stay away from me!' Crystal shouted, when the fever left her body and her breathing returned to normal. 'I know what you've done. I can see you're holding my friend captive.'

Forusian's resolve slipped away.

'I'm very sorry you feel so upset, and yes, I do have your friend staying with me. How clever of you to use your power to detect him. How did you do it, did you read my mind? Nonetheless, it is all quite simple. Agree to marry me and I will free him at once; however, if you still wish to play these silly games and refuse to be my wife, then I will have no alternative but to have him executed. It's your choice at the end of the day, take it or leave it.'

There, he had done it. He would make her bend to his will; after all, he was the one holding the trump card and she was the kind of person who put others before herself. She would not want her friend to suffer, or worse, die.

He touched a glass panel with his fingers and waited for the door to open. He saw the glint of hatred still wild in her eyes when the door closed behind him. His two guards grunted when they saw him approach, and taking a step back they watched him fly by like a scolded cat. He mounted his horse, pulling at the reins and causing her to whinny in distress.

'Hurry, for I have a wedding to arrange!' he yelled, when his guards ran to his side. He whipped the horse when she reared but she kicked out her legs in retaliation. Her hooves hit the ground and Forusian put his boot to her belly, forcing her to move on. While his mind spiralled out of control, he told himself he would feel better once he had her temper firmly under wraps.

# *Chapter 15*

After Forusian left her, Crystal sat deep in her own thoughts for quite some time. She knew she must escape and find Matt as soon as humanly possible, aware she was responsible for their dire circumstances and she repeatedly cursed herself for bringing them to this terrifying place.

She had studied the room meticulously over the last couple of days and knew every crack and crevice, but had found no way out. The room was hidden underneath the ground, making it impossible for her to escape, having no windows to break out of or roof to climb onto and as far as she could see the only way out was the same way she had come in – through the door.

She had seen how it worked. On several occasions she had watched Forusian press his thumb onto a shiny panel cut inside the wood and magic always appeared to scan the very tip. She had tried her own many times, watching the bright light skim her fingers, but nothing ever happened and to her dismay, the door always remained sealed. To make matters worse, she never saw the servant who came with her daily supplies. Forusian wasn't stupid and had purposely built a narrow chute measuring approximately twelve inches wide, just large enough to have someone pass down her food on a rope each day. There was simply no way out.

Feeling restless, she crossed the floor with the two empty teacups in her hands. She glanced down at Forusian's cup and saw the shimmer of an imprint left on the side of the rim. Her eyes lit up with sparks of hope and crossing the room, she moved towards the magic panel.

Holding the rim of the cup up towards the glass, she rotated it from right to left. Forusian's thumbprint was distinctly on the edge of the cup, and the natural grease from his fingers had left an impression so clear that she could see the friction ridges and furrows. There was a swish when the thumbprint was accepted and the door flew open, revealing a long, dark corridor.

'I don't believe it!' Crystal cried out loud, dropping the cup and cringing when she heard it smash on the ground. Without a second thought, she entered the darkness. The door closed immediately behind her, and she felt a moment of panic before hurrying down the uneven passageway to try and find her way out.

She came across a solitary torch that was still alight when she reached a set of stairs and she reached up and unhooked it from the wall. She carried on with desperate haste until she stepped out into the forest and the torch soared with a sudden fiery glow and the euphoria she was feeling immediately evaporated. The dark night enfolded her like long, dark arms and the air was damp and bitterly cold. She realised what a fool she had been not to bring her cloak and was therefore unable to stop the chill from seeping through to her bones and she stumbled blindly into the unknown, unsure which way to turn.

A disgruntled owl hooted an unexpected warning, and the whoosh of its wings flapped overhead while it searched for food, startling her. The shadows cast by the flames of the torch made the bird look gigantic and she flinched when a wing appeared only inches from her face, and she dragged the torch closer until she heard the owl screech in triumph when it took its evening meal back to its nest to be devoured.

She felt so alone and vulnerable, believing a million tiny eyes were watching her from the seclusion of the trees, causing her courage to weaken with every step she took. Her fear was starting to make her breathing sound staggered and her palms were moist with sweat. She fretted over being recaptured, realising the torch could probably be seen for miles and so she dropped the sconce to the floor and stamped it out with the heel of her shoe until the flame fizzled and died. Tiny sparks flew in the air and drifted away on the breeze like a mass of golden fireflies and she felt a moment of relief when all she could see was darkness.

She realised her main priority was to find somewhere to hide for the night, but the forest was deep and unyielding. Her steps were clumsy and she walked like a blind woman, her arms outstretched, afraid of the elongated twigs and branches that repeatedly assaulted her flesh. With every footstep she took, her fear grew, until she was totally convinced someone was lurking in the bushes, waiting for the right moment to make their attack. Her fear allowed her imagination to run riot and elaborate thoughts of her assailants caused her throat to constrict, the terror in her eyes eventually clouding her better judgment.

Unable to endure the black abyss any longer, she was at the edge of delirium when she suddenly stumbled across a small hollow in the trunk of a tree. Finding sanctuary saved her sanity and she climbed inside, thankful to be protected from the danger she thought still loitered outside. She curled into the foetal position, trying to keep the cold at bay and she prayed that when the sun rose she would still be alive. Crystal had never felt so lost in her entire life. She was so afraid of the darkness and what the daylight would bring and unable to hold back her terror any longer, she allowed a heavy stream of tears to fall. With her mind full of anguish, she sobbed uncontrollably for what seemed like hours and the sound of her frantic tears were carried along by the four winds of the forest.

The echo of her cries stretched for miles and was heard by a forest dweller out late collecting a few pieces of firewood. On hearing the sobbing, the dweller guessed it was a young one who had lost their way and on dropping the kindling to the forest floor, she followed the winding path that wormed through the forest to find them. In her hand she held a common oil lamp and a tatty shawl was drooped around her chiselled shoulders while her skirt which was old, and faded, dragged along the floor.

The forest dweller knew the path like the back of her hand. She had trodden on this rich soil many times and was acquainted with every twist and turn. She was not troubled by the darkness or what it could hold, but she sensed whoever was crying was very afraid.

It took her only a few minutes to find the hollow where Crystal was hiding herself away. The lamp shone brightly, breaking the shroud of obscurity, and Crystal shielded her eyes when the light dazzled her, petrified the soldiers had somehow found her.

'Come with me,' said a voice from within the darkness. 'No point sitting in there unless you want to die of cold.'

Crystal was shocked to hear a woman's voice. But when the light started to fade, she clambered out of the hole and staggered towards the glow.

'Wait for me!' she called, when the light grew small, 'I'm right behind you.' Her feet were not so surefooted like the stranger's, and she stumbled more than once in her attempt to keep up.

The woman didn't slow her pace on hearing her cry and with the lamp still swinging in her hand; she turned from the path and in seconds was almost out of sight. Crystal scrambled after her. Her feet were aching and her knees hurt from the constant whipping of the thickening undergrowth but she refused point blank to be left behind. She finally caught up with the dweller, breaking into a small clearing and the woman approached a tumbledown shelter.

'You'd best stay the night,' said the woman, beckoning for her to enter.

'It's so kind of you to take me in like this,' said Crystal, following her inside. 'I'm really very grateful.'

'Tell me, child what were you doing out there?' asked the stranger, placing the lamp on a wooden table. Crystal's blue eyes filled with uncertainty. Where should she begin? What was she going to say? She felt she owed this stranger some kind of an explanation, but felt immensely intimidated by her. They stared at one another, sizing each other up, until the woman grew self-conscious and moved away. She reached out and picked up a beaker; filling it full of water from a pitcher standing close by. She offered it to Crystal and watched her lift it to her lips, drinking thirstily.

'What's your name?' the woman asked, when she saw the girl was trembling.

Crystal's mind thought only of protecting herself, aware of keeping her real identity secret for the time being. She had already had the sense to realise her host could well be an ally of Forusian's, or worse, simply prepared to betray her for a few gold coins. She thought quickly on her feet.

'My name is Nienna,' she said, dropping her gaze towards the floor.

The woman's eyebrow arched.

'Mmm, I see you're not from these parts?' she said in a rather matter of fact tone.

'Er, no,' agreed Crystal, shaking her head, 'you're right, I'm not from anywhere near here.'

The woman did not press her, but instead pointed to a sack which had been filled with horse hair and was used as a chair.

'Do you mind, if I ask what I should call you?' asked Crystal, placing the empty cup on the table.

The woman seemed to ponder over this question for a moment before giving her an answer.

'I go under many names,' she said at last, her voice sounding distant, 'but the one I have used for most of my life is Amella.'

Crystal smiled. 'That's a really nice name,' she said, with genuine warmth. 'And it's very pretty,' she added, still shaking from cold.

Amella shrugged, unsure of her visitor and not used to compliments. 'You'd better go and make yourself comfortable,' she said throwing her gaze at the chair.

Crystal nodded, dropping like a stone into the hairy sack.

'I sense you're running away from someone,' said Amella with a twitch. She crossed the small room and started to light the makeshift stove.

Crystal bit her lip. There was no way she could tell her the truth, but if she didn't tell her something she would be unable to ask for help. Amella busied herself preparing a light meal for her guest, but it wasn't long before Crystal noticed how Amella's movements were almost graceful. She studied her host with sudden fascination, surprised at her hidden elegance until the room filled with wonderful smells and her stomach growled with hunger.

'Come on, eat up,' said Amella, passing Crystal a simple wooden bowl. 'It's only feefalas and a few woodland vegetables, but it'll keep your hunger at bay and help to warm you up.'

'Thank you, you're very kind,' said Crystal, taking the bowl with both hands. 'It's so very good of you to give me something to eat as well as a bed for the night.'

Her host eyed her warily. It was becoming obvious to her that her guest was not some mere peasant like she had first thought and once Crystal had eaten; Amella came and sat by her side.

The oil lamp was smouldering in the furthest corner, making the shadows dance along the walls; cloaking the room in a shroud of mystery and Crystal couldn't help wonder how long Amella had lived like this.

She also realised Amella was not quite as old as she had first thought but there were obvious signs the woman had endured a hard life. Her hands were ingrained with years of dirt and her skin showed signs of exposure to the sun; however, her face was still youthful and very beautiful. Crystal saw her hair was thick with natural hazelnut highlights which shone like copper whenever it caught the light, but her hair was left to hang over her face like a dark curtain, almost hiding her away.

'So, tell me Nienna, who are you running from?' asked Amella breaking her train of thought and offering her a ragged, old shawl.

'Oh, from King Forusian,' said Crystal, accepting the garment and then closing her eyes to conjure up his image. 'He kidnapped me and then for some strange reason decided to try and force me to marry him, but I obviously refused, and he hid me away in the forest. By sheer luck I managed to escape and now I am free, I have just got one more thing to do, then I can go home.'

She opened her eyes and saw Amella staring at her.

'Where is home?' asked the woman.

'Erm, The Kingdom of Nine Winters,' Crystal lied, dragging her eyes away and feeling a moment of unease.

'Really?' said Amella, stiffening. 'You don't appear to have many characteristics of an elf, but then it's been many years since I entered the realm of King Gamada and you are of a new generation.' She glanced straight at Crystal's ears, but they were covered by her long, thick hair causing tension to flare over Amella's face.

'You know King Gamada?' asked Crystal, intrigued by her revelation.

The woman's eyes clouded and her mood changed unexpectedly. Hidden barriers made their presence known and Amella left Crystal's side to reach for a solitary bottle sitting high up on a shelf.

'I'm afraid I can't help you find your way back to the Kingdom of Nine Winters,' she said, filling her glass and taking a huge mouthful of the amber liquid. She placed the bottle back on the shelf without offering any to her visitor.

'Oh, no,' Crystal cried. 'You don't understand, I don't want to go back to my kingdom, I want to go back to Forusian's castle and free my friend, Matt.'

'That's simply absurd, you won't stand a chance against Forusian's men and you don't even know how to get out of the forest, let alone into the castle,' Amella flounced.

Crystal felt a bolt of stubbornness rip through her spine.

'Perhaps not,' she answered in retaliation. 'But one thing's for sure, I'm willing to try. I won't just sit back and let him kill my friend without a fight.'

'Brave words from one so weak,' said Amella, swinging round to stare at Crystal as though seeing her for the first time.

'What do you mean?" asked Crystal becoming infuriated. 'Why do you judge me so?'

The woman's lips tightened.

'I'm not judging you,' she said, her eyes wide with surprise. 'I'm merely telling you the truth. How do you intend to fight the guards, let alone the king? I am puzzled by you. You have no weapon and know no wizardry with which to protect yourself. An elf of your breeding should know more magic and sorcery than you appear to possess, yet you seem more '*worldly*' than a mere innocent of your kind should be.'

Crystal wriggled in her seat.

'Please stop analysing me. I realise I'm not quite what you think I should be, but the issue here is rescuing my friend. I've managed to save Matt's life once before and I am willing to try again,' she added still squirming under her gaze. 'Forusian needs to learn that not everyone will lie down and die just because he has commanded it, and he cannot have everything he wants just because he has power and has taught the Nonhawk to fear him.'

'You're very courageous for one so young,' said Amella with a sigh. 'You know, it's strange, but you remind me of someone I once knew, someone I thought to be brave and kind but turned out to be only weak and spineless. Let's hope you don't fail like the friend I once held dear.'

'I'm sorry about your friend, but I'm not like them,' snapped Crystal, raising her chin in disdain. 'I must get Matt out of the castle and back to Nine Winters.'

'You're right,' said Amella, placing her drink on the table, 'but you're going to need help to kill King Forusian.'

'Hey, wait a minute,' said Crystal, shaking her head in despair, 'I never said anything about killing him.'

Amella laughed a hearty laugh, leaving Crystal feeling foolish.

'You *have* to defeat him,' Amella told her, 'or you will never see your friend alive again. Forusian will not allow you to just take him, and when he finds out it is you who has turned against him he will not rest until you are dead too.'

Crystal gulped.

'I will do whatever it takes,' she said, folding her arms across her small chest. 'I will save Matt at any cost.'

'Very well,' said Amella, throwing her a moth-eaten blanket and downing the last of her drink. 'I had better make you a bed and let you get some sleep if you are so intent on changing both of our destinies tomorrow.'

# *Chapter 16*

Despite Nekton feeling much better it was apparent he was slowing the group down. Time was of the essence, and so it was agreed they should take an alternative route and stop in the realm of the dwarves so that Nekton could rest and fully recover. They entered without any resistance and rode through the marketplace, stopping at a tavern renowned for its hospitality to strangers. The wizards were impatient to be on their way and did not wish to sample any of the delights the dwarves openly offered and Amadeus felt genuine despair when the time came to bid his new friend, farewell.

'Remember to visit me in Fortune's End,' said Nekton, trying to clear his throat of any trace of emotion.

'Of course, I will,' answered Amadeus, giving him a heart-warming grin. 'Where else would I get such cheap entertainment? And anyhow, I must return the king's horse to him before you're accused of being a thief.'

They laughed the laugh that new friends share when parting, before hugging each other with a firm grip. The wizards' horses became restless and Amadeus sensed it was time to leave. With a heavy heart, he mounted his steed and without looking back spurred it on to re-join the others.

Nekton watched the band of mages ride off to meet their destiny and a crushing wave of regret washed over him when he realised he would never be a part of it. He had always been the keeper at Fortune's End, and had never known any other life. Now he'd had a taste of adventure he longed with a burning desire to go with the group on what he believed to be an invigorating quest.

The dust settled and with it his racing heart steadied. He shook his head, admitting he was being a silly, old fool and he turned towards the tavern on hearing the merriment inside. His eyes sparkled when a buxom female wearing little more than a smile caught his roaming eye and he grinned, deciding it wouldn't be quite so bad staying here after all. His thoughts swept back to Amadeus. If nothing else, he could take from this journey a new friendship, a friendship that would remain with him for the rest of his life and with this thought in mind; he indulged himself with far more than a few tankards of ale...

*

The five wizards continued along the dusty road on their way to the Kingdom of Nine Winters, with Amadeus riding by their side.

'I've never been to the elf kingdom before,' muttered Amafar to Voleton once they had reached the open plain.

'Neither have I,' replied Voleton, still keeping a watchful eye, 'but it's time we made it clear that they have crossed the line this time.' Amafar considered the implications of the wizards entering the elf realm uninvited.

'We may have bitten off more than we can chew,' he said, kicking his horse on when it decided to slow. 'Gamada is no fool, and we're unsure as to who he has allegiances to these days. I don't know if there is a connection between

Forusian and Gamada, but I can taste changes ahead and I'm uncertain it's a good omen. One thing is for sure though; Bridgemear will not rest until he has his vengeance on Gamada, and this could be just the excuse he's been waiting for.'

A sudden burst of laughter caused him to lower his voice.

'I think we're heading for a very rocky ride,' Voleton said, stealing a glance at Bridgemear. He gripped his reins tighter. 'However, whatever happens when we reach the Kingdom of Nine Winters I promise you, I'll stand by him. He's our blood and he's our brother, and I will not allow anyone to try and take him down because of his past.'

Amafar nodded.

'You're right,' he said, with a flow of solidarity sweeping through his bones. 'We are one and one we shall remain. No one will beat back the mages' who hold Oakwood blood in their veins. The power of the magician's wrath hasn't been felt in over a hundred years. Yes, you're right, I too can feel the change which is so imminent amongst us, and I embrace it. If it means a fight then I will fight at Bridgemear's side too.'

'So be it,' said Voleton, kicking his horse to spur it on. 'Our allegiance has been set once and for all. For the honour and pride of the wizards of Oakwood we will fight to the death, and hell will have to wait until eternity ends to claim its prize.'

*

King Gamada watched for the return of his trusted messenger, Amadeus, with growing anticipation. He had been gone far too long and with each passing day Gamada saw the return of Crystal slipping away. In desperation he had sent Phaphos to find him, who had previously returned with Arhdel and the boy from the ordinary world, but now they too had disappeared and a dark foreboding crept unwillingly down his spine.

He was sat in his luxurious dining room eating alone when one of his servants came to his side and placed a small silver platter before him. On it lay a piece of parchment folded into the shape of a cone. He picked it up and inspected the vellum, before dismissing the servant with a wave of his hand. The strange letter was sealed with wax, and he noted the bond had been made by a small, circular signet. His name was written in black, flowing letters, but the handwriting was unfamiliar to him.

He reached for the crystal letter opener, shaped like a slither of ice and slid it across the seal. Scanning the few scanty lines, King Gamada took an inward gasp, his eyes opening wide when he digested the contents of the letter. Hate and envy lurked uninvited within his darkening soul. It was just as he feared; Crystal had been captured by the mad King Forusian and was holding her prisoner, along with his faithful warrior Arhdel. The words were bold, demanding a substantial amount of money if he wished to see them both alive again.

The letter stated a rendezvous would be held at the Tower of Leddour. His kidnapper pulled no punches; he must come alone, and if he was followed his captives would die. With a strong hand he crumpled the letter into a tight ball. His frustration fuelled a hot fire in his belly, one he realised he could not put out, not until he had Crystal back where she belonged. He felt his fury rise, knowing he had no choice but to meet the demands of the Nonhawk king.

After a moment's thought he got up and crossed the room to look out of the large dome-shaped window which gave him a splendid view of his city.

'Damn Forusian,' he cursed, watching a mounted flag blow fiercely in the wind. The bright, masterful colours were bold and distinctive, but gave the king little comfort. He lowered his gaze and returned to his chair. He rubbed his temples when tension stabbed him behind his eyes like an invisible blade. He had been watching the Nonhawk king for some time, and Forusian's plans to start a war against him had been filtering back to him through his own spies.

He slammed his fist on the table while he fought with what was left of his conscience, trying in desperation to think of a way to defeat Forusian without the need of Crystal. His thoughts were interrupted by a sudden commotion followed by the doors to the dining room being flung aside to reveal the magician Elveria. He was followed closely by several other magicians.

'Forgive the intrusion,' Elveria bellowed, making his way to the king's table, 'but we need to speak to you urgently.'

'Well, well, well, this is an unexpected surprise,' said Gamada, forcing a watery smile. He relaxed his clenched fists and left the table to greet the magicians, leaving the crumpled letter unattended on his plate.

'You're always welcome in my realm,' he said, trying to stop his eyes from narrowing, 'but tell me, what brings you all the way out here?'

Elveria made quick work of the tale. Finishing with, 'And we cannot believe that you have brought Crystal back to our land; on whose authority did you seek to do so? I'm sure you can see it from our perspective, and it all looks extremely suspicious.'

Gamada's eyes hardened. 'This is neither the time nor the place to discuss why I have summoned Crystal,' he said, trying to keep calm.

A troubled expression spread across Elveria's face while he digested the king's words.

'I can assure you this is exactly the time and place,' said a voice from somewhere behind him, a voice the king deemed somewhat familiar.

Gamada lifted his gaze and his eyes searching the many faces and it was then that he spied Bridgemear. He recognised the handsome face immediately; time had not altered his chiselled good looks and a stab of resentment crept into his bitter heart.

Elveria noticed the look of distaste that was spreading over the king's face and he made his way to his side in an attempt to distract his attention away from the once disgraced magician.

'I know what you're thinking,' he hissed in the king's ear, flashing him a warning look, 'but we are not here to bring up any more of the past than we need to.'

The king felt a sharp chill fill his bones when he spoke.

'There is trouble brewing within the Nonhawk kingdom and Crystal may become our only hope in keeping peace within our realms,' he said, beckoning to his servants. 'But you're right; the rest of what happened all those years ago has become ancient history.'

Elveria looked pacified.

'Bring me food and wine for my guests,' called the king to his servants. 'I'm sure they are in great need of sustenance.'

The wizards grinned, pleased they were to be made welcome, and relief filled Elveria's tense features. The food was brought out quickly and King Gamada guided his guests to his enormous table, enticing them with the delicious aromas of exquisite meats.

'Tuck in and fill your empty bellies,' he said sounding jubilant; however, out of the corner of his eye he spotted Amadeus lurking in the shadows.

'Excuse me a moment,' he said, placing a cup of wine in Elveria's hand. 'I have just noticed that you have brought with you one of my good men.'

He made a gesture for Amadeus to approach.

'Where have you been?' he hissed, trying to stay calm.

Amadeus bowed low.

'Sire, there are things amiss; it's a long story, but I was taken by Forusian's men once I reached Fortune's End. They captured me and took me to Forusian's castle but I managed to escape. With the help of the keeper, I was able to track down Bridgemear to give him your message concerning his daughter, hence why he has returned with me.'

Gamada pulled Amadeus to one side, his grasp firm and strong.

'Never mind all that. Is it true Forusian has captured both Crystal and Arhdel too?' he demanded, unconsciously digging his fingers into the warrior's flesh. Amadeus dropped his gaze.

'I was not aware Forusian held Crystal, sire,' he said, his face clouding like dark rain. 'I assume therefore that he intercepted the wagon at some point?'

Gamada let out a huge sigh of frustration.

'Yes, of course he did,' he said sounding weary, 'and no one has seen or heard from her since.'

While the king was talking to Amadeus, Mordorma sat himself on a soft cushioned chair next to where the king had been sitting when they arrived. He noticed the crumpled letter left discarded, lying temptingly on the dinner plate and glancing around, checked he wasn't being observed before he used his magic to unravel the wrinkled paper.

The parchment rocked on the platter and then disentangled itself before becoming perfectly flat and smooth. Once again, Mordorma checked he wasn't being watched prior to sliding the letter under his nose. He swiftly read the contents and absorbed the startling demands. Once fully digested, he was both concerned and alarmed by what he'd read. He immediately changed the letter back to its original state and sat there pale faced, unsure of how to react to such shocking news.

King Gamada and Amadeus re-joined the wizards'; the mood was mellow and the mages' tucked into the multitude of fine dishes with a ravenous appetite.

'More food!' called King Gamada, slapping Voleton on the back. 'Please eat as much as your bellies can muster.'

Bridgemear had fallen silent since his meeting with the king. Bitterness simmered deep within his heart and he had to use all of his willpower to stop himself from letting the grief he felt inside, rip free. He knew he must play it cool, but he saw Gamada only as a weak minded king who'd turned his back on his daughter at a time when she'd needed him the most. Since entering Nine Winters, Bridgemear had done nothing but scan the faces of anyone who passed by, in the hope it would be his beloved Amella. He knew she would not enter back into the realm without the 'Spirit of Eternity', but he searched their faces in sheer hope that she'd somehow returned.

He felt the room had a tense, guarded atmosphere. The king appeared to wish to pacify his guests a little too much for his liking. The crafty old elf was hiding something, he could sense it and he watched Elveria stand up and whisper something in the king's ear once he returned to the table.

Gamada paused in mid-sentence and then rose from his chair.

'Please excuse us,' he said, leaving the table. 'Elveria and I have things to discuss in private.'

'What things?' asked Voleton, giving him a look of surprise, 'what is this trickery you set amongst us?'

Before Gamada could answer, Bridgemear also rose from his chair and positioned himself between Elveria and the king.

'Anything you have to say can be said right here,' he said, with a defiant glint in his eye.

Elveria's wrinkled eyes appeared to crease a little more.

'No, Bridgemear, we have important business to discuss which we do not wish to divulge until we have decided on the correct course of action.'

This time it was Mordorma who interrupted.

'What is there to say which cannot be said in front of us? We have come here in solidarity to revenge our forefathers and find out what has happened to Bridgemear's child. We respect you as the eldest wizard, but you do not represent us all here today.'

A rush of anger filled Elveria. He stared hard at Mordorma, livid that the wizard had dared to challenge his authority, but Mordorma was not alone; the other wizards rose from their seats to stand beside him, an unusual alliance growing between them.

'Very well, as you wish,' said Elveria, identifying a change in allegiance and swallowing his pride. 'You're right, we should stand as a solid unity and I apologise for forgetting my place.'

'We just want the truth, Gamada,' Mordorma demanded hitting the table hard with his fist and allowing his eyes to glow. 'Tell us why did you bring Crystal back after all that has happened?'

The king was unsure of how much they knew, until he caught Mordorma staring at the crumpled letter. He cursed himself for his carelessness at leaving it in view; for someone who thought themselves clever he was certainly making himself look a fool. He realised he had no choice but to divulge the information contained inside it and so he gestured for the magicians' to take to their seats.

All their eyes were upon him and he inhaled deeply, realising he would look more of a fool if he tried to deceive them again.

The king cleared his throat and then he said, 'the truth is the outer realms as well as my own are in serious trouble.' He looked across at Elveria and on seeing his goblet was empty, signalling for the elder mage to help himself to more wine.

An eerie hush crept over the mages' and Gamada's mind whirled in a fretful wave of anxiety, unsure of how this meeting would end.

'I took council with the Elders and it was eventually decided that I would send one of my shape-changers into the ordinary world in the hope of bringing back Bridgemear's daughter.'

'How come you knew where to find her?' asked Bridgemear intrigued.

The king looked uncomfortable and the magician found that he could not meet his stare.

'If you remember, I was one of the original council members who decided her fate. I was privy to where she now lived and therefore sent Tremlon back to seek her out.'

'So, you're telling us he went to the ordinary world and told her about us?' shot Amafar in despair. 'What, after everything that was declared to us at that time?'

'Yes, yes, and I'm sure you think we have gone mad, but we are heading for desperate times which means taking desperate measures.'

Rage was burning deep within Bridgemear and Amafar saw the fury ignite inside his eyes. He left his seat to place a hand of reassurance upon his brother's shoulder, but Bridgemear was already rising from his chair.

'You had no right to go to her without my permission,' he hissed, taking a step closer to the king, 'no right at all.'

'It's too late to get angry now,' said Elveria, sliding over to Bridgemear and gripping his arm. 'What's done is done, you cannot change that.' The king looked pained.

'Look, what can I say?' he said, clearing his throat. 'I learned through my spies of plans made by King Forusian to assemble a new army. We are in peaceful times and our own army is small, we would never survive such an assault. The Elders were knowledgeable to why Crystal had been banished, for she will become a sorceress stronger than any of us in her own right. You are all aware Crystal was born with immense magic inherited from both of her parents and when she matures she will ultimately have the power of at least ten wizards, a sorceress like no other. Crystal is our only hope for the future; without her we will all be lost.'

'Such nonsense,' Mordorma snapped looking perplexed. 'Why, she's barely sixteen and without training in the ways of magic, tell us, what actual help could she possibly be?'

'Isn't it obvious?' gasped Gamada in surprise. 'We believe even though she is so young and inexperienced she has the power to destroy King Forusian with her transcendental magic alone. Don't you see, we don't need to go to war and risk losing so many good elves, not with Crystal by our side, for she would be able to stop Forusian with a single throw of her hand, and as far as I am concerned that could still be possible.'

'So where is Crystal now?' asked Elveria, feeling a stir of unease.

Gamada looked ruffled, clearly growing more uncomfortable with each passing moment.

'Unfortunately, the wagon which was bringing her here was intercepted. Forusian is holding Crystal captive and is demanding gold for her release, which doesn't make much sense to me. I have heard from my sources that he wishes to copulate with her so he can start his own bloodline, but I don't think he realises just how powerful she really is; but then having said that, we don't know that for sure. We assume he sees her merely as breeding material of a magical kind, one which he perhaps hopes will see him king over all other realms one day. With her by his side and his immense army he will be able to stop at nothing and destroy those who willingly fight against him, enabling him in time to rule our world with his kind forever.'

'We hadn't realised things had grown so serious,' barked Voleton, when the enormity of the situation turned heavy.

'I can't believe Crystal's not here,' said Bridgemear, moving towards the fire. 'I have travelled far to see my daughter only to find she is gone once again.' He placed his hands on the mantel and hung his head, staring down at the burning embers. 'You know, none of this is making sense. Why would Forusian hold her to ransom when he clearly wishes to keep her for himself?' He allowed a wave of sadness to wash over him; to think his daughter was now at the mercy of an evil tyrant.

'Come back to the table,' coaxed Gamada waving his hand in the air. 'We must all decide on a plan of action that will enable us to defeat Forusian and bring Crystal back to where she belongs.'

Bridgemear turned to face the man who had stolen his life. His eyes burned red with fury while they rested on Gamada, his body knotting with tension when the physical pain seared through his psyche like a hot blade thrust deep into his soul.

'You are unbelievable!' Bridgemear hissed. 'You stand there, calm and composed and ask for our help after what you have done to my daughter. Because of your stupid pride you told us nothing, preparing instead to use your own granddaughter, your own flesh and blood, as a pawn in some half-hatched plan to win a battle which could, in effect, destroy every realm in the land.'

His eyes flickered to Elveria, before returning back to the king. He pointed an accusing finger straight in his direction.

'I find this all just a little ironic,' he said with bitterness running through his voice. 'You, the king, who punished me all those years ago for breaking the most ancient of laws, now wish to use the fruit of my loins to help defeat Forusian; my, how the tide has turned.'

'Enough!' shouted Elveria, clearly irritated by the wizard's outburst, 'we must fight together, or no one will defeat him.'

'Damn you, I will have no part of it!' Bridgemear shouted back in a sudden rage. 'As far as I am concerned, you started this without me so you're on your own.' Before anyone could reason with him, he made for the door.

'Running away will not solve a thing,' Gamada hissed, his voice filled with resentment, but his words were unable to penetrate through Bridgemear's pulsating skull. Instead, the mage turned and looked at Mordorma, whom he saw as his only ally.

'I will find my daughter and bring her back to the realm of Raven's Rainbow,' he said when their eyes locked. 'Crystal is my only concern now. I betrayed her once and lost the love of my life because of it, but I will make amends for what I did and make sure it never happens again.'

With a defiant gesture he swept his cloak across his shoulders and vanished from sight. Silence engulfed the remaining magicians' until Elveria beckoned to Amadeus.

'Follow him,' he instructed, 'do not lose sight of him; he is angry and this will only blind his senses. However, be wary of his temper and keep downwind. Take Mordorma with you, he will use his magic to keep us informed of his whereabouts.'

'Very well,' said Amadeus, when Gamada nodded his agreement. 'But I think he will know we are following him.'

'Of course he will,' Elveria snapped, almost losing his temper. 'However, he cannot do this alone, no matter what he thinks right now. This journey he feels he has to take will put his life in jeopardy and his daughter's too; therefore we must help him all we can. Whether he realises it or not, he *will* help us to defeat Forusian, because he's the only one who can.'

# *Chapter 17*

Brilliant sunlight streamed through the trees and awoke Bridgemear early next morning. He had camped for the night in the surrounding woodland, his bed a mere mattress of dried leaves and soft mosses. He cast his gaze upwards to soak up the warmth of the sun's rays, which fell in ribbons of light on his chilled body and thought what an idiot he had become.

His anger abated and in its place sat only regret. He had been too quick to judge the king's reasoning, but what he had done was wrong; to use his daughter in such a way to win his war was a despicable trick to play and he couldn't get the feeling of betrayal out of his head.

Frustrated, he rolled up his cloak which he'd used as a blanket and set to building a fire. He knew he was not alone, for he sensed Amadeus and Mordorma watching his back and it gave him some much needed comfort.

He wasted little time collecting wood and wisps of kindling and used no magic to light it. Breakfast consisted of little more than a few dried crackers and a cup of tepid water.

He could have made himself a feast fit for a king if he'd used his magic, but he felt the need to punish himself.

Once he had eaten, he was ready to ride and heading out, his mind whirled with cunning plans and new formed ideas. He was no fool, and understood that to challenge Forusian on his own turf would not be wise but not impossible. However, he knew he was not alone, Mordorma and Amadeus were with him, and if he guessed correctly the other wizards would not be far behind.

Birds sang in the trees overhead while others foraged by his feet for an easy meal. The woodland was becoming alive with activity and many animals as well as birds scurried between the leaves along with other woodland creatures. The tension Bridgemear felt yesterday diminished and he rode in the saddle of his horse with much confidence, winding in and out of the dense trees with smooth, natural movements with only his tangled thoughts for company.

A pair of small, brown eyes watched the wizard pass by. The well-camouflaged creature, both inquisitive and meddlesome chuckled inwardly at finding a new playmate and followed Bridgemear through the forest for most of the day. Fear was not a feature of this creature's genetic chemistry and with silent footsteps kept close to the mage.

After several hours, Bridgemear leant over to reach for his water bottle held in a pouch on the rear of his saddle. His hand searched for his drink and he stopped his horse abruptly when he couldn't find it. He turned his horse and retraced his steps, peering on the ground in search of the container. The path lay empty with no sign of it, and confused, Bridgemear headed once again in the direction of Forusian's castle. Seconds later, his cup and plate fell from the straps that held them secure and they dropped noisily to the ground, clattering together on impact. The noise startled the horse and Bridgemear's reaction was to draw his sword wondering what mischief was about.

A fleeting shadow in the bizarre shape of a wisp of leaves shot past the corner of his eye. Bridgemear became guarded and dismounted. He scanned the undergrowth and thick bushes for an indication of an intruder, but could see no trace. He noted the time of day, twilight. He also recognised the type of trees that dominated the forest. Oak, ash and hawthorn grew in abundance and the telltale signs of his troublesome stalker soon became apparent.

He placed his sword back into its sheath, no longer troubled, and decided to rest for the night. The place he had stumbled upon was quite charming: the soft grass sat like a bright-green cushion on two lush banks of earth and a large brook opened up and created a small, freshwater pool. The water looked inviting, but Bridgemear knew better than to contemplate a swim with something devious hiding in the shadows. Once again he built a fire and waited for his trickster to play yet another prank; knowing this time he would be ready.

As darkness began to descend upon the forest and wrap it dutifully in black, the silence was momentarily broken by Bridgemear using his magic to create a force field around himself. It was not something he would normally do, for to use his magic out of his own realm would be frowned upon and small spells were his usual limit; however, for peace of mind and a good night's sleep he had no choice but to use a spell that was usually not permitted.

His force field was invisible to the naked eye, and while Bridgemear wandered the grassy area surrounding the brook, it travelled with him. He bent over and cupped his hands into the sparkling water, splashing it on his face and washing away the dust and grime of the day. Once refreshed, he settled on a broken log, eaten away and crumbling with old age. Hunger bit at his empty belly and soon after he had ample meat roasting on a spit.

From the seclusion of the trees, two watchful eyes were becoming irritated and impatient. While time ticked slowly by, temptation became too much for the intruder to bear. He had waited as long as he could muster, eager to strike and steal whatever he could from the weary traveller. There came a rustle in the undergrowth and then a painful howl exploded into the forest, frightening a pair of nesting birds.

Bridgemear felt no alarm when the painful screech penetrated the night air and he sat eating his meal, while a slow smirk danced at the corners of his mouth. At his feet a small creature lay in a daze outside the force field, its nose bleeding and its front tooth looking slightly loose.

'Good evening, wood sprite,' said Bridgemear, allowing a stern note to creep into his voice. 'I hope you haven't done any serious damage to yourself?'

The wood sprite, his vision blurred from the blow to his head when he crashed into the force field, was speechless for only a matter of seconds before regaining his high-jinx attitude. Standing up on his wobbly legs, he pressed his hands on his hips, his lip already swollen and his face swelling at one side.

He was a mere three feet high and of agile stature. His small eyes were clear like glass and his mouth fixed in a firm grimace. Wood sprites are created by Mother Nature to protect the foliage and live within the heart of the trees. They are made of plant tissue, and sap runs through their veins instead of blood. The lines on their faces coincided with the shapes of leaves, and their skin is green and made of living matter. Wood sprites were renowned for their mischievous misbehaviour and exasperating habits, and anyone with an ounce of sense did not intentionally get on the wrong side of one.

'Are you talking to me?' the wood sprite asked, pointing a finger that looked like a stick of asparagus to his chest.
Bridgemear carried on eating, finding him easy to ignore.

'You're not allowed in these parts,' the sprite insisted, shaking the same finger crossly, 'and what's more, you're certainly not allowed to use that kind of magic in here.'

'Oh really?' said Bridgemear, glancing up and raising an eyebrow. 'So how do I stop thieving little sprite's like yourself stealing my supper?'

The sprite appeared shocked by his words and displayed a wounded expression on his leafy face.

'If that's for my benefit, I wouldn't bother,' said Bridgemear, gnawing hungrily at his food. 'I have met your sort before.'

The sprite moved his shifty gaze and wandered around the force field, measuring the width of it using his feet to calculate the length.

'What are you doing?' asked Bridgemear watching his every move.

The sprite looked up. His feet were in an odd position and the ends of his shoes curled up in a strange way.

'Nothing,' he said, looking rather sweet, 'I was just curious as to how big your force field is.'

'What does it matter?' asked Bridgemear, becoming irritated by the spirits presence.

'Well,' he replied, touching his chin, 'you know you can tell a lot about a wizard by the size of his force field!'
Bridgemear almost choked.

'Why, you cheeky little pile of compost.'
The sprite giggled, showing a row of bright green teeth; it was clear it gave him great pleasure to taunt new visitors to the forest.

'Be off with you!' commanded Bridgemear, already bored with the rude little fellow.

The sprite ignored him; this was more fun than sitting by himself watching the woodworms digging holes in his favourite tree. He sat down adjacent to the wizard. He clicked his fingers and a beautiful mass of fireflies buzzed golden around his head, their glowing bodies lighting where he sat like someone had just switched on a stadium of light.

'What's your name?' probed the sprite, always burning with curiosity.

Bridgemear pretended not to hear him and took a drink from his cup, which bore a sharp dent in the outer rim from its fall earlier.

The sprite caught his gaze and used it to his advantage.

'My name is Bracken,' he revealed with a wide grin, 'so aren't you gonna tell me yours?'

Bridgemear kept silent and moved to the sanctuary of the water's edge. Naturally, the wood sprite followed.

'It's Bridgemear, now sod off!' the magician bellowed, becoming ill-tempered when Bracken continued to follow him like a stunted shadow. 'I do not want your company this night, or any other night come to think of it, so get lost!'

Bracken was unfazed by the wizard's grumpy attitude and simply skipped from one slippery stone to the next, following him everywhere he went. Happily toying with the idea of falling into the water, his aim was to grab the wizard's full attention but Bracken decided against it because he didn't fancy having to dry out, and besides that it would make his skin crisp and flaky.

The forest was settling for the night and Bridgemear decided to do the same. Perhaps in the morning the sprite would have tired of his latest victim and moved on. The evening was one of beauty. The night sky was not quite pitch black and the stars twinkled their existence to anyone who wished to peer so far. There was no wind to blow the phantom shadows away and so they sat alone, unable to dance in the moonlight.

Bridgemear stamped out the fire with a hard stomp from his metal-plated boot. The fire fought to stay alight, but he grounded the flames into the dirt, cutting off the oxygen supply until it crackled and eventually died away. He used his cloak yet again for a blanket and settled down in a spot near the water's edge. He listened to the gentle tinkering of the water as it ran by and brought with it gentle memories of the waterfall in Raven's Rainbow.

The sprite was disappointed with the wizard for wanting to retire so early so he sat with his legs crossed on a mossy patch, which overlooked where Bridgemear lay and hoped he would change his mind.

'Do you mind turning off your fireflies!' shouted Bridgemear, still sounding cross. 'Some of us are trying to get some sleep.'

'Oops, sorry,' Bracken said, chuckling to himself, 'I forgot all about them.'

He turned his head and blew gently on his halo of light, and each fly touched by his breath immediately vanished.

'Is that any better, grumpy?' he yelled, when darkness descended, but Bridgemear merely grunted and wrestled with his covers, concerned only for his comfort throughout the night.

Bracken noted how much frustration engulfed the wizard and sensed he needed to find inner peace. As Bracken sat watching the wizard settle for the night he decided he would tag along for the next few days and see what mischief he could unravel. He knew every nook and cranny within the forest and could live in any woodland of his choosing as long as he had one of his sacred trees to hide inside. He felt confident to admit he could be an invaluable asset to the mage while he journeyed through the forest, so with this in mind, he snuggled inside a bed of leaves and drifted off to sleep.

Mordorma and Amadeus watched with amusement from their hiding place amongst the shadows, before creeping away and returning to their own camp. They had watched the little sprite wind Bridgemear up as tight as a coiled spring and they'd half expected him to be turned into a pile of wood shavings for his efforts.

They hadn't retired early unlike Bridgemear, and instead talked until the early hours of the morning, a bond forming between them through their mutual understanding of each other's dire situation. They would not let any harm come to Bridgemear; he may have acted hot-headedly on more than one occasion, but his heart was good and his loyalty to his realm undisputed.

As dawn broke and a new day beckoned, they each rose from their beds, aware that Forusian's castle was only one more day's ride away.

# *Chapter 18*

It wasn't until he heard the hollow footsteps behind him that Voleton realised he was no longer alone in the Tower of Leddour. It had been agreed between the remaining three wizards that he would be the one to ride to the tower covered by a powerful spell, a spell which changed him into King Gamada's double.

Voleton spun round, vaguely aware of a pair of unfamiliar eyes watching him from close by.

'Show yourself,' he demanded, drawing his sword in anticipation and staring into the semi darkness. The clip of the intruder's heels sounded out across the bare stone floor and he held his breath in expectation.

'My lord,' came the reply, 'what are you doing here?'

Voleton was confused; the person who had walked from the safety of the shadows was not a young girl as he expected and he was unsure whether Forusian was using the same kind of spell, in an effort to trick Voleton into admitting his own true identity?

'Oh it's you,' Voleton answered, not wishing to give the game away. 'Why are *you* here?'

The soldier hung his head in shame before answering whom he thought to be King Gamada.

'Sire, I do not know why I am here. I was captured by Forusian's men and thrown into a chamber awaiting my demise, and then I was told I was to be released. I had no idea you would be here waiting for me, my lord, indeed I am deeply ashamed I did not manage to bring Amadeus back to you.'

Voleton's neck almost snapped when he raised his gaze to scrutinise the soldier who spoke of Amadeus. This just wasn't making any sense; why had Forusian not appeared for the gold and instead sent one of King Gamada's own men in the place of Crystal?

*Oh no*, he thought in horror, *this was just a decoy*. He stared wide-eyed at the soldier. 'What's your name?' he shouted, replacing his heavy sword in the sheath and retracting the spell which would turn him back to himself.

The soldier's face flooded in confusion and he backed away from the mage, becoming afraid.

'Where's the king?' he shouted. 'Who the hell are you?'

'I am a friend of the kings,' Voleton explained. 'I am the wizard Voleton and your king is now in great danger. I ask you again, what is your name?'

'My name is Phaphos,' the soldier answered, placing his hands unclenched by his side.

'Then we must return to your kingdom, for I fear Forusian is there already.'

Without another word uttered between them, they raced down the stone steps, tripping and jumping two at a time. They both flung themselves out onto the sand which surrounded the single stone tower, but to Voleton's horror his horse was nowhere to be seen.

'Damn Forusian,' he cursed. 'He's taken my horse as well as the gold. Now I have no choice but to use my magic and get to the kingdom as quickly as possible. Phaphos, you will have to go on foot; I'm sorry, but I cannot take you with me.'

'Don't worry,' said Phaphos pointing to the horizon, 'I can run the distance. I may be too late to assist you, but I will make it back.'

'Very well,' said Voleton, nodding his head. 'I can cast a spell which will give you the energy to run as fast as the wind.'

Voleton touched the soldier's shoulder and the magic flowed from his hand and straight through his body, giving Phaphos a sudden rush of adrenalin.

'Go swiftly,' Voleton urged, 'for we have much to do.' He closed his eyes muttering something under his breath and he mutated into a magnificent, golden hawk, his wings already outstretched and he flew high into the sky.

Phaphos sneered outwardly when he watched the mage fly away. It had been so easy to trick the wizards' and now he could return and resume his traitorous activity as a spy for King Forusian. With evil intent running through his veins, Phaphos made his way back to his realm, a realm he had so cunningly betrayed.

*

Elveria and Amafar were keeping watch at the top of an outward built turret for the return of Voleton, assured that Forusian's greed would be enough to make the exchange. King Gamada was resting in his chamber believing none of it. He had been consumed with an overwhelming guilt ever since Bridgemear's display at his table and his thoughts were consumed by his only daughter, whom he had not seen since Crystal's birth. He had never expected Amella to give the child the amulet therefore stopping her returning home. How he wished he could turn back time, but no magician, no matter how powerful, could ever do that.

He sat on his bed and pulled his legs up to rest them on top of the satin cover; then he lay down and stared up towards the colourful ceiling. Beautiful paintings of cherubs and young maidens stared back at him.

*At least they do not judge me, unlike so many,* he thought, to himself still feeling miserable.

He barely heard his chamber door open and at first did not register the slight draft which drifted his way. Busy wallowing in his own self-pity, he didn't raise his head to see the figure drawing closer to the bed, and when a gloved hand pressed against his mouth, his fingers were slow to react.

With lightning speed there came a shimmer of cold steel while the sunlight cast itself upon the blade. A king with as much magical power as Gamada could not be killed with an ordinary sword, but his assailant carried no ordinary blade. His murder happened within the briefest of minutes, the cold metal flashing a fatal warning before the Sword of Truth burnt a searing arc of pain into the kings lower abdomen.

The blade was pushed up into his chest and the impact forced a shudder through the metal, which sliced through flesh and bone and within the realm of darkness, Abbadon was beckoned to the extraordinary world. King Gamada who'd been caught by the element of surprise could only gasp in sheer horror while he watched the enchanted sword slice its way between his ribcage in search of his heart. No amount of magic could save him now; he had been ill-prepared for such a vicious attack.

Forusian finally let go of the sword and watched the king with morbid curiosity clutching frantically at his chest in an attempt to remove the blade. A hideous wail filled the chamber when Death entered and hovered over the dying king. The room's temperature dropped and the stench of Death was overpowering. Abbadon reached out and touched Gamada, using his skeletal fingers to stop his beating heart, but Gamada would not give in, refusing to die so easily.

Forusian's eyes turned to slits and the corners of his mouth hung in a deep frown. With the strength of the damned he pulled the sword from the king's chest and blood splattered onto Forusian's face causing him to flinch, but he quickly recovered his composure and grabbed a shirt, folded neatly on a nearby chair. He wiped his face clean, furious that the blood had marked his clothing, before cleaning the blade with it.

'You were always so pathetic,' he snarled, placing the sword back into its sheath. 'Did you really think you could outfox me? For all your magic and knowledge of this world you really are a bitter disappointment. I had hoped you would have been a bit more of a - challenge.'

He bent towards the dying king and placed his lips close to his ear.

'You know, I *will* marry your granddaughter,' he hissed, watching horror fill the king's dark eyes. 'She's being a little 'difficult,' but I'm sure that's all about to change, and besides,' he added, pulling a look of genuine distaste, 'I just couldn't possibly see you as my in-law.'

Gamada slipped in and out of consciousness and Forusian looked without remorse towards Death's shadowy figure.

'He's all yours,' he said, taking a step back and almost slipping on the pool of blood which was congealing at his feet. 'My part of the bargain is complete.'

Forusian turned and left the room as quietly as he had entered content in the knowledge that he was one step closer to his goal.

While King Gamada clung to the last threads of his life, he watched his bedclothes turn into a sea of crimson. In desperation he dragged himself to the edge, followed closely by Death and he fell with a heavy thud onto the hard surface of the floor. With the shaky hand of a dying man he spelt out the word 'Forusian' smeared in his own blood, the word creating a bright scarlet stain on the floor.

'Amella,' he croaked, but the word came out only as a gurgle of blood upon his lips and with one last agonising intake of breath, his head fell back and he was dead.

Upon the king's sickening demise, a ghostly green apparition floated above his body. Abbadon's chest swelled in triumph, filling the room with dark malice. With a bloodcurdling howl he sucked in the green matter until it became caged with the rest of his terrified souls. His master would be very pleased with his majestic prize, a prize he had been promised for so long.

It was at that moment when Elveria felt the cold hand of Death brush his senses and he looked with concern at Amafar, who showed by the look on his face that he had sensed it also. A look of horror blew across their faces and they hurriedly left their lookout post and ran with baited breath to King Gamada's chamber. They pushed open his bedroom door, but only an eerie silence welcomed them in.

'King Gamada!' Elveria called out, trying to hide the panic in his voice when he took a step inside. He'd only just made it over the threshold before he saw the king's lifeless body lying on the bedroom floor. Beside him the word, 'Forusian' was written in his blood; evidence that there could be no doubt as to who had done this wicked deed.

Elveria put a shaky hand over his eyes; his feet stood stone still but his legs wobbled like jelly. Amafar moved with haste to the king's side, taking his pulse and examining him closely.

'He's dead,' he pronounced, lowering his gaze.

'I can see that,' snapped Elveria bringing his fist to his mouth. 'He's been murdered in cold blood right under our very noses.'

Amafar looked again at the grey face of King Gamada. Waving his hands over the body, he closed his eyes in meditation. Using his magic, he relived the last moments of the king's life. After a few moments, his body was rocked with such immense pain that pierced straight into his heart that he was unable to stop the cry which left his trembling lips. Dropping his arms down by his side, he collapsed to the floor, and although the pain subsided, he felt Death linger.

Elveria was distraught.

'How could I have been so blind?' he wailed, watching Amafar get to his feet. 'Forusian had every intention of making sure King Gamada was out of the equation, I should have seen this coming,' he gasped and with his spirit shattered, he knelt beside the king.

'I never truly believed Forusian would stoop so low,' he told the dead king with genuine sorrow filling his eyes. 'And for my stupidity, you have paid with your life.'

Amafar placed himself by Elveria's side and put a gentle hand on his shoulder, a gesture of comradeship.

'You were not to know,' he said, trying to soothe him, but he knew Elveria spoke the truth.

Finding no comfort in Amafar's words, Elveria left the king's side and started to pace the floor, his eyes searching for clues. Elveria turned to Amafar, the lines on his face appeared much deeper.

'Bridgemear's daughter is in great danger,' said the elder mage, aware of the seriousness of his words. 'I believe Forusian knows far more than we first thought. I think he has a hidden agenda.'

His eyes narrowed and the wisdom of his years began to show.

'Crystal is also second in line to the throne of Nine Winters,' he continued. 'Think what that could mean if he were to somehow become her husband and Amella is never found.'

A shrill cry came from outside the window. Both Elveria and Amafar were startled, but Amafar was the first to recover, reaching out to open it. A darkening silhouette choked the light from the room before the body of a hawk entered the chamber. It flew inside, perching on the bedstead, its feathers ruffled and its beady eyes focused on the dead king. A strange vibration filled the room when Voleton changed back into his human image.

'I am much too late,' he cried, when he was finally able to speak. He cast his eyes towards the king's body, before holding Elveria's stony gaze.

'What? You knew this was going to happen?' asked Amafar in dismay.

'No, of course not,' Voleton answered, feeling the piercing eyes of Elveria burrow into his skull.

'Forusian tricked us all. He placed one of King Gamada's own men inside the tower and while I wasted time guessing what Forusian had done with Crystal, someone was taking the gold and my horse.'

'And he took Gamada's life,' added Elveria watching Amafar move towards the chamber door.

'I will send for the guards,' Amafar told him, ignoring his cold stare, 'they can at least take him to the healer, Sawbones.'

'And what good will that do now?' sighed Elveria, pulling his cloak close to try to stop the chill which filled his old bones.

Amafar shrugged his shoulders.

'They will need to take care of his body and get him ready for burial,' he said, watching Elveria's mouth set in a tight line.

'Very well,' stated the elder mage, looking grave. 'Indeed, it is time they learnt what has happened and how we failed to protect their king.'

'You are being too harsh,' snapped Amafar becoming tense. 'The king should have told us sooner of Crystal's return and perhaps this could have been avoided.'

For a moment the two magicians appeared to study each other with open resentment until Elveria coughed and cleared his throat.

'Do you really think we could have saved him?' Elveria asked, pointing a bony finger towards the dead king. 'Do you honestly believe this could have been so easily averted? My, how ignorant of the times you are my young mage.'

Amafar flashed an angry scowl and stormed off, not wishing to start a fight.

'What's the next step?' asked Voleton, bending down over Gamada's body and placing a large flat coin on top of each eyelid.

'We have no choice but to ride to Forusian's castle and meet with Bridgemear. I fear we are heading towards a great battle of which I know nothing of the outcome.'

Voleton rose from his knees and looked out of the window.

'Do you want me to saddle the horses?' he asked.

'Yes, we cannot stay; we must concentrate on this new task set before us.'

'But what will we do about the burial of the king? We cannot leave without paying our last respects.'

'We have lost our respect,' hissed Elveria, hanging his head in shame. 'We must leave and find our honour once more, for we have the humiliation upon us for allowing Forusian to kill the king right under our very noses. We must revenge his death and only then will we have enough dignity to pay our overdue respects to him.'

'It isn't all our doing,' said Voleton, his eyes turning hard.

'It goes deeper than that,' said Elveria. 'Someday perhaps I will speak of it.'

'Is it because of what happened to Crystal?'

'Partly,' admitted Elveria, 'but now is not the time to discuss my failures.'

'Very well, I will see to the horses,' said Voleton, heading towards the door.

'Thank you, my friend,' said Elveria nodding his head. 'We ride the moment they are ready.'

# *Chapter 19*

Crystal slept fitfully on Amella's makeshift bed. The following day at early dawn, Amella woke her with the distinct smell of something burning. Her neck was stiff from the uncomfortable night's sleep and her mouth was dry and furry.

'What's on fire?' she asked, sitting up and rubbing the sleep from her eyes.

'Breakfast!' came Amella's flustered reply, and Crystal watched her grab an old cloth and waft the billowing smoke towards the door.

Crystal stifled a yawn and stretched.

'Er, no thanks,' she said, returning her head back to the lumpy pillow. 'I'm not really hungry.'

'Come on, up with you!' Amella scolded, rushing towards her and pulling roughly at her pillow. 'As my father always said, time enough for sleep when you're dead.'

Crystal pulled open her eyes to see Amella standing over her with her hands planted firmly on her hips.

'So, do you want something to eat or not?' Amella clucked.

'Well, no, not if it's cremated,' Crystal replied, pulling a face that caused Amella to give her young guest a glare of irritation. She moved back towards the stove, picking up a plate and proceeded to shove it under Crystal's nose.

'Look, not all of its burnt,' she insisted with a sniff. 'The feefalas is a bit over cooked I admit, but everything else is fine.'

Crystal looked down at the bright yellow egg yolk and the juicy button mushrooms and instantly changed her mind.

'In that case I would be most grateful,' she said, jumping out of bed and allowing a smile to play mischievously upon her lips. The protective barrier that had been between them the previous night when she had first arrived was beginning to crumble away, leaving the contours of a new friendship in its place. It was also obvious that Amella was becoming more tolerant of her new friend and once she had filled her own plate, she wasted no time tucking in.

Crystal stared at Amella, noting how she ate like a lady even though she lived as a common hermit. The precisely cut pieces of food were placed with grace towards her lips and Crystal felt a slight tingle of suspicion prickle the back of her spine. It was clear to her that Amella had not always lived a life of solitude in these bleak and lonely woods and she became curious.

They soon cleared their plates away and busied themselves with settling the hut ready for Amella's imminent departure. Once satisfied everything was secure, Amella stood outside her somewhat meagre home and surveyed her surroundings with a critical eye. Leaving all that she owned behind didn't cause Amella to worry; this place had only ever been somewhere to shelter from the cold and she turned away ready to start a new chapter in her life.

In one of her hands she carried a small oil lantern and in the other a thin blanket that she tied into a bundle containing a chunk of fresh bread, a soft, brown paste and a flask of fresh spring water. Her clothes were ordinary and tatty, but her outwardly manner was smart and resolute. Her eyes shone with anticipation and her nostrils flared with a sense of excitement.

'Come on lets go,' she said, her voice bright. 'It's time we made haste and rescued your friend.'

Her pace was swift and tireless and Crystal found it difficult to keep up with her. The morning sun was glaring between the trees, causing her to sweat and make her eyes seem somewhat bleary.

'Please slow down,' Crystal moaned, when a sharp stitch pierced her side, 'we don't have to kill ourselves before we get there!'

Amella ignored her whining and continued with the quick pace, realising time was of the essence and aware her plan would only work in the light of day.

By mid-morning they came upon a tree; it was a magnificent specimen of a giant oak, its bark deeply etched with the age of time. Amella bent down and scraped away the soil with her bare hands to reveal an object wrapped up in a piece of torn linen and tied with string. The string was knotted, and she used her nimble fingers to swiftly unravel it. Pulling away the cloth she revealed an astounding piece of jewellery. It was a large brooch in the unusual shape of a black raven, and in each eye sat an exquisitely cut diamond, as large as a pea. It had two feathery wings, which could be manipulated by hand to become outstretched, and its body was made of a mineral that shone like jet. With a sudden hint of mischief, the sunlight caught the sparkling gems within its bright rays. A rainbow of colour shot from the raven's eyes, producing a kaleidoscopic beam which rested close to where they stood.

'Quick,' urged Amella, scrambling to pick up their provisions. 'The raven has created a doorway for us to enter, but we don't have much time. Please hurry and go and open it.'

Crystal was surprised, but she did not falter, and in one swift step she reached the spot where the colourful beam rested upon the ground. She took only a second to focus beyond the bright light and see a dark circle protruding from the earth. She entwined her fingers around a heavy ring which appeared before her eyes and with a twist of her wrist pulled sharply. The soil gave way underfoot and a doorway fell open to reveal a dark tunnel.

Amella moved to Crystal's side and urged her protégé to get into the hole. Crystal hesitated afraid of the unknown, but Amella wasted no time dallying and with a gentle push, forced her inside.

The entranceway immediately closed above their heads, smothering out the daylight and Amella lit the lantern and the tunnel filled with a golden glow. Once her eyes adjusted to the light, Amella folded the wings of the raven back into place before placing the brooch into the safety of her skirt pocket.

'Where are we?' Crystal asked, looking around and seeing nothing but dark soil and walls of earth.

'We're in a forest chamber,' Amella explained, taking the lead. 'If we're lucky it should take us somewhere close to the castle walls,'

'I must say, what you just did with that brooch was pretty impressive,' stated Crystal, her eyes still sparkling with wonder. 'I've never seen a brooch like that before.'

'It's a very rare jewel,' Amella agreed. 'However, I must tell you that the magic contained inside only works with the power of natural daylight.' Crystal was still impressed.

'Where did you get such a brooch?' she asked, wishing to know more about the jewel.

Amella fell silent, but her thoughts flew back to a single moment lived many years before when the love of her life sat next to her by a sparkling waterfall glowing with the love they shared, exchanging gifts. She had given her lover a traditional elfish present of a brooch filled with jewels the colour of her eyes. He in return had offered her a similar gift, knowing how much it would mean to her. However, his gift was extra special, concealing a magic spell within its beauty. The raven held a means of escape, a gift Bridgemear felt she may need in time.

Pain crushed Amella's chest, causing her to gasp. Bridgemear had given her this brooch in case she should ever encounter danger, but he'd never intended for her to use it in such a way.

They carried on until a halo of bright light shone before them.

'Look, there's our exit out of here,' Amella cried, adjusting the oil lamp. 'Let's make our way back towards the sun as quickly as we can.'

Relief flooded Crystal's mind; she hated the darkness and was suffering the effects of Amella's black mood and so she ran ahead wanting to reach the daylight first. Crystal clambered out of the tunnel and greeted the fresh air which blew against her skin with a grateful smile. Amella soon emerged, pulling herself out of the hole and she shielded her eyes when the sun appeared to blind her.

The castle loomed in the foreground, with its evil proprietor concealed for the moment from view and Amella dusted off her skirt and shook fine particles of dirt from out of her hair, with one eye forever watchful on the fortress of depravity.

Within minutes they were climbing a deep incline; their exit from an overgrown iron grate remained concealed within a grassy bank.

'We haven't got much further to go,' Amella said when Crystal became short of breath. 'We are virtually a stone's throw away from the castle entrance.'

'What do you mean?' Crystal huffed. 'You're not seriously expecting us to just walk through those huge gates unchallenged are you? I mean, wouldn't that be like the lamb jumping up on the slab and offering the sacrificial knife in its hoof in preparation for its own slaughter?'

'That's just it,' explained Amella with a sudden twinkle in her eye. 'Forusian will never expect you to enter via the front door.'

'But I'll be instantly recognised; we don't exactly blend in, do we? No, that's a terrible idea, sorry, but you're going to have to think of something else.'

Amella ignored her words and started to untie the thin blanket.

'Come and sit down here,' Amella said, placing herself in a shallow dip concealing them from view. She felt Crystal's eyes bore into the back of her head and she turned and patted the ground wanting her to do as she was told.

Crystal finally obeyed, her immaturity showing in her youthful eyes.

'Look, let's have something to eat before we try and make it into the lion's den.' Amella urged, placing the food directly onto the blanket.

Crystal shrugged her shoulders acting like a stubborn child.

'I'm not in the least bit hungry,' she said, lifting her nose in the air. 'In fact, food is the last thing on my mind, because I'm feeling a little sick.'

'Here, take a piece, it will ease your queasiness,' said Amella, offering her a large chunk of bread.

Crystal had to admit the fresh baked dough smelt good, and before she knew what she was doing she was reaching out and taking an unintentional nibble. The bread was layered with a thin, brown spread which tasted delicious, and she swilled it down with the spring water, which was as cold as when it had first been filled from the stream.

She felt the sun's golden ray's burn down on her body and with it came a strange sensation, which started in her mouth. Her tongue went slightly numb and her lips swelled and became puffy. She was not too alarmed at first, but then the sensation travelled through her body causing her to feel bloated and uncomfortable. Pressure was rising in her head and her blood was pumping around her brain at a dramatic rate causing a migraine to blast pain into her eyes. Panic set in when she felt her face grow itchy and her nostrils flare. Her look of alarm rested heavily on Amella, who simply pressed her hand to her shoulder to help keep her calm.

'Don't worry, you're going to be fine,' she said, realising the child's dilemma, 'that'll be the magic in the pâté working. I know I should have told you what my plan actually consisted of, but I knew you would have refused me if I had told you what I was really going to do.'

As Amella spoke, Crystal felt her body transmute. Her arms and legs appeared to grow shorter and she noticed her hands melted together to form small hooves.

Seeing the fear in her eyes, Amella continued to try to reassure her.

'You won't stay like that for long,' she soothed. 'The spell will only last for a short while, but it will give us enough time to smuggle you into the castle without suspicion.'

Crystal flailed her arms about in a mad dance; her voice disappeared and tears streamed down her hairy face.

'Why are you acting this way?' asked Amella, becoming slightly worried at Crystal's reaction to the spell. 'Why, you must have changed into another creature at some point in your life?'

With light fingers Amella helped Crystal off with her clothes.

'I will wrap them inside the blanket for later,' she explained, grabbing the cloth. 'Don't fret; I know you are angry with me right now, but this was the best idea I could think of at such short notice.'

Amella folded her clothes into a neat pile before rolling them up into a tight ball.

'You said yourself how you couldn't blend in, so I have made it easier for you to do so, for I have changed you into something no one will ever suspect is you.'

Crystal had lost none of her senses and opened her mouth to declare Amella's insanity. She had been caught off guard and felt utterly stupid, but instead of words coming out of her mouth she only made a bleating sound and instantly shut her mouth in dismay. The shock of what had happened to her filled her with fury, but she realised she had no choice but to trust Amella.

'You will forgive me,' said Amella, tying a thin piece of rope around Crystal's neck. 'But if you carry on bleating like that you will draw unwanted attention to us,' she chided. 'Now, what we are going to do is give the impression I am going to the castle to sell livestock. This will not only get us inside the castle, but give us access to the kitchens. Now listen and listen carefully, for we will only get one shot at getting inside. Stay by my side at all times; on no account must you wander off and no matter what you see or hear you must not alert them to your spell or they will know that we are infiltrators and kill us on the spot. Do you understand?'

Crystal opened her mouth, but again only a bleat escaped her fur-covered lips.

'We can do this,' Amella said, 'but we can only do this together. Remember, brave one, Forusian is an evil man who doesn't know the meaning of forgiveness, and no matter what happens there will be no turning back.'

With a heavy heart Crystal bleated her alliance. She raised her small round eyes towards heaven and watched the clouds swirl in the sky like the many thoughts drifting through her mind. Amella pulled unexpectedly at the cord around her neck and she jerked her head, pulling back in protest, hoping against hope that no one in the future would ever learn how she had suffered such an indignity as being turned into a goat.

# *Chapter 20*

Matt was losing all sense of time and only the edge of reason was keeping him from going insane. He had been separated from Arhdel soon after his first encounter with Forusian and held in a dungeon close to where the king slept. For some strange reason, Matt wasn't clasped in chains like so many, but suffered his confinement in a damp and mouldy fleapit all the same. The walls were bare stone; the air bitter cold and the only thing to wrap themselves around him were the feelings of loss and desperation.

On arrival, he'd been given a tatty blanket to help stop the damp reaching his skin and a small, metal plate, dented and unwashed. His plate now sat on the floor next to the door, a reminder of the pathetic scrapes of food he was offered each day. A small flap cut into the lower part of the door lay closed, yet it was his only link to the outside world and it was barely left open.

Matt quivered uncontrollably when continuous screaming pierced the darkness each and every night. He recognised the cries to belong to Arhdel and recoiled in horror, cupping his hands over his ears to try and stop the noise mashing his brain to pulp. It was clear Forusian's fury at losing Crystal could not be quenched and his anger fell at the bloodied feet of Arhdel and as each day rolled into the next, Matt heard the moans grow weaker until only silence echoed around him.

Forusian, meanwhile, sat on his bed trying to scratch out the last parts of his plan. He had decided not to treat the boy as harshly as the soldier, realising that when he reclaimed the princess she would look upon him with more favour if the boy had been unharmed. He smiled to himself at the thought of having her back, it wouldn't be long now he was sure of it and he was more than willing to force her to become his wife when he did. His smile faded; he'd wanted her to marry him of her own freewill but it was obvious that this was never going to happen now.

He'd sent many soldiers out in search of her shortly after he had returned to his lair to find that she'd somehow escaped. The Nonhawk searched for a night and a day, but by the end of it they had returned empty-handed and the consequence had been their immediate slaughter. The cliff became stained once again with their blood, and its jagged rocks and the rough vicious sea could not wash away its shame quickly enough.

Forusian became obsessed with finding Crystal, and sent three of his most competent soldiers to enter the forest covered by a magic spell of the woodland in the hope of tracking her down. They could enter any dwelling, constructed of wood or of a natural origin, and go undetected; enabling them to spy on anyone – unseen, but Forusian gave them a grave warning: return only when they had news of her whereabouts or taste the bitter reward of death.

The three soldiers' left the castle and rode their horses fiercely; confident they would find the princess with the help of Forusian's magic. They hadn't taken his warning lightly and knew that if they failed to bring her back it would mean their ultimate death. With his violent words ringing in their ears, they vowed not to return empty-handed.

They came upon many huts and cabins hidden within the lush, green trees and with the day turning into night they slipped undetected in and out of each dweller's home. They invaded the hovels of creatures of misfortune, folk that had been forced to live a life of squalor and destitution, exiled by their own people for crimes against their realms. The soldiers' sharp ears laboured relentlessly, listening to idle gossip and careless snippets of conversation, hoping someone would lead them straight to the princess. But as time passed by the soldiers became disgruntled by the sheer lack of information and so they pushed on until they came upon a hut that was closed up and showing no signs of life.

They encircled the small cabin before entering through the front door. Once inside, they dispersed their spell and showed themselves to all but an empty room.

'Search the place,' commanded the Nonhawk leader, knocking the table bare of most of its meagre tableware while he searched for vital clues. He wore the black livery of Forusian and his metal fist hit the surface of the table, shattering what was left of the shabby crockery.

His eye caught sight of the makeshift bed and he made his way towards it. With a sharp tug, he pulled the covers back and glanced down at the lumpy mattress, resting his eyes upon something that resembled dark, silken thread, lying on the pillow.

Pulling off one of his leather gloves he enabled two of his podgy fingers to pick up the single strand of auburn hair. He sniggered outwardly, before calling his companions to his side.

'She was here!' he said, producing the strand and holding it up to his torch. It shone a thousand shades of copper and grunts of welcomed satisfaction came from each of their hardened mouths.

'Whose hut is this?' the leader demanded. The two soldiers shook their heads, unsure.

'No matter,' he said, carefully placing the evidence inside a piece of torn linen which he spotted lying on the floor. 'We will find out who owns this place the minute we get back, for this hut is on King Forusian's land.'

Within minutes the soldiers were back in the saddle and making their way to Forusian's castle. They travelled through the night and when they reached the castle, thousands of torches had been placed around the towers, lighting up the night sky to create a blaze of firelight.

'It is our welcome home,' shouted one of the soldiers, pulling at his horses reins to make him slow his pace. 'We are going to be made heroes.'

Once inside the castle they were announced to the king and Forusian didn't hesitate to offer his men a welcoming drink when they were shown into the drawing room. The ambience gave the impression of warmth, but Forusian's expression was ice cold.

'What news do you bring of the princess?' the king asked staring at them with hardening eyes.

'My lord,' said the leader, taking a low bow. 'We have found evidence of where the one you seek has been sheltering.'

'And where would that be?' asked Forusian, forcing his lips tight.

'A hard day's ride from here, deep in the forest.' Forusian rolled his eyes. 'So damn close,' he cursed aloud. 'I knew she couldn't have gotten far.'

He edged his way towards a nearby carafe and filled his goblet to the very brim, downing the liquid in one mighty gulp.

Forusian looked sharply at the soldier.

'So, what proof do you have of this?'

Without delay, the commander moved to the king's side. With shaking hands, he reached inside his pocket and drew out the cloth.

'Come on, man,' Forusian snapped clearly losing his patience, 'I haven't got all day.'

Without further delay the soldier unfolded the small piece of torn linen to show his master his prized possession.

'Where did you find it?' Forusian asked moving closer, his voice turning to a whisper when he reached out and touched the fiery strand with his newly manicured fingers. He felt a tremendous burst of elation; there could be no doubt that the familiar auburn thread, glistening in the light was indeed a stand of Crystal's hair.

'We found it in a small hut near the area called Sorin's Corpse, sire,' the soldier explained, looking pleased.

Forusian gave him a long, cold stare. 'Are you sure she wasn't still there, hiding somewhere?'

The commander looked resolute.

'No sire, there was no signs of life.'

'Who owns that piece of land?' the king asked, taking the hair from the soldier's outstretched hand and rubbing it between his thumb and forefinger.

The soldier hesitated and the blood drained from his face.

'We don't know the dweller's name, sire, but we thought you would have some record of them in your deeds of ownership.'

For a moment, Forusian fell silent and the atmosphere crackled with mounting tension.

'Well done, men,' Forusian said at last, turning to face them with a dazzling smile. 'You have found me a lead although not the girl, I will make sure you are well rewarded.'

A look of relief registered on all the soldiers' stricken faces and they each broke out into toothless grins.

Forusian absentmindedly chewed the inside of his cheek in concentration, a habit he seldom displayed in public.

'Leave me!' he ordered, shooing them like flies towards the door. 'You have done all you can – for now.'

Without hesitation, the soldiers' made their leave, filing out one by one and heading for their billets. Forusian called to the main guard.

'Have those imbeciles' executed,' he commanded, his eyes turning black with evil intent. 'Yet again they fail me.'

The guard left and Forusian made his way down the stone staircase and straight to his vault. Once inside, he lit several sconces and the room blazed with bright light. His eyes soon adjusted to the glare and he flashed his gaze cross the interior, checking all was as he had left it.

The vault throbbed like an Aladdin's Cave, bursting at the seams with many stolen artefacts and trinkets. It had been divided into three sections, each committed to one division of his wealth. These sections consisted of gold, (including jewels), magic spells and land.

He walked over to a small box, opened it and quickly removed the contents. He retrieved a piece of jewellery and placing it between his fingers, stroked the magnificent work of art. Mesmerised by its beauty, his eyes gleaming, he drank in its wealth and took an involuntary breath when the exquisitely cut stone set in its centre sent a radiant pyramid of colour straight through his fingers and he felt the surge of its kinetic force. He wished he knew how the amulet worked, but he also knew he would never know its secret. Closing his eyes, he tried to connect to its power but felt no tingling sensation and he became infuriated. The amulet could be his greatest weapon but only if Crystal helped him to use it.

He pulled a face, his mind flooding with images of the princess and then his half-made army and the blue slimy body parts of the gruesome goblins flashed before his eyes pushing thoughts of Crystal aside. His latest experiment was cultivated from pieces of dead tissue from those he'd had murdered in the past and he needed the power from the amulet very soon or everything he had dreamed of would die of decay and be destroyed. Pressure was building behind his eyes and with some reluctance he dropped the amulet back into the box and promptly closed the lid.

His day of triumph would come soon enough he vowed and when he married Crystal, the necklace and its power would be his for the taking, for he would force his bride to use the amulet once she became his queen. A desperate stench poured from his mouth when he produced a sudden roar of laughter caused by his darkest desires.

He turned and made his way to a darkened corner that resembled a small library. Row upon row of long, wooden shelves held much in the way of brown leather-bound books, books which calculated his vast fortune and ill-gotten wealth, including extensive documentation on all his tenants and owners living on his land.

A small ladder lay forgotten on the floor and he clicked his fingers and the wooden steps flew to his hand. He grasped them firmly and then placed them in the very centre of the bookshelves. Each row represented a county within his own realm and he called out to the volume which contained the details of Sorin's Corpse.

A large book flew from one of the shelves and levitated in front of him, the pages were used as wings while it sat poised in mid-air, making the air stir with the faintest of breezes.

Snatching the book with his fingers, he placed the heavy tome under his arm and made his way back down the ladder. He reached out and expertly extinguished the torches one by one before leaving the vault with a lighter step. Filled with enthusiasm, he made his way to the comfort of his chamber. His lips were set firm when he closed the door and heading for his desk slammed the volume down before grabbing a seat. He meticulously turned over each page, drinking in long forgotten information and while the moon began to glow, he smiled a somewhat chilling smile when he placed his finger upon a name.

'Oh, my lord,' he gasped, remembering long years past. He snapped the book closed and immediately called for his guard.

# *Chapter 21*

The sun was almost set when Bridgemear reached the kingdom of the Nonhawk. An orange glow was throwing itself against the outer walls of the castle, giving the evening some added warmth and Bridgemear envied those who would have time to sit and enjoy it.

He kicked his horse on and drew his sword tighter around his waist, checking to see if his cloak still hid it from view. He knew he would not be made welcome within the castle walls, but they would not refuse him entry. Bracken was not far from sight, having followed at a safe distance. There was something magnetic in Bridgemear's mannerisms which drew Bracken to him and he felt curious of the wizard and now ceased playing tricks, keeping a close watch over the mage instead.

Bridgemear nodded to the sprite when he left the safety of the trees and made his way to the main gatehouse. He toyed with the idea of covering his face and using his cloak to hide his identity as well as his sword; but to most he was already a stranger and so he hid the blade instead. A rush of air brushed against his leg and Bridgemear looked down to see the wood sprite at his feet.

'What are you doing here?' demanded the mage, annoyed at seeing the sprite. 'Were you not told to stay in the forest?'

Bracken set his mouth in a firm scowl, staring fiercely upon the outer walls, which were littered with silver helmets.

'You shouldn't go in there,' he muttered, folding his arms against his chest. 'You know, it's far too dangerous.' Bracken turned and faced the wizard without fear of reprisal. Their eyes locked, and for a brief moment Bridgemear was able to observe the courage harboured deep behind them.

'You're being followed too, were you aware?' Bracken added, when the wizard still refused to answer.

Bridgemear sighed.

'Yes, I am aware, but it's nothing for you to worry about.'

'Aren't you the least bit scared?' asked Bracken, his eyes wide in confusion.

'No, of course not, because those who are following me are hopefully my friends, but thank you for your concern.'

'Are you sure?' Bracken asked, still unconvinced, 'because they've been following you for quite some time.'

'Yes, I'm sure, but again, thanks for bringing it to my attention.' Bridgemear nodded, patting the sprite's head like a loyal hound, somehow touched by the creature's sincerity towards him.

'Go home, little one,' he advised, nudging his horse forward. 'There's nothing here for you but trouble.'

'Why do you feel you have to do everything alone?' Bracken suddenly snapped, becoming cross. 'Why won't you let me help you?'

Bridgemear pulled sharply on the reins, causing his horse to throw its head. He turned in his saddle to face the sprite, his hard expression, softening.

'It is not that I wish to do it all alone,' he explained with a sigh, 'it's just that I am used to being alone and that's something completely different.'

'Then let me help you,' Bracken pleaded, making his way once again to Bridgemear's side.

'Why are you so insistent?' asked Bridgemear, almost wavering from his decision, 'You know you owe me nothing.'

Bracken's eyes became hooded.

'I simply believe in your kind and all that you stand for,' he said, relaxing his shoulders. 'Isn't that enough?'

Bridgemear shook his head.

'This isn't the forest,' he said pointing towards the trees. 'This is not a game I can stop when the going gets tough. Go, my friend, keep yourself safe and be glad you have the chance to live another day.'

Once again Bridgemear kicked his horse on, but this time it broke into a trot, leaving the sprite rooted to the spot. Bracken called out to the magician when the distance between them grew vast.

'I will wait for your return, and if you need to hide within the forest I will be there to shelter you,' he shouted. 'Simply call my name and I will come to your aid.'

There was no reply from the wizard and Bracken sniffed. Still, he meant what he said. He would wait in the seclusion of the trees for Bridgemear to leave the castle just in case he needed his help. Moments later, he melted into the trees and became invisible once again to the naked eye. He would watch for those who followed the mage, those Bridgemear claimed were his friends and should the need arise and they wanted his help, he would be ready and waiting to lend a hand.

*

Not long after Bracken returned to the forest, Bridgemear found he had entered the gates to the castle without much fuss. The Nonhawk guards watched all who entered, their eyes alert and heavy with distrust and they glared at the stranger with suspicious eyes, but saw nothing to alert them to any danger; believing he was not a wanted man.

Once inside the castle walls, Bridgemear noted the wave of activity which seemed to follow him through the gates. He guided his horse between the narrow streets and the intolerable swarm of village people, while trying to find somewhere half decent to stay for the night. Almost everyone he passed acknowledged him in some way, born of respect; he received many a courteous nod from a noble born or a low bow from the servants who adorned the busy streets, but nothing but blank expressions from the Nonhawk soldiers themselves.

He eventually dismounted and entered a dark lobby, and without taking off his cloak he made his way to a tatty desk. He studied the layout of the building, noting its disrepair and inwardly felt displeased.

A nervous creature pulled himself from behind a discoloured red curtain and bowed in greeting. It was obvious he had once been tall, but his twisted spine had seen to that and Bridgemear thought his eyes were far too close together giving him the uncomplimentary resemblance of a street rat.

'Keeper, a room,' Bridgemear demanded, with a sharp edge to his voice.

'Certainly, sire, will that be just for the night?'

'No, a few days.'

'Oh, not just passing through then?'

'Yes, exactly; do you mind, the key?'

'Sorry, where are my manners? Please follow me and I will take you straight to your room.'

The inn keeper's trembling hand grabbed a brass key from off an old, wooden peg, which he attempted to shine with the cuff of his shirt sleeve. The owner appeared to walk with a strange stoop and his neck looked as displaced as his spine.

Bridgemear wondered how this creature had managed to survive living within the Nonhawk community. The Nonhawk's were not known for their caring nature or willingness to help anyone less fortunate than themselves, and Bridgemear's instincts led him to believe that things were perhaps not quite what they seemed.

'I have friends who will be following shortly,' Bridgemear stated, climbing the stairs two at a time. 'Can you put them close by?'

'Will there be many?'

'No, no more than two.'

'Consider it done, my lord; for I have plenty of rooms at my disposal,' acknowledged his host.

Bridgemear tossed three gold coins up into the air and they landed in the keeper's outstretched hand.

'You're very gracious,' said the landlord, slipping them into his pocket and tapping it with his hand.

'Your room is ready and right this way.'

He took the wizard to the second floor and opened the first door on the right. The door wouldn't open easily and the keeper had to push hard with his shoulder to gain entry.

'It's a little stiff,' he said, his face turning scarlet, 'I will bring something to fix it, once you are settled.'

'No need to bother me, the room is fine,' Bridgemear said, stepping inside. He found it to be clean and tidy and smelling distinctively of lavender.

'My woman's idea,' said his host, sniffing the fragrance like a dog sniffs a bone. 'It's supposed to help you stay calm and have a peaceful night's sleep.'

Bridgemear nodded, looking unimpressed and walked over to the window. He slid the thin, laced curtain to one side and peered out into the street, watching the world below bustled by at a swift pace. Nonhawk soldiers swarmed the alleyways and streets, and the everyday folk were often seen pushed aside in their haste. Bridgemear's tension increased, feeling unnerved by the huge mass of Nonhawk soldiers. He thought of Forusian; perhaps he was now ready to invade his beloved Amella's lands? He shifted his gaze and rested it upon the keeper, who was still standing by the doorway, looking a little hesitant. Bridgemear thought his stoop appeared to have worsened with climbing the stairs. The creature caught his eye, lifting his finger when he could see he had his full attention.

'By the way, my name is Snitterby for anyone who has the desire to know it,' he told the mage with a hint of mockery in his voice. 'May I ask if you require anything else before I leave you?' he added, tilting his head to one side as though straining to listen for a reply.

'No, you may go,' Bridgemear answered, with a flurry of his hand, 'I have everything I need for the moment.'

'Very well, sire as you wish and when your friends arrive, I will let you know,' he said, giving a slight bow.

'Yes, that would be appreciated,' said Bridgemear, grateful the landlord was finally leaving.

On closing the door, the magician made his way across the room and turned the key in the lock, but on hearing it 'click' he found it didn't ease the tension that crept up into his shoulders. Something wasn't right, it was as though he had been expected and if that was the case then he doubted if he had much time before he was placed under arrest, or worse if Forusian had his way.

Bridgemear was right, as soon as he was able to leave, Snitterby made his way as quickly as his curved spine would allow, heading with haste, straight to the king. His feet sounded noisy when they hit the cobbled stones and he kept glancing over his shoulder, convinced he was surely being followed by the ill-tempered wizard. The streets were still crawling with bustling citizens, concentrating on the activities of market day. The air was heavy with desperate cries from the many traders, each trying to tempt the ignorant passers-by with their mountain of irresistible wares.

The keeper ignored them all, trying not to catch anyone's eye for fear of being recognised and he slid like an unknown shadow through the busy, main streets, knowing how cruel the Nonhawk could be to him with him being crippled, if the mood so took them.

Only a short time later his nervous body stood waiting for an audience with King Forusian. Sweat poured like rain from his clammy forehead and he wiped the constant stream away with a long, trembling hand. His nervousness grew while he waited and when the huge doors opened to allow him entry, he couldn't help shiver. A solitary guard brought him into the Great Hall to where Forusian was sitting on his throne, surrounded by his council.

'What news do you bring?' asked Forusian, staring at the ugly face standing before him. 'What stranger have you in your house?'

The keeper kept his eyes focused on the floor and bowed.

'Your excellence, I bring news of the wizard Bridgemear; he has entered the castle walls.' Forusian's head almost snapped back when his words perforated his brain, and his eyes sharpened like broken glass. He jumped from his throne, his withered legs almost causing him to stumble and he made his way to his spy's side.

'Are you sure it's him?' he asked, peering in his face, looking slightly suspicious.

'Yes, sire, it is he.'

'When did he arrive?'

'Little more than an hour ago, sire.'

'Is he alone?'

'For the moment, but he speaks of two others who will be joining him.'

'Tell me what else?'

'There is nothing more my lord, your guard simply ordered me to come to you the moment either Amella or Bridgemear were seen, but she is not with him and the mage appears on edge.'

Forusian's face broke into a sly grin.

'And so he should be,' he said, unable to stop himself from sneering.

He paced the hall with his withered legs trembling. His council watched him with curious eyes, their hands filled with unsigned papers and their mouths agape with indignation from the unwelcome intrusion.

'Leave us!' Forusian commanded the council when he caught their penetrating stare. 'I will deal with those trivial matters later.'

Tight-lipped, the council obeyed, but a look of distaste was flashed in Snitterby's direction.

'Damn Bridgemear,' Forusian spat, with malice. 'He thinks I have the girl and that is why he's here.'

His eyes became hard like pieces of flint, his once flamboyant characteristics no longer on display, replaced with a chilling mask of resentment instead.

'I will have to act quickly and try and kill him before the others arrive,' he stated, showing clear signs of agitation. He stopped pacing the floor and stared into the unremarkable face of Snitterby.

'Go back and watch his every move. I want an hourly update,' the king insisted.

'As you wish, my lord,' said the keeper, bowing and making his leave.

He felt the doors close behind him and Snitterby breathed a sigh of relief. He had no real loyalty to the king and his allegiance had been cast through fear and my, how he feared Forusian. Once he became calmer and his heart quietened enough to ease the loud thumping noise within his ears, he wasted no time in making his way back home.

Back in the seclusion of the Great Hall, Snitterby was soon a distant memory in Forusian's mind. He thought only of his future and how close he was to reaching his goal. He'd killed King Gamada to make way for himself on the throne, and he just had one more elf with royal blood to destroy; then, as soon as he married Crystal, the elf realm and all its empire would be legitimately his for the taking.

He retracted his steps back to his throne. Now Bridgemear had arrived, he felt the first sharp prick of apprehension. He knew the sorcerer would not rest until he'd killed the Nonhawk king and so time was of the essence; he must act quickly. He knew what he had to do; he must kill Bridgemear before this day came to a bloodthirsty end.

# *Chapter 22*

Through her closed eyelids the light glared painfully upon her dilated pupils. Crystal raised her hands to cover her face and recoiled when she realised she still bore hooves. The spell was, however, beginning to wear off and with it came the pain of the transformation back into her human form. Crystal could see the distinct colour of red behind her eyes and an unwelcome feeling of nausea sloshed about inside her empty stomach. Her pulse throbbed in her temple and she cursed, wondering how much longer she was going to suffer the consequences of her naivety.

With some reluctance she opened her eyes, unprepared for the bright light that hit her full force and she squinted, feeling white pain exploded inside her brain and she cried out. She lay helpless on a cold stone floor for what seemed like an age, the floor covered only with thin matting to stop the damp from seeping through to her bones.

It took a while, but once the pain subsided, she sat upright and found herself to be tethered to a wooden pole. She tugged at the rope fastened around her neck, but she couldn't get it to untie with still having hooves. Her brain was fuzzy, but thankfully her body was almost back to normal now. She stared down at her naked flesh and felt a huge wave of embarrassment crash over her. Where the hell was Amella with her clothes?

The room was in semi darkness, with only one small window allowing in light. The light fell onto Crystal's trembling body and she was grateful for the slight warmth it gave her cold skin.

While her eyes adjusted to the gloom, she began to notice red stains upon the walls and a small channel built into the ground to allow drainage to run the full breadth of the butchery. The air was filled with a sickly, sweet aroma which filled her nostrils and she was aware of the distinct smell of fresh blood. She suffered a moment of panic when she realised she'd been placed in an area used for the slaughter of animals and a noise behind her caused her to freeze.

A huge shadow teased the cold stone and Crystal's throat tightened in fear. In desperation, she swept her eyes along the ground in search of something she could use as a weapon, but there was nothing she could hold on to; she was helpless. She frantically tried to pull at the cord around her neck, but she couldn't get a grip and the rope dug deeper into her flesh, causing her to wince in pain. She closed her eyes and listened to the footsteps that were drawing near; they were soft, almost undetectable, but Crystal didn't miss a step. She knew she must act quickly and use her powers to defend herself. But it was too late; the sound was closing in on her and Crystal shrank back in fright.

A distinct outline was growing along the wall and Crystal turned, staring down at her hooves which were barring her escape and Crystal couldn't help cowering, awaiting the fatal blows to her head.

A cold hand touched her shoulder and Crystal pulled away, screaming.

'Shut up, you silly girl,' snapped a sharp voice in her ear, and a hand came from nowhere and covered her mouth.

Recognition ignited in Crystal's eyes and she let out a deep sob of relief.

'Oh, thank god, it's you!' Crystal cried, when Amella dropped her hand away. 'I thought you were the cook and you'd come to bash my brains in!' She shuddered at the mere thought, thankful she had been rescued in time, but her eyes still shone with anxiety.

Amella untied the rope from around her neck.

'We must get out of here, before we are caught,' she said, throwing the rope to the floor. She then placed a small bundle next to her feet and her nimble fingers tore at the threads tied around it, revealing Crystal's clothes.

'Quickly, get dressed,' she ordered. 'The cook *will* be here shortly and I don't want us to be anywhere near here when she arrives.'

Crystal did as she was told and Amella took in her surroundings and suffered a nauseating shiver. Many a hand had placed their mark against the stone and the walls were gnarled with violence.

'We must head for the dungeons if we want to find your friend,' Amella whispered, glancing down and realising Crystal was struggling to get her hooves through her sleeves.

'Your hands should be back to normal very soon,' she said, helping her to dress and then examining Crystal's hooves with her own hands.

'I don't know why, but that always seems to happen when I create a creature spell,' she said, appearing baffled.

'Do you have any idea how frightened I was when I couldn't undo the rope?' Crystal hissed, pulling her hands from Amella's tight grasp.

'It couldn't be helped,' Amella muttered, unperturbed by her furious tone. 'But at least I got you inside the castle.'

Crystal shook her head in exasperation. Didn't anyone born in the extraordinary world realise when someone was angry with them? It was growing obvious to her that they all appeared to possess rather thick skins.

Once dressed, Crystal and Amella made their way out of the slaughter house, thankful to be leaving behind the oppressive gloom and stench of death.

'I've got to rest,' said Crystal, when her legs buckled underneath her. 'I feel really weak and my legs are like jelly.'

'Shush!' hissed Amella, placing a finger to her lips. 'We can't rest here, it's far too dangerous.'

Crystal was too weak to argue and found herself sliding to the floor. The spell had finally given her back her hands, but in return it had taken the rest of her strength. The corridor they'd just entered was quiet, but plainly accessible to the guards. Amella's agitation showed in her face and Crystal took a deep breath in order to try and stand.

A noise caught Amella's attention and she grabbed Crystal's hands, pulling her to her feet. In desperation, she looked for somewhere to hide; Crystal noted the look of panic in Amella's eye's and pointed to a large painting hanging on the wall to the left.

'Over there, behind that picture, there's a door which leads to Forusian's dressing room,' Crystal gasped, still trying to stand on her own two feet.

Strong hands dragged her to the end of the corridor and Amella cautiously opened the dressing room door and took a fleeting peek inside. The room was empty, and with one swift movement she dragged Crystal inside. Loud voices could be heard approaching and both Crystal and Amella felt a slither of panic as they glanced around for somewhere to hide. In one corner sat a large satin screen and they rushed behind it, just in time to hear the door open and they both held their breath, not knowing if they had been seen or not.

Amella glanced at Crystal, who was turning white, and she reached out and placed her hand on hers, giving her reassurance. She slipped her free hand into her clothing and pulled out a knife. The tip glistened when it caught the light and for a brief moment Amella feared that whoever had entered the room might have seen it glimmer.

'So, everything is ready?'

Crystal instantly recognised Forusian's voice and she started to tremble.

'Yes, my lord, I have the men assembled and they await your command.'

'Phaphos, you have done well. When I become the king of the elves, I will ensure you are rewarded for your loyalty.'

Amella in return recognised the voice of Phaphos; he had been one of her father's most trusted aides. It was clear Phaphos had betrayed him and her soul wept for his sins while she vowed to slice a dagger through his deserving heart. Forusian cleared his throat.

'So, you fully understand the plan for tonight? I want no mistakes and I want no evidence either, do I make myself perfectly clear?'

'Very clear, sire.'

'Good, then I will see you later; now leave me.'

The echo of footsteps and the door closing told both Amella and Crystal of Phaphos' departure. Amella raised her arm with the knife securely in her hand. She went to take a step forward, ready to strike, when a rap at the door caused her to shrink back and lower the blade.

'What is it now?' Forusian shouted.

'Sire, the keeper Snitterby has arrived with more news.'

Forusian's good mood could be heard in the trill of his voice.

'Excellent news,' he said. 'I will see him in the drawing room.'

The door was heard to close and it became clear after a minute or two that Forusian had left.

'What do you think he's up to?' Crystal whispered in Amella's ear.

'I don't know,' Amella replied, hiding the knife back inside her skirt, 'but he is sick and his wickedness runs deep; all he wishes to do is conquer everything in our world.'

They made it to the door and once the coast was clear, resumed their hunt for Matt. Crystal's knowledge of the castle was very limited because she had been restricted whilst staying at the castle and her memory failed her for she'd only toured the corridors and passageways on her first day of capture. She vaguely remembered certain areas but relied on Amella's instincts most of the time.

Eventually, they turned in the right direction and headed straight for the dungeons. Amella noted there were few guards around, which she thought unusual, and it suddenly dawned on her they could well be in the field ready to attack her father's realm and she shivered uncontrollably.

She pulled herself together and followed the stone steps, chipped away with time, to descend into the bowels of the castle. The smell of decay stung their nostrils and Crystal found she was covering her nose to help stop the putrid stench reaching her stomach. Cautiously, they made their way to the first stone cell and looked inside but to their dismay, they found it was empty. No guards were to be seen and Amella started to feel slightly uneasy. They moved to the next cell and then the next, but to no avail; there were no prisoners at all in Forusian's dungeons.

'Where the hell is Matt?' cried Crystal, trying hard not to become hysterical. 'I know he's here somewhere.'

Amella pulled a face.

'Forusian obviously expected you to try and get him out. He may still be in the castle, but where is another story. Can you think of anywhere he may hide him? Did he show you any secret chambers or a place where he could hide someone indefinitely within these walls?'

Crystal became upset.

'No, he didn't show me anywhere like that, but I know he does have secret chambers inside the castle.'

'Then we have no choice, we will have to use magic to find him and this could make us vulnerable to Forusian. Now you must help me conjure an image of Matt to show us where he's being imprisoned.'

Crystal shrank back.

'I can't do magic,' she stammered, tears spilling down her face. 'I don't know how.'

'Yes, of course you do,' said Amella while her eyes flashed with surprise. 'The spell we will use is weak and only works within the place where the person is dwelling. We must find out where Matt is quickly, otherwise we could be searching forever.'

With some reluctance, Crystal came and sat next to Amella, who had cleared away a small area of the floor and was drawing a pentangle by scraping into the stone with her knife.

'This is the symbol of our magic and each corner represents the four elements of life: earth, air, fire and water. The four points placed below represent the physical being, but we are unable to find the physical being and therefore we must seek the spiritual one instead.'

She placed a candle she'd found lying on a table inside the centre of the pentangle, she threw her hand and a flame left her fingers and the wick ignited.

'We must hold hands and you need to visualise Matt's face,' encouraged Amella, grasping Crystal's hands. 'I will use the magic you generate to show us where he is being kept prisoner.'

Crystal was nervous. She knew she could not do what Amella asked, but was too afraid of letting her down to tell her the truth. She held onto Amella's hands and closed her eyes. Focusing on Matt, she remembered the last time she had seen him and became overwhelmed with the pain of losing her friend once again. His image was growing stronger in her mind and she felt Amella's grip tighten. A low chant rose from her lips and strange symbols were swimming about inside her brain and becoming entwined with her images of Matt. The chanting grew more urgent, and with it her vision was more intense.

'Open your eyes,' Amella commanded.

Crystal did as she was told and to her amazement, the picture in her head appeared to float above the candle. Matt's surroundings had changed from what her mind had visualised and she could see he was surrounded by solid stone walls.

'Excellent work!' Amella exclaimed. 'I knew you could do it. Look, he's in the castle, just as you suspected. Wait a while and he will walk the corridors within his own mind to show you where he is being held captive.'

Sure enough, the vision floating above them left the place where he was being incarcerated and walked the corridors to show them the way to his cell. Crystal gave a gasp of delight.

'I know where he is,' she laughed, jumping to her feet. 'He's close to Forusian's own chamber.' Amella smiled.

'Well done, my sweet child, now we must hurry, the day is almost night and with it comes the danger it so willingly holds, for without the daylight I cannot use the brooch to get us out of the castle and away from here.'

Without another word, Crystal climbed the stairs two at a time, her energy levels soaring in the knowledge that Matt was alive, and with added gusto she headed straight for Forusian's corridor of vile chambers, in the hope of setting Matt free.

# *Chapter 23*

It seemed to Matt that he had only been dozing a short while when he awoke to find it late afternoon. He forced himself out of his flea-ridden blanket and made his way to the door and looked down at the maggot-filled stew wriggling on his plate, feeling his gut retch.

The rest of his resolve slipped away. He believed Arhdel to be dead, and a wave of utter despair washed over him. He fell to his knees, curled up into a ball and allowed his suppressed tears to finally fall. His cheeks burned and so did his eyes; he had never known such grief before but once his tears were spent, he rose from the floor and washed his face with the last of his drinking water.

Curious sounds were infiltrating the stone walls and he stiffened, his senses alerted when he heard a blur of female voices trail along the passageway.

'Matt, are you in there?'

His green eyes gazed blearily at the door, his face pensive and solemn. It was obvious to him that he was hallucinating. As far as he was concerned, Crystal had no knowledge of this place and would probably never see him alive again. The metal flap at the bottom of his door flew open and he jerked his head back, when two familiar eyes peered inside.

'Matt, it's me!' Crystal rasped, trying to keep her voice low, 'are you alright?'

She couldn't reveal her name with Amella standing so close by and prayed he wouldn't blurt it out when he realised who it was calling his name.

He blinked, focusing upon her face. She looked so real, her beauty vibrant, and he was astounded what the brain could do when suffering acute distress.

Crystal rose and her skirt swished in the dirt, she looked worriedly at Amella.

'What's the matter with him?' she asked confused, 'why's he acting so weird?'

Amella shrugged.

'Wouldn't you be a little weird if you'd been locked inside there?'

'Damn Forusian!' Crystal cried, her eyes blazing with contempt. She paced the area for something she could use to get the door open.

'Here, use the brooch,' said Amella, throwing it to her. 'The clasp can be used as a key; it will open any lock.'

Crystal opened the pin and pushed the sharp needle inside, listening to the lock turn.

'It really works!' she cried, stuffing the brooch in her pocket and then pulling back the door and rushing inside. She threw her arms around Matt and hugged him tight.

'Thank God you're alive,' she declared, feeling him respond to her tender embrace and Matt came to his senses reassured by her touch, the warmth of her skin melting into his own.

'I can't believe you're here,' he gasped, swallowing back his longing to kiss her. A sudden burning ignited in his belly before rushing through his veins as quick as fire. He tried to hold her fast but she pulled way.

'We've got to get out of here,' she told him, dragging him to where Amella stood watching them with open curiosity.

His fingers gripped her wrist, causing her to cry out in pain.

'No! We can't leave, not until I know for sure whether Arhdel is alive or dead. He took care of me when we became separated and I look on him as a friend.'

His voice cracked and a sob escaped his lips. 'Forusian tortured him in ways I have never seen or heard of before. I can't leave here, not until I know the truth.'

Amella's expression turned to one of despair as she listened to Matt's allegations.

'I know Arhdel, and he is a fine warrior. I must agree with you, we cannot leave until we have found him. Do you have any idea where he might be? He's not in the dungeons; we've already searched there looking for you.'

Matt relaxed his grip. Crystal shuddered and rubbed her arm, shocked at the change in him.

'No, I don't, but he can't be far, because I was able to hear his screams clear enough,' he said, with a chill in his eyes.

'Then we don't have a moment to lose,' said Amella with a frown. 'Are you fit to walk?'

'Yes, of course. I'm a little weak, but don't worry, I'll keep up.'

'Good, then follow me. I have a slight inkling as to where Arhdel might be.' Crystal held Matt back.

'You mustn't call me Crystal,' she insisted, watching Amella check for guards. 'It's a long story, but she thinks my name is Nienna.'

'Who is she?' he asked, with growing concern.

'She's a recluse who took me in when I managed to escape from Forusian. She found me the night I was trying to hide in the forest. She has a hut hidden within the trees and she gave me shelter. I was frightened of her at first, but I've come to trust her. She's the only person I know who was willing to help rescue you.'

'Is she an elf?'

'Yes, I think so, but she's very guarded about it. I get the impression something really bad happened to her like Gzhel, and she never talks about her past.'

Amella turned, hearing their voices rising, and gave them a cold stare.

'Have you forgotten where you are?' she hissed. 'We are not out of danger yet.'

They fell quiet, following her in silence and when a guard appeared, they flew into the safety of the shadows. The soldier didn't see them and they carried on but Amella stopped and drew a deep breath. She turned towards them and her eyes darkened with sadness.

'I'm guessing this is where I think Arhdel might be. I need you both to be brave when you enter here, for I don't know what we're about to find behind these walls.'

Matt came forward, trembling.

'If he's dead, I'll –'

A wave of sympathy almost swamped Amella's hard exterior and, shaken, she took a moment to recover.

'You must expect the worst,' she told him, stepping forward and with her hand called a flame to the torch pole set outside. The wind licked at the flame when they entered the passageway and the dark walls pressed close, creating a measure of claustrophobia. Countless doors chiselled deep into the stone loomed on each side and Amella pulled the first deadbolt back to reveal nothing but bare stone walls. Each chamber was empty, and Amella feared the worst.

'He's got rid of all the bodies,' she whispered, when she opened yet another door to find nothing inside but cold air.

There was only one chamber left. Her hands were shaking as she stretched her fingers around the bolt and drew it back. To her horror, Arhdel lay manacled face down on a table. His back had been slashed; his skin invisible through a sea of crimson welts, and the floor was awash with his blood. Matt and Crystal froze in terror.

'Nienna, you have the brooch, unfasten the manacles,' Amella commanded, rushing to his side and checking his pulse. 'Look, he's barely alive.'

Crystal snapped into action and ran to the warrior's side, unlocking the manacles with two swift clicks.

Matt went to help, but the blood had congealed on the floor and he slipped.

'Get up!' cried Amella, as she put one of Arhdel's lifeless arms around her neck, 'I need you to hold him for me.'

Suddenly angry shouts penetrated the corridor.

'Oh shit, they know I've escaped,' Matt blurted, dragging the unconscious body away from his chains.

'Then we must work quickly,' gasped Amella, already out of breath. 'Nienna, come here and hold Arhdel while I use the brooch to open a doorway.'

Crystal ran to her side and immediately changed places.

'Damn it, there's no natural sunlight in here. We must go back into the corridor, I'm sure I saw a window out there.'

'But the guards are coming!' roared Matt in blind panic. 'If they reach us they'll kill us where we stand.'

'Matt, we don't have a choice. Either we head for the corridor or we simply stand here and wait for them to kill us.'

'Get out!' shouted Crystal, realising it was their only chance. 'Amella's right, if we go now, we just might make it.'

Matt felt her eyes bore holes into his and found himself heaving Arhdel's body through the doorway with Crystal's help. Amella ran in front and found the window. She opened the brooch, manipulating the eyes of the raven to capture the last of the sunlight. A small shimmer created the gateway they so desperately needed, and Amella crouched down and pulled open the muddy grate.

'Hurry,' she urged, on hearing the soldier's shouts getting louder, 'they're almost upon us.'

Amella jumped into the tunnel first. Arhdel's unconscious body was pushed into the hole and landed on top of her, winding her and Matt followed, helping to manoeuvre his heavy frame from off her. Crystal climbed in and used her nimble fingers to lock the doorway. A cry rang out as the soldiers were heard arriving at Arhdel's chamber and then the doorway closed.

'They were too late,' laughed Amella in triumph. She turned to face Crystal. 'You must make your way to the healer Sawbones if you wish to save this warrior. You may find it hard to gain entry into the Palace of Nine Winters without your key, but Arhdel doesn't need one.'

'What key?' asked Crystal, feigning ignorance.

Amella almost choked with surprise.

'Why your key is the amulet every elf from the Imperial Palace is given upon their birth. I can see the resemblance to the king himself in you; therefore you must be a child of the realm.'

Matt gulped and Crystal flashed him a look that chilled his bones.

'Oh, that amulet,' said Crystal, a little too casually. 'Forusian took it from me when he captured me.'

A look of horror flew to Amella's face.

'This is worse than I first thought. If he has your amulet, then he will want to use it for his own gain. I am not strong enough on my own to overthrow such a powerful king; we need the power of the Guild behind me.'

Amella began to pace the floor and her mind raced ahead. If only she could get the Oakwood wizards here, surely they would be more than a match for Forusian. A sudden chill ran down her spine. What if Forusian already knew how to use the amulet?

'We are all in grave danger,' she said, clasping her hands together with worry. 'We must leave here and get help immediately.'

Slowly, they moved down the tunnel, hindered by Arhdel's broken body. The evening was not so bright and their journey ended abruptly.

'Damn it,' said Amella when she hit a wall of earth, 'we have run out of sunlight.'

The iron grate they came upon was heavy and not so easy to move but once Amella checked the area was safe, she forced the gateway open.

'To hell with Forusian,' she cursed under her breath. 'We are still within the castle walls and the doorway has given us only a short passage out. The sun has gone, so we cannot use the brooch again today so we must hide and keep low until the morrow, then I will be able to get us out of here.'

'What about Arhdel?' Matt pressed, 'he may not live for much longer if we don't seek help.'

'Then we must do the best we can. I will scout about and see if I can find an indiscriminate healer. As long as one of us stays in the tunnel it will not close. But be very careful, and on no account must you draw attention to yourselves whilst I'm gone.'

Amella was soon winding her way through the streets as the last remnants of daylight disintegrated into early dusk. The alleyways were now much calmer; the market traders were home and the only sound came from a stray hound, howling while the darkness descended.

Cautiously, she walked amongst the few with her hair covering her face and her drab clothing gave no clear indication of who she really was. She headed in search of anyone who'd provisions to heal, and although there were no clear painted signs to guide her, she fell upon such a dwelling without much difficulty.

The healer was a renowned black witch, known to most to have an unpredictable temper and Amella checked she had not been followed before lifting the strange woven curtain the witch used as a door and stepping inside.

The room was in darkness except for a cluster of candles that illuminated a small corner. The dwelling was rather peculiar, and with every flicker of a candle Amella's silhouette bounced against the walls, to create long, sinister shadows.

With growing anticipation, Amella strained her eyes in search of the healer. The room was filled with strange aromas and Amella glanced down at an assortment of herbs, lying on a table. She brushed her fingertips over a stem of pretty flowers and then recoiled when the petals changed into hissing vipers that stretched their mouths, trying their best to sink their fangs into her flesh and bite her. She immediately stepped away and banged straight into a chair. Her heart was in her mouth and she turned to see a row of glass jars filled with large hairy spiders and long-legged creepy crawlies staring right at her. The air turned still and then a solitary figure loomed out of the semi-darkness, taking her by surprise.

'What do you want?' spat the witch, sweeping closer. Her body was bent almost double and she wore a black hooded cloak that masked her old, wizened face.

Amella felt a stab of apprehension.

'I need some herbs,' she said, clearing her throat of fear.

'Speak up,' demanded the old woman. 'I take it you've come for something in particular?'

'Why, yes,' answered Amella, filled with unease. Her voice sounded strange to her, and she realised she was trembling.

'Do not fear me, elf woman, for I wish you no harm.'

'I am not afraid,' Amella said, jutting out her chin. 'I just need a few things from you so I can make a potion.'

'And what's wrong with one of mine?' snarled the witch, insulted.

'Nothing at all,' Amella answered honestly. 'It's just a concoction I created myself.'

The witch eyed her with a sudden curiosity.

'So what is it that you require?'

'I need the shavings of cedar, a handful of hyssop and a small number of juniper berries.'

'Hmm,' said the witch with a spark of interest. 'So you need cedar, which is known for its healing powers and courage, hyssop will give protection and purification, and the juniper berries will give extra protection and a speedy recovery.'

Amella instantly felt stupid. She should have known the witch would know why she wanted such specific ingredients and cursed herself for acting so dim. The old woman moved around the wooden table and with agile fingers began to prepare the ingredients Amella needed.

'You will need six to eight flower whorls from the hyssop bush if you friend is in a bad way,' said the witch looking Amella straight in the eye. 'You are foolish to take what belongs to Forusian for he will destroy all that is yours in return.'

Amella was ill-prepared for the witch to speak so bluntly and she quickly broke eye contact.

'I'm sorry, I don't know what you're talking about,' she mumbled, 'you must have misunderstood why I'm here.' The witch broke out into a toothless grin when she turned her attention to some drying leaves.

'I speak only the truth,' she said, parcelling up the ingredients with her old, wizened fingers.

Amella stood tight-lipped.

'I'm done,' said the old woman at last. 'Make sure you use these as soon as possible; if you let them dry out they will lose their healing powers.' Her outstretched hand held three parcels, which she dropped into Amella's palm.

'Do you have a silver bowl?'

'No, do I need one?'

'Yes, I have one here somewhere.' She reached out and pushed a few particles of dried leaves and decaying bark to one side, revealing a small, dirty bowl.

'Here, take it,' she commanded.

'You're very kind,' Amella told her.

'I only do what I'm paid for,' said the witch, becoming cross. 'However, even I can regret what I have done in the past.'

'Whatever do you mean?'

The witch cocked her head, studying the other woman's face more closely.

'She will look like you, but will have his eyes.'

'What are you babbling about, old woman? You don't know me.'

'But I know of your child.'

Amella felt a flutter of panic build around her heart. The mere mention of her daughter forced an overwhelming pain to form in her chest and swiftly recovering part of her composure, placed two small coins in the palm of the old woman's hand.

'Thank you for the herbs and the silver bowl,' she said, tucking the parcels safely into a hidden pocket sewn into the lining of her skirt.

'There's no safe place to hide,' muttered the old witch, when Amella turned to leave.

Pulling back the curtain, Amella left without uttering another word. The witch gave a hiss of irritation before she fell back into the shadows and allowed her poisonous tongue to finally fall quiet.

The night had finally fallen, and with it came a biting wind which stung Amella's face. She wasted no time dallying, but her thoughts were elsewhere as she turned a corner and collided with full force into the arms of a stranger.

'Hey, what's your hurry?' someone asked, alarmed.

She was startled and unprepared and she tried to smile, relieved it wasn't a Nonhawk guard.

'Are you alright?' he asked, his eyes narrowing with concern. He brushed the mass of hair away from her face and saw the panic in her large, green eyes. Recognition was also instantaneous.

'By all the gods!' the stranger roared, 'Amella, is that you?'

Terror flew to her throat at the sound of her name and she tried to loosen his grip, but the stranger held her fast.

'Amella, it's me, Amadeus! Have I changed so much that you don't recognise a faithful soldier of your father's anymore?'

For a moment she did not register what he was trying to say, wishing only to run to the safety of the tunnel, but then recognition ignited in her eyes. It had been many years since she had seen Amadeus, and memories of the past brought back the reality of why she'd left her kingdom. The pain was suffocating her and the brief conversation with the witch was playing over and over in her head. She fought the ache, but consumed with grief her mind turned black and then the lights went out, and she fell into an abyss of darkness.

Amadeus felt her weight fall against him. Deeply concerned, he swept her off her feet and carried her in his strong arms, hugging the shadows while he made his way back to the lodging house.

Mordorma looked up in surprise when his comrade crashed through the door with a dishevelled woman in his arms.

'I could have found you one a little better if you'd asked,' teased Mordorma with a chuckle.

'Don't be so stupid! This is Amella,' Amadeus cried. 'I literally ran into her.'

He stood with his feet apart to help balance the weight. He gave a pleading look at Mordorma, not knowing quite what to do with her.

'I think she's fainted,' he said in desperation, 'or perhaps gone into shock.'

'Lie her down on the bed,' said the mage in astonishment. 'I can't believe it's her.'

'No, nor can I, I wonder what's she doing here?'

Mordorma shrugged his shoulders unsure and followed him to the bed. Once she was settled, he placed a blanket over her body to help keep her warm. He lit a candle, which he found in one of the small cupboards, and began to meditate. Amadeus watched a blue light circle over her body, before slowly dying away.

'She'll be fine,' Mordorma soothed. 'It's all been a bit too much for her seeing you again. I feel she is under immense strain, but just give her a little time and she will awaken feeling refreshed.'

'We must tell Bridgemear at once,' said Amadeus in a panic.

'No!' said Mordorma sharply. 'He mustn't know of her. They are forbidden to see each other ever again.'

'But that was so long ago,' said Amadeus. 'Surely with everything that's happened, events cannot stand as they once did?'

'We are not here to judge who is right or wrong,' insisted Mordorma, feeling a sharp stab of tension build in his shoulders. 'Until the Elders decide their fate, we are not to interfere.'

A deep moan cut short their discussion and they both turned to see Amella regaining consciousness.

'Where am I?' she asked, her voice still sluggish with sleep.

'You're safe and that's all that matters,' said Amadeus, glaring at Mordorma. 'We only wish to help you.'

Amella sat bolt upright and scanned the room, unable to take in any of its features.

'You must come with me and help bring Arhdel here,' she babbled. 'He is seriously ill, but I have managed to obtain ingredients to help make a potion. He is with two others in a tunnel, just at the edge of the castle walls.'

Mordorma and Amadeus grabbed their weapons whilst helping Amella to her feet. Each hurried down the stairwell as they headed into the night. Amadeus shielded Amella with his sword and Mordorma clung to her side.

Snitterby watched them leave. He was unsure of what was happening, and decided it would be in his best interests to wait and bide his time. He didn't want to run to Forusian with half a tale and find himself at the mercy of the king. Wasn't it Forusian, after all, who had told him that everything comes to those who wait? And waiting was something he was eager to do, if he was to get this just right.

# *Chapter 24*

They were left alone for what seemed like forever and the bitter wind made cause for Crystal and Matt to huddle together for warmth. Arhdel was in a sorry state and they had bound him with a few strips of their own clothing to try and help keep him warm and stem the flow of blood, but still the warrior remained at death's door.

'I wonder where Amella's got to?' said Crystal, shivering and placing her arms around Matt's waist, nuzzling into his chest. It was bony against her cheek, but she was only aware of the comfort it brought and snuggled in a little closer, but then footsteps were heard approaching and the two friends broke free from their embrace.

The wind was howling against the grid, causing the bars to rattle, but they dared not move and take a peek for fear of being detected. Their breathing was lost in the swish of the wind and Crystal sensed intruders were very close and then the grid was hoisted up and an unknown face peered inside.

Without hesitation Matt punched the assailant straight on the nose, sending him reeling back in surprise and a squeal escaped his lips. Matt saw the spark of pride in Crystal's eyes but before he could say anything, Amella was at the forefront of the hole and calling out for Matt to calm himself, only narrowly missing a right hook.

'What were you thinking?' she hissed, making her way into the tunnel. 'That's certainly not going to help anybody.'

'How was I supposed to know he was with you?' Matt snapped in his defence. 'That was a pretty stupid idea to send a stranger first, don't you think.' Amella nodded, raising her hand in submission before heading towards the warrior.

'Okay, I guess you're right, but come here and help me get Arhdel to his feet, we have to get him out of here.'

The mouth of the tunnel was at least six foot high and pushing the warrior out of it proved to be a real struggle without the use of magic, but after much tugging and shoving, they heaved him out of the hole and then rested his head on a clump of soft earth.

Amadeus was still smarting from being caught off guard by the young man's punch; however, Mordorma was more concerned about Arhdel's welfare and drew a shuddering breath when he saw his broken body.

'He's in a bad way,' Mordorma stated, looking down at the heavy frame of the warrior. Amadeus nodded his head and sighed deeply.

'You're right, what a mess. Why, some of the wounds are almost to the bone and he's lost so much blood he's nearly run dry. The sooner we get him back to the inn, the better.'

Crystal came and stood beside them. She was cooling down from the exertion of getting Arhdel out of the tunnel and was starting to feel the cold. She shivered involuntarily.

'Here, take my cloak,' said Mordorma, going to her side and unfastening it from his throat. 'It will help to keep the chill at bay.'

Grateful, Crystal swirled the cloak around her shoulders and placed the hood over her thick mountain of hair to warm her frozen ears. She smiled at him in gratitude and he acknowledged her thanks with a bow of his head.

'It's time we moved on,' said Amadeus, gesturing to Mordorma to help lift Arhdel. 'It's too dangerous to loiter; we must get him out of sight.'

Amella and Crystal helped raise Arhdel to his feet and then followed close behind. Matt kept watch and they were thankful that the moon stayed covered with thickening cloud, hiding them well. Once they arrived back at the inn, Arhdel was hustled upstairs while they tried to shield him against the ever-watchful eyes of the keeper.

Snitterby however, had seen them return and he licked his dry lips in triumph when he thought how pleased Forusian would be when he told him all that was transpiring under his roof. A bell rang above his head and he jumped to his feet; realising one of Bridgemear's associates was calling for his services. As quickly as he could, Snitterby climbed the wooden stairs and rapped lightly on the door. The bedroom door opened, showing only Amadeus in the doorway and Snitterby almost cried out with joy when the warrior invited him in, but the door was barely closed when he was hit from behind with a heavy instrument and the lights immediately went out.

With Snitterby out of the way, the room became a hive of activity. Amella worked quickly to make the potion, but Arhdel's lips stayed firmly closed when she tried to administer the strange concoction, allowing only a few drops to seep down his throat, giving Mordorma little time to prepare his own magic. He needed the support of another wizard, worried he might be too late to save the warrior, but although

Bridgemear was only a few doors away, he knew he could not ask him with Amella being at his side.

The curtains were pulled tight across the window so as not to allow the outside world the smallest glimpse of what was going on inside and then magic burst from the mage's fingertips, landing like long, white veins of lightening, upon Arhdel's broken body.

Matt sat in a corner and watched in awe, picking at the fibres of his chair to keep his hands occupied. He stroked the raw materials and felt the coarseness of the fibres scratch the palm of his hand. Their roughness gave him little comfort while he watched the mage try and save his friend's life.

Mordorma glanced at Matt, his eyes becoming anxious.

'We'll have to wait a while,' said the magician, when the light from his fingers faded, 'only time will tell if he will make it.'

'Let's eat while we wait then,' said Amella, rubbing her stomach, 'I don't know about you, but I'm famished.'

Amadeus agreed.

'There'll be enough food for everyone down in the kitchen,' he said, pointing to the door, 'and with the keeper in no position to argue we can eat our fill.'

Mordorma smiled, dryly.

'I guess it's been quite a while since his guests have helped themselves to his larder.'

'Indeed,' said Amadeus, turning and pointing to Matt. 'Hey you, go and find us some food.'

Matt caught the warrior's eye and glared at him.

'My name's Matt,' he snapped, his eyes filling with indignation, 'and don't ever talk to me like that again, I'm not your servant!'

Without waiting for Amadeus to respond, Matt jumped from his chair and flew out of the door, heading down the stairs.

'I didn't mean to offend him,' said Amadeus, looking flummoxed.

Amella shook her head and sighed.

'He's not from our world and he's suffering a great strain just being amongst us. Please treat him with respect; he may be young, but so far he has shown great courage way beyond his years.'

Amadeus merely shrugged his shoulders, but remained silent.

Mordorma cleared his throat.

'Once we have eaten you must both try to get some sleep,' he said, looking directly at Amella and Crystal. 'Amella, you, Matt and Nienna must leave in the early hours; Forusian must not find you within these walls or there could be much bloodshed.'

'But I don't understand,' Amella gasped, 'why should he care about my whereabouts after all these years? I am no threat to him.'

Mordorma placed his words carefully upon his lips.

'Because Bridgemear is here and Forusian knows of your past.'

His words sliced through Amella like a vicious sword and a dark shadow crept across her face making her pain, plain for all to see. The mere mention of Bridgemear's name brought its own anguish, and the loss of losing the one she had once loved, bubbled to the surface until she found herself falling on her knees.

'Be strong!' urged Mordorma, rushing to her side and holding her tight. 'Perhaps it is best if you leave tonight and return to your realm.'

'I cannot go back,' she wailed, allowing a river of tears to roll down her face, 'and you know the reasons why.'

'Times have changed,' said Mordorma, his tone softening, 'I'm sure you would be allowed into your kingdom, especially with all that is happening now.'

A sudden crash startled them all as the door was knocked completely off its hinges and hit the floor only narrowly missing Amella. Both shocked and surprised by the attack, no one had time to respond to the sheer mass of soldiers who swarmed upon them like locusts. Amadeus managed to draw his sword, but had no time to use it.

'We have them, sire!' cried a Nonhawk soldier, dragging Amella to her feet.

'Excellent work, men,' boomed a voice that caused Crystal's blood to run cold. 'Let me see who we have uncovered hiding in there,' said Forusian, entering the room and wearing a smile that split his face from ear to ear. 'Well, well, well, what have we here?'

He made his way to Amella, but failed to recognise her with her curtain of long dark hair still hiding most of her face.

'Whoever she is, take her away,' he ordered with a casual flick of his hand. 'She may be of some use to me later.'

The guards dragged Amella outside placing her roughly into an awaiting cart. Back in the room, Arhdel lay motionless on the wooden cot tucked in a corner by the window, his breathing was still almost undetectable and Forusian eyed him with distaste, before glaring at the magician.

'I had no argument with you, Mordorma, or you, Amadeus, yet you shelter criminals within my walls. These acts of treason make you as guilty as the rest and I therefore have no choice but to arrest you. Guards, seize them!'

Mordorma tried to protest, but his words fell upon deaf ears.

'Save your breath,' said Forusian, forcing a bitter smile. 'You cannot escape your fate.'

Suddenly a Nonhawk warrior ran to his king.

'Have you found Bridgemear?' asked Forusian, pushing his dark hair from his eyes.

The soldier grunted.

'No, sire, his room is empty.'

'No matter,' said Forusian, showing signs of contempt, 'he will come to me in time.'
Forusian's caught sight of a wave of red hair and unconsciously sucked in his breath.

'Crystal, is that you?' he babbled, allowing his hard mask to slip away like silk. Crystal pressed her lips tight, refusing to answer and he took a step closer, pulling at the hood to reveal her face.

'Oh my word, my joy has no bounds at finding you again,' he said, sounding slightly docile. He looked to have a fever and his palms were moist with sweat.

Mordorma and Amafar were shocked into silence; they had had no idea they had been travelling with Crystal, and wondered simultaneously if Amella had actually been aware of Crystal's true identity.

'Take them to the dungeon's,' Forusian commanded while his eyes were feasting on the princess. 'Come,' he said, sliding his body closer to hers and causing her to shudder. 'You're riding with me.'
Forusian turned and looked down at Arhdel.

'Leave him to die,' he ordered the soldiers, giving a sour smile. 'He won't be in this world for much longer and I don't want his carcass rotting in my jail.'

Moments later he left, and the noise of horses' hooves striking the uneven cobblestones were heard when the magnificent beasts were burdened with a heavy load of prisoners. As they were pulling away, a pair of watchful eyes, well hidden from sight, espied them in the darkness of his hiding place, and with growing trepidation, watched the group being taken away.

The inn was buzzing with the travellers who came to see what all the commotion was about and to discuss what they had heard but not seen. Snitterby now dazed and confused, sat in the corner cursing aloud and Bridgemear entered the place, where moments ago both Amella and Crystal had stood.

'Where are my comrades?' Bridgemear demanded, watching the keeper rub the back of his head with the palm of his hand.

'Why are you asking me?' snapped Snitterby, pulling a surly face. 'It's not like I'm their mother!'

Bridgemear scanned the four walls and saw what looked to be the lifeless body of Arhdel, lying abandoned on the cot.

'Make arrangements for his body to be taken to the Kingdom of Nine Winters and I will ensure you are well paid,' he told the keeper, allowing a touch of despair to sweep into his voice.

'As you wish,' said Snitterby, getting to his feet. 'It will be easy enough to arrange.'

Just when Bridgemear was about to turn and leave something caught his eye and made him pause, mid-step. With swift reflexes he knelt before the warrior and watched his eyelids flutter. Startled, he moved a little closer, staring at Arhdel and willing him to live until the warrior opened his dark, green eyes and looked up at him.

'Welcome back,' said Bridgemear patting the warrior's shoulder with relief. He pressed his hand onto Arhdel's chest and felt his heart beating as strong as ten men. Arhdel tried to move.

'Hey, steady on,' said Bridgemear, pushing him back down. 'I don't think you'll be quite so keen to get up from your resting place, once you realise just how injured you are.' Arhdel chose to ignore the mage and Bridgemear found himself helping the warrior to his feet before demanding that the keeper go and get water to press against his dry lips.

'You must rest and recover before you even think of going anywhere,' said Bridgemear a short while later. 'Even I cannot be sure of the extent of your injuries.'

Arhdel remained silent but once his lips were moist and his throat not quite so dry, he spoke for the first time.

'It has been many years since our paths have crossed,' he said, letting his mind drift back to a time when life had been so very different. A dark shadow crept behind his eyes and he made his way on wobbly legs to a small table, before pouring himself a large goblet of wine which Snitterby had just brought in. Remembering his manners, Arhdel offered it to Bridgemear, who merely declined and Arhdel saw only his look of concern.

'You know what we have to do,' stated Arhdel, almost to himself. 'Forusian must be stopped at any cost.'

With one swift gulp the wine was gone and making its way down inside his belly. Arhdel's strength was returning, and his body was becoming powered with energy and dexterity through Amella's earlier potion.

He turned to Bridgemear.

'We must leave immediately and end this once and for all, for he is a dangerous man who will be content only when he has destroyed our lives and become ruler of the extraordinary world.' Arhdel's eyes filled with horror as he remembered what he'd seen being made deep within the castle walls.

'We are in serious trouble,' he said, making his way back to Bridgemear's side and landing heavily on the threadbare cushion, placed beside him. 'I have seen his evil creations and the horror which is in store for us all.'

Bridgemear sighed, shaking his head.

'I have seen it,' Arhdel insisted. 'He has created a mass of dead limbs, body parts that look like goblins and what's more,' he said, his voice trembling, 'I believe he's trying to make them come alive.'

Their eyes locked and Arhdel refused to look away.

'I also have a notion as to why he wishes to claim Crystal of all the daughters of magic. You see Crystal will one day have complete supremacy and with the help of the amulet she can make his dream a reality and therefore we must find her before it's too late.'

Bridgemear's eyes hardened.

'He will destroy her if she fails to give him what he wants.'

Arhdel dropped his gaze.

'And if she does, we are all doomed.'

Their conversation was interrupted when someone came running through the broken doorway.

'You're alive!' Matt cried with obvious joy at seeing the warrior. He stood quite still, unable to believe his eyes. Arhdel's own eyes lit up like fiery beacons.

'Yes, my young friend,' he said, when a smile made its way to his lips, 'it does appear that way, doesn't it.'

# *Chapter 25*

In his private chamber, Forusian poured himself wine and tried to control the loathing he was suppressing deep inside. On reflection, he felt it had been a serious mistake not to have successfully captured Bridgemear for hadn't this been the sole reason why he had attacked the lodging house in the first place? But then his failure was not completely without its reward; after all, didn't he have Crystal back in his grasp?

He refilled his goblet and stood by the hearth with his feet planted slightly apart and his long coat swaying against his wispy legs. The flames were soft and colourful but the warm glow did nothing to penetrate his mood. He turned, accidentally spilling wine down the sleeve of his coat. The red liquid soaked into the expensive material, ruining the luxurious garment but Forusian had more pressing matters on his mind. His thoughts were of his future, wishing only to taste sweet victory and so he made a conscious decision that this night would be the night when his dreams became a reality.

He moved towards the window and focused on the sky. It was Hallows' Eve, an evening acknowledged by both worlds, and he remembered how mortals were forever fearful of the magic and mayhem it so often conjured. He hated them all, men, mages, elves alike and with an animalistic roar he ran from his chamber and headed towards the tower. With his confidence suddenly ignited, he felt his excitement grow. His breath was short when he arrived at the anatomy unit, stopping only to regain his composure.

He entered to an array of sharp smells and bright flashing lights and he waited until his eyes grew accustomed to the glare before strolling between the caskets and checking to see if the fleshy parts they harboured were showing any signs of deterioration. On finishing his inspection, he made his way to the back of the room. It was an area completely void of caskets and held a distance of around fifty square feet.

He stood there with his arms outstretched and his eyes closed, concentrating only on clearing his mind and then he whispered a forbidden spell. As soon as the words left his lips a deep growl came from within the stone. The noise was so loud it made his ears hurt and then a large part of the floor broke away, creating a massive hole where the ground had been seconds earlier. The hole was vast, at least thirty feet wide and in retaliation, the ceiling shuddered and cracked and particles of dust and small pieces of debris rained down inside it, causing Forusian to shield his eyes and turn his head away. Within minutes the vaulting disintegrated, and when he was brave enough to peek, Forusian watched the solid structure of the ceiling rip apart to reveal to him the dark, night sky. When he looked up at the stars they were dim and grey, shrouded by a choking mist but he was pleased to see that the moon was full.

He scurried like a rat towards a narrow stone pathway held together by broken rocks and sods of earth that led to the centre of the pit. He reached the pinnacle and peered down to see the chasm filling with the magic liquid he had stored inside the huge vat below the anatomy unit. He rubbed his hands together with glee when a golden river poured into the gaping hole and gallons of seemingly bubbling lava slithered around him until it almost touched the tip of his toes.

The heat soared and the temperature rocketed and Forusian felt beads of sweat form on his forehead and then quickly dry up and burn his skin. He shifted to the very centre of the chasm and a sudden stab of contentment filled his darkened heart. Flinging his arms out before him, he called to the malignant spirit who was waiting to be summoned and with a rush, the caskets started turning on their axles. The caskets began to move, making their way towards the pit and once they reached the edge, their precious cargo was tipped inside. Arms, legs, torsos and twisted heads dropped into the gaping hole, and Forusian looked on in fascination while his sanity slipped away. He watched all the disgusting, blue limbs bounce and dance in the enchanted river, a river which washed them with black magic. He laughed aloud, for now all he needed was a sacrifice...

*

Crystal was taken by surprise when Forusian made a sudden entrance into her cell. He appeared agitated and rather aggressive and his behaviour was totally out of character for him, causing a wave of suspicion to wash over her.

'I've come to ask you one last time if you will marry me,' he said, looking disgruntled.

'Never in a million years!' She exclaimed, sensing danger but unable to stop her mouth in time. 'You know as well as I do that I would rather die than marry you.'

The air cracked with tension and Forusian looked at her through murderous eyes. Without warning, he lunged at her, taking her completely by surprise and he grabbed her around the throat, pressing his thumbs down onto her windpipe, choking her until she became pliable. She fell to her knees, and he suddenly let go.

Gasping for air Crystal had no time to react before he was twisting his fingers deep into her scalp and dragging her along the floor by her hair. Terror exploded inside her brain and sharp pain shot down her throat, neck and spine. With fumbling hands she tried to grab at her hair in an attempt to loosen his grip, but she found she could not free herself and he smacked at her hands like a naughty child.

'Enough!' Forusian roared, stooping so close to her face she could see the madness dancing in his eyes. 'You had your chance to be with me and you blew it.'

Tears poured down her frightened face when he dragged her through the corridors and past a few guards without showing an ounce of mercy. He took her to where her amulet lay amongst his vast fortune of gold and jewels and once satisfied she could not escape, he released her. He threw her onto the ground; the charming Forusian was no more and in his place stood a vile and terrifying sorcerer.

'Get up and put the necklace on,' he demanded, causing spittle to fly through the air. His breathing was laboured but it was clear to her that he was very much in control of himself. The amulet was dangling from his fingertips like an expensive titbit and although she was numb with shock, she outstretched her hand and took it from him. She found her fingers were trembling so much she couldn't fasten it around her neck. The clasp was tricky and she watched the amulet slip from her grasp and land at her feet on the floor. Anger sprang across Forusian's face and she felt panic rise in her chest when she saw the flash of his ring and his hand flying towards her. He slapped her so hard across the face he made her teeth rattle and she gasped in open disbelief. His lips curled back in mockery and she was terrified to see his eyeballs were turning black. Her cheek burned with pain, but she held back the cry that filled her throat and she grabbed the amulet and somehow managed to put it on.

As soon as the necklace was around her neck, Forusian snatched her hair again and she screamed out in desperation. He ignored her pleas to let her go and stretched out his arm to retrieve a golden spear instead. The arrowhead was carved with strange looking symbols and decorated with tendrils of platinum and he brushed his thumb over the very tip and then pressed down hard, drawing blood.

'My future waits,' he hissed, smearing a drop of his blood across her forehead. 'My time has come to be ruler of all, and you *will* be the one to help me fulfil my destiny.'

*

Bridgemear wasted no time breaking into Forusian's living quarters but was alarmed to find his aura weakening the minute his feet made contact with the floor. Leaning back against the cold, stone wall, he pulled his sword swiftly from his belt. His mind swirled inside his head like morning fog and he soon became dizzy, causing the acid in his stomach to bring a wave of bile to his throat and he panicked thinking himself sick. He looked down and saw his hands tremble and he clenched his fists when the power drained from his fingertips. His ice-blue eyes flickered when he realised his powers were diminishing and he felt almost naked, such was the feeling of exposure and his thoughts flew to Forusian and the knowledge that he had created a weakening spell.

His sword was heavy in his large hands and his strong, muscular legs seemed to find difficulty in putting one foot in front of the other. He reached out and held onto the back of a chair for support and he cursed Forusian's foresight. It was clear the Nonhawk king was no fool, but Bridgemear was also aware of those who were depending upon him and something inside his soul ignited. He was determined he would destroy Forusian and somewhere deep within, he set alight his inner strength.

Cautiously, he made his way to the door and opened it - a slither. He caught sight of two soldiers guarding the main staircase and he crept out of the room, clutching his sword tight afraid it would fall from his grasp. He brought the hilt crashing down on the head of the first sentry and the second soldier turned when a faint cry left his comrade's lips. Surprise filled his eyes when a sword sliced through his belly and he fell to the ground like a puppet severed of its strings, blood covering his hands and a second later, he was dead.

Bridgemear stepped over the bodies, careful not to get blood on his boots, and was relieved to see his power and strength was returning. He headed straight for the dungeons. The castle's layout was well known amongst most of the people who lived within its walls, and in the lodging house one person in particular had been more than eager to share his knowledge, for a price.

Bridgemear's steps were calculated and his eyes sharp. He soon reached the main part of the castle, which held the dungeons and within the darkness of the shadows he watched the guards come and go until he was able to slip on by like a ghost in the night. When he came to a stairwell, he heard male voices carried by the echo of emptiness; he listened and heard the distinct mutterings of Mordorma cursing his imprisonment and he silently thanked Snitterby for his treachery towards Forusian, for it had been he who had given him a map.

Checking for guards, the mage made his descent and kept his body close to the wall like a fleeting shadow and when he reached the bottom of the stairwell, a silhouette of a Nonhawk soldier slid into view with a large circle of iron keys hanging from his leather belt. There was a flash of cold steel, a solitary cry, and then the sound of clinking metal brought Amella, Mordorma and Amadeus scurrying to their feet while relief flooded their faces when the door flew back to reveal the solid bulk of the magician.

Amella caught sight of his handsome face, one she had not seen for so many years and found herself grappling at the wall for support. Bridgemear nodded to his comrades before resting his gaze on the woman with her mass of wild, red hair. He thought she looked oddly familiar, and then he was rushing to her side and moving her matted mane away from her face to reveal to him her identity. His throat tightened and he took an involuntary gasp when he realised it was Amella standing before him. He so desperately wanted to take her in his arms and kiss her trembling lips, but he dared not, not after everything he had caused her and he faltered. He saw her beautiful skin was etched with fine lines, especially around the eyes, and he noted her hands were stained with dark, ground in dirt. His mind conjured the misery of what she must have endured because of him and he felt himself weep inside.

She let out a wail that was so deep it wounded him as though a thousand swords had pierced his heart and because he couldn't bear the sound she made, he instinctively cupped her mouth with his hands. Her eyes shone with longing and he found he could hold himself back no longer. He bent his head and kissed her lips and when he felt her respond, he pulled her swiftly into his arms.

Eventually he let her go and his voice was soft and husky when he said to her, 'my dearest Amella, what on earth are you doing here?'

She opened her mouth to speak, but before she could get her breath back, Amadeus was interrupting.

'I'm sorry to have to say this, but we must leave immediately,' he said with glowing cheeks. 'I know there's a lot for you to discuss, but it's far too dangerous to stay here.'

Bridgemear's eyes narrowed.

'Very well, but before we leave there is something I must tell Amella, something I cannot keep secret from her a moment longer.'

He turned to see a look of panic sweep over her face and it was clear from her expression that she was waiting for an emotional blow.

'Go on, what is it?' she gasped, searching his face for some kind of clue. Bridgemear took a deep breath, feeling his heart beat violently against his ribs.

'I must tell you that Forusian has taken our daughter Crystal, she is a prisoner here in this very castle and the reason why I'm here.' He thought she had not heard him for she did not respond and so he repeated the sentence once again. This time her eyes told him she had digested every word and the shock of it looked as though it had dealt her a physical blow.

'You're crazy,' she finally choked, unable to stop the tears which were spilling down her pale cheeks. 'How can you say such a terrible lie?' she rasped, pulling further away from him.

'It's no lie,' he said unable to stop her leaving his arms. 'Your father commanded her to be brought back from exile.'

'That's simply not true!' she cried, turning furious. She snatched her hand away when he tried to take it in his own and held her fingers to her chest as though she would catch some infectious disease if he touched her.

'You of all people know that would never happen in a thousand years,' she hissed, allowing bitterness to rise from her belly, but Bridgemear stood his ground.

'Amella, I understand your misconception,' he insisted, taking a step closer. 'However, it *was* your father who brought her here.'

A crack of thunder broke overhead.

'We must hurry and leave this terrible place,' said Mordorma repeating Amadeus's warning. His face was strained with worry and he began to bite his lower lip, in agitation.

'Amella, its true what he's saying.'

He hesitated, and then took a deep breath.

'I clearly don't know how all this mess has landed at my feet,' he added, making it obvious he feared that he was about to be blamed, 'but Bridgemear is right, your daughter *is* here in this castle, but she must have escaped Forusian at some point only to be recaptured.'

'And there's more,' said Amadeus, unable to look Amella in the eye. 'We believe the elf child you know as Nienna to actually be your daughter Crystal.'

Amella turned on him then, her face set in an accusing glare. Her jaw flexed, her expression nothing less than murderous.

'I don't believe a word,' she hissed, throwing her hands in the air in disbelief. 'Surely I would know my own flesh and blood!'

'No, not necessarily,' Amadeus insisted. 'She has not been among us very long and acts more like a mortal than a daughter of magic.'

Amella's face froze and then she paled as recognition finally unmasked itself to her.

'Of course,' she gasped. 'Those startling blue eyes and that luscious, red hair... how could I have been so blind. Tell me, does she know who I am?'

'I have no idea,' Mordorma replied, still looking uncomfortable. 'We only found out who she was when Forusian raided the inn and took us captive; it was then we realised she had been travelling under another name. Amella, you know we are bound by our oath of the Oakwood wizards not to allow you contact with your daughter, and to be honest we just didn't know what to do. As for your question whether she knows if you are her mother, I can only guess from her aloofness towards you at times that she did not know who you are. I am truly sorry for all this torment, but it is not for us to decide your fate with her.'

'You must pull yourself together,' said Amadeus, placing his hand gently on her arm. 'We understand this is all too much to take in, but we must leave this place or we will undoubtedly die at the hands of Forusian.'

'Never!' she cried, her voice sounding shrill. 'I allowed my daughter to leave my side once before, but not this time.' She turned and stared straight at Bridgemear, her eyes shining like huge, glass baubles and her lips were set in a firm line. 'I won't leave this place if our daughter's held captive. If what Mordorma says is true, then I cannot abandon her again.'

With a swish of her skirt, Amella turned her back on him and made her way towards the door. He called to her and she turned to face him once again but before he could utter another word she silenced him with the look of courage that was burning in her eyes.

'I won't change my mind Bridgemear no matter what you may say or do. All these years I have yearned for my child, believing I would never see her again, and then, out of the blue, I learn she has been by my side all along and I never even knew it. She found me and I let her go, but believe me when I say that it will not be the Elders who decide my fate with my daughter again, for I will make amends with her and shall have my daughter back. Now, I either do it with or without your help, but either way I *will* save my daughter from Forusian.'

Before they could stop her, Amella spun on her heels, leaving them standing with their mouths agape and their faces staring into space.

'Damn that woman,' said Mordorma, when she started climbing the stairs. 'She always was a feisty one.'

'She's only doing what any half decent mother would do in her situation,' Bridgemear murmured in her defence.

Mordorma nodded his agreement and they left the dungeon with sudden haste. Amadeus stopped to pick up the sword from the dead Nonhawk, wiping away the blood that was already starting to congeal against the blade. He had known all along it would come to this; the elf child must be saved to secure the future of his people. With a deep foreboding, he too climbed the stone steps and prayed that by the end of the night their mission would have been accomplished and Crystal would be free once and for all from the evil clutches of King Forucian.

# *Chapter 26*

High above Forusian's castle sat a huge mass of crimson fog. A swarm of thick, red clouds were gathering in between the turrets and stone walls and the castle dwellers were becoming frightened. Shouts of fear and confusion filled the busy streets and those with families watched the demon clouds descend and immediately rushed to their homes to protect those they loved, barricading themselves inside.

Voleton sat on his horse on the top of a hill and watched the storm clouds suffocate the last of the evening stars. Elveria and Amafar were by his side and each was struck by the knowledge that they would never be able to gain entry to the castle now. The castle was unapproachable by foot or by horse, for at least a thousand soldiers were positioned outside the walls, protected by a magical ring of fire. The castle shimmered with its power and Voleton wept inside, for it was obvious to him that they had arrived too late.

Just a few feet away a tiny hand swept a spindly shrub aside and two bright eyes shone from the undergrowth. The wood sprite watched the three wizards with interest. He believed these mages' where also following Bridgemear and he stared at them with mistrust shining in his eyes. The three wizards pulled back their horses and started to engage in conversation and Bracken listened to their every word, deciding whether they were dependable and found he disliked Elveria's tone. The wood sprite sensed the elder wizard's bad mood not liking his air of authority and so he kept himself hidden and listened in a little more...

*

Crystal awoke to find herself in the anatomy unit, tied to a large wooden stake. She had fainted when the pain had become too much for her to bear and she looked down and saw her hands were bound behind her back. She tried to free herself but the invisible threads cut into her wrists and she winced when she felt her flesh burn.

She looked up and saw Forusian standing close by and she let out a scream when she realised she was standing on the very edge of a pinnacle and her feet were also bound. The king turned to face her, his eyes still nothing more than black holes and she saw his lips move, but his words were smothered by the loud cries coming from inside the pit. The cries were of agonising pain, like that of lost souls and Crystal found their voices to be almost unbearable to hear.

Sweat poured down her face from the intense heat that surrounded her and soon her clothing stuck to her skin. She tried again to escape her bonds; she was so frightened, terrified that Forusian was going to kill her, but her struggles were all in vain. Forusian continued to mouth silent words and then the stake began to stir and vibrate down her back. Screaming wildly, Crystal was petrified when she flew up into the air. She screamed over and over again from pure terror, realising she could not break free and her eyes searched for someone to save her before she tumbled to her death. The stake stopped suddenly in mid-air to levitate above the river and the swell of broken limbs appeared to jump up and try and touch her feet.

Forusian laughed and pointed the golden spear towards her as though he was about to throw it and pierce her heart and he saw the hurt and look of bewilderment etched on her young face. She saw a moment of regret, but it was only a moment, before he was once again chanting forbidden magic and watching the centre stone of the amulet turn black.

*

Bridgemear looked down at the map and was unsure where the anatomy unit was kept. Arhdel had been left behind to look after the boy; they had both agreed he would be of no use while his broken body still recovered from his ordeal but now Bridgemear wished he'd come along. Arhdel had done his best to explain what he believed Forusian was planning and while Bridgemear guided the others along the corridors of the castle he informed them of what he thought to be Forusian's intentions.

Amella wasn't listening. She was still suffering with the revelation of Nienna being her daughter and she was angry with herself too. How on earth could she not have noticed such vital characteristics of her daughter's genetic make-up? Her mind whirled with explanations and excuses until she could stand it no longer and it was Bridgemear who kept telling her it was not her fault, holding her in his arms whenever he could until her mood appeared much calmer.

After several twist and turns in the wrong direction they found themselves on the metal overhang that Arhdel had come across, perched at least twenty feet in the air. Bridgemear peered down over the rail and looked into the huge vat which Arhdel had told him was full of golden liquid and found that it lay empty of its contents. Amadeus caught his eye and he shook his head in despair aware this meant trouble and the warriors grip tightened on his sword.

The group started to climb the stairs, and it wasn't long before they arrived on the first level.

'What is your plan?' asked Mordorma suddenly. 'You know we are no match for Forusian without our staffs.'

Bridgemear's eyes narrowed.

'Have I ever let you down before?' he said, with almost a trace of humour.

Mordorma looked into Amella's face and Bridgemear's humour slipped away.

'You're going to have to trust me,' Bridgemear snapped, pushing Mordorma aside.

Mordorma grabbed Bridgemear firmly by the shoulder.

'I do trust you, brother,' he said, refusing to lower his gaze, 'I did not mean to offend you, but we cannot go in there without a plan.'

Bridgemear held his stare, but his expression showed he knew Mordorma spoke the truth.

'I know we have very limited powers here,' he warned them all. 'Forusian is clever and has somehow drawn the dark side of magic to him, and this force could well be greater than our own. But we do have the element of surprise and our internal magic so we can still fight. If we're lucky the others will come in time, but until then we must hold off whatever plans Forusian has in store for our realms and my daughter.'

'And if they don't come?' asked Mordorma gravely.

'You know the answer to that,' said Bridgemear, taking a deep breath. 'You know as well as I do the consequences should we fail.'

His eyes flicked over to Amella. She appeared unaware of his gaze and he watched her nervously bite her fingernails. He knew they would probably not make it out alive and for that he felt deep regret. Not for himself, he was beyond that feeling now, but for the woman and the child who had been bound together with an invisible love which his own selfishness had almost destroyed.

'Let's get going,' he said, placing his hand on the door which he believed led to Forusian. 'The time has come for us to fight, so let the battle of the mages' commence.'

# *Chapter 27*

The three wizards sitting outside the castle no longer watched the devilment which protruded from inside the castle. They had set up camp for the night on the brow of a hill having no fear of being seen, and busied themselves building a fire to warm their chilled bones.

'I know your mind burns with frustration,' said Amafar to Elveria, 'but we have no choice, we must sit this one out.'

Elveria spun on his heels to glare at him. The shimmer from the fire struck his face at such an angle as to allow Amafar the impression of narrow eyes and a sneering mouth. He looked away and down at the floor for he had never liked Elveria.

'Just listen to me, you young whippersnapper!' said Elveria, in an indignant tone. 'We are not going to simply sit here while Bridgemear and Mordorma struggle to try and bring Crystal back.'

'So what would you have us do?' snapped Voleton, looking very serious. 'Tell us, how can we help from way out here?'

A rustle in the undergrowth made them all turn and draw their swords, becoming one unity whenever danger surfaced.

'Are you friends of the magician, Bridgemear?' asked a voice from out of the darkness.

'Who wants to know?' called out Amafar. He stole a glance at the others, who eyed him back with tension gripping their faces.

'Show yourself!' demanded Elveria, his mouth set in a firm scowl. 'Are you friend or foe?'

'Begging your pardon my lord, I come to give you my help,' replied Bracken, looming out of the shadows. Elveria relaxed at the sight of the wood sprite and one by one the mage's replaced their swords.

With a light, rustling step Bracken made his way closer.

'Would you care to join us?' asked Voleton, walking back to the sanctuary of the fire and sitting down.

Bracken looked closely at the flames which flickered and danced mischievously towards the sky. He knew how easy it would be for his dry leaves to catch alight and he quickly shook his head.

'I'll stay here if you don't mind,' he said with a tight smile, 'but please go ahead and warm yourselves, there's a chilly wind surrounding us tonight.'

Elveria eyed the wood sprite and sniffed, crinkling his nose with distaste and Bracken felt the leaves on his spine bristle and he sniffed back, only louder. Amafar chuckled and his eyes flashed to catch Elveria's reaction but before the elder mage could chastise the cheeky fellow, a flash of bright light illuminated the night sky high above them and Elveria turned to see the profile of a huge bird glowing silver, appear from the centre of the castle.

'Is that who I think it is?' said Voleton, rising to his feet.

The others cast their gaze towards the light and as they watched, the image of Mordorma materialised right before their eyes. The beacon shone for the benefit of the sorcerer's and the magicians' gave a loud hoot of euphoria when they realised what it actually meant.

'Mordorma's inside!' Amafar said with a huge grin, slapping Amafar on the back from sheer delight. Elveria nodded, looking almost happy but then the image faded abruptly and their laughter died in their throats.

'What has happened?' asked Voleton looking worried. He turned and looked at Elveria for an answer and when none came he kicked at the dirt, sending stones flying across the ground, narrowly missing the sprite.

Bracken seized the moment.

'My lords,' he said, placing a leafy finger to his lips, 'I think I might be just the answer you seek.'

Elveria stopped in his tracks and grew angry.

'Be off with you, wood sprite,' he hissed, shooing him away like some pesky fly. 'We have no time for your childish games.'

But Bracken appeared unperturbed by the wizard's unsociable behaviour and simply stood his ground. He grinned instead, showing his earthly, green teeth.

'I know a way into the castle,' he said, pulling himself up to his full height.

Elveria's mouth moved into a deep frown.

'What nonsense this is,' he scoffed, making his way to his horse.

'I'm serious, if you wish to gain entry into the castle this night you had better follow me,' Bracken persisted. 'I'm your only hope.'

The wizard turned back to face the sprite and was surprised to see the look of determination on his small, green face. Amafar and Voleton moved swiftly to Bracken's side and this made it clear that he was the only one who thought the sprite was not sincere.

'Will you show us the way?' asked Voleton, adding a hint of urgency to his voice. 'You know it is imperative that we get inside.'

'Yes, I will take you,' said Bracken, his eyes flashing with indignation and his tone was firm when he directed his voice to Elveria.

'You know, if you are ever in need of help from the forest again I suggest you have a little more respect for those who are deemed less important than you, for one day your greatness may well be the pinnacle to your downfall and you will only have yourself to blame.'

Elveria was shocked into silence for he could not believe his ears. A nerve began to twitch against his temple and humiliated, he spun on his heels, his mind already overloaded with resentment at the wood sprite's words. He turned ready to give the sprite a lashing with his tongue, but he tasted only bitter disappointment when he realised Bracken had already melted back into the seclusion of the darkness.

'What is wrong with you?' asked Voleton in disgust. He brushed past the sorcerer and almost knocked him off his feet as he made his way to his horse. Elveria stood and watched Voleton place his boot inside the metal stirrup and then climb upon the beast.

'Come on,' Voleton urged him, noting Amafar had already mounted. 'You have little time to smart from the sting of his words; we must follow him if we are to succeed at all this night.' He kicked his horse and turned full circle.

'Elveria, you are not the great wizard here and the sprite is probably wiser than you think.'

Something snapped inside Elveria's brain and his fury rested at Voleton's feet. He reached up and seized the reins, giving them a sharp tug, causing the horse to rear up. Before he knew what was happening, Voleton was on the ground and Elveria was on top of him, pummelling him with his huge, great fists. Punches rained down on his head and body, taking the younger mage's breath away and blood burst from his lip when an indiscriminate punch hit him full force on the mouth.

'Damn you!' shouted Amafar, dragging Elveria away. 'We should not be fighting amongst ourselves.'

Elveria allowed Amafar to pull him away and with some resistance, backed off. His breathing was laboured from the exertion of the fight and his energy had been replaced with despair. Amafar offered his hand to Voleton who gratefully took it. He jumped to his feet and cricked his neck from side to side and then checked his jaw for any sign of a fracture. Once satisfied he would live to fight another day, he walked over to his horse and grabbed the reins. Hatred flashed from his bloodshot eyes towards Elveria and for a second the elder mage felt a slither of shame.

Eventually, the three wizards mounted their horses and with some reluctance from Elveria, followed Bracken into the forest. The wind was howling between the trees, spooking the horses, but the sorcerers themselves felt nothing except the adrenalin that shot fire through their veins. Riding in between the trees they dodged twisted roots and several low branches, gripping their horse's thick manes until they arrived at the north side of the castle. They caught their breath and then they dismounted. Surprisingly, the undergrowth was still quite dense and Bracken stood close to a large elm tree. He looked rather confident while his body rustled in the strengthening breeze and he was clearly unaffected by the harsh ride the wizards endured, for he had been carried along by the wind.

'You can get inside the castle through there,' said Bracken, clapping his hands to bring a halo of fireflies to his side. He nodded towards the forest and they flew off into the direction of where his finger now pointed. They lit the way for the others to follow and in the midst of a dark patch of tangled ivy and wild roses they showed them a door which lay hidden.

Bracken's chest swelled.

'Forusian has dozens of these hiding places all through the forest, but only this one is actually linked to the castle itself.'

'Where in the castle does it lead?' asked Amafar.

'That I cannot tell you, my lord,' said Bracken, shrugging his shoulders. 'I am bound to the forest therefore I have never been able to go so far.'

'How do we get inside?' asked Elveria, when he pushed at the door and it didn't move.

'The opening is there for the trained eye,' said Bracken, with a smug grin; it was clear he was enjoying being the centre of attention, and his dislike for Elveria was no longer contained.

He brushed Elveria to one side and once the mage had stepped away he reached up and grabbed hold of the ivy without breaking the vine. There came a strange swish from the leaves before the ivy started curling around the wood sprite's hand. Bracken twisted the vine and pushed at the door and this time the door fell away to reveal a dark corridor. The three wizards hesitated for only the briefest of seconds before lunging forward and entering it, but Bracken did not follow.

Voleton turned and caught the sadness in the young sprite's eyes.

'You have done well, my young friend,' he said, understanding his plight.

'Just tell Bridgemear it was me who showed you the way in,' he said, suddenly beaming. 'I told him he couldn't do it alone and I was right.'

Voleton smiled and shot a quick glance behind him to check on the others progress.

'He needs us all,' he said, drawing his sword, 'but I will ensure he knows what you have done for us this night.'

Bracken grinned. 'I'm always willing to help,' he replied, but Voleton was gone.

He touched the ivy with his fingertips and the creeping vines and tendrils wrapped themselves around the door and pulled it shut, removing any trace of the entranceway and he turned away feeling a moment of contentment. A sudden gust of wind blew towards him and he exploded into a thousand billowing leaves before vanishing once again into the very heart of the forest.

*

Bridgemear sensed they were doomed. They had crossed the threshold into the anatomy unit and entered a place which was way beyond anything they could have ever imagined. As sleek as cats, they each slipped between the empty caskets without a sound and Bridgemear was not the only one to notice they were all lacking their hideous cargo.

'I feel a bad omen,' said Amella when her eyes caught his.

Bridgemear nodded looking grim.

'Try not to be afraid,' he said, reaching out and squeezing her hand. 'We must at least try and get through this together.'

She gave him a weak smile, her face was pale and her hair was damp with moisture. Beads of sweat ran down her cheek and she wiped them away with the back of her hand and then brushed her hair away from her face, revealing her beautiful green eyes.

Bridgemear held his breath; she was all he had ever wanted and he could have so easily whisked her into his arms and taken her to somewhere safe, but instead he tightened his grip on his sword and beckoned for them to move on.

'Look, it's all gone!' cried Mordorma, pointing towards the ceiling.

They all looked up and sure enough where there was once a vast roof, only a gaping hole remained. Mordorma saw the crimson clouds and he called out to the others to turn back.

'We must leave at once,' he said in a panic, 'don't you see, demons are being summoned.'

A distant chanting reached his ears and he touched Bridgemear's arm to grab his attention and warn him that he could see Forusian, but it was clear by Bridgemear's expression that he had seen him too. With their senses heightened, they each made their way closer to where Forusian stood with his back towards them.

As they approached, the air turned thick and their throats became as dry as sandpaper. Bridgemear was the first to spot a young girl with long, red hair suspended in the air and he realised she was tied to some kind of stake. He watched her floating before the evil king and heard her weeping and he felt his gut twist. He was still quite far away, but he instinctively knew without question that the girl was his own flesh and blood.

He tried to stop Amella from seeing Crystal by blocking her view and pressing his hand to her chest but she pushed his hand away and forced herself past him to see and as soon as her eyes fell on her daughter her whole body turned to jelly. She made a tiny whimper and Bridgemear grabbed her and cupped her mouth with his hand and she bit his finger so hard to stop the scream that was trying to explode in the back of her throat that she drew blood. Her legs collapsed beneath her but he held her fast, dragging her back into the shadows and holding her there until he thought it was safe to let her go.

Eventually when she was much calmer, Bridgemear allowed her to return to where Mordorma and Amadeus were waiting for them and they each saw how the clouds were penetrating the tower and descending in from the sky. At first it had given the impression of a fine mist but now something far more sinister was heading towards Crystal's body. Then out of the blue came a horrific crack of thunder and a spear of lightening bolted inside the tower and hit the stake where Crystal was still tied. Bright coloured sparks flew like fireworks into the atmosphere and Crystal screamed in terror when the smell of burning flesh filled the air.

Bridgemear saw an aura of pure, white light surround Crystal's body and he looked aghast.

'He's going to take all her powers for himself,' he gasped sounding incredulous. 'For all that is magical, we must never let that happen!'

Mordorma couldn't stand it a moment longer and was the first to take matters into his own hands. He drew away from the shadows to force a beam of light from his fingertips out into the night sky. The light was so bright it was blinding and the menacing clouds rushed to suffocate the beam but the glow was much too powerful and he managed to hold the clouds at bay long enough to signal his whereabouts to Elveria and the others.

'How did you escape!' shouted Forusian when he espied Mordorma out of the corner of his eye. He turned to face him, his eyes searching for Amadeus and his black pupils shone like jet.

'Never mind that, what the hell do you think you are doing?' demanded Mordorma, walking briskly towards him. Forusian moved away from the centre of the pit and his long coat swished madly around his legs.

'Wouldn't you like to know, but then why should I waste my time with someone who is nothing more than an ignorant fool,' he hissed when Mordorma was no more than twenty feet away. 'Do you really think I have time for this?'

'I will not let you continue with this atrocity against the girl,' shouted Mordorma, making a run for it. Forusian laughed like a mad man. 'Oh really Mordorma and do you think you're going to stop me? Why you are no match for me!'

'I may not be strong enough to destroy you on my own, not with the evil that possesses your soul, but there are others who will come and crush you into fine dust.' Anger was making Mordorma sweat but he continued to deliberately distract Forusian to enable the others to move closer without hopefully being seen.

Forusian allowed himself a sly smile.

'Your kind have had it too good for too long, it's time I put you in your place,' he hissed. 'You've all spent too many years cosseted by the rules of the Elders, with all your terrible secrets tucked away in other worlds in the hope that no one would ever find out.'

'And you had to be the one to open Pandora's Box?'

'Oh yes, for as you now realise, I had the most to gain.'

He raised the golden spear which he still held in his hand and pointed it directly at Mordorma's chest. He tossed his head and a gobbet of fire shot from the spear and knocked Mordorma straight off his feet. The surprised mage looked down and saw his clothes were set alight. Panic filled his throat when he realised he was on fire and it seemed like an eternity until he came to his senses and rolled over in the dirt, smacking at the flames with his bare hands until he forced them out. He was winded but he scrambled swiftly to his feet, his eyes bright with fury.

Mordorma's hand produced a powerful force of energy and Forusian circled the spear in the air to produce his own. Both elements of magic clashed together, but the spear's magic was far stronger and Mordorma was thrown into the air by its power. His arms shot above his head and he was thrown bodily to a pinnacle high up in the stone and was instantly shackled to what was left of a wall of rock. Furiously he fought to free himself, but it was no use for his bonds dug deep into his flesh causing him to wince in pain, and the more he fought the tighter they became until he could no longer feel his wrists.

'You should not have come here,' said Forusian, lowering the spear to his side. 'This was never your fight and now I have no choice but to end what is turning out to be a very tiresome interlude.'

Amadeus watched what was happening and a trickle of fear sweat ran down his spine and he made himself ready to fight. He knew he was no match for the sorcerer, but he could not stand by and do nothing. Bridgemear signalled to him to stay put and Amadeus's eyes flashed in defiance before the look on Bridgemear's face forced him to do as he was told. Reluctantly, he forced a nod of acknowledgement and moved closer to Bridgemear's side. When he was close enough, Bridgemear grabbed him by the scruff of the neck, dragging him closer to the shadows. The blood drained from his face when he saw red fury burning in Bridgemear's eyes.

'You do nothing without my say so,' Bridgemear hissed through gritted teeth. 'You're no use to anyone dead.'

A bloodcurdling shriek caused them all to snap their attention towards Crystal. A strong wind entered the anatomy unit, the cold brushing against their skin when Abbadon flew down and entered through the gaping hole which once held the roof. He soared and swooped around Crystal's body, howling with pleasure when he recognised his latest victim, sending her into a terrified panic, for she had met this terrible demon once before and Gzhel's warning ran through her tortured mind. Death shivered with pleasure, for he'd stumbled upon the one who'd taken the boy from him and now she would pay for doing so.

Forusian watched with interest while the demon terrorised his sacrifice until he started to grow bored.

'There's really no need to frighten her to the extreme; come, stand by my side so we can begin,' he said, beckoning the demon with his index finger.
Abbadon ignored him, still overcome with euphoria at finding the girl so soon.

'I demand you, come to me!' snapped Forusian, beginning to lose his temper. 'We have struck a deal,' he shouted, baring his teeth like a wild animal. 'Now let's get down to business or I will find another to do my bidding!' The icy chill in his voice made Abbadon hesitate, but not before he had tasted her fear with his foul tongue.

'Very well,' he howled, 'I am ready to take her for my own.'

Abbadon flew to his side and took the spear from Forusian's grasp and dropped it to the ground. The floor was covered with debris and he brushed some of the small stones to the side with his skeletal feet and then drew seven symbols which matched the ones imprinted on the spear into the dirt. He shut his eyes tight and let out a piercing howl.

A ghoulish cry burst from the pit, and the spear exploded, raining a thousand glistening shards of magic upon the stone. Each crudely drawn symbol glowed golden, embedded with the remnants of the bewitched lancet. The glow intensified and then images of seven demonic creatures materialised before their very eyes.

Forusian leaned forward to get a closer look, fascinated by what had manifested before him and the atmosphere crackled with anticipation.

Crystal's body broke into a violent spasm the second the demons fixed their burning gaze upon her and she felt her body shake with protest when they tried to force their way inside her. Her vision blurred and her eyes flickered from side to side before she was forced into a deep trance. Her body started to revolve, turning ninety degrees and she hovered, face down over the pit. The jewel clasped securely around her neck started to glow to protect her and the demons were unable to enter her body and so they tried to sap her life force from outside of her instead.

The light from the necklace became so bright that it sent a beam of light towards the pit, and as soon as it touched the red-hot liquid, something changed. A wave rose and washed over the bouncing limbs and the body parts rushed together and became joined. Legs found needed torsos and arms splashed about for a head. Within minutes gruesome bodies were climbing out of the chasm, grotesquely deformed and hideous to the eye, they formed into ranks like soldiers. Their hands were enormous, as were their heads, but their bodies were of different sizes with twisted spines and dislocated limbs, all disgusting freaks of Forusian's making.

Up in the air, Crystal's body was convulsing, enough it seemed to push her into unconsciousness. The power the demons were taking from her through the amulet was too much for her young body to bear and she fell into a deep sleep.

Bridgemear and Amella looked on aghast; Forusian was killing their daughter right before their very eyes and there was nothing they could do to save her. Then something snapped inside Bridgemear's head. His gaze never wavered when he ran full force from his hiding place, leaping over one of the caskets and landing right behind Forusian. He raised his arm and stabbed the king straight between his shoulder blades with his sword. He heard the sickening sound of bone crunching against the blade as the sword severed his spinal cord. He took a step back, believing this act alone would be enough to stop the evil sorcerer.

There followed a shriek of fury while Forusian turned to face his attacker.

'Damn you Bridgemear!' Forusian cursed, while his fingers searched for the source of pain.

The look of triumph quickly faded on Bridgemear's face when Forusian twisted the blade until it was free from his body, and with the weapon firmly in his grasp he was quick to turn upon the wizard.

'You can't kill me with one swish of a blade,' he barked, goading Bridgemear with his own sword. 'I cannot die so easily and you cannot save your daughter by trying. You are all doomed. As I speak my army is getting ready to fight. You and your kind are going to know what it's like to be ruled by the most powerful being in the whole universe.'

Bridgemear roared with fury and went for him, punching Forusian just above the jaw. The sound of his cheekbone disintegrating against his fist filled him with much-needed adrenalin, and he grinned with pure delight when he saw the look of agony sweep over the king's face.

'Ha-ha,' he crowed, 'you may not die so quickly but you still feel the pain of your wounds just like the rest of us.'

Forusian's eyes blazed; he had no time for this, he had serious work to do. He took a step forward, the cheek along with his spine already starting to heal. He waved the sword in the air and took a strike, but Bridgemear was far too quick and bolted out of the way.

Abbadon was furious with the unexpected interruption and barked orders for the demon creatures to continue with the ritual while Forusian dealt with the wizard. But Amadeus had waited long enough and rushed into view, throwing his body into the centre of the ring of demons, flaying his sword as he cut the apparitions with his blade.

'It's no use,' he shouted to Amella, when his sword did nothing to disperse the phantoms, 'I cannot kill what is not alive.'

'We need to stop the power of the amulet,' screamed Amella in answer. She felt herself teetering at the very edge of hysteria again and she tried hard to pull back from its darkening grip. She ran towards the pit, but she caught

Death's attention and with a whoosh; he was there at her side.

'She will never be yours,' he sneered, dropping down and scooping her up by the throat.

Amella felt herself rising from the floor and she grappled with the long, bony fingers which threatened to choke the life out of her, but he was too strong and she felt her eyelids turn heavy and then everything went black.

Bridgemear caught sight of what was happening to Amella out of the corner of his eye and he spun around to see Abbadon let go of her and let her fall. Forusian seized his moment and brought the sword down hard, slicing the flesh of Bridgemear's arm. The magician gasped from the bone-deep gash, the bright red bloodstain, visible against his clothing. He jumped back and Forusian followed him, wielding the weapon to and fro above his head like a madman.

'It's time to die!' the evil king cried, brandishing his sword in the air, but Bridgemear was far more skilled and manoeuvred him nearer to the pit. He saw the abominations of evil standing in silent rows, lifeless and unmoving; the incantation was not yet finished and the breath of life that they needed to exist had not yet been injected into their slippery bodies.

'We must stop the ritual!' he cried out, watching Amadeus still slicing at the demons.

'But how?' shouted Amadeus turning to face him in desperation.

'It's the necklace!' Bridgemear shouted. 'We must somehow stop the amulet!'

Amadeus looked at Crystal's sizzling body and realised what he had to do. As light as the wind, he left the circle of demons and ran towards the chasm. For a moment it seemed everyone stopped to stare as he rushed past, dropping his sword within easy reach of Bridgemear. Death barked a warning when he realised what he was about to do, but Amadeus was already one step ahead of him. With his eyes focused on Crystal, he leapt from the centre of the pinnacle, his arms flaying widely as he jumped into the air; his aim was nothing more than perfect. He landed with a 'thud' on Crystal's body and he immediately grasped at her shoulders to stop himself from falling into the pit. Then, with one arm wrapped around her waist he used his other hand to cover the powerful stone. The heat from it seared through his skin and he cried out with the pain, but he refused to let go until it died away. Frantically, he searched at the back of her neck for the clasp and when he found it, he unfastened the amulet from her throat. Death was furious when he saw what was happening and flew to attack, but he knew he was already too late. The second the stone died, the spirits spun into dust.

'You cannot harm me now, evil one,' Amadeus said with a smirk, 'you have failed. Be gone, and take your evil doings with you.'

For the first time in a century, Abbadon didn't know what to do; without the necklace and the girl's immense life force they could not continue to bring the soldiers to life. He looked over at Forusian and cried for him to do something, but Forusian was still preoccupied.

Bridgemear's pale skin glistened with sweat when he bent down to retrieve Amadeus's sword. Forusian's eyes were gleaming with fury having realised his dream was in serious peril and he lunged for the magician with madness dancing in his eyes.

Bridgemear swung his sword and the noise of clashing metal filled the air. They both turned full circle but Bridgemear was the better swordsman and before he knew what was happening he had Forusian pinned up against the wall.

'It's over,' Bridgemear said, pointing his sword at Forusian's heart. 'Surrender now before more blood is shed.'

'I still have your daughter,' Forusian hissed. 'She is not out of the woods yet.'

'You can do her no more harm,' said Bridgemear, shaking his head. 'Your days of being king are well and truly over.'

As he spoke, the torches suddenly seemed to burn a little too bright and a strong gust of wind blew at the flames causing them to flare, momentarily distracting the wizard. It was all it took for Forusian to slice his own sword deep across Bridgemear's belly. The magician looked shocked and then fell to his knees, unable to believe Forusian had been able to wound him so. Not used to feeling such pain, his sword slipped from his grasp and Forusian kicked it away with the heel of his boot while Bridgemear tried to stem the flow of blood. He soon realised his inner strength was not enough to save him and he tried to pull at the wound with his bare hands.

'Wish you hadn't done that,' Bridgemear said, swallowing hard and cursing the lack of magic in his fingertips.

Forusian smiled down at him.

'I warned you not to interfere, but you would insist upon it,' he said swinging the sword above his head. The metal glistened as it wavered in the air and Bridgemear closed his eyes, waiting for the fatal blow. He realised he was a failure, and at that moment the dismay he felt abolished all fear. The blade sliced the air and he braced himself, but the swish of the blade never reached him. A piercing howl bellowed from Forusian's mouth instead, and like a dragon caught by the dragon slayer his eyes opened as wide as saucers and his sword slipped from his fingers, landing with a sharp clatter upon the stone floor.

Bridgemear stared dumbstruck when Forusian fell to the ground twitching and writhing before him. He couldn't comprehend what was happening and Forusian reached out towards him as though he thought he could save him. Recoiling, Bridgemear watched in shocked surprise when tendrils of smoke smouldered all over Forusian's body, before igniting and turning him into a human torch. Orange and gold flames licked viciously at his flesh and the repugnant smell of cooked tissue caused Bridgemear to almost throw up when it filled his nostrils.

'No! This can't be happening!' screamed Forusian, when his flesh melted away to reveal bone. 'My handsome face, my beautiful skin, it's not my time to die!' The flames consumed him in his entirety and within minutes he was unrecognisable.

'Help me,' he gurgled, when his blackened lips crumbled and turned into dust, 'for you have not seen the last of...'

He fell upon the floor, like a tree felled in the forest, his eyes lifeless. His limbs disintegrated when they made contact with the floor and he fell apart in large chunks; his fingers, already stiff, curled inwards looking like broken stumps. He lay dead, there at Bridgemear's feet, and what was left of his remains hardened into a charcoal effigy. Bridgemear stared wide-eyed at the cremated torso of King Forusian, unable to digest what had just happened, his own pain momentarily forgotten.

In a flash, Abbadon was by his side salvaging what he could. He hadn't expected things to turn out quite this way and, wasted no time in devouring the fine, green mist which appeared above the dead king. Bridgemear felt another wave of nausea hit what was left of his stomach.

'Be off with you, you sick creature of darkness!' he gasped, furious that Death should take such advantage. 'Go back to the dark one and tell him you have lost your fight this night.'

Abbadon howled in retaliation, but retreated when he saw the anger flare in the magician's eyes. He was furious at being unable to reap Crystal's soul for that had been the bargain between his master and Forusian, but there would be other times and other chances, and this thought gave him comfort. She would be his one day, of that he was sure. With a shriek that left the blood running cold, Abbadon made his way out of the tower, taking with him the dark clouds and suffocating air.

Clutching his belly, Bridgemear tried to stand but found it impossible; then a gloved hand came towards his face. There were no longer dark shadows to hide the mysterious person who had saved his life and Bridgemear looked directly into the red eyes of Tremlon. His pale skin looked just as white as he remembered but his grip was far stronger. Tremlon pulled the magician to his feet and Bridgemear glanced over to see the shape-changer was still holding the blade that dripped with Forusian's blood. He recognised the blade immediately for it was the magnificent - Sword of Truth.

'You saved my life,' said Bridgemear, when Tremlon let him go.

'I owed you,' said Tremlon, tight-lipped. 'All these years I have lived with the knowledge that I was the one who betrayed your love for Amella, and because of what I did she was cast out and her child taken away. Now it is time to make amends; King Gamada is dead and Amella must return home to us and rein as queen.'

Bridgemear fell silent, unable to digest the shape-changer's words. In the distance someone was yelling, but his mind was still reeling from the revelation that King Gamada was dead.

'There they are!' shouted a number of familiar voices.

Bridgemear managed to snap his attention towards those whom he had openly condemned.

'Help me!' called Amadeus, when he recognised the face of Elveria. 'We must get Crystal down from here, for she will die if we do not hurry.'

Bridgemear stared open-mouthed when Elveria, Voleton and Amafar took control and, with their own spells cast, brought Crystal back to safety. With Forusian dead their powers were once again united and he felt his muscles ache as his body responded to the power of self-healing. His flesh tingled when the gaping wounds closed, and his sliced intestines stung like a belly full of wasps until they placed themselves back inside his abdomen. He winced and gritted his teeth so as not to cry out until the pain eventually subsided.

'There is one more thing I must do,' Tremlon said, fixing his gaze upon the rows of hideous creatures who stood waiting for the breath of life that would never come. His boots sounded dull upon the ground as he turned and faced the goblins. He swung the magical sword above his head, and as he reached the first victim he placed his opening strike against its neck. The body fell to the ground with its head completely severed. Tremlon didn't wait; instead, he swung the sword again and the glistening of the metal shone each time it made contact, slicing the head off each and every grotesque figure. Although his arms ached, he didn't stop until he had slaughtered every last one.

Amella stirred, then sat bolt upright. She blinked, realising the scene was not as she remembered. She had been dragged away from the pit and she sensed the presence of another close to her.

'It's all over,' said Bridgemear softly in her ear. He watched her turn to him and saw the look of bewilderment fill her eyes and he put his arms around her, giving her a strong embrace.

'Take a moment to rest,' he said, stroking her wild hair. 'Everything's going to be fine, because against the odds we somehow saved our daughter.'

# *Epilogue*

Seven days had passed with Crystal resting in her chamber in the Kingdom of Nine Winters. Amella stepped from behind a marble pillar and watched her daughter sip from a challis filled to the brim with a potion made from her own special recipe. A hearty fire crackled in the corner and the sweet aroma of fresh herbs filled the air.

'I have someone to see you if you're up to it?' she said, folding her arms against her chest. Crystal smiled and her face lit up.

'Who is it?' she asked, smoothing the crumpled sheets, unable to hide her excitement.

Amella clapped her hands and a servant opened the bedroom door.

'Matt!' Crystal cried with pleasure. 'My God, is it really you?'

Matt grinned sheepishly.

'Yeah, it's me,' he said, feeling shy.

'How are you?' she asked, patting the bedclothes, her eyes turning bright.

'Shouldn't I be asking you that question?' he teased drawing nearer. 'After all, you're the patient not me.' They both burst out laughing when he jumped on the bed, the atmosphere alive with their happiness at seeing each other again.

Amella heard the swish-click of metal against armour and cricked her neck to spy Arhdel wavering at the chamber door. She signalled him to enter, but he hesitated.

'Come in, come in, you're more than welcome here,' she insisted, ushering him inside.

'Is that Arhdel?' asked Crystal, waving him closer.

'I am glad you're safe,' he said when he approached. His voice took on a compassionate note when he saw her look of joy and it warmed his heart.

'And I am so glad you're alive,' she laughed, sliding her dainty hand into his.

Arhdel swallowed and he squeezed her delicate fingers between his.

'Me too,' he said in a gruff tone.

'Right, everyone, time to let our little heroine get some rest,' said Amella with a light smile.

She walked to the window and forced the drapes closed. The sunlight vanished and the room became instantly dark.

'Close your eyes and go to sleep,' she commanded, raising her eyebrows and rounding up the visitors, hustling them out of the door.

'But I feel fine,' Crystal moaned, watching her friends leave and forcing a pout.

'Good, then taking a little nap will make you feel even better,' Amella insisted, sliding the door closed behind her.

'You haven't told her, have you?' said Arhdel, when they stepped into the drawing room and Matt was out of earshot. Amella wrung her hands and started to pace the floor. She found she could not look him in the eye.

'No,' she admitted, 'how can I?'

'If you leave it any longer it will be too late. Tomorrow she returns to her old world, and what will you do then?'

'Perhaps I should let Bridgemear tell her. After all, we're in this mess because of him.'

'That's not quite true is it, Amella? It does take two to make a baby.'

Amella's cheeks burned with embarrassment; she had asked for that.

'The child needs to know,' he said, lowering his voice when he saw Matt draw close. 'Time is of the essence,' he added, leaving her side and taking his leave.

Sometime later Crystal awoke, her head feeling much clearer from the effects of the potion and revitalised, she threw back the covers, eager to get out of bed. She thought back to the last few days. She couldn't remember much after Forusian had tied her to the stake and for that she was secretly relieved. She remembered her first lucid day in Amella's kingdom though. She had awoken from a fretful fever to find many strangers peering down at her, causing her to become frightened. Then Amella had appeared and tried to explain to her how she had become queen and was ruler of the Kingdom of Nine Winters. The king, Amella's father, had been murdered by Forusian's hand and Crystal felt a wave of sadness wash over her; she had never met him, yet she felt his passing with genuine grief.

Amella had explained the sudden departure of Elveria and the others, who had been sent back to Raven's Rainbow on important business, allowing only Bridgemear to remain. Inside, she sensed *she* was the important business but didn't press the new queen for more information.

She padded to the foot of her bed and found a luxurious robe and put it on. The material was soft and warm, making her feel relaxed and secure. Her delicate feet slipped into her new jewelled slippers and then she made her way to the door.

She noted there was no one about as she closed the door behind her. She was not familiar with the palace, but felt safe enough to explore. She found the interior of the palace truly amazing, and was soon mesmerised with all its rich beauty. Her eyes sparkled with the light reflected from the petrified chandeliers and she was unable to concentrate on where she was going. Familiar voices wafted by her senses and without hesitation she reached out and pushed open a door. She suddenly stopped dead in her tracks. A half-finished sentence, one that was still hanging in the air and not made for her ears was digested.

'Crystal is our flesh and blood, our daughter, we must...'

Crystal felt her brain go numb.

'What did you just say?' she whispered pushing the door aside. She saw Amella and Bridgemear stiffen as though turned to stone and found she could not move for fear of falling. Her knees were starting to shake and she reached out and held onto the doorknob for some kind of support. She cast her gaze from Amella to Bridgemear and the pain she saw in their eyes was mirrored in her own. Bridgemear's face turned pale and tears spilled down Amella's cheeks like falling raindrops.

'I'm so sorry,' she cried, taking a step forward. 'I never wanted you to find out like this.'

Crystal shook her head.

'I don't understand, there must be some mistake, I must have misheard you. How could you possibly be my mother and father?'

'It's no mistake,' said Bridgemear clinging to what was left of his composure. With purpose, he walked over to her and placed his arm around her shoulders. He waited for the rebuff, but none came, and he exhaled with a sigh of relief.

'Crystal, we have much to tell you, Amella and I; please come and sit by the fire, you look frozen.'

Crystal allowed him to lead her to the nearby chair and he placed her like a babe in its cradle. Her beautiful blue eyes, so like his own, looked up at him in total bewilderment.

'I think it's time you knew the truth,' he said, pulling a chair close. 'I think it's time we told you who you really are...'

*

Matt sat in his bedchamber with Arhdel as his only companion.

'What's going on?' he asked, pushing his food around his dinner plate. 'Why can't I see Crystal?'

'There's been a development,' said Arhdel frowning. He walked over to Matt and with a swift movement took the plate away.

'They're her parents, aren't they?' Matt said, peering into Arhdel's face. 'I guessed,' he added with a sigh, when he saw the warrior turn pale.

Arhdel tried to change the subject.

'Look, tomorrow you will be leaving us,' he said, trying to sound light hearted, 'so why don't you just enjoy what little time you have left with us.' Matt shook his head and Arhdel walked over to the window, letting out a deep sigh. From this high vantage point, he could see something huge and black hurtling towards him. Instinctively he knew it was Elveria returning from his meeting with the Elders and his blood ran cold. He turned away from the window, pretending to have not seen him, but all too soon the heavy caw of the bird was heard, demanding entrance. Arhdel choose to ignore his cry; knowing that whatever his news, it could wait a while longer.

'There's a big, black bird at the window,' said Matt looking up in surprise.

'Is there? Oh, well, let it find its own way in.'

'But it wants to get in here.'

'Really? Then let him know what it's like to want.'

'You said him, who is it?'

Irritated by the boy's probing questions, Arhdel snatched the door handle to make his escape. The beady eye of the raven twitched towards him and its wings flapped while Elveria clamoured for his attention. Arhdel flicked his gaze to rest upon the bird who he could see was growing more and more impatient but he still refused to open the window and so Elveria flew away.

'Come on, we might as well go downstairs and meet the others, there will be an assembly once the bird has gained entrance.'

'Will it be about Crystal?'

'Yes it will; hurry boy, so we can be there first, I don't like walking in halfway through.'

They entered the hall as the assembly was starting to gather and Matt was guided close to the front by the firm hand of his mentor.

Amella stood alone next to her throne and she watched Matt take his place before observing the entourage of the royal courtiers and council members who were following close behind. Her mouth was dry with nerves for she was waiting for Elveria to bring news from The Guild of Elders. She realised she was pacing the floor and her thoughts flew to Bridgemear wishing she could have him by her side. Her courage was failing yet she knew she dare not show it, for those assembling before her would like nothing else than to devour her if she showed any signs of weakness.

The select few fell silent when Elveria's boots echoed his arrival against the highly polished floor. The click of his heels grated upon Amella's nerves, causing her to wince.

'You're Royal Highness,' Elveria cooed, throwing back his cloak and kissing her outstretched hand.

'What news do you bring?' she asked, ignoring his friendly manner and pulling her hand away.

He drew himself up, acknowledging the unexpected rebuff.

'Where's the girl?' the elder mage demanded, throwing a quick glance towards the council members.

'My daughter,' Amella stated, flashing him a warning look, 'is with her father.'

'So the child has been told then?'

Amella lowered her eyes, her lashes hiding what her eyes could not withhold. She finally brought her stare towards him.

'Yes, she has been told. Now enough of these questions and tell us instead, what the Elders have to say.' She moved away from him then. Her long, slender body looking radiant dressed in an exquisitely, jewelled gown. The soft swish of her garments could be heard as she sat on her newly appointed throne and the emeralds from her slippers danced like green fire in her eyes.

'She is to leave,' said Elveria, dropping his head but unable to hide the tone of satisfaction from his voice.

'But she can return?' Amella gasped and her eyes creased with worry.

Elveria's own narrowed and he looked up to display a tight smile playing at the corners of his lips.

'I am here only as a messenger.' he said, unable to wipe the smirk from his face. 'The Elders have decreed that Crystal, your illegitimate daughter, cannot be a part of this world. They have declared this order to stand, regardless of the fact that they'd agreed with King Gamada to bring her back to help fight Forusian. Her return was never to be permanent, she is not one of us and so their decision is to be written in the 'Scroll of immortals' and Crystal is to never return here again.'

His voice turned hard, and he shook his hand in the air as he continued.

'Let it be a warning, the Elders still decide the laws of these lands.'

'That's enough!' shouted a voice from somewhere behind Amella.

Everyone turned to watch Bridgemear appear from the shadows and take his place at Amella's side. His blonde hair stood out against the dark backdrop of silk and his ice-blue eyes shone as clear as glass.

'What are you doing here?' hissed Elveria in disgust. 'How can you show your face, you are not welcome here especially after what you have done?'

'I have done nothing to be ashamed of,' Bridgemear said raising one of his blonde eyebrows. He reached out and touched Amella's hand and she smiled, showing him she was reassured by his presence.

'Oh and as for not being welcome. Here sits the lady I have always loved, the woman who gave birth to my child. I believe I most definitely have the right to be here. All my life I served the Elders and their laws,' Bridgemear continued. 'Yes, it's true, we did break the ancient scriptures, something which, I have to say, cost us both dearly.' Elveria squirmed under his gaze.

Bridgemear broke eye contact and placed his hand on his belt. His fingers moved to his side and he grappled within his tunic. Elveria watched Bridgemear pull out a small scroll and saw him quickly untie a strap holding it together. Bridgemear caught his stare and their eyes locked. He waited an age before looking away, refusing to be intimidated by the elder mage and then he started to speak.

'To all here present, I should warn you now that the Elders are unaware and will not learn of how I have acquired the information of which I'm about to reveal to you,' he said, addressing first the Council and then Elveria. His lips twitched in a faint smile and his legs appeared to tremble with excitement. 'The source of how I came to have this evidence in my possession I will never betray, but I now hold in my hands the means to tell *you* what is going to happen with our daughter.'

Elveria spotted Tremlon hovering in the wings and a wave of suspicion washed over him. With a loud, clear voice, Bridgemear began to read from the tatty piece of vellum.

> *...And if the child who has been born of mixed blood, should be wronged and brought back to the extraordinary world, then the Elders must break the claim they hold over the child and grant her freedom in both of her parents' realms, for the pact will have been severed by another's greed and the child must know of their true birthright and be allowed back into the bosom of their family...*

Still holding the parchment, Bridgemear walked up to Elveria and thrust his face within inches of his.

'What pact was this?' he asked, suddenly shaking his evidence in the air. Elveria looked aghast, but remained tight lipped.

'Were you one of those who knew my child never had to leave in the first place?'

Elveria shuffled his feet and averted his eyes, but Bridgemear hadn't finished.

'I had no need to give my daughter to the ordinary world, did I, Elveria? Come on, tell them all the truth!'

Something inside Elveria snapped; why should he take all the blame?

'You dishonoured your people, you had to be punished,' he snarled. 'You were born to be a part of the elite magicians of Oakwood, yet you abused your place in our society. It was the chosen ones who made the decision to punish you for your crimes; I was merely the advocate. The Elders used the forgotten scrolls from our ancestors to deliver your punishment. You had to give a living part of yourself to another, or you would have been banished to live in an indeterminate state forever or taste the sword of death.'

'Such despicable lies!' spat Bridgemear. 'None of you had a reason to be so cruel. The Elders knew I had already fulfilled your pact when I gave Amella my child, as the child grew in her belly that was already a living part of me. All I had to do was give Crystal to Amella, but you knew that already, didn't you! Instead you gave our daughter to someone else!'

'You had to suffer for your crimes against your own kind, it is the law, and we cannot have mixed blood here.'

'No, my daughter, an innocent child, was the one who suffered, not me. And for that alone, I can never forgive you.'

'You are a fool, my lord, you have no jurisdiction here,' Elveria scoffed.

Amella could contain herself no longer and rose from her throne.

'Oh yes he does,' she broke in, her face aglow with indignation, 'because Bridgemear is my husband.'

A gasp echoed for several seconds around the hall.

'Say it is not so,' said Elveria in dismay. 'These stupid games you play are not amusing,' he added, noting the room had turned thick and warm.

'Don't you think he makes a fine king?' Amella teased.

'What is this abomination I hear against our ways?' Elveria shouted, his face having become so red it looked ready to explode.

He turned away and the council members stared at him as though he had gone mad. The Rank Master quickly left his seat and walked with a brisk pace to where Elveria stood. The atmosphere was nothing more than electric.

'Is this nonsense true?' he demanded towards the queen. 'Have you taken a wizard as your husband?'

'It is not nonsense, Rank Master, and I do not care for your tone. You are quick to forget *our* laws, which clearly state I can choose anyone to be my husband once I have taken my place as queen.'

'Yes, but...'

'No buts. I have chosen the father of my child to rule by my side and that is the end of the matter.'

Looking composed, Amella moved closer to her husband, taking his hand when he offered it to her. She entwined her fingers within his and their eyes locked for a fleeting moment before she turned to face the council one last time.

'We are retiring and preparing our daughter to go back to the ordinary world, where she will once again hold the Spirit of Eternity. Crystal will be a part of our lives from this day forth and will visit the extraordinary world as a free citizen whenever she wishes. This is my decree as queen.'

Turning her back on her audience, she allowed Bridgemear to escort her back to their daughter. As the royal council left in silence, Elvcria stood alone, staring blankly at the empty throne.

'So be it,' he said, when his frozen blood began to thaw, 'but beware Queen of Nine Winters, for you have not heard the last of this.'

*

Outside the great doors and along the sweeping corridors, Amadeus stood waiting. He smiled when the handle was released and an elf warrior entered his room, but his smile did not reach his eyes.

'Hello, Phaphos,' he said, giving a menacing glare and his sword glistened like silver in the light. 'Glad you could make it, you see, it's time I settled an old score...'

*Coming Soon…*

*Betrayers of Magic*

Lightning Source UK Ltd.
Milton Keynes UK
UKOW05f0027010813

214701UK00001B/4/P